My
NEW YORK
Marathon

SEBASTIEN
SAMSON

Life Drawn

SEBASTIEN SAMSON
STORY & ART

VÉRONICA LOPEZ
COVER COLORS

*

MONTANA KANE
TRANSLATOR

*

FABRICE SAPOLSKY
& ALEX DONOGHUE
US EDITION EDITORS

AMANDA LUCIDO
ASSISTANT EDITOR

VINCENT HENRY
ORIGINAL EDITION EDITOR

JERRY FRISSEN
SENIOR ART DIRECTOR

FABRICE GIGER
PUBLISHER

Rights & Licensing - licensing@humanoids.com
Press and Social Media - pr@humanoids.com

For Milo, Eve, Isaïe, Baptiste and Théo, my five lungs.

MY NEW YORK MARATHON
This title is a publication of Humanoids, Inc. 8033 Sunset Blvd. #628, Los Angeles, CA 90046.
Copyright © 2018 Humanoids, Inc., Los Angeles (USA). All rights reserved.
Humanoids and its logos are ® and © 2018 Humanoids, Inc.
Library of Congress Control Number: 2018944648

Life Drawn is an imprint of Humanoids, Inc.

First published in France under the title "*Le Marathon de New York à la petite semelle*"
Copyright © 2016 La Boîte à Bulles & Sébastien Samson. All rights reserved. All characters, the distinctive likenesses
thereof and all related indicia are trademarks of La Boîte à Bulles Sarl and / or of Sébastien Samson.

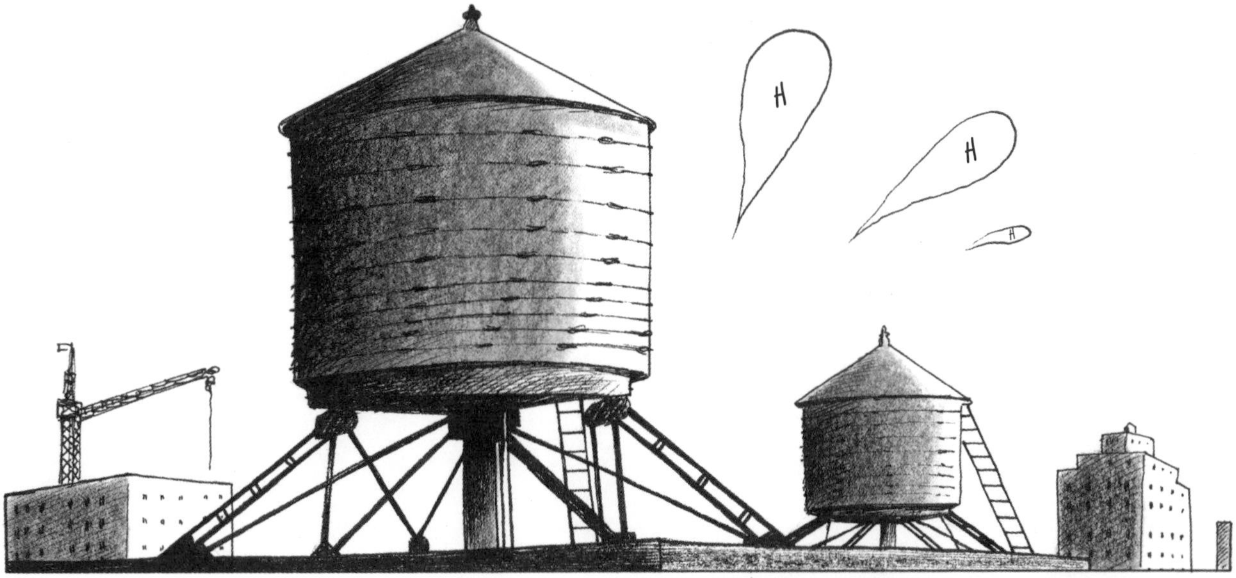
H
H
H

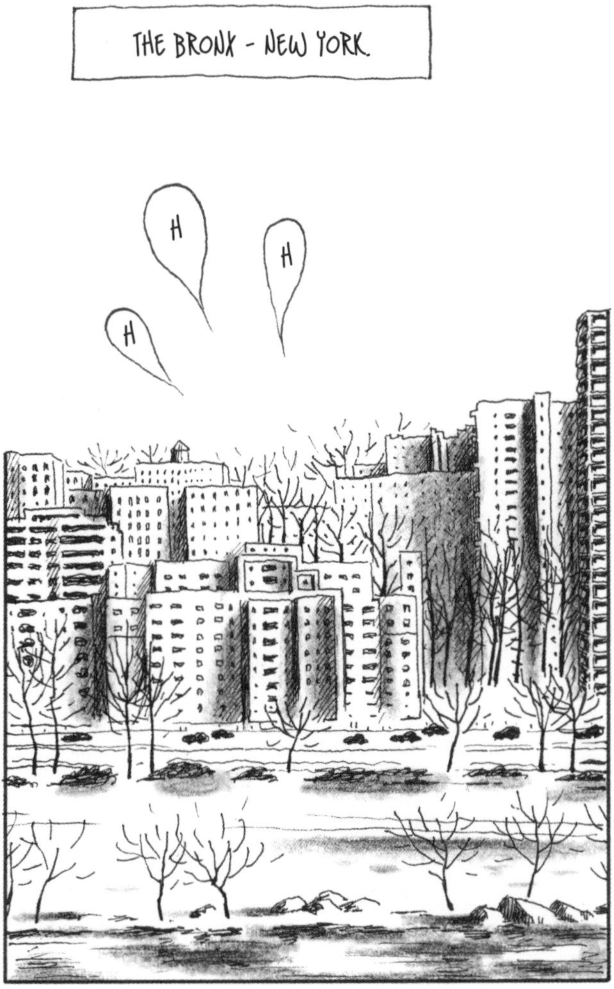
THE BRONX - NEW YORK.
H
H
H

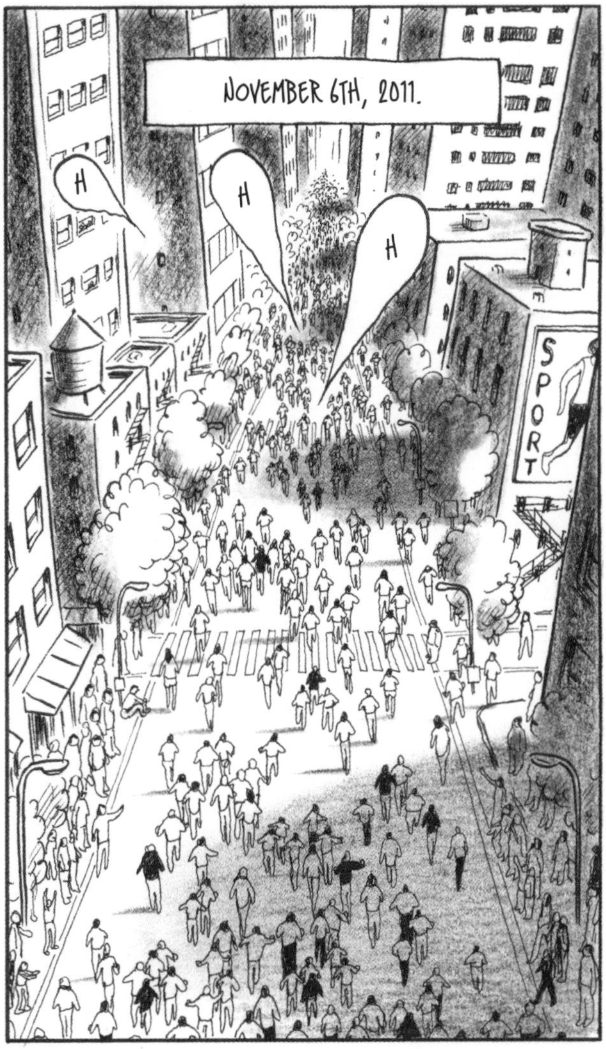
NOVEMBER 6TH, 2011.
H
H
H
SPORT

MILE 20 MARKER.

COME ON!

H

H

GO GO GO

RUN!

FRANCE

WHAT THE HELL WAS I THINKING, EMBARKING ON SOMETHING LIKE THIS?

?

RUN FOR Voices

Daddy, I love

OKAY, STOP! I'VE HAD ENOUGH, I'M IN SO MUCH PAIN...

1.
CARL
LEWIS
Unfit for Duty

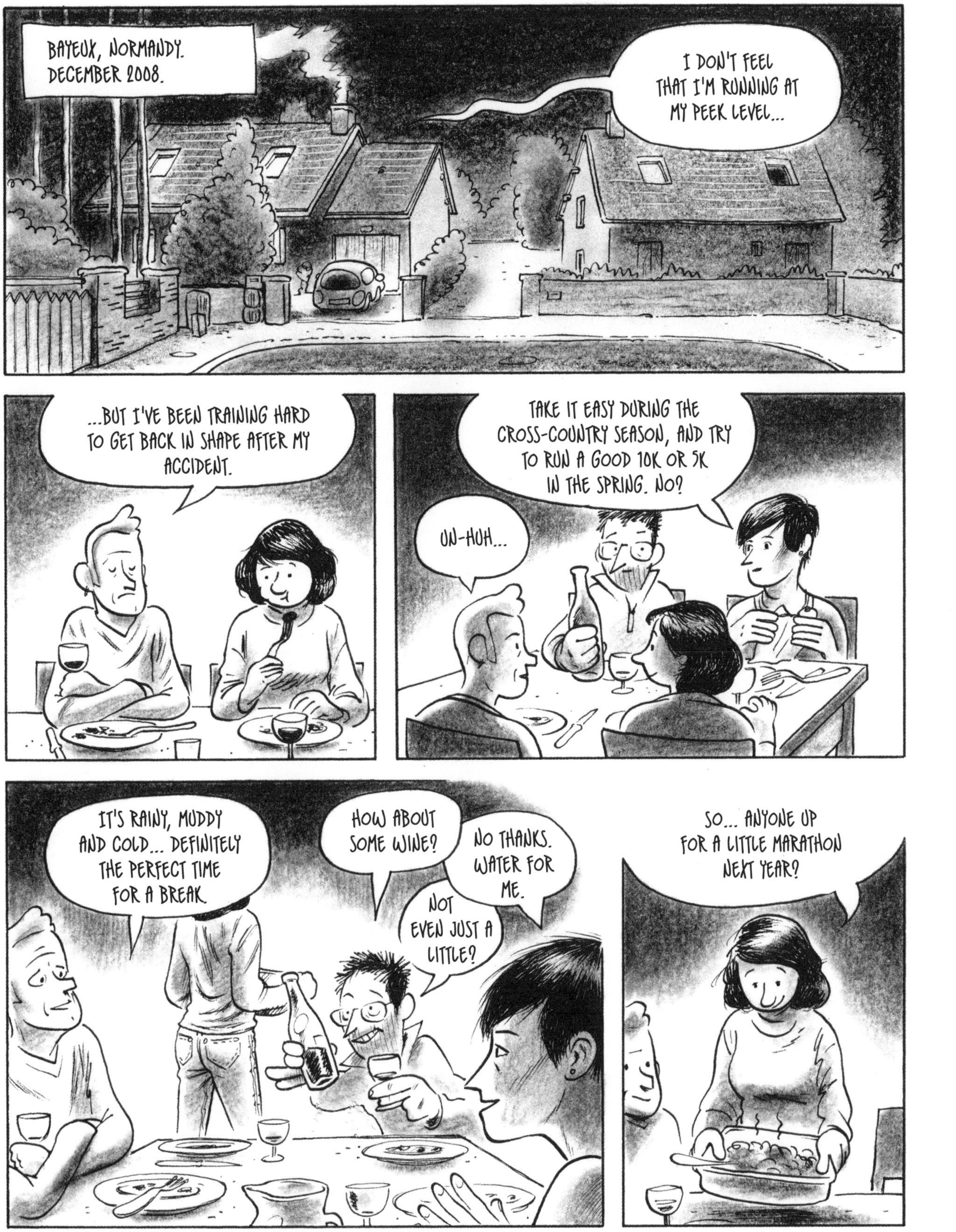
BAYEUX, NORMANDY. DECEMBER 2008.
I DON'T FEEL THAT I'M RUNNING AT MY PEEK LEVEL...
...BUT I'VE BEEN TRAINING HARD TO GET BACK IN SHAPE AFTER MY ACCIDENT.
TAKE IT EASY DURING THE CROSS-COUNTRY SEASON, AND TRY TO RUN A GOOD 10K OR 5K IN THE SPRING. NO?
UN-HUH...
IT'S RAINY, MUDDY AND COLD... DEFINITELY THE PERFECT TIME FOR A BREAK.
HOW ABOUT SOME WINE?
NO THANKS. WATER FOR ME.
NOT EVEN JUST A LITTLE?
SO... ANYONE UP FOR A LITTLE MARATHON NEXT YEAR?

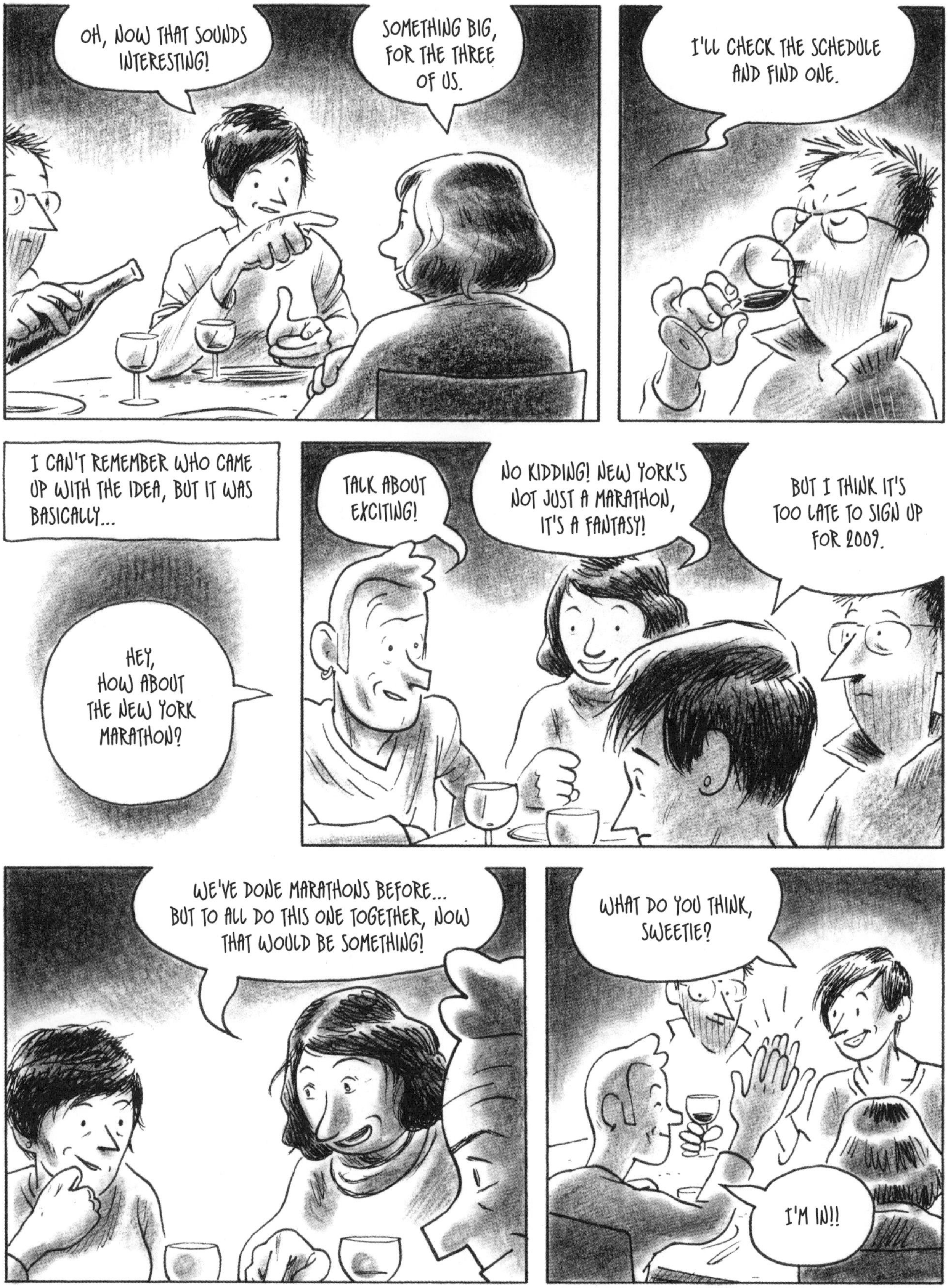
OH, NOW THAT SOUNDS INTERESTING!
SOMETHING BIG, FOR THE THREE OF US.
I'LL CHECK THE SCHEDULE AND FIND ONE.
I CAN'T REMEMBER WHO CAME UP WITH THE IDEA, BUT IT WAS BASICALLY...
HEY, HOW ABOUT THE NEW YORK MARATHON?
TALK ABOUT EXCITING!
NO KIDDING! NEW YORK'S NOT JUST A MARATHON, IT'S A FANTASY!
BUT I THINK IT'S TOO LATE TO SIGN UP FOR 2009.
WE'VE DONE MARATHONS BEFORE... BUT TO ALL DO THIS ONE TOGETHER, NOW THAT WOULD BE SOMETHING!
WHAT DO YOU THINK, SWEETIE?
I'M IN!!

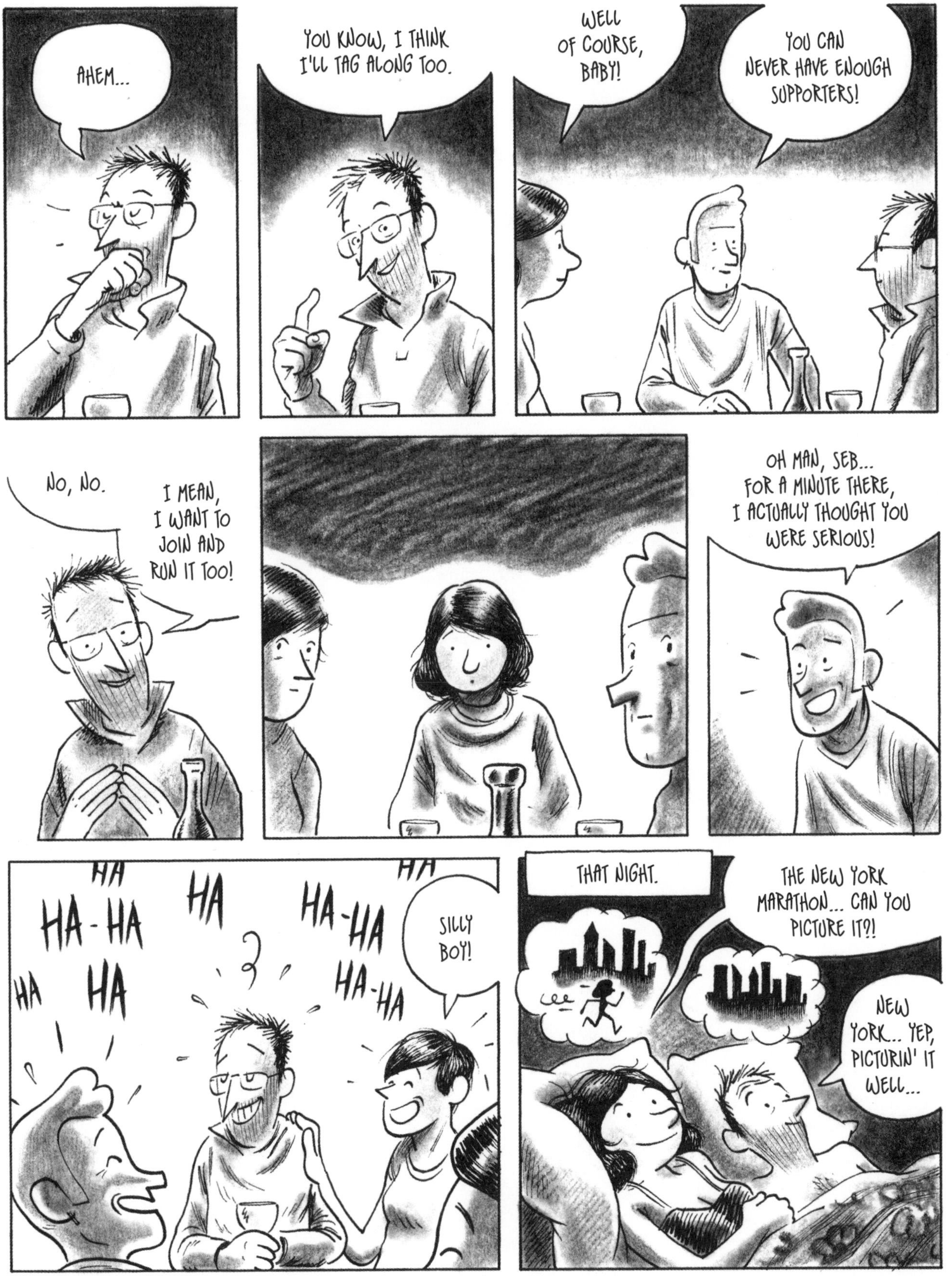
AHEM...
YOU KNOW, I THINK I'LL TAG ALONG TOO.
WELL OF COURSE, BABY!
YOU CAN NEVER HAVE ENOUGH SUPPORTERS!
NO, NO.
I MEAN, I WANT TO JOIN AND RUN IT TOO!
OH MAN, SEB... FOR A MINUTE THERE, I ACTUALLY THOUGHT YOU WERE SERIOUS!
HA
HA-HA
HA
HA
HA
HA-HA
HA-HA
HA
SILLY BOY!
THAT NIGHT.
THE NEW YORK MARATHON... CAN YOU PICTURE IT?!
NEW YORK... YEP, PICTURIN' IT WELL...

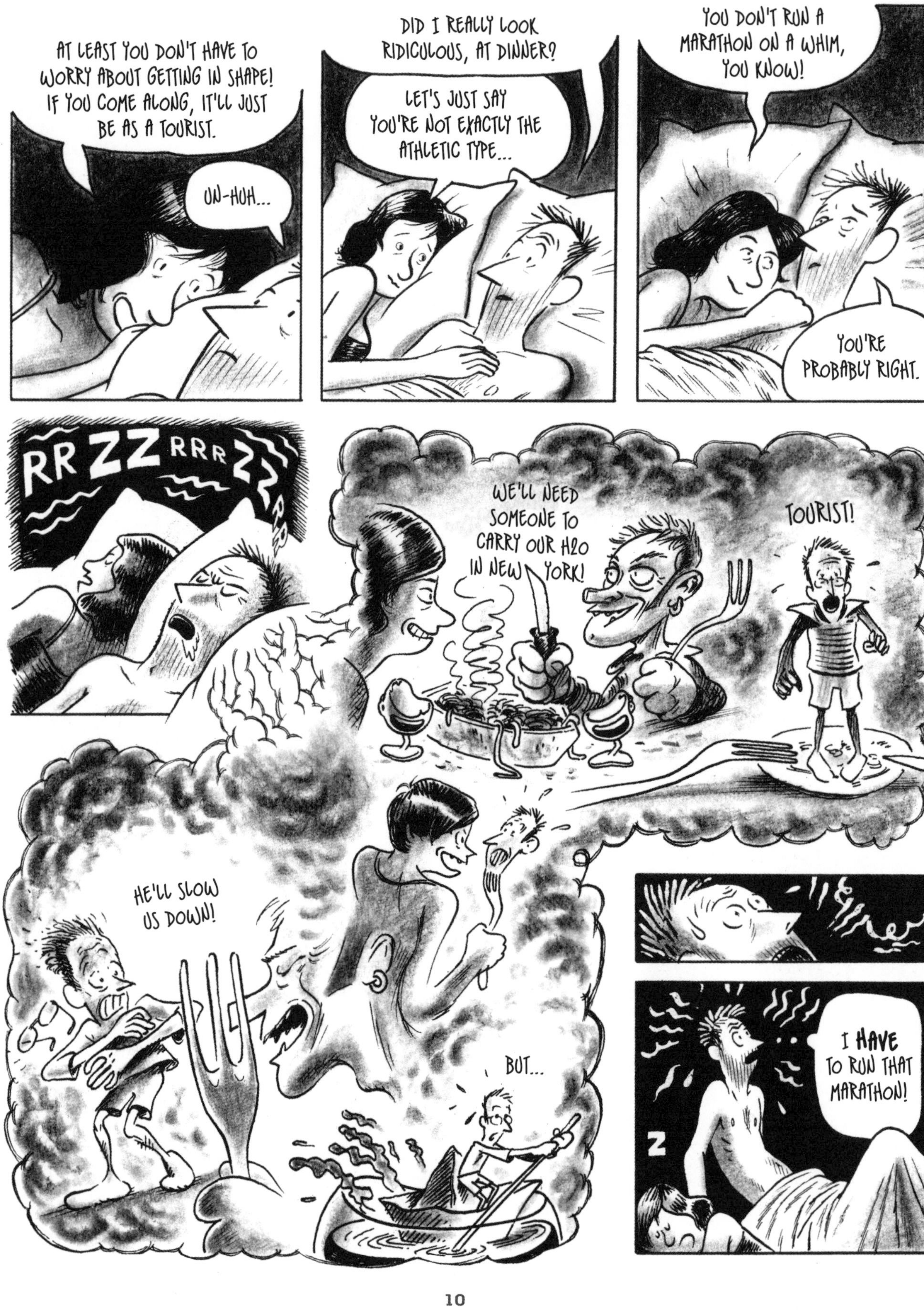
AT LEAST YOU DON'T HAVE TO WORRY ABOUT GETTING IN SHAPE! IF YOU COME ALONG, IT'LL JUST BE AS A TOURIST.
UH-HUH...
DID I REALLY LOOK RIDICULOUS, AT DINNER?
LET'S JUST SAY YOU'RE NOT EXACTLY THE ATHLETIC TYPE...
YOU DON'T RUN A MARATHON ON A WHIM, YOU KNOW!
YOU'RE PROBABLY RIGHT.
RR ZZ RRR ZZ RR
WE'LL NEED SOMEONE TO CARRY OUR H2O IN NEW YORK!
TOURIST!
HE'LL SLOW US DOWN!
BUT...
I HAVE TO RUN THAT MARATHON!
Z

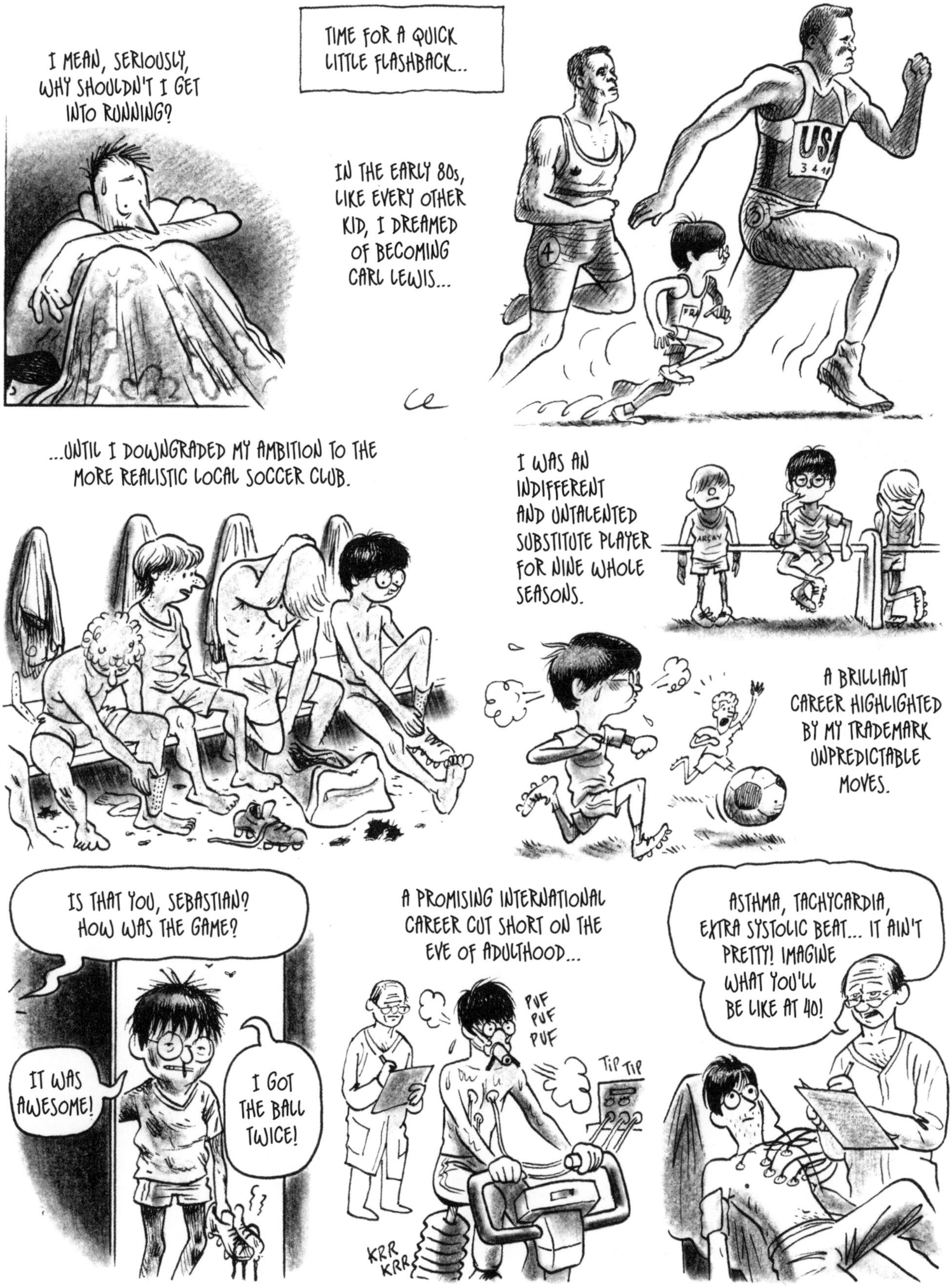

I MEAN, SERIOUSLY, WHY SHOULDN'T I GET INTO RUNNING?
TIME FOR A QUICK LITTLE FLASHBACK...
IN THE EARLY 80s, LIKE EVERY OTHER KID, I DREAMED OF BECOMING CARL LEWIS...
USA
...UNTIL I DOWNGRADED MY AMBITION TO THE MORE REALISTIC LOCAL SOCCER CLUB.
I WAS AN INDIFFERENT AND UNTALENTED SUBSTITUTE PLAYER FOR NINE WHOLE SEASONS.
A BRILLIANT CAREER HIGHLIGHTED BY MY TRADEMARK UNPREDICTABLE MOVES.
IS THAT YOU, SEBASTIAN? HOW WAS THE GAME?
IT WAS AWESOME!
I GOT THE BALL TWICE!
A PROMISING INTERNATIONAL CAREER CUT SHORT ON THE EVE OF ADULTHOOD...
PUF PUF PUF
TIP TIP
KRR KRR
ASTHMA, TACHYCARDIA, EXTRA SYSTOLIC BEAT... IT AIN'T PRETTY! IMAGINE WHAT YOU'LL BE LIKE AT 40!

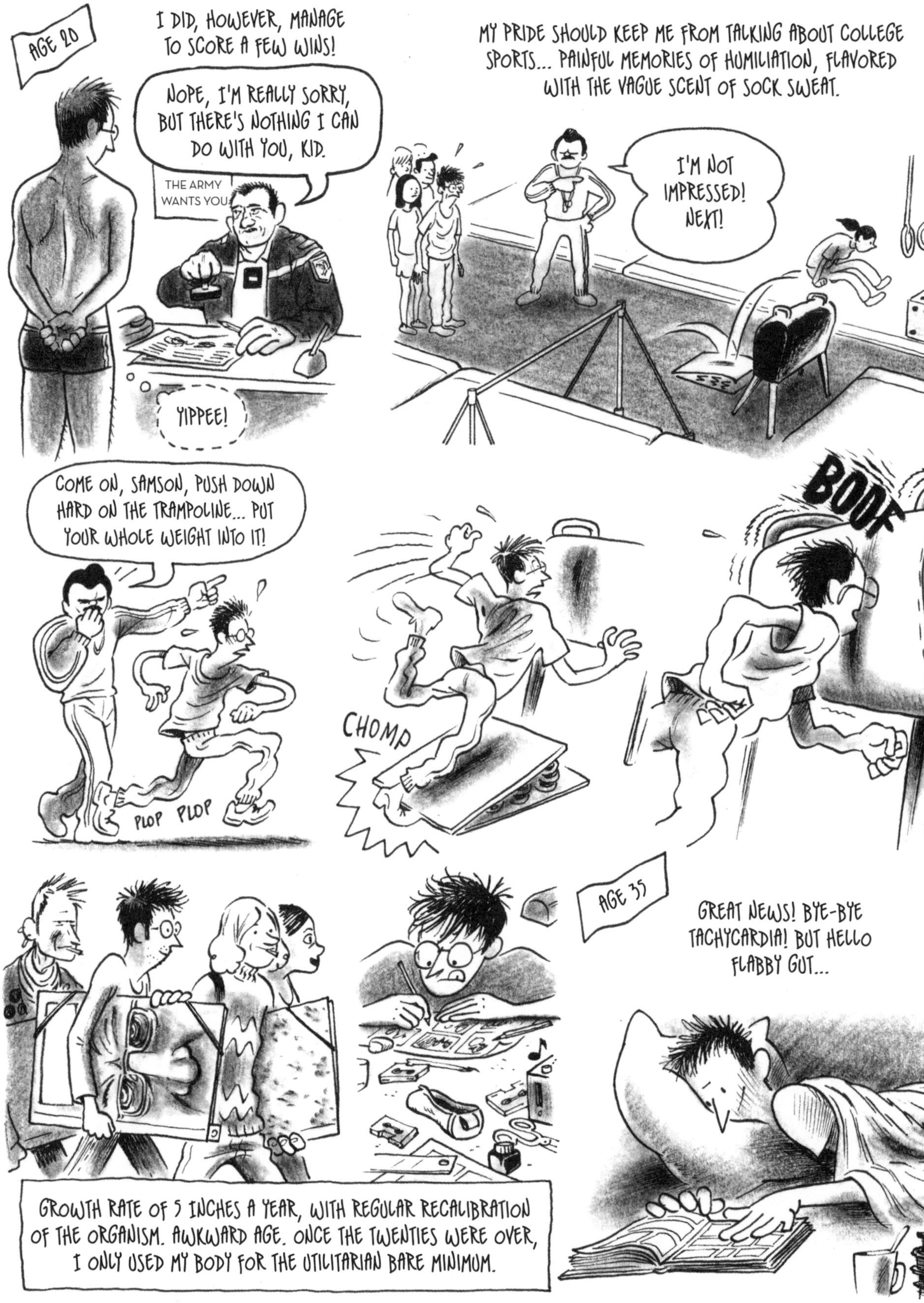
AGE 20
I DID, HOWEVER, MANAGE TO SCORE A FEW WINS!
NOPE, I'M REALLY SORRY, BUT THERE'S NOTHING I CAN DO WITH YOU, KID.
THE ARMY WANTS YOU!
YIPPEE!
MY PRIDE SHOULD KEEP ME FROM TALKING ABOUT COLLEGE SPORTS... PAINFUL MEMORIES OF HUMILIATION, FLAVORED WITH THE VAGUE SCENT OF SOCK SWEAT.
I'M NOT IMPRESSED! NEXT!
COME ON, SAMSON, PUSH DOWN HARD ON THE TRAMPOLINE... PUT YOUR WHOLE WEIGHT INTO IT!
PLOP PLOP
CHOMP
BOOF
GROWTH RATE OF 5 INCHES A YEAR, WITH REGULAR RECALIBRATION OF THE ORGANISM. AWKWARD AGE. ONCE THE TWENTIES WERE OVER, I ONLY USED MY BODY FOR THE UTILITARIAN BARE MINIMUM.
AGE 35
GREAT NEWS! BYE-BYE TACHYCARDIA! BUT HELLO FLABBY GUT...

2.
STIFF
On The Cliff

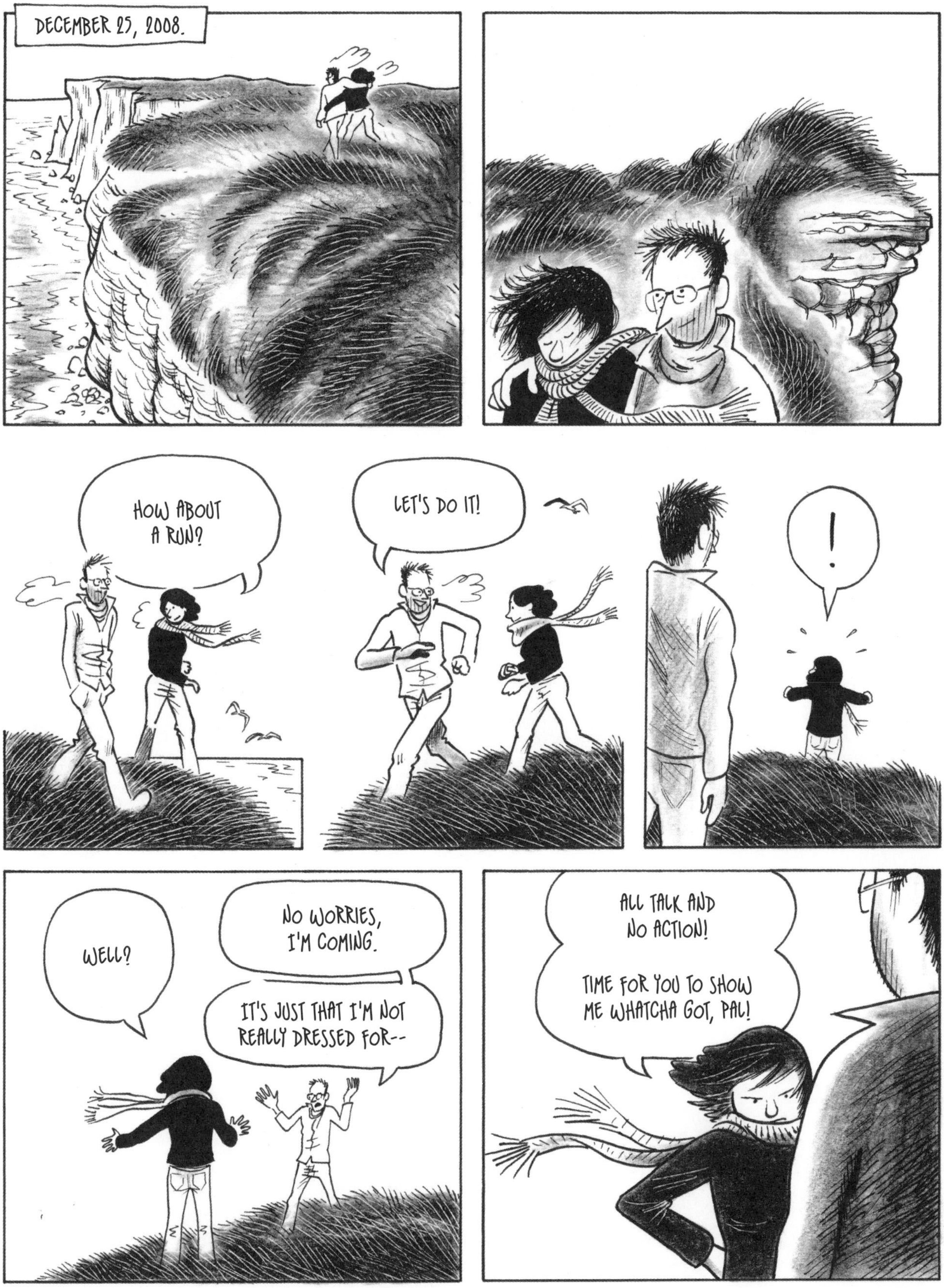
DECEMBER 25, 2008.
HOW ABOUT A RUN?
LET'S DO IT!
!
WELL?
NO WORRIES, I'M COMING.
IT'S JUST THAT I'M NOT REALLY DRESSED FOR--
ALL TALK AND NO ACTION!
TIME FOR YOU TO SHOW ME WHATCHA GOT, PAL!

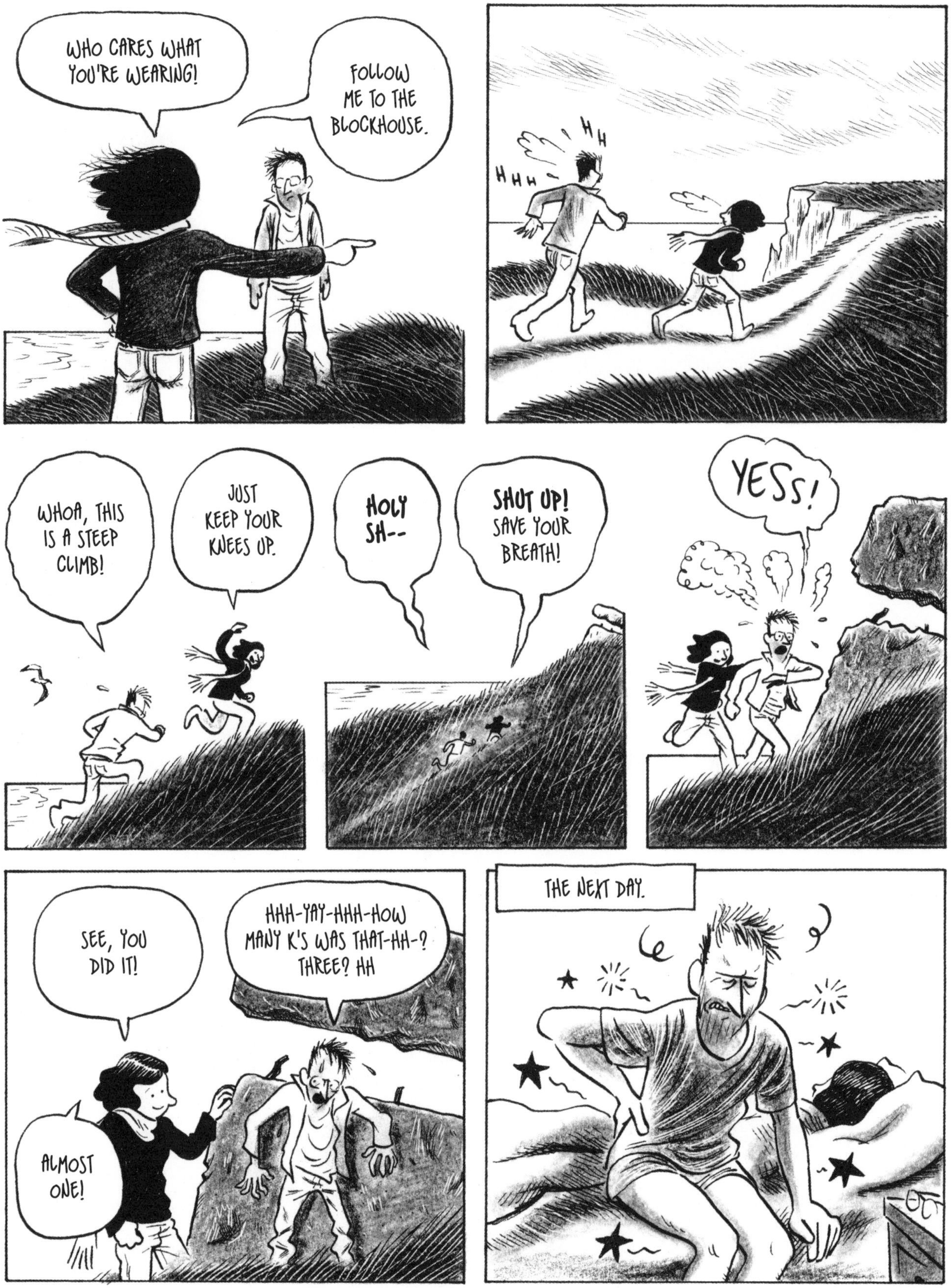
WHO CARES WHAT YOU'RE WEARING!
FOLLOW ME TO THE BLOCKHOUSE.
HH
HHH
WHOA, THIS IS A STEEP CLIMB!
JUST KEEP YOUR KNEES UP.
HOLY SH--
SHUT UP! SAVE YOUR BREATH!
YESS!
SEE, YOU DID IT!
HHH-YAY-HHH-HOW MANY K'S WAS THAT-HH-? THREE? HH
ALMOST ONE!
THE NEXT DAY.

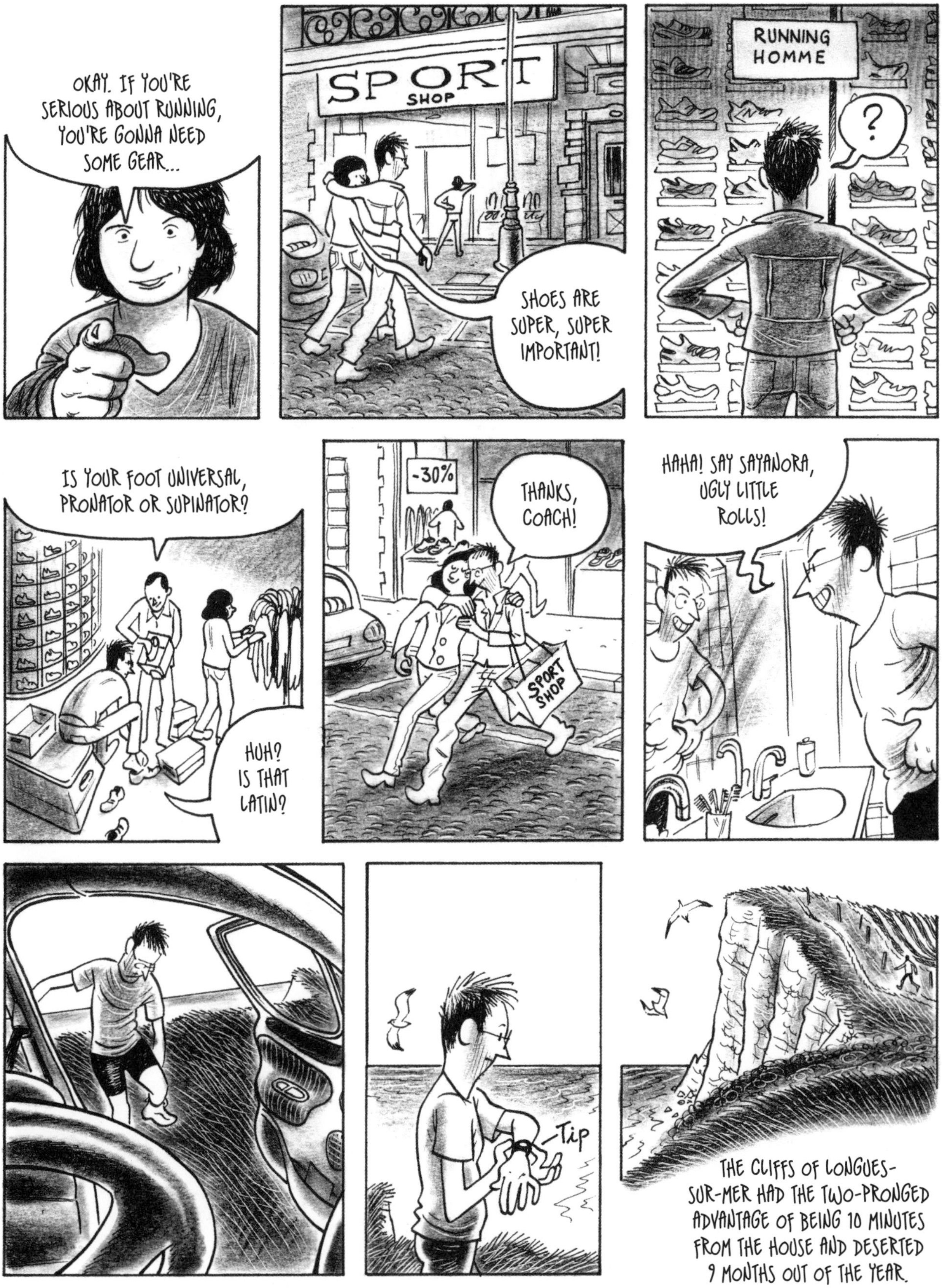
OKAY. IF YOU'RE SERIOUS ABOUT RUNNING, YOU'RE GONNA NEED SOME GEAR...
SPORT SHOP
SHOES ARE SUPER, SUPER IMPORTANT!
RUNNING HOMME
?
IS YOUR FOOT UNIVERSAL, PRONATOR OR SUPINATOR?
HUH? IS THAT LATIN?
-30%
THANKS, COACH!
SPORT SHOP
HAHA! SAY SAYANORA, UGLY LITTLE ROLLS!
-Tip
THE CLIFFS OF LONGUES-SUR-MER HAD THE TWO-PRONGED ADVANTAGE OF BEING 10 MINUTES FROM THE HOUSE AND DESERTED 9 MONTHS OUT OF THE YEAR.

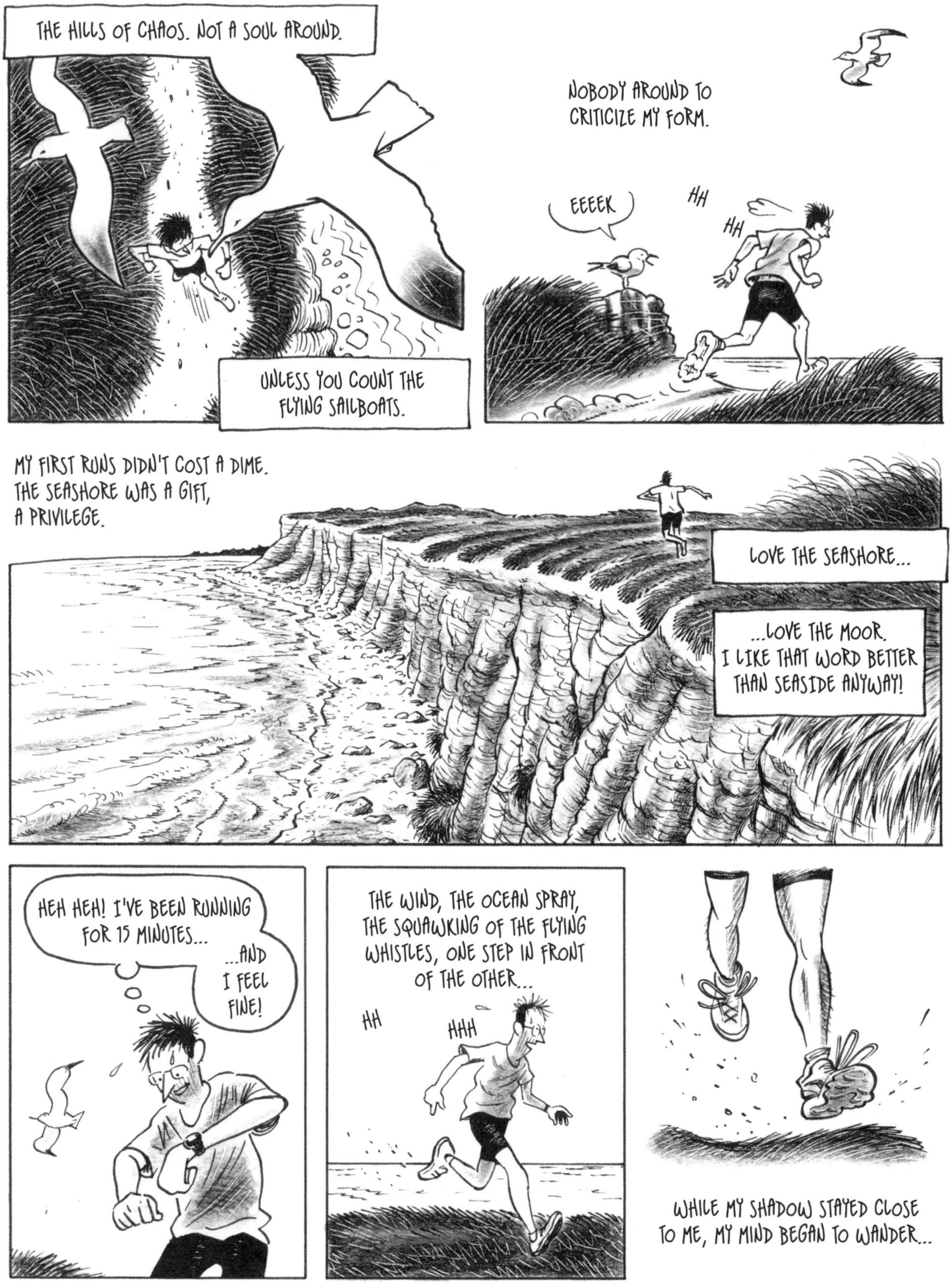
THE HILLS OF CHAOS. NOT A SOUL AROUND.
UNLESS YOU COUNT THE FLYING SAILBOATS.
NOBODY AROUND TO CRITICIZE MY FORM.
EEEEK
HH
HH
MY FIRST RUNS DIDN'T COST A DIME. THE SEASHORE WAS A GIFT, A PRIVILEGE.
LOVE THE SEASHORE...
...LOVE THE MOOR. I LIKE THAT WORD BETTER THAN SEASIDE ANYWAY!
HEH HEH! I'VE BEEN RUNNING FOR 15 MINUTES...
...AND I FEEL FINE!
THE WIND, THE OCEAN SPRAY, THE SQUAWKING OF THE FLYING WHISTLES, ONE STEP IN FRONT OF THE OTHER...
HH
HHH
WHILE MY SHADOW STAYED CLOSE TO ME, MY MIND BEGAN TO WANDER...

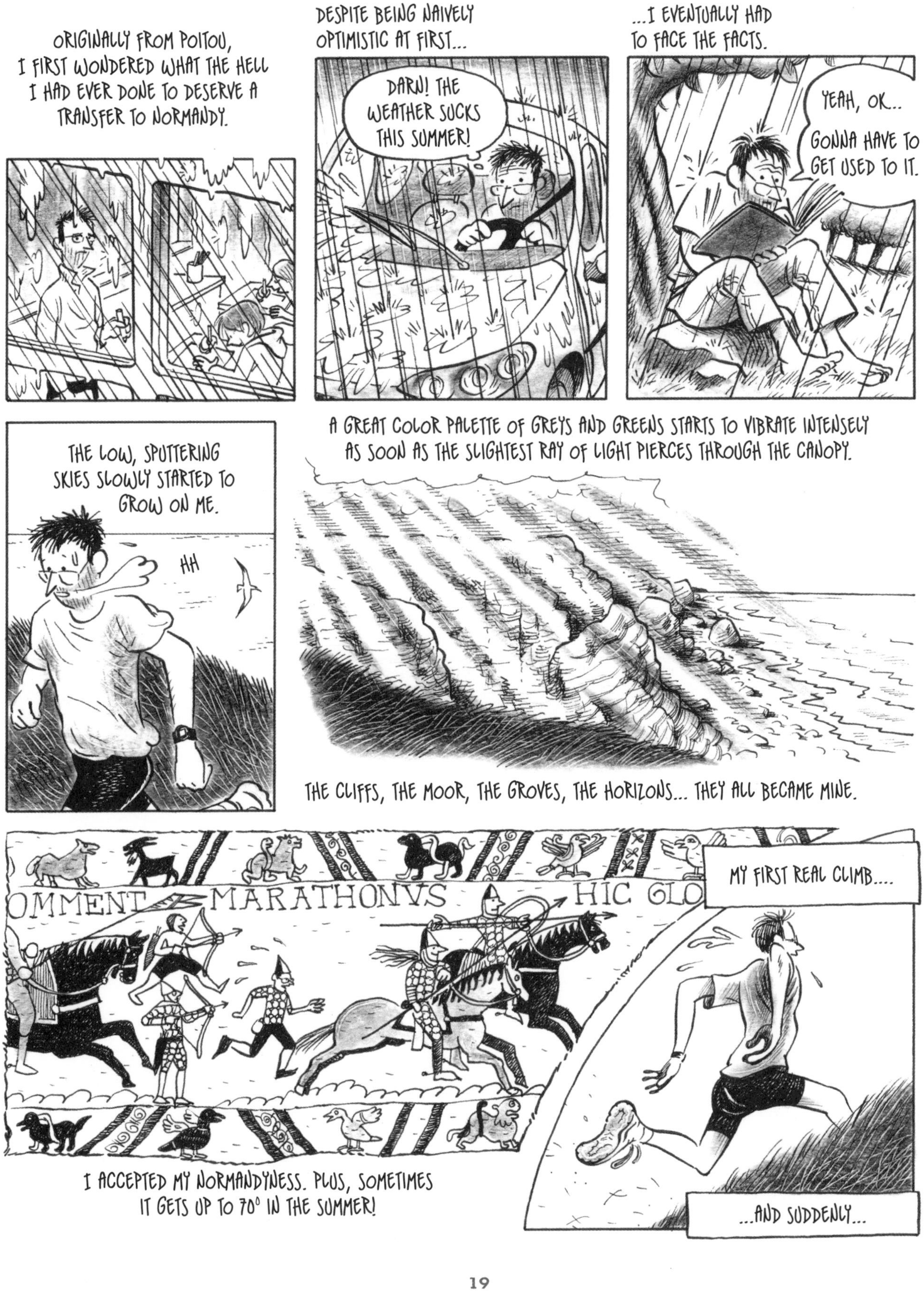
ORIGINALLY FROM POITOU, I FIRST WONDERED WHAT THE HELL I HAD EVER DONE TO DESERVE A TRANSFER TO NORMANDY.
DESPITE BEING NAIVELY OPTIMISTIC AT FIRST...
DARN! THE WEATHER SUCKS THIS SUMMER!
...I EVENTUALLY HAD TO FACE THE FACTS.
YEAH, OK...
GONNA HAVE TO GET USED TO IT.
THE LOW, SPUTTERING SKIES SLOWLY STARTED TO GROW ON ME.
HH
A GREAT COLOR PALETTE OF GREYS AND GREENS STARTS TO VIBRATE INTENSELY AS SOON AS THE SLIGHTEST RAY OF LIGHT PIERCES THROUGH THE CANOPY.
THE CLIFFS, THE MOOR, THE GROVES, THE HORIZONS... THEY ALL BECAME MINE.
OMMENT
MARATHONVS
HIC GLO
I ACCEPTED MY NORMANDYNESS. PLUS, SOMETIMES IT GETS UP TO 70° IN THE SUMMER!
MY FIRST REAL CLIMB....
...AND SUDDENLY...

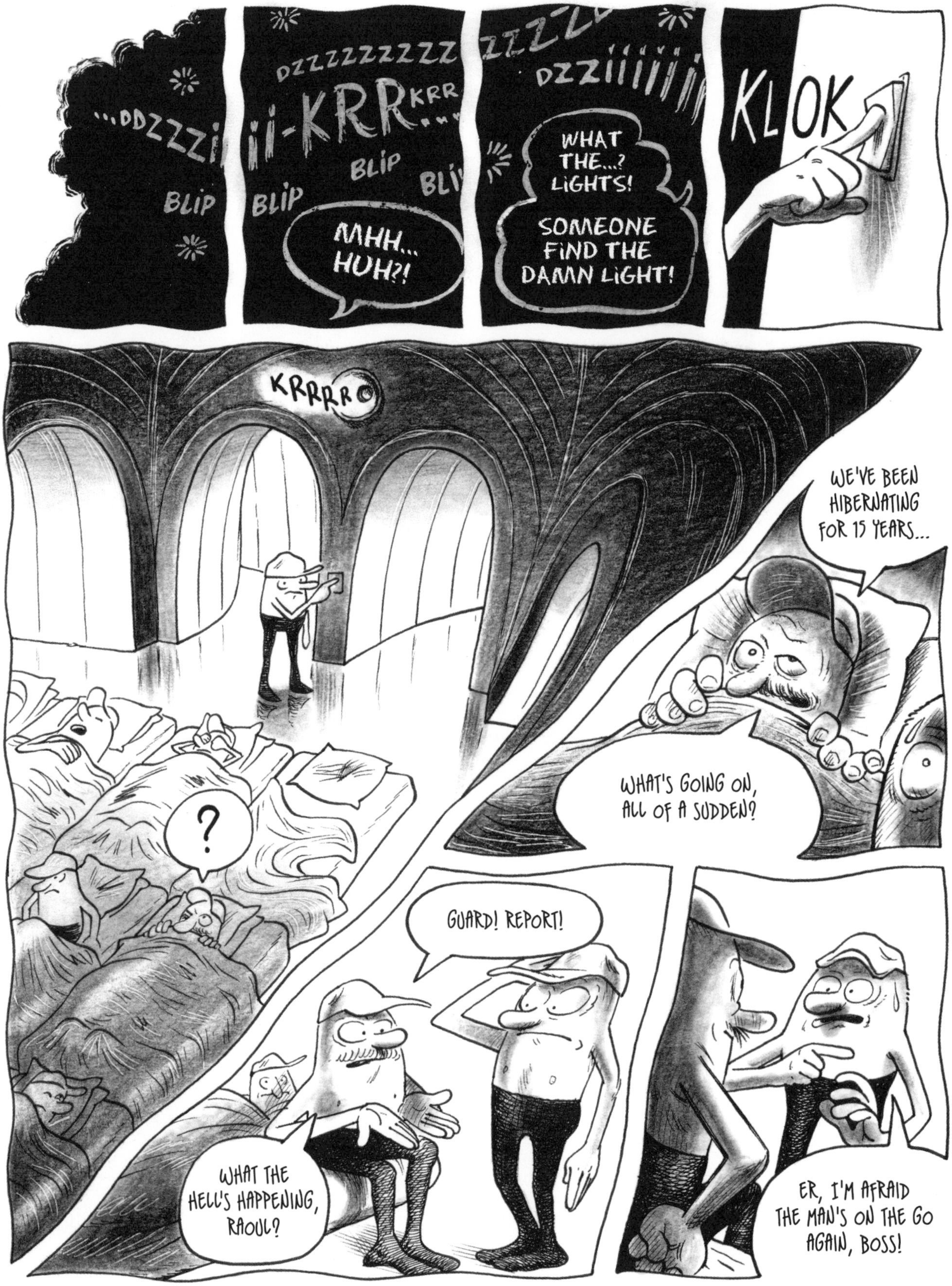
...DDZZZZi
BLIP
DZZZZZZZZZ
ii-KRRKRR...
BLIP
BLIP
BLI
MHH... HUH?!
ZZZZZ
DZZiiiiiii
WHAT THE...? LIGHTS!
SOMEONE FIND THE DAMN LIGHT!
KLOK
KRRRRO
?
WE'VE BEEN HIBERNATING FOR 15 YEARS...
WHAT'S GOING ON, ALL OF A SUDDEN?
GUARD! REPORT!
WHAT THE HELL'S HAPPENING, RAOUL?
ER, I'M AFRAID THE MAN'S ON THE GO AGAIN, BOSS!

OUR MONITORS SHOW INTENSE CARDIAC ACTIVITY AND AN EXCESSIVE OUTPUT OF SWEAT, BOSS.

COULD IT BE THAT THE MAN IS SIMPLY FEELING ESPECIALLY AMOROUS?

NEGATIVE, BOSS! OUR TECHNICIANS HAVE INDEED RECORDED A MASSIVE FLOW OF BLOOD TOWARD THE LOWER ORGANS...

...BUT NOT A HECTOLITER TO THE GROIN AREA!

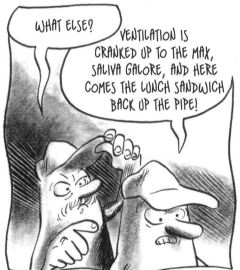

WHAT ELSE?

VENTILATION IS CRANKED UP TO THE MAX, SALIVA GALORE, AND HERE COMES THE LUNCH SANDWICH BACK UP THE PIPE!

YIKES! WHAT KIND OF STUNT IS HE PULLING, HERE?

LET'S SWITCH TO VISUAL.

FOLLOW ME.

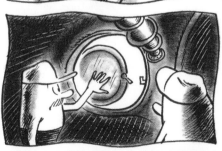

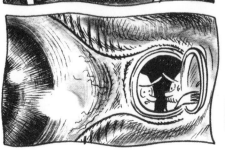

WHEW! MAN OH MAN!

21

MY POETIC REFLECTIONS ON THE BEAUTY OF THE LANDSCAPE QUICKLY DISSIPATE AS I HIT A ROUGH PATCH.

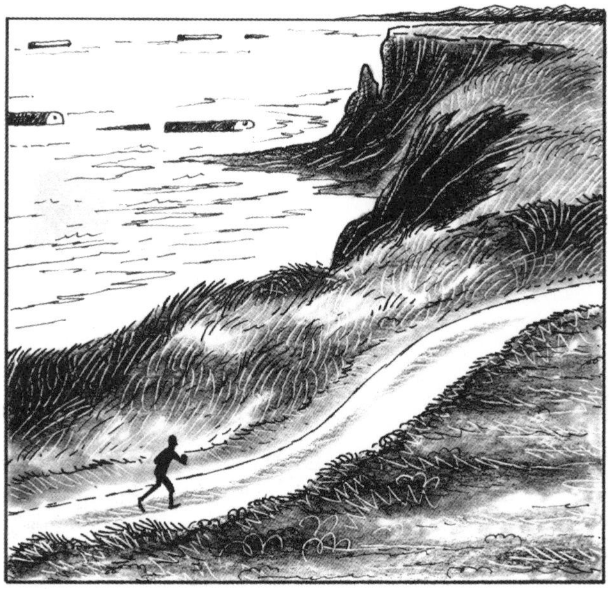

THE PAIN APPEARED LIKE A SERIES OF WARNING LIGHTS INDICATING AN ENGINE MALFUNCTION AND REQUIRING AN URGENT STOP.

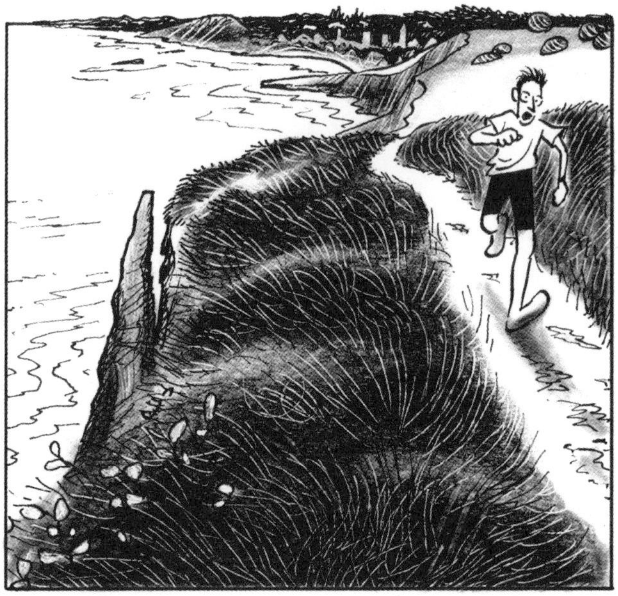

I COULD FEEL THE WEIGHT OF MY ENTIRE BODY AND OF ALL THOSE YEARS OF INACTIVITY WITH EVERY STEP. WHY WERE MY LUNGS EJECTING MORE CARBON MONOXIDE THAN THEY WERE INHALING OXYGEN?

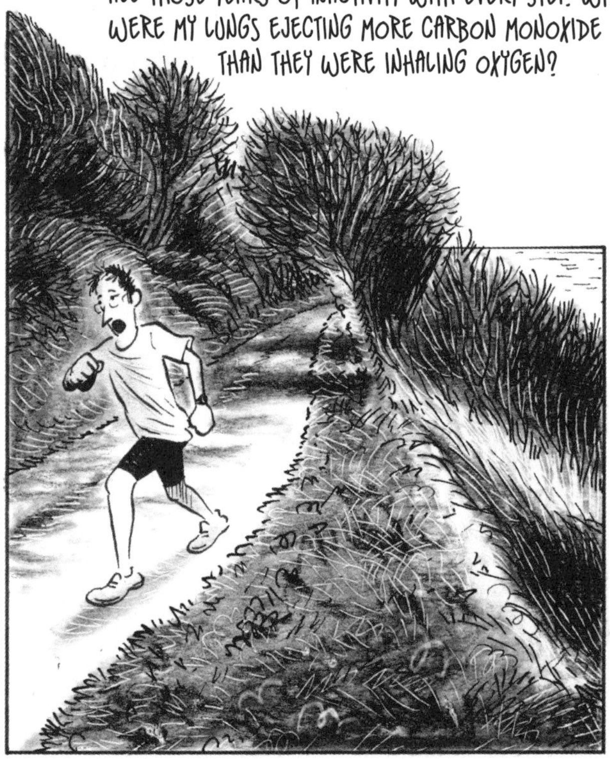

I WAS GETTING THE DISTINCT FEELING THAT THE ENGINEERING WASN'T UP TO TASK IN THERE!

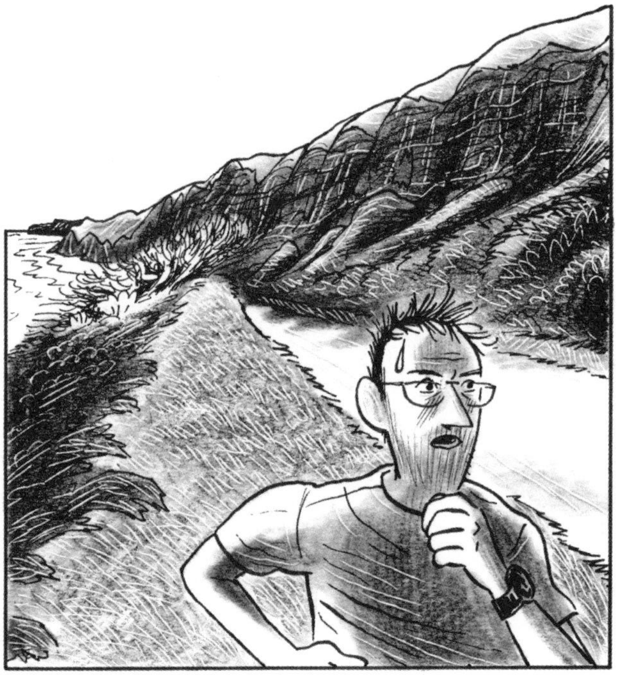

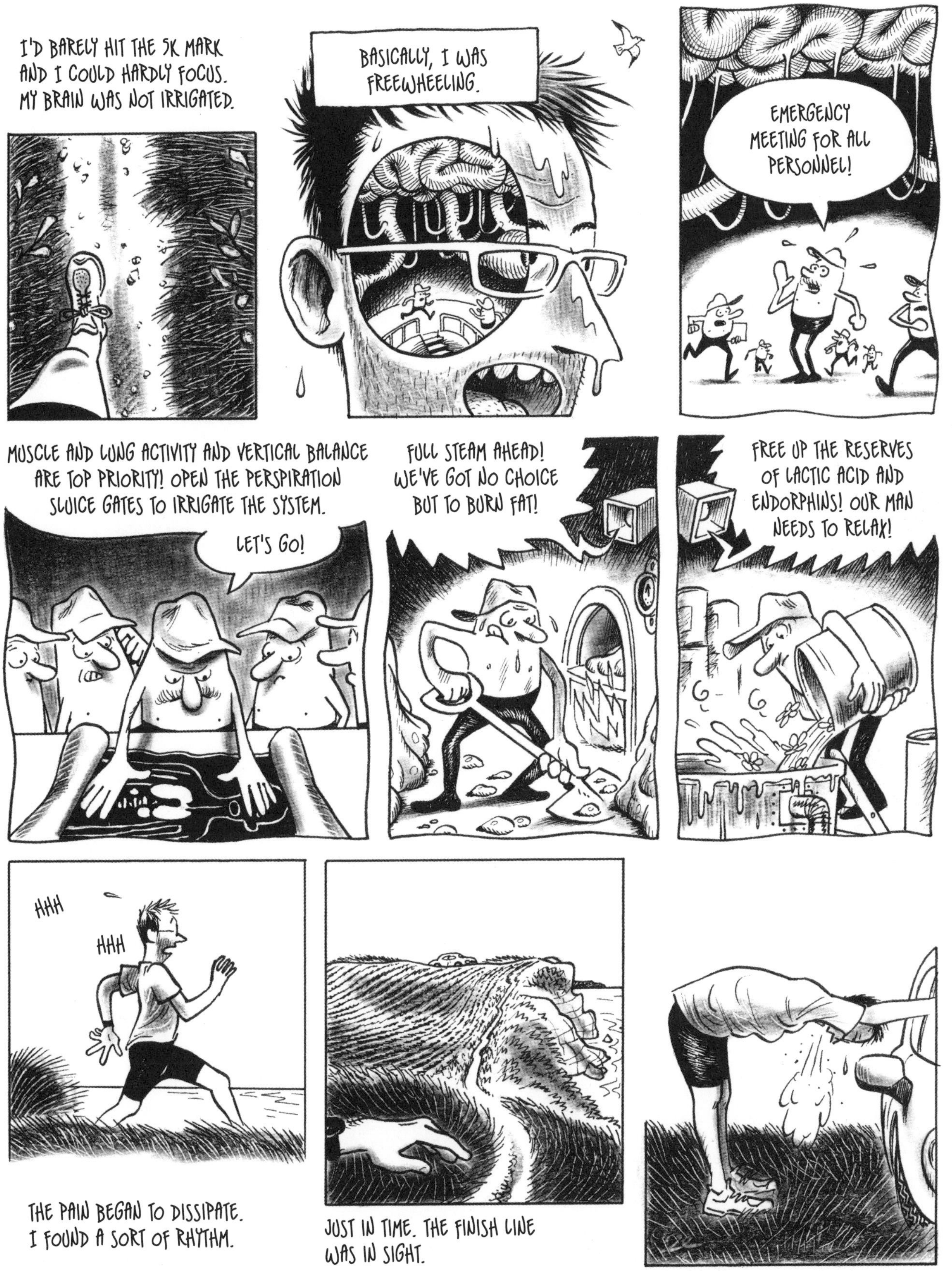
I'D BARELY HIT THE 5K MARK AND I COULD HARDLY FOCUS. MY BRAIN WAS NOT IRRIGATED.
BASICALLY, I WAS FREEWHEELING.
EMERGENCY MEETING FOR ALL PERSONNEL!
MUSCLE AND LUNG ACTIVITY AND VERTICAL BALANCE ARE TOP PRIORITY! OPEN THE PERSPIRATION SLUICE GATES TO IRRIGATE THE SYSTEM.
LET'S GO!
FULL STEAM AHEAD! WE'VE GOT NO CHOICE BUT TO BURN FAT!
FREE UP THE RESERVES OF LACTIC ACID AND ENDORPHINS! OUR MAN NEEDS TO RELAX!
HHH
HHH
THE PAIN BEGAN TO DISSIPATE. I FOUND A SORT OF RHYTHM.
JUST IN TIME. THE FINISH LINE WAS IN SIGHT.

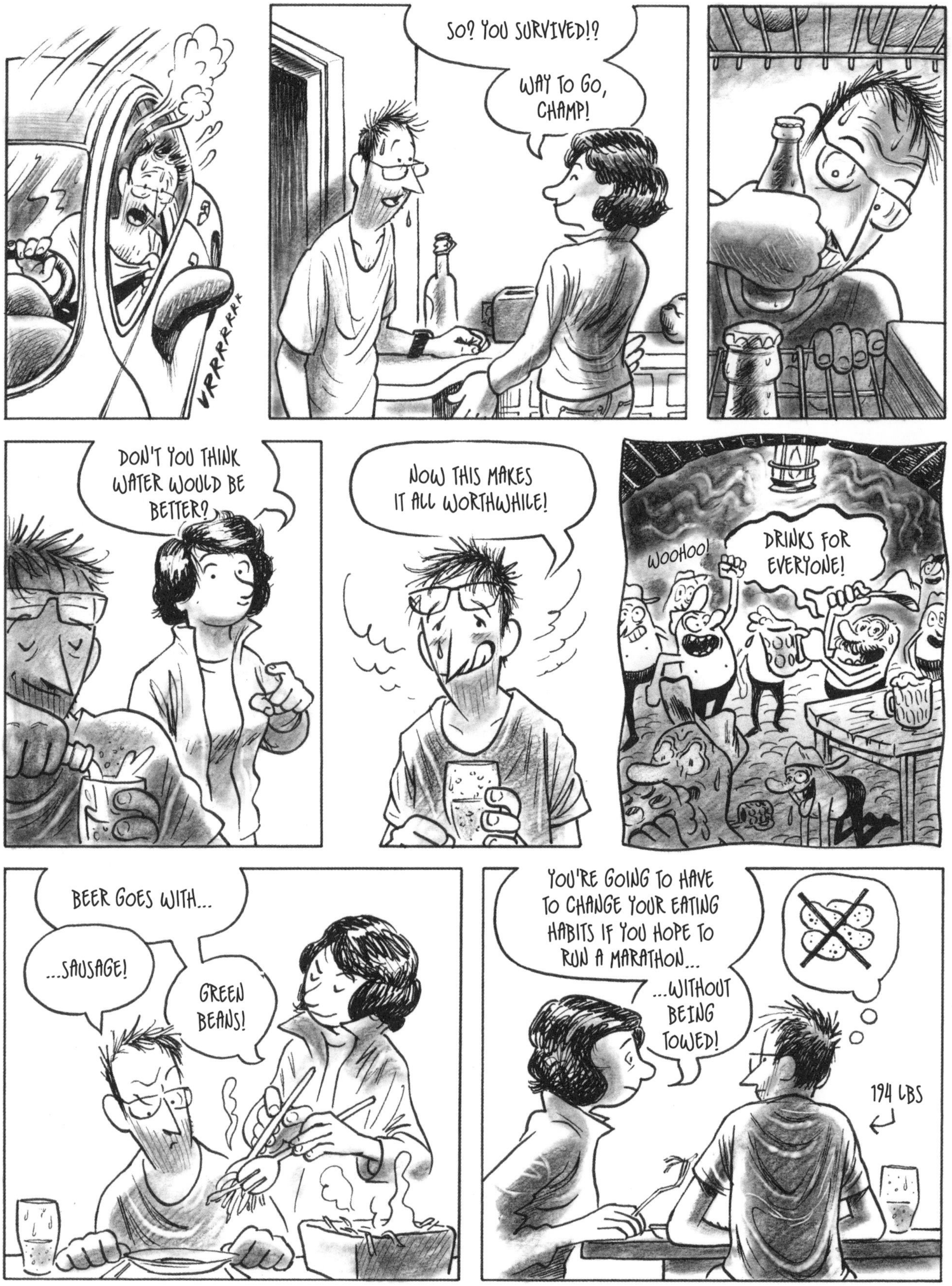
VRRRRRRR
SO? YOU SURVIVED!?
WAY TO GO, CHAMP!
DON'T YOU THINK WATER WOULD BE BETTER?
NOW THIS MAKES IT ALL WORTHWHILE!
WOOHOO!
DRINKS FOR EVERYONE!
BEER GOES WITH...
...SAUSAGE!
GREEN BEANS!
YOU'RE GOING TO HAVE TO CHANGE YOUR EATING HABITS IF YOU HOPE TO RUN A MARATHON...
...WITHOUT BEING TOWED!
194 LBS

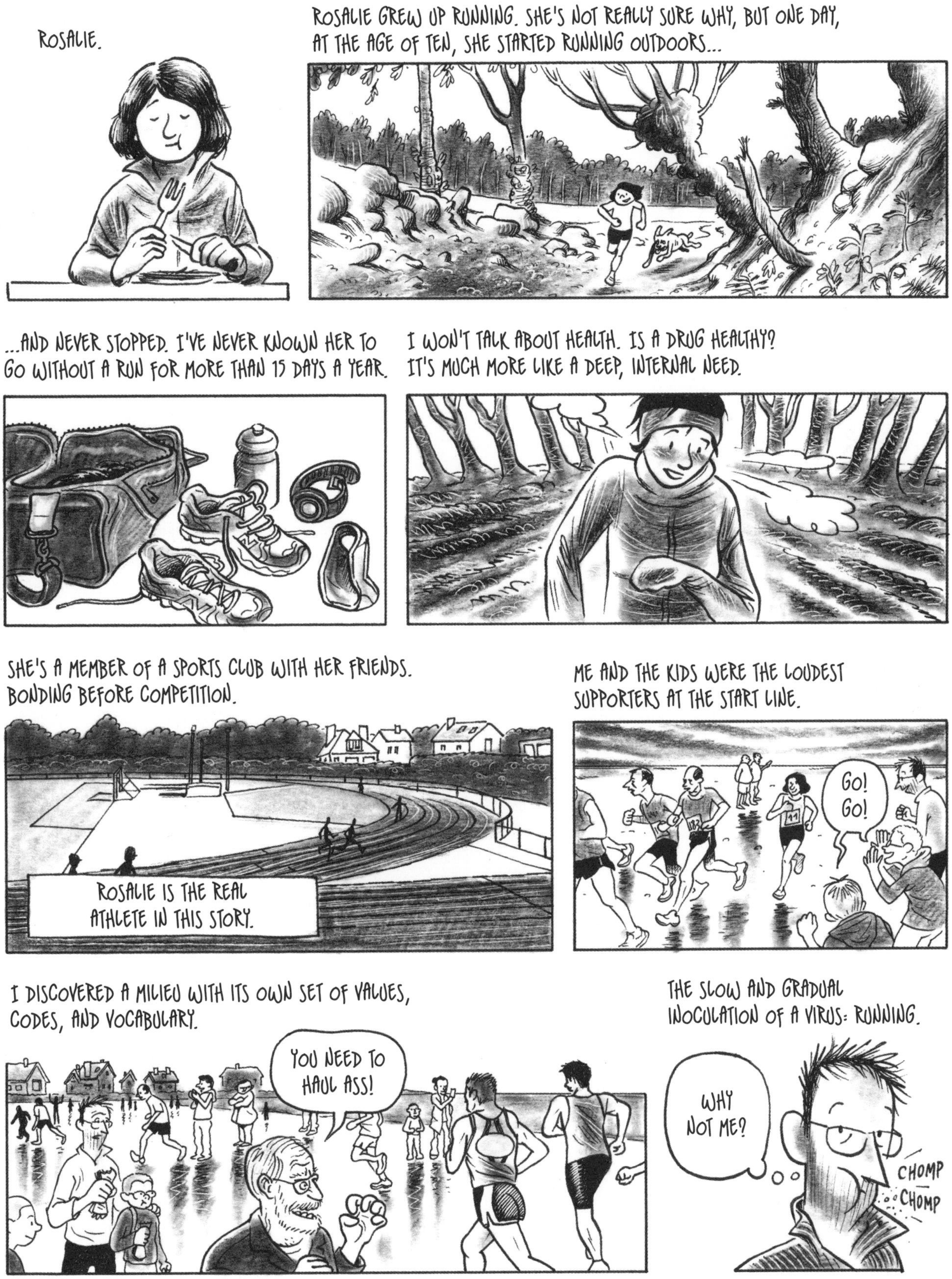
ROSALIE.
ROSALIE GREW UP RUNNING. SHE'S NOT REALLY SURE WHY, BUT ONE DAY, AT THE AGE OF TEN, SHE STARTED RUNNING OUTDOORS...
...AND NEVER STOPPED. I'VE NEVER KNOWN HER TO GO WITHOUT A RUN FOR MORE THAN 15 DAYS A YEAR.
I WON'T TALK ABOUT HEALTH. IS A DRUG HEALTHY? IT'S MUCH MORE LIKE A DEEP, INTERNAL NEED.
SHE'S A MEMBER OF A SPORTS CLUB WITH HER FRIENDS. BONDING BEFORE COMPETITION.
ROSALIE IS THE REAL ATHLETE IN THIS STORY.
ME AND THE KIDS WERE THE LOUDEST SUPPORTERS AT THE START LINE.
GO! GO!
I DISCOVERED A MILIEU WITH ITS OWN SET OF VALUES, CODES, AND VOCABULARY.
YOU NEED TO HAUL ASS!
THE SLOW AND GRADUAL INOCULATION OF A VIRUS: RUNNING.
WHY NOT ME?
CHOMP
CHOMP

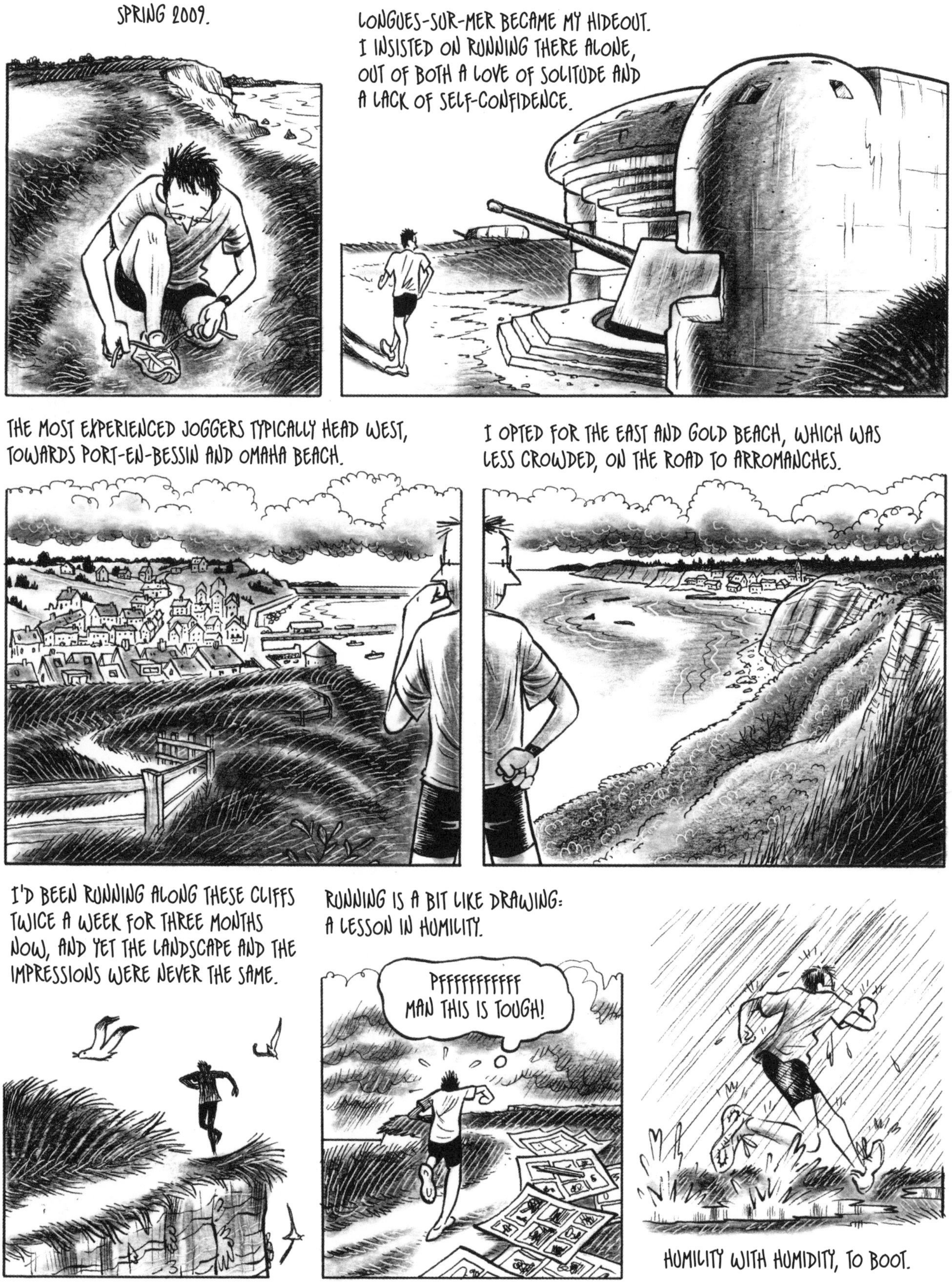
SPRING 2009.
LONGUES-SUR-MER BECAME MY HIDEOUT. I INSISTED ON RUNNING THERE ALONE, OUT OF BOTH A LOVE OF SOLITUDE AND A LACK OF SELF-CONFIDENCE.
THE MOST EXPERIENCED JOGGERS TYPICALLY HEAD WEST, TOWARDS PORT-EN-BESSIN AND OMAHA BEACH.
I OPTED FOR THE EAST AND GOLD BEACH, WHICH WAS LESS CROWDED, ON THE ROAD TO ARROMANCHES.
I'D BEEN RUNNING ALONG THESE CLIFFS TWICE A WEEK FOR THREE MONTHS NOW, AND YET THE LANDSCAPE AND THE IMPRESSIONS WERE NEVER THE SAME.
RUNNING IS A BIT LIKE DRAWING: A LESSON IN HUMILITY.
PFFFFFFFFFFF
MAN THIS IS TOUGH!
HUMILITY WITH HUMIDITY, TO BOOT.

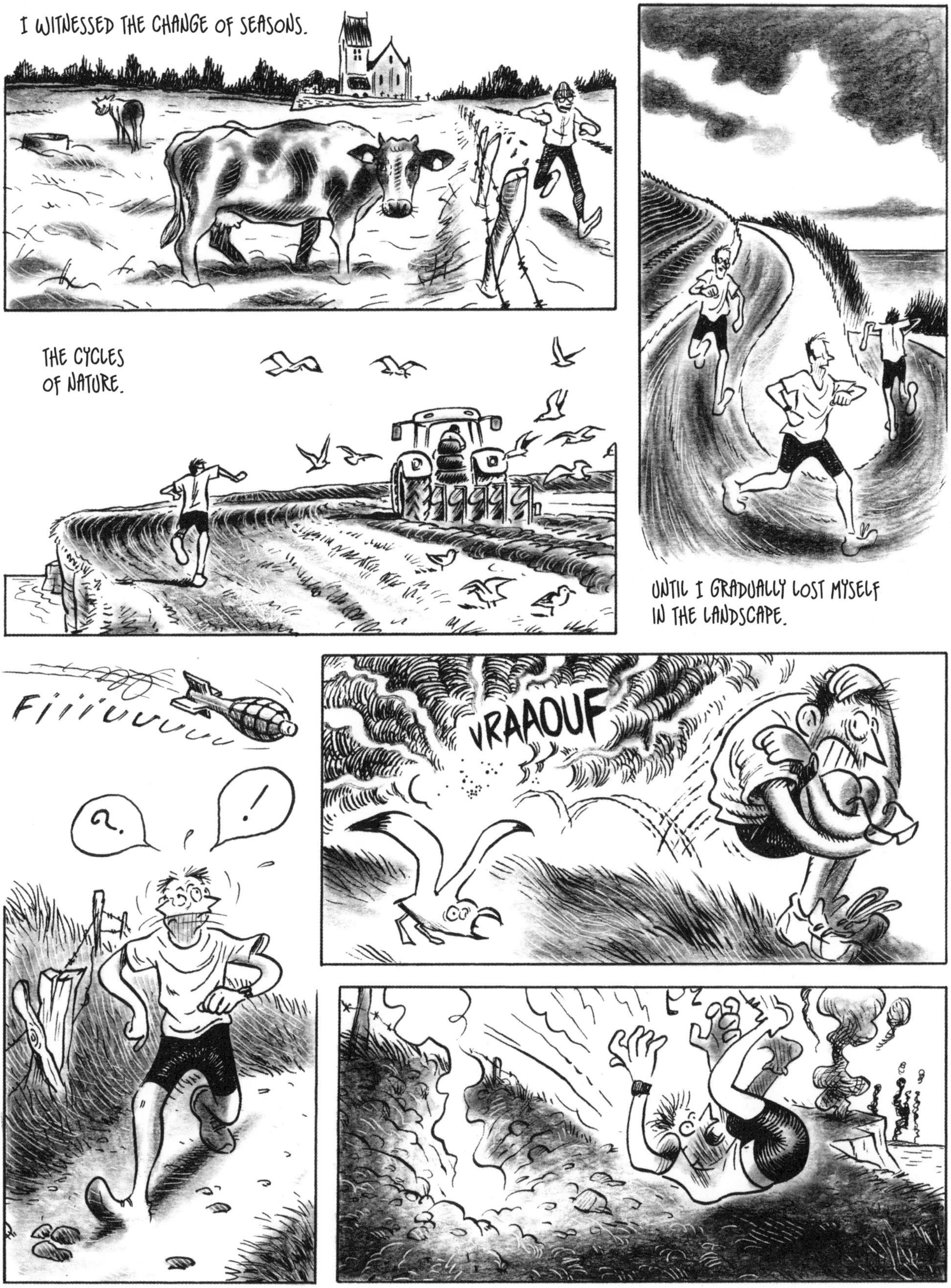
I WITNESSED THE CHANGE OF SEASONS.
THE CYCLES OF NATURE.
UNTIL I GRADUALLY LOST MYSELF IN THE LANDSCAPE.
FIIIUUUUUU
?
!
VRAAOUF

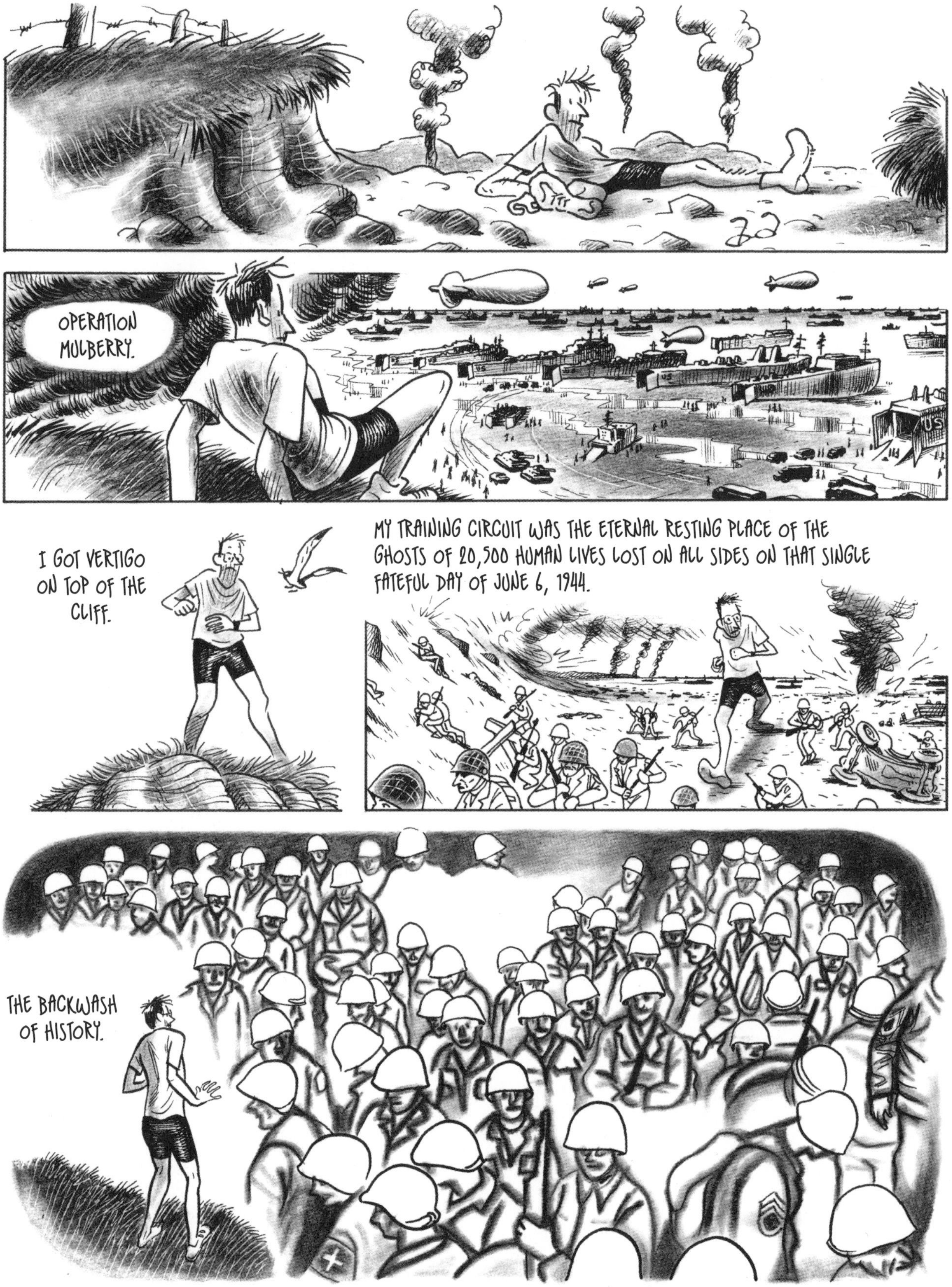
OPERATION MULBERRY.
I GOT VERTIGO ON TOP OF THE CLIFF.
MY TRAINING CIRCUIT WAS THE ETERNAL RESTING PLACE OF THE GHOSTS OF 20,500 HUMAN LIVES LOST ON ALL SIDES ON THAT SINGLE FATEFUL DAY OF JUNE 6, 1944.
THE BACKWASH OF HISTORY.

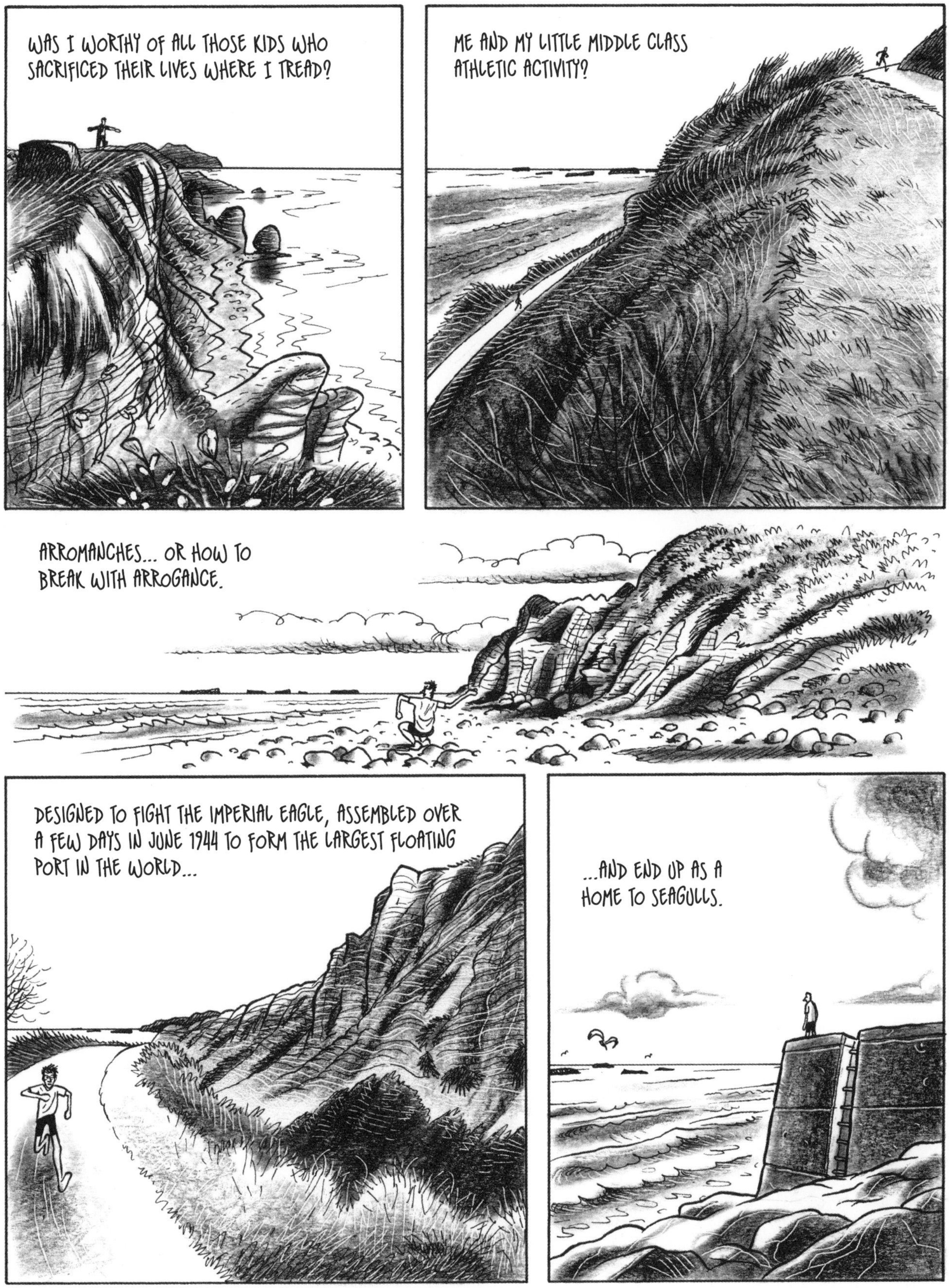
WAS I WORTHY OF ALL THOSE KIDS WHO SACRIFICED THEIR LIVES WHERE I TREAD?
ME AND MY LITTLE MIDDLE CLASS ATHLETIC ACTIVITY?
ARROMANCHES... OR HOW TO BREAK WITH ARROGANCE.
DESIGNED TO FIGHT THE IMPERIAL EAGLE, ASSEMBLED OVER A FEW DAYS IN JUNE 1944 TO FORM THE LARGEST FLOATING PORT IN THE WORLD...
...AND END UP AS A HOME TO SEAGULLS.

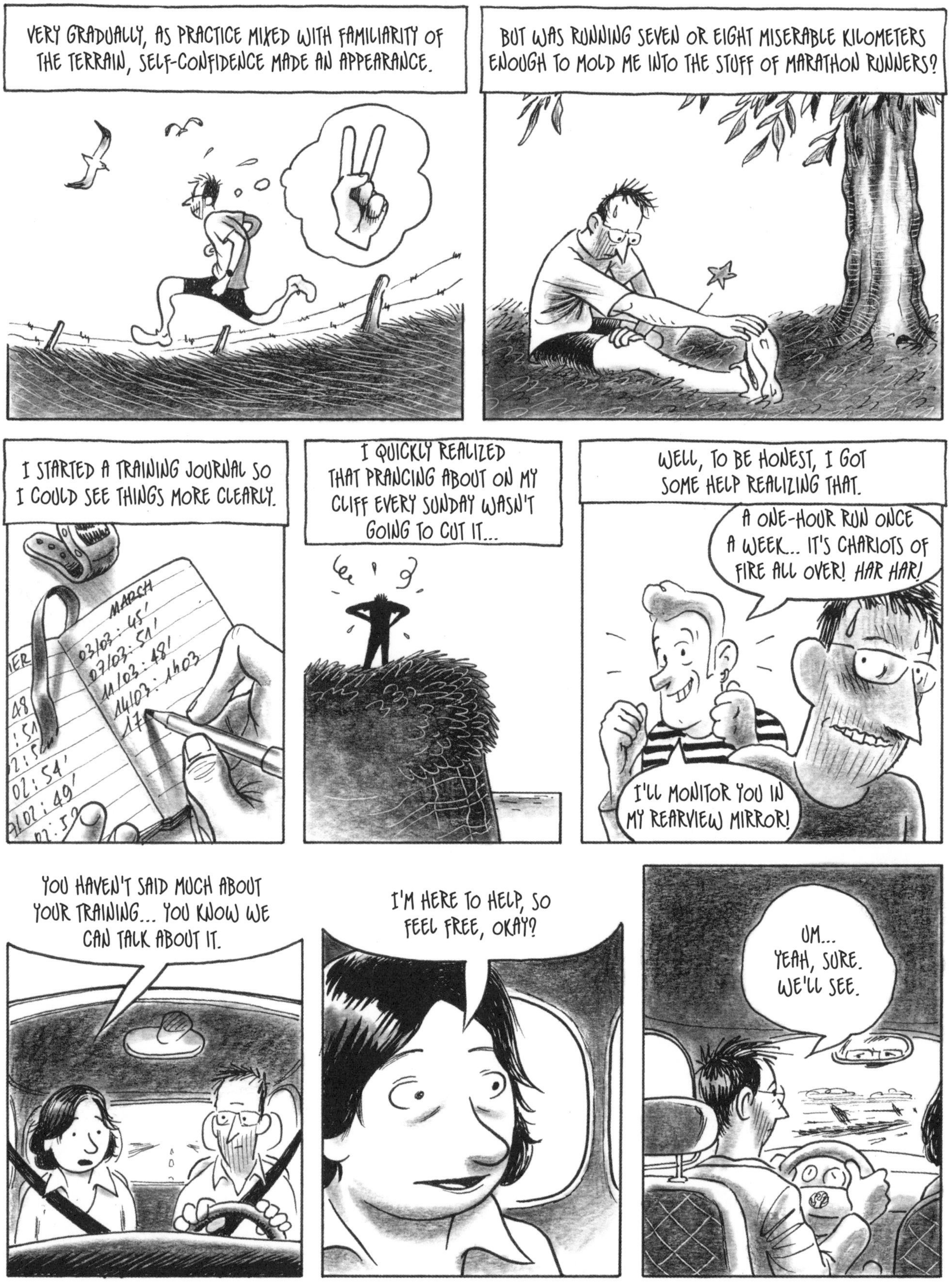

VERY GRADUALLY, AS PRACTICE MIXED WITH FAMILIARITY OF THE TERRAIN, SELF-CONFIDENCE MADE AN APPEARANCE.
BUT WAS RUNNING SEVEN OR EIGHT MISERABLE KILOMETERS ENOUGH TO MOLD ME INTO THE STUFF OF MARATHON RUNNERS?
I STARTED A TRAINING JOURNAL SO I COULD SEE THINGS MORE CLEARLY.
MARCH
03/03: 45'
07/03: 51'
11/03: 48'
14/03: 1h03
17
I QUICKLY REALIZED THAT PRANCING ABOUT ON MY CLIFF EVERY SUNDAY WASN'T GOING TO CUT IT...
WELL, TO BE HONEST, I GOT SOME HELP REALIZING THAT.
A ONE-HOUR RUN ONCE A WEEK... IT'S CHARIOTS OF FIRE ALL OVER! HAR HAR!
I'LL MONITOR YOU IN MY REARVIEW MIRROR!
YOU HAVEN'T SAID MUCH ABOUT YOUR TRAINING... YOU KNOW WE CAN TALK ABOUT IT.
I'M HERE TO HELP, SO FEEL FREE, OKAY?
UM... YEAH, SURE. WE'LL SEE.

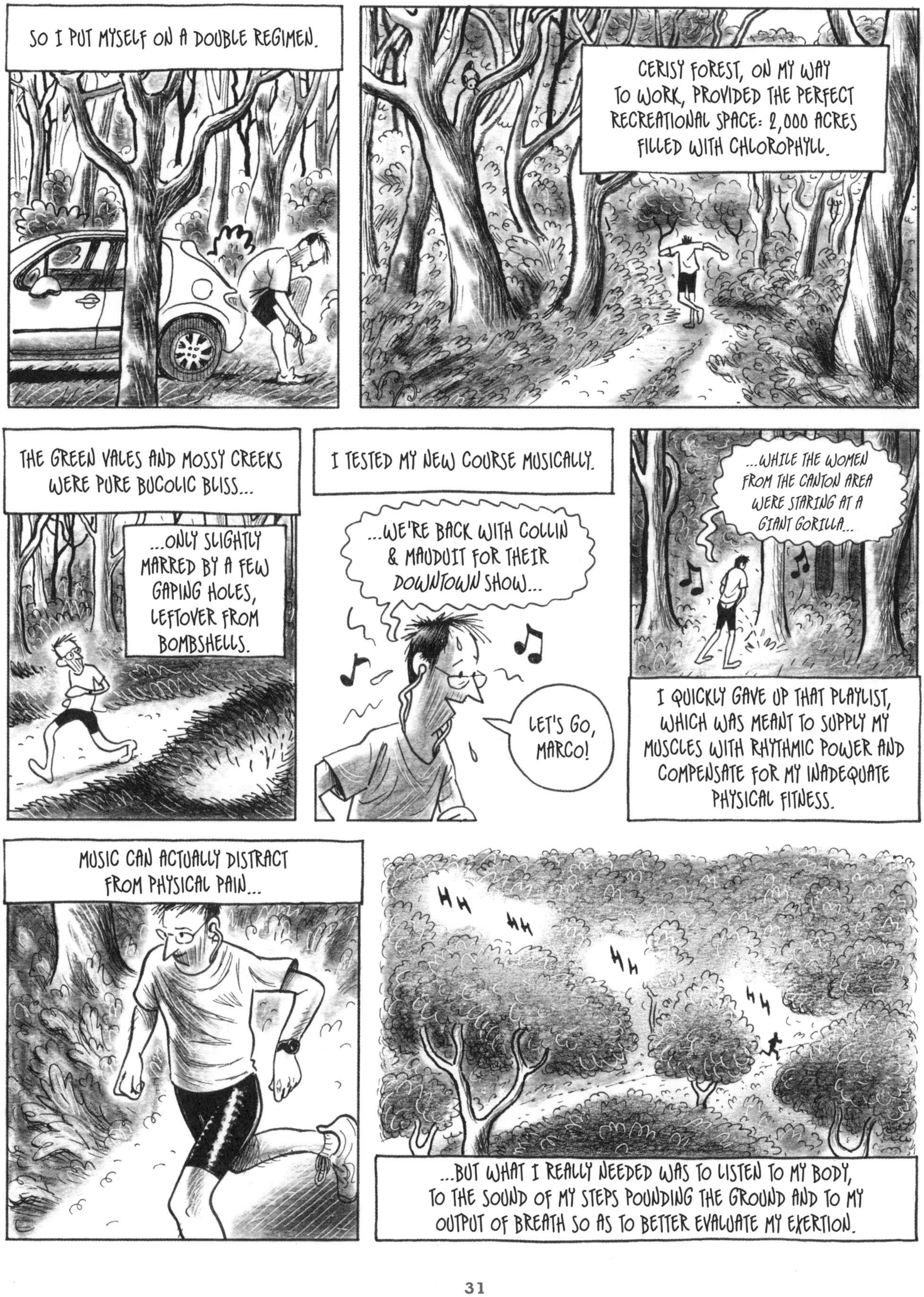
SO I PUT MYSELF ON A DOUBLE REGIMEN.
CERISY FOREST, ON MY WAY TO WORK, PROVIDED THE PERFECT RECREATIONAL SPACE: 2,000 ACRES FILLED WITH CHLOROPHYLL.
THE GREEN VALES AND MOSSY CREEKS WERE PURE BUCOLIC BLISS...
...ONLY SLIGHTLY MARRED BY A FEW GAPING HOLES, LEFTOVER FROM BOMBSHELLS.
I TESTED MY NEW COURSE MUSICALLY.
...WE'RE BACK WITH COLLIN & MAUDUIT FOR THEIR DOWNTOWN SHOW...
LET'S GO, MARCO!
...WHILE THE WOMEN FROM THE CANTON AREA WERE STARING AT A GIANT GORILLA...
I QUICKLY GAVE UP THAT PLAYLIST, WHICH WAS MEANT TO SUPPLY MY MUSCLES WITH RHYTHMIC POWER AND COMPENSATE FOR MY INADEQUATE PHYSICAL FITNESS.
MUSIC CAN ACTUALLY DISTRACT FROM PHYSICAL PAIN...
HH
HH
HH
HH
...BUT WHAT I REALLY NEEDED WAS TO LISTEN TO MY BODY, TO THE SOUND OF MY STEPS POUNDING THE GROUND AND TO MY OUTPUT OF BREATH SO AS TO BETTER EVALUATE MY EXERTION.

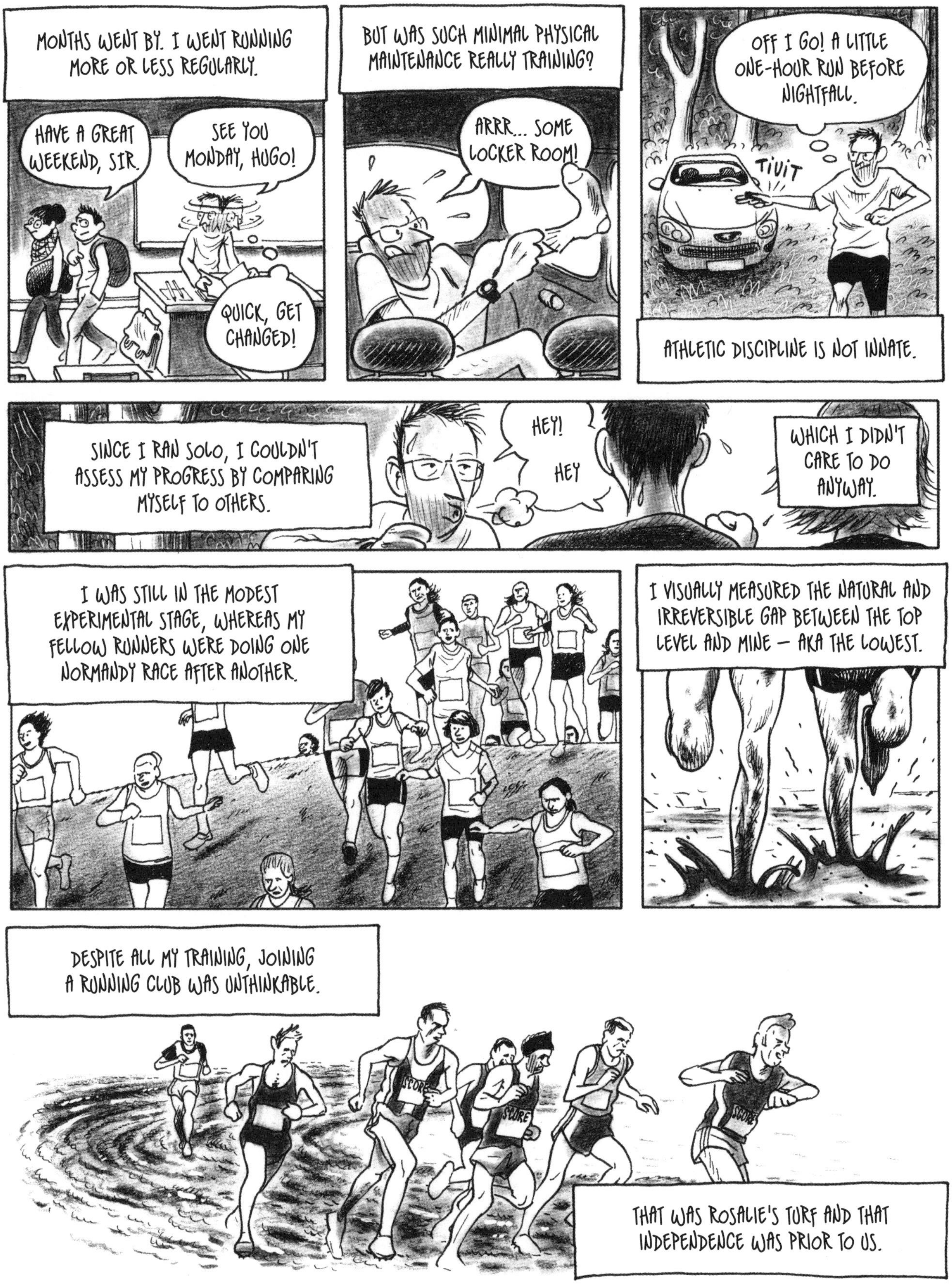
MONTHS WENT BY. I WENT RUNNING MORE OR LESS REGULARLY.
HAVE A GREAT WEEKEND, SIR.
SEE YOU MONDAY, HUGO!
QUICK, GET CHANGED!
BUT WAS SUCH MINIMAL PHYSICAL MAINTENANCE REALLY TRAINING?
ARRR... SOME LOCKER ROOM!
OFF I GO! A LITTLE ONE-HOUR RUN BEFORE NIGHTFALL.
TIVIT
ATHLETIC DISCIPLINE IS NOT INNATE.
SINCE I RAN SOLO, I COULDN'T ASSESS MY PROGRESS BY COMPARING MYSELF TO OTHERS.
HEY!
HEY
WHICH I DIDN'T CARE TO DO ANYWAY.
I WAS STILL IN THE MODEST EXPERIMENTAL STAGE, WHEREAS MY FELLOW RUNNERS WERE DOING ONE NORMANDY RACE AFTER ANOTHER.
I VISUALLY MEASURED THE NATURAL AND IRREVERSIBLE GAP BETWEEN THE TOP LEVEL AND MINE — AKA THE LOWEST.
DESPITE ALL MY TRAINING, JOINING A RUNNING CLUB WAS UNTHINKABLE.
SCORE
SCORE
SCORE
THAT WAS ROSALIE'S TURF AND THAT INDEPENDENCE WAS PRIOR TO US.

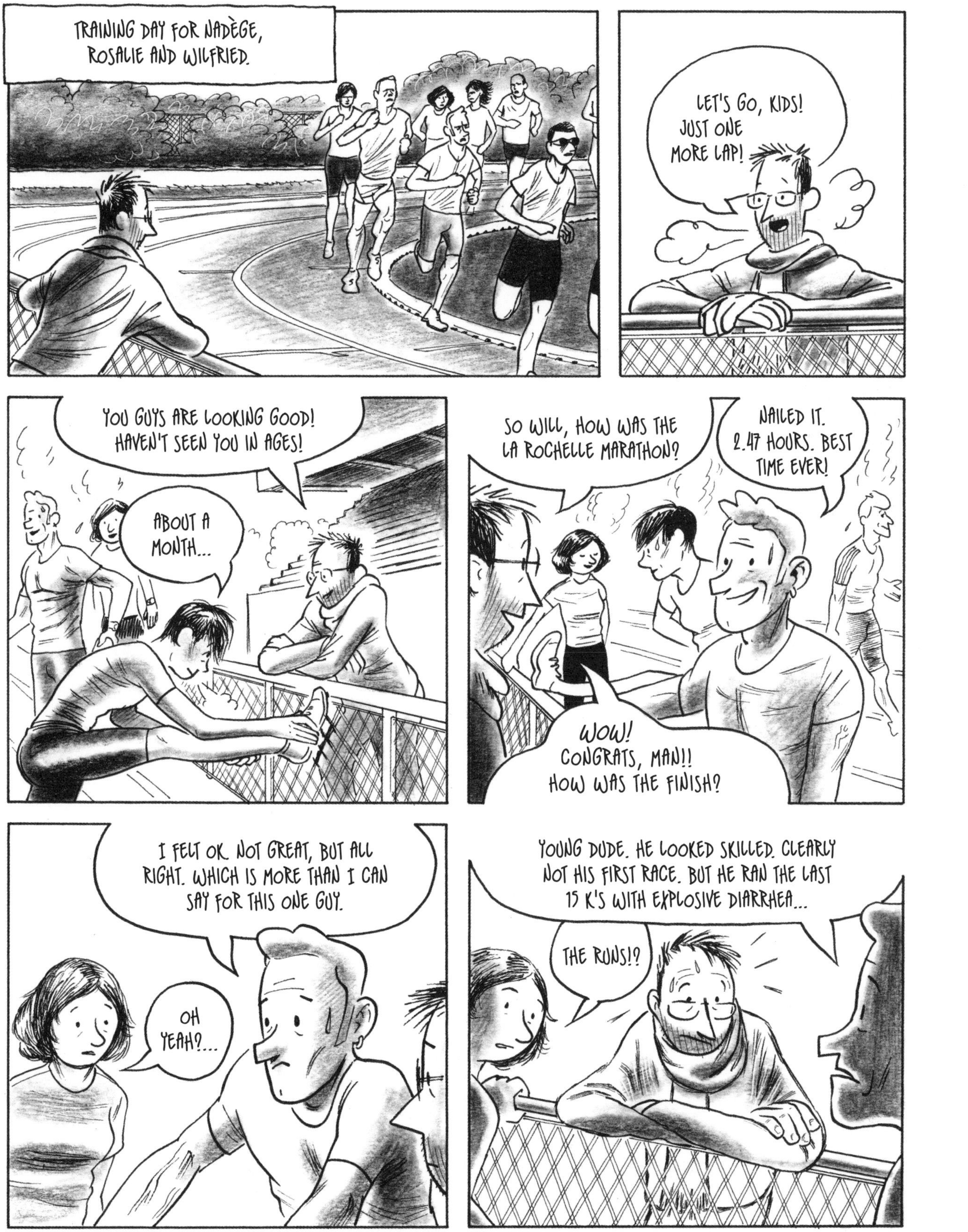
TRAINING DAY FOR NADÈGE, ROSALIE AND WILFRIED.
LET'S GO, KIDS! JUST ONE MORE LAP!
YOU GUYS ARE LOOKING GOOD! HAVEN'T SEEN YOU IN AGES!
ABOUT A MONTH...
SO WILL, HOW WAS THE LA ROCHELLE MARATHON?
NAILED IT. 2.47 HOURS. BEST TIME EVER!
WOW! CONGRATS, MAN!! HOW WAS THE FINISH?
I FELT OK. NOT GREAT, BUT ALL RIGHT. WHICH IS MORE THAN I CAN SAY FOR THIS ONE GUY.
OH YEAH?...
YOUNG DUDE. HE LOOKED SKILLED. CLEARLY NOT HIS FIRST RACE. BUT HE RAN THE LAST 15 K'S WITH EXPLOSIVE DIARRHEA...
THE RUNS!?

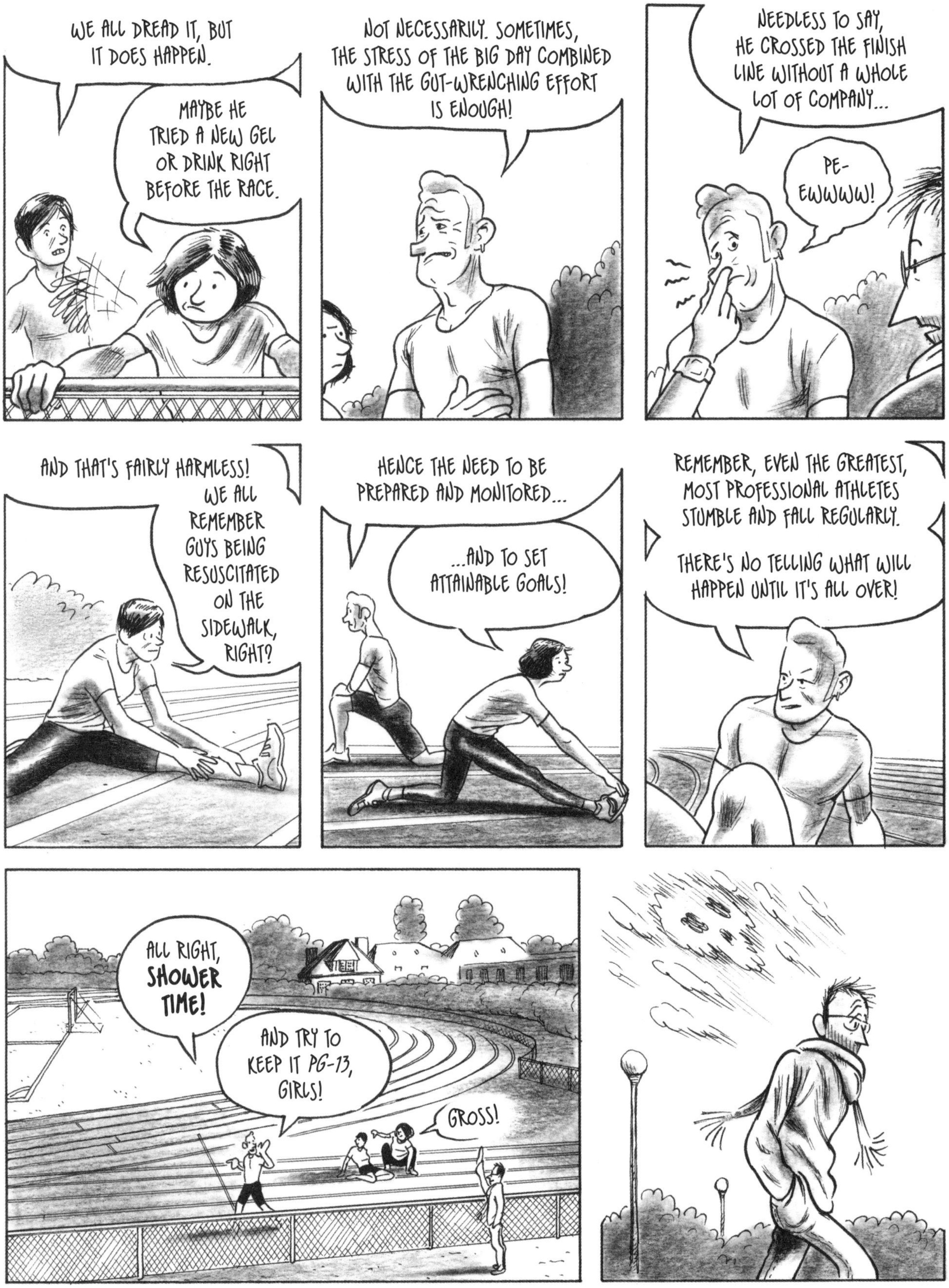
WE ALL DREAD IT, BUT IT DOES HAPPEN.
MAYBE HE TRIED A NEW GEL OR DRINK RIGHT BEFORE THE RACE.
NOT NECESSARILY. SOMETIMES, THE STRESS OF THE BIG DAY COMBINED WITH THE GUT-WRENCHING EFFORT IS ENOUGH!
NEEDLESS TO SAY, HE CROSSED THE FINISH LINE WITHOUT A WHOLE LOT OF COMPANY...
PE-EWWWW!
AND THAT'S FAIRLY HARMLESS!
WE ALL REMEMBER GUYS BEING RESUSCITATED ON THE SIDEWALK, RIGHT?
HENCE THE NEED TO BE PREPARED AND MONITORED...
...AND TO SET ATTAINABLE GOALS!
REMEMBER, EVEN THE GREATEST, MOST PROFESSIONAL ATHLETES STUMBLE AND FALL REGULARLY.
THERE'S NO TELLING WHAT WILL HAPPEN UNTIL IT'S ALL OVER!
ALL RIGHT, **SHOWER TIME!**
AND TRY TO KEEP IT *PG-13*, GIRLS!
GROSS!

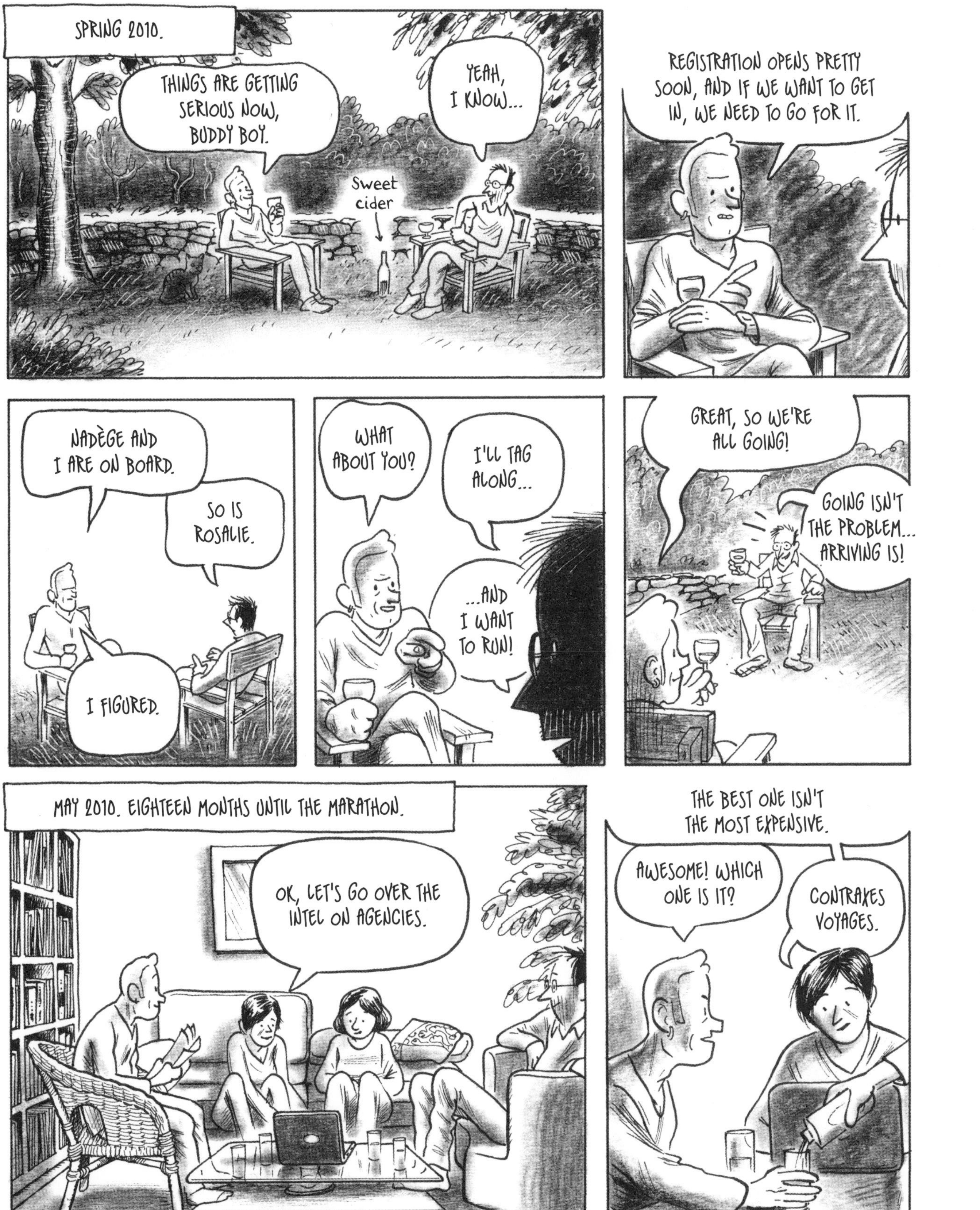
SPRING 2010.
THINGS ARE GETTING SERIOUS NOW, BUDDY BOY.
YEAH, I KNOW...
Sweet cider
REGISTRATION OPENS PRETTY SOON, AND IF WE WANT TO GET IN, WE NEED TO GO FOR IT.
NADÈGE AND I ARE ON BOARD.
SO IS ROSALIE.
I FIGURED.
WHAT ABOUT YOU?
I'LL TAG ALONG...
...AND I WANT TO RUN!
GREAT, SO WE'RE ALL GOING!
GOING ISN'T THE PROBLEM... ARRIVING IS!
MAY 2010. EIGHTEEN MONTHS UNTIL THE MARATHON.
OK, LET'S GO OVER THE INTEL ON AGENCIES.
THE BEST ONE ISN'T THE MOST EXPENSIVE.
AWESOME! WHICH ONE IS IT?
CONTRAXES VOYAGES.

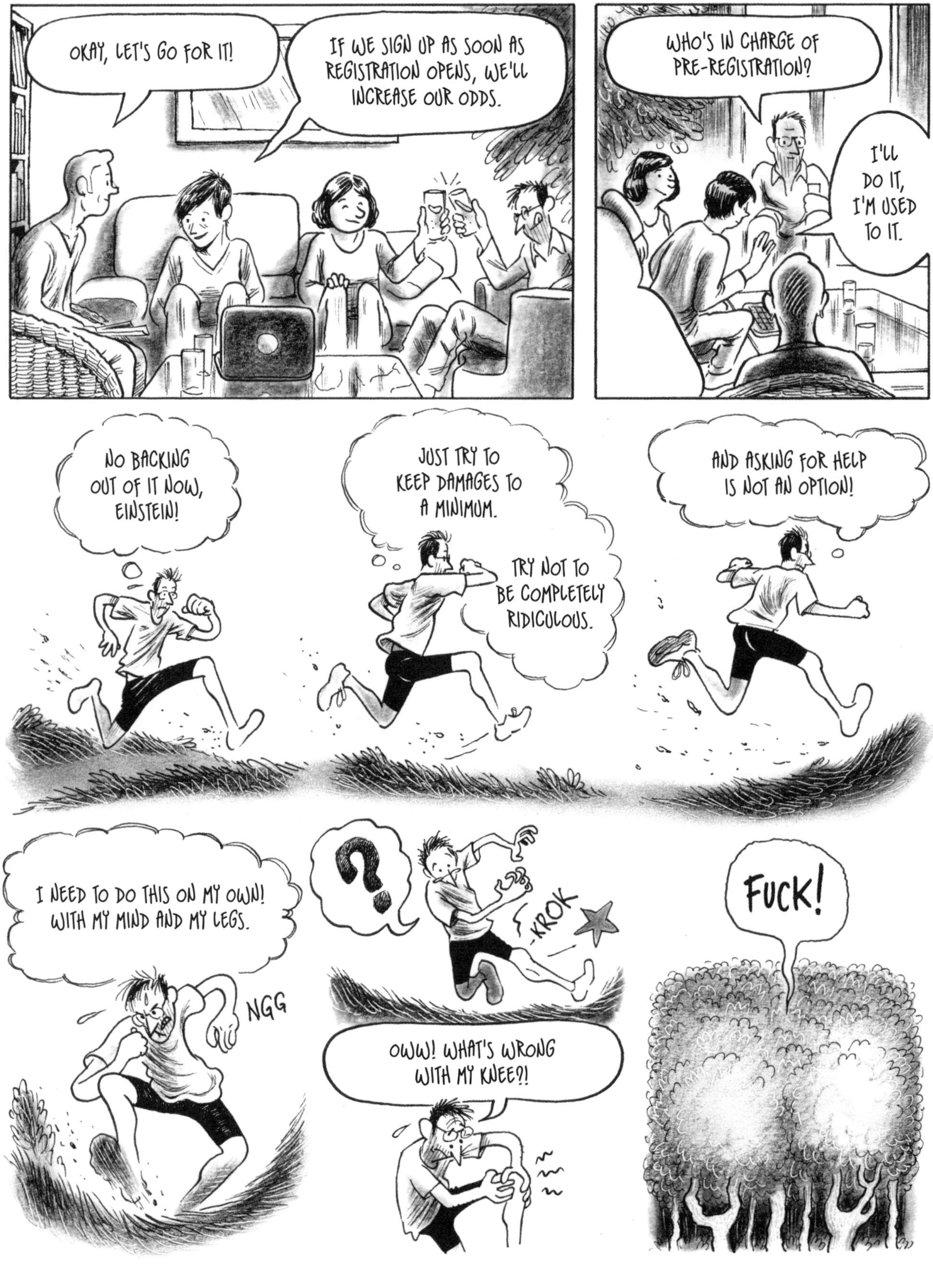
OKAY, LET'S GO FOR IT!
IF WE SIGN UP AS SOON AS REGISTRATION OPENS, WE'LL INCREASE OUR ODDS.
WHO'S IN CHARGE OF PRE-REGISTRATION?
I'LL DO IT, I'M USED TO IT.
NO BACKING OUT OF IT NOW, EINSTEIN!
JUST TRY TO KEEP DAMAGES TO A MINIMUM.
TRY NOT TO BE COMPLETELY RIDICULOUS.
AND ASKING FOR HELP IS NOT AN OPTION!
I NEED TO DO THIS ON MY OWN! WITH MY MIND AND MY LEGS.
NGG
?
KROK
OWW! WHAT'S WRONG WITH MY KNEE?!
FUCK!

3.
ONE STEP
At a Time

YOUR SPEED IS

09.5 KM/H

GO FASTER!

I WAS FAR FROM BEING LIKE THOSE SEASONED ATHLETES...

...AND VERY FAR FROM HAVING THEIR RIPPED, CUT, MUSCULAR BODS...

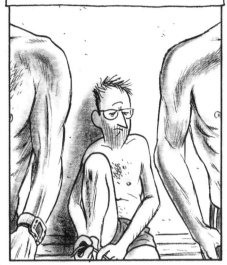

NEVERTHELESS, I DID OBSERVE SOME NOTICEABLE CHANGES TO MY FIGURE.

NOTHING TOO DRASTIC, THOUGH. JUST A FEW TRIMMED DOWN BULGES...

BEFORE (194 LBS)

AFTER A FEW MONTHS (178 LBS)

HAHA!

NOT SO SMUG NOW, ARE WE?

OUCH!

EASY FOR YOU TO SAY!

...AND NIGHTS-MORE RESTORATIVE THAN EVER.

KRRRR

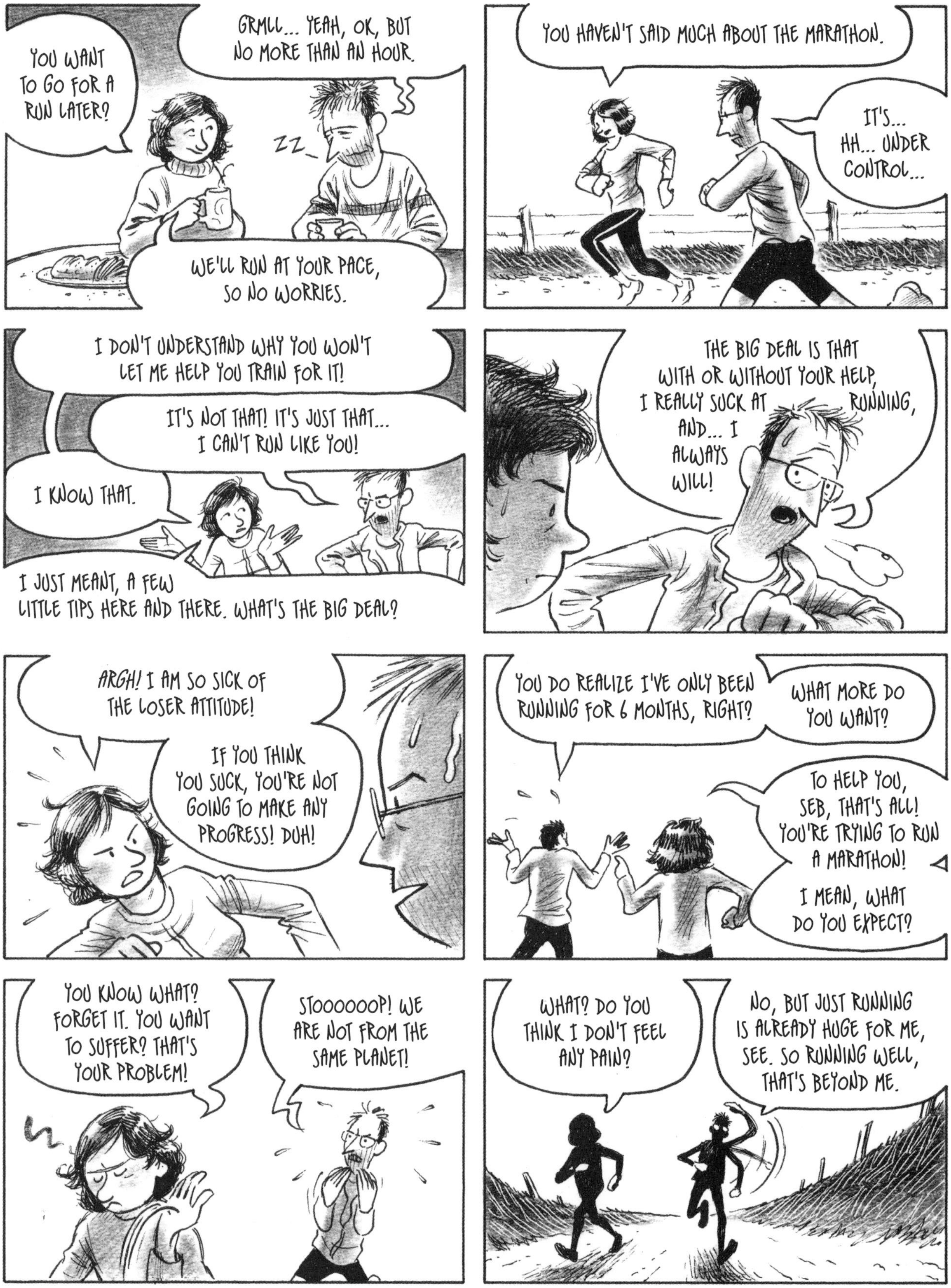

YOU WANT TO GO FOR A RUN LATER?
GRMLL... YEAH, OK, BUT NO MORE THAN AN HOUR.
ZZ
WE'LL RUN AT YOUR PACE, SO NO WORRIES.
YOU HAVEN'T SAID MUCH ABOUT THE MARATHON.
IT'S... HH... UNDER CONTROL...
I DON'T UNDERSTAND WHY YOU WON'T LET ME HELP YOU TRAIN FOR IT!
IT'S NOT THAT! IT'S JUST THAT... I CAN'T RUN LIKE YOU!
I KNOW THAT.
I JUST MEANT, A FEW LITTLE TIPS HERE AND THERE. WHAT'S THE BIG DEAL?
THE BIG DEAL IS THAT WITH OR WITHOUT YOUR HELP, I REALLY SUCK AT RUNNING, AND... I ALWAYS WILL!
ARGH! I AM SO SICK OF THE LOSER ATTITUDE!
IF YOU THINK YOU SUCK, YOU'RE NOT GOING TO MAKE ANY PROGRESS! DUH!
YOU DO REALIZE I'VE ONLY BEEN RUNNING FOR 6 MONTHS, RIGHT?
WHAT MORE DO YOU WANT?
TO HELP YOU, SEB, THAT'S ALL! YOU'RE TRYING TO RUN A MARATHON!
I MEAN, WHAT DO YOU EXPECT?
YOU KNOW WHAT? FORGET IT. YOU WANT TO SUFFER? THAT'S YOUR PROBLEM!
STOOOOOOP! WE ARE NOT FROM THE SAME PLANET!
WHAT? DO YOU THINK I DON'T FEEL ANY PAIN?
NO, BUT JUST RUNNING IS ALREADY HUGE FOR ME, SEE. SO RUNNING WELL, THAT'S BEYOND ME.

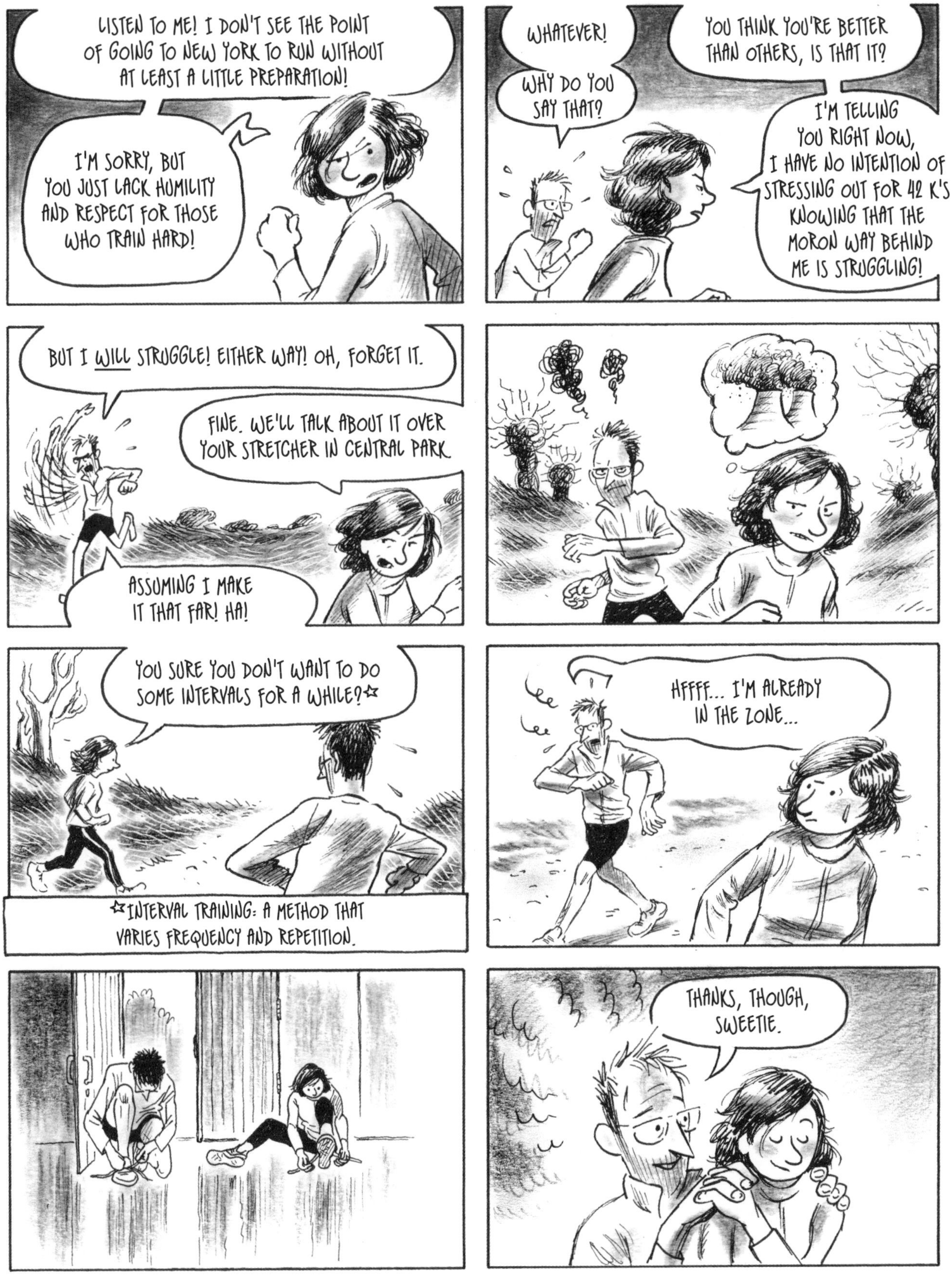
LISTEN TO ME! I DON'T SEE THE POINT OF GOING TO NEW YORK TO RUN WITHOUT AT LEAST A LITTLE PREPARATION!
I'M SORRY, BUT YOU JUST LACK HUMILITY AND RESPECT FOR THOSE WHO TRAIN HARD!
WHATEVER!
WHY DO YOU SAY THAT?
YOU THINK YOU'RE BETTER THAN OTHERS, IS THAT IT?
I'M TELLING YOU RIGHT NOW, I HAVE NO INTENTION OF STRESSING OUT FOR 42 K'S KNOWING THAT THE MORON WAY BEHIND ME IS STRUGGLING!
BUT I WILL STRUGGLE! EITHER WAY! OH, FORGET IT.
FINE. WE'LL TALK ABOUT IT OVER YOUR STRETCHER IN CENTRAL PARK.
ASSUMING I MAKE IT THAT FAR! HA!
YOU SURE YOU DON'T WANT TO DO SOME INTERVALS FOR A WHILE?☆
☆INTERVAL TRAINING: A METHOD THAT VARIES FREQUENCY AND REPETITION.
HFFFF... I'M ALREADY IN THE ZONE...
THANKS, THOUGH, SWEETIE.

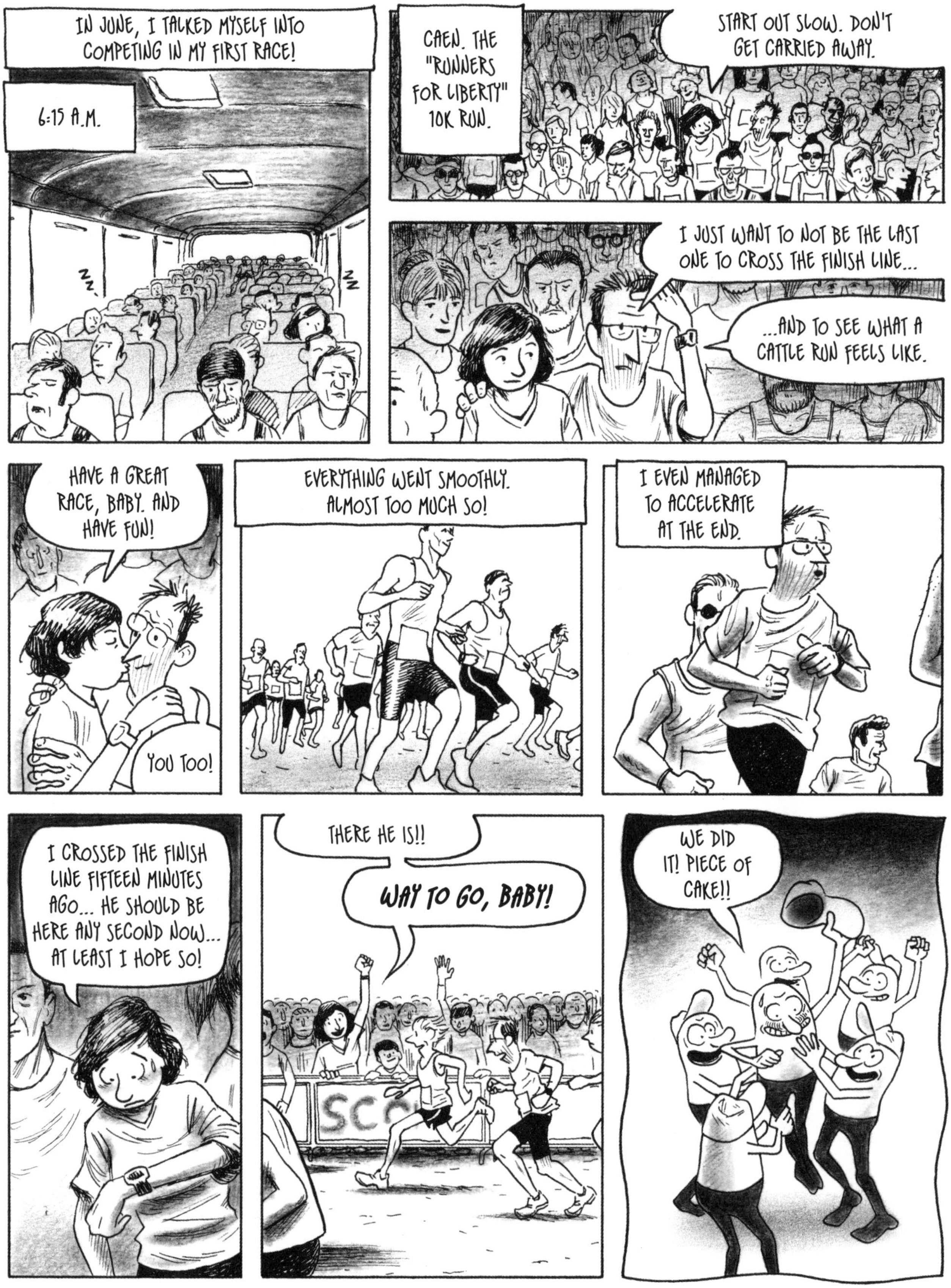
IN JUNE, I TALKED MYSELF INTO COMPETING IN MY FIRST RACE!
6:15 A.M.
ZZ
ZZ
CAEN. THE "RUNNERS FOR LIBERTY" 10K RUN.
START OUT SLOW. DON'T GET CARRIED AWAY.
I JUST WANT TO NOT BE THE LAST ONE TO CROSS THE FINISH LINE...
...AND TO SEE WHAT A CATTLE RUN FEELS LIKE.
HAVE A GREAT RACE, BABY. AND HAVE FUN!
YOU TOO!
EVERYTHING WENT SMOOTHLY. ALMOST TOO MUCH SO!
I EVEN MANAGED TO ACCELERATE AT THE END.
I CROSSED THE FINISH LINE FIFTEEN MINUTES AGO... HE SHOULD BE HERE ANY SECOND NOW... AT LEAST I HOPE SO!
THERE HE IS!!
WAY TO GO, BABY!
WE DID IT! PIECE OF CAKE!!

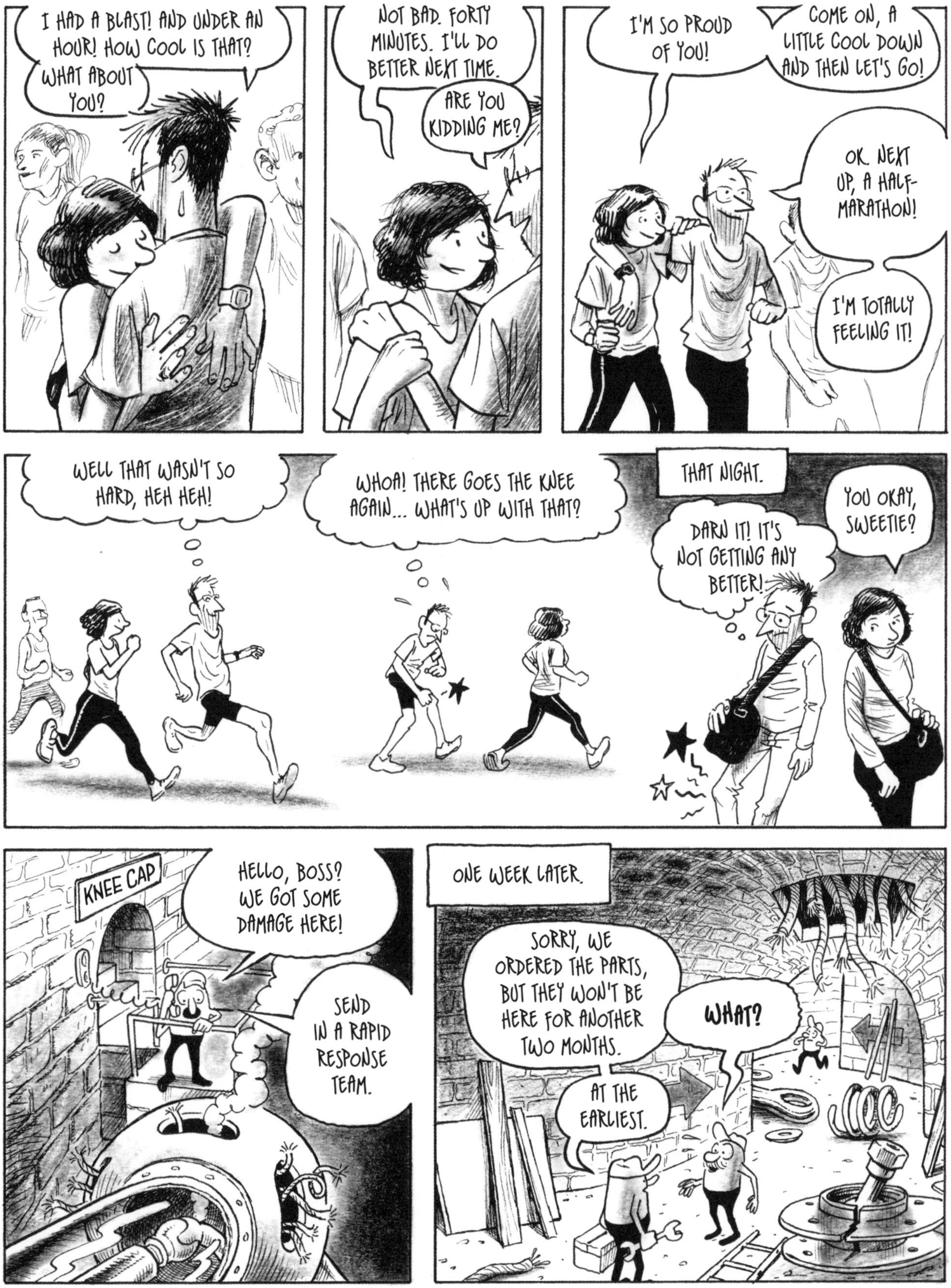
I HAD A BLAST! AND UNDER AN HOUR! HOW COOL IS THAT?
WHAT ABOUT YOU?
NOT BAD. FORTY MINUTES. I'LL DO BETTER NEXT TIME.
ARE YOU KIDDING ME?
I'M SO PROUD OF YOU!
COME ON, A LITTLE COOL DOWN AND THEN LET'S GO!
OK. NEXT UP, A HALF-MARATHON!
I'M TOTALLY FEELING IT!
WELL THAT WASN'T SO HARD, HEH HEH!
WHOA! THERE GOES THE KNEE AGAIN... WHAT'S UP WITH THAT?
THAT NIGHT.
YOU OKAY, SWEETIE?
DARN IT! IT'S NOT GETTING ANY BETTER!
KNEE CAP
HELLO, BOSS? WE GOT SOME DAMAGE HERE!
SEND IN A RAPID RESPONSE TEAM.
ONE WEEK LATER.
SORRY, WE ORDERED THE PARTS, BUT THEY WON'T BE HERE FOR ANOTHER TWO MONTHS.
AT THE EARLIEST.
WHAT?

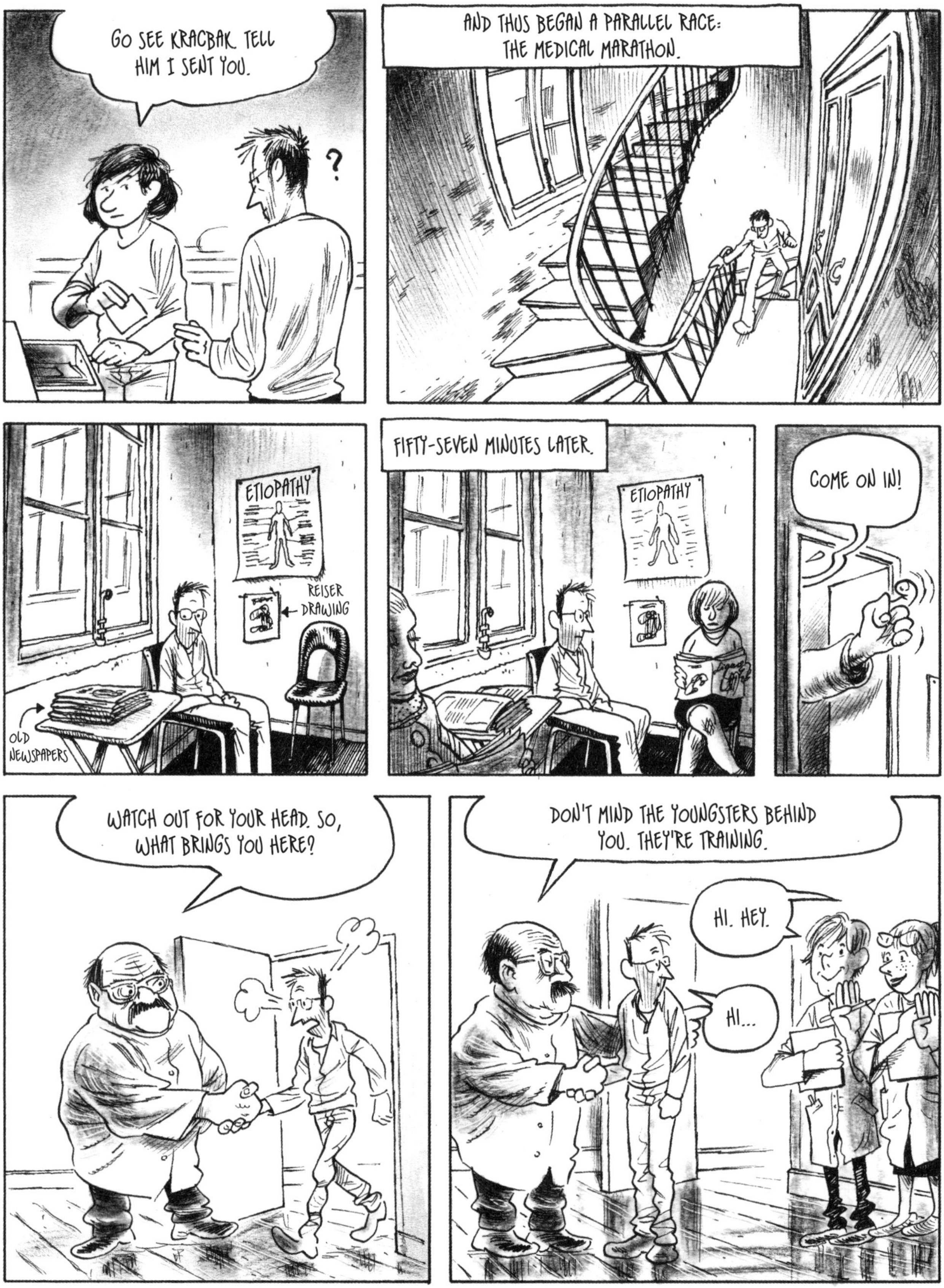
GO SEE KRACBAK. TELL HIM I SENT YOU.
?
AND THUS BEGAN A PARALLEL RACE: THE MEDICAL MARATHON.
ETIOPATHY
REISER DRAWING
OLD NEWSPAPERS
FIFTY-SEVEN MINUTES LATER.
ETIOPATHY
COME ON IN!
WATCH OUT FOR YOUR HEAD. SO, WHAT BRINGS YOU HERE?
DON'T MIND THE YOUNGSTERS BEHIND YOU. THEY'RE TRAINING.
HI. HEY.
HI...

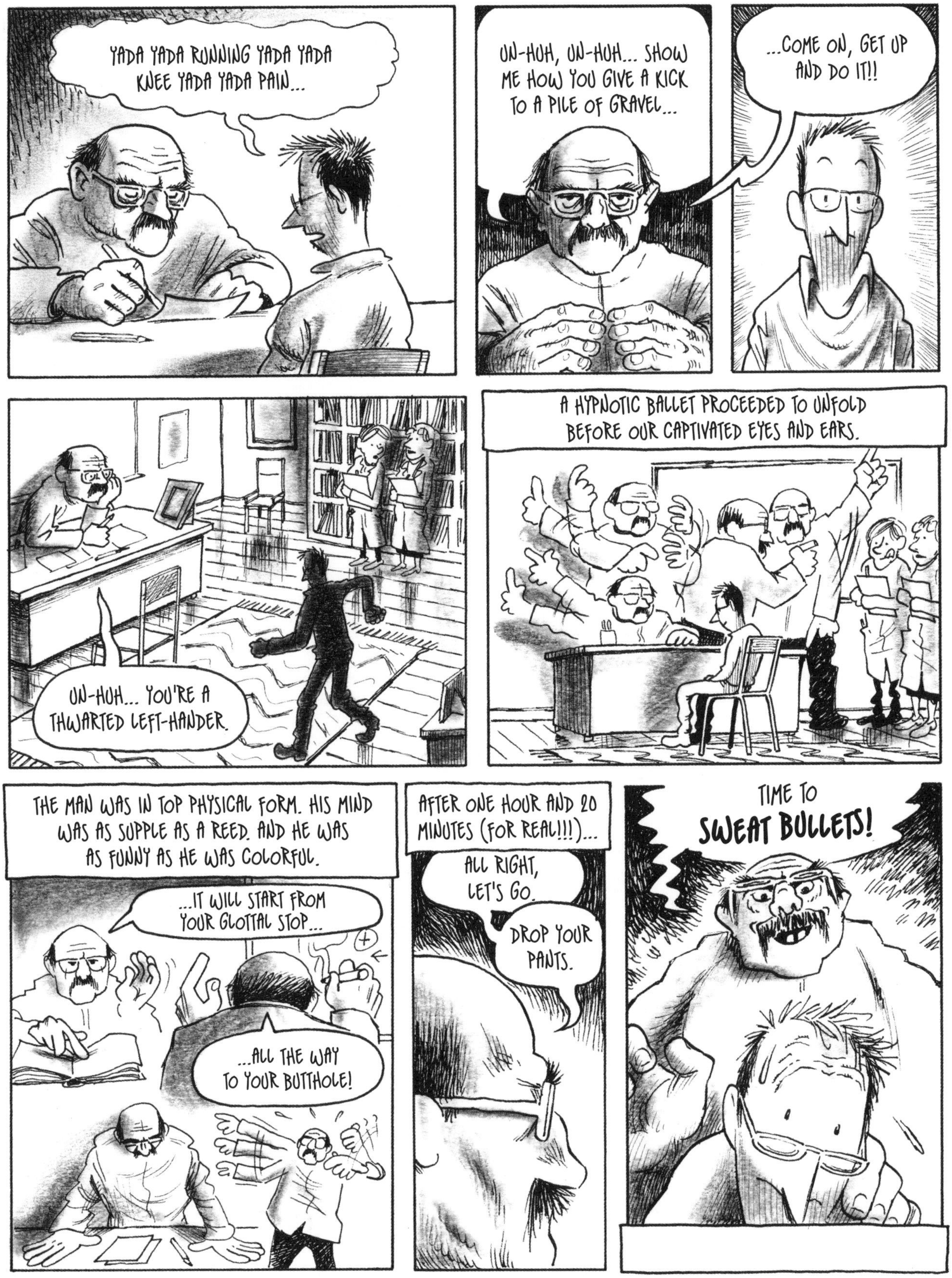
YADA YADA RUNNING YADA YADA KNEE YADA YADA PAIN...
UN-HUH, UN-HUH... SHOW ME HOW YOU GIVE A KICK TO A PILE OF GRAVEL...
...COME ON, GET UP AND DO IT!!
UN-HUH... YOU'RE A THWARTED LEFT-HANDER.
A HYPNOTIC BALLET PROCEEDED TO UNFOLD BEFORE OUR CAPTIVATED EYES AND EARS.
THE MAN WAS IN TOP PHYSICAL FORM. HIS MIND WAS AS SUPPLE AS A REED. AND HE WAS AS FUNNY AS HE WAS COLORFUL.
...IT WILL START FROM YOUR GLOTTAL STOP...
...ALL THE WAY TO YOUR BUTTHOLE!
AFTER ONE HOUR AND 20 MINUTES (FOR REAL!!!)...
ALL RIGHT, LET'S GO.
DROP YOUR PANTS.
TIME TO SWEAT BULLETS!

I BET THIS HURTS RIGHT HERE, RIGHT?
YES!
GULP!
WHEN I PUSH HERE, BETWEEN THE FLANK AND THE FILET, YOU DON'T FEEL ANYTHING, RIGHT?
ER, NO...
WHAT ABOUT WHEN I POKE YOU HERE?
AAHOU!
NATURE IS ANYTHING BUT LATERAL.
MPFF!
HEE!
LIE DOWN, DUCKY! HEAD ON THE CHOPPING BLOCK!
FLAF
BUCKLE UP, GUYS! IT'S GONNA GET BUMPY!
GRMPFF ...

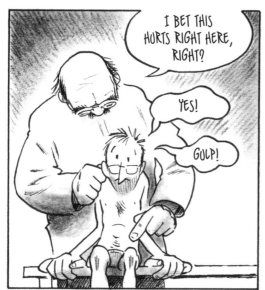

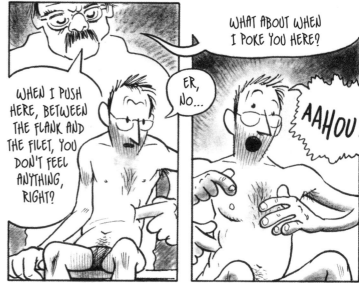

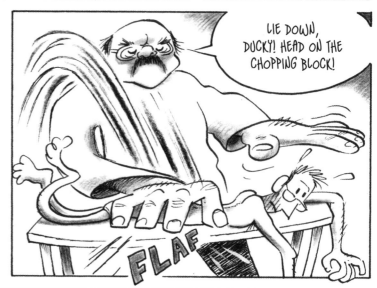

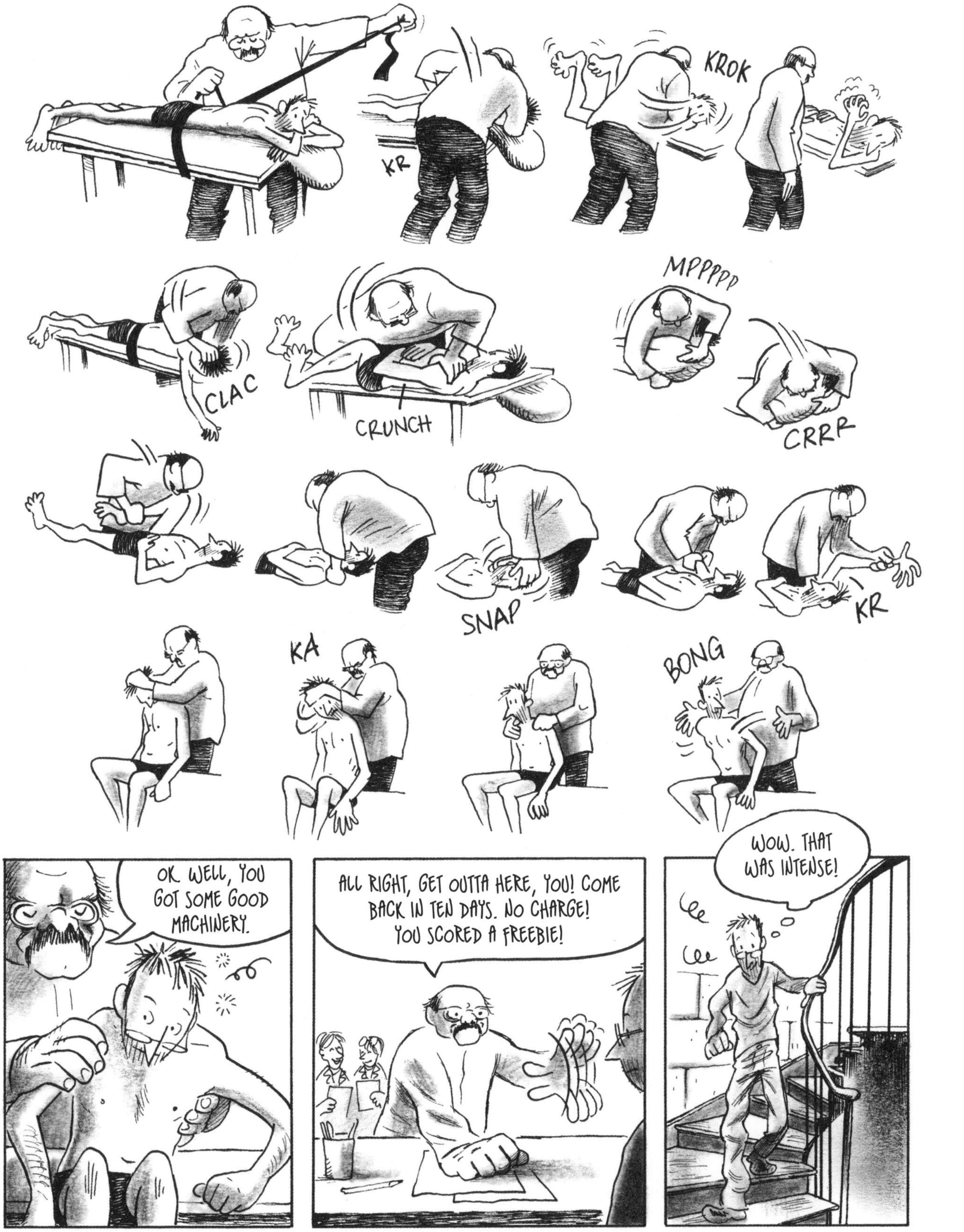
KR
KROK
CLAC
CRUNCH
MPPPPP
CRRR
SNAP
KR
KA
BONG
OK. WELL, YOU GOT SOME GOOD MACHINERY.
ALL RIGHT, GET OUTTA HERE, YOU! COME BACK IN TEN DAYS. NO CHARGE! YOU SCORED A FREEBIE!
WOW. THAT WAS INTENSE!

I SLEPT LIKE A LOG THAT NIGHT.

IF I TOUCH YOUR BACK, WILL YOU QUACK?

I FELT LIKE JELL-O OVER THE NEXT FEW DAYS.

You can mix white, yellow and red to get a flesh tone...

I COULD RUN AGAIN...

...BUT MY BODY STILL ACHED.

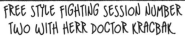

FREE STYLE FIGHTING SESSION NUMBER TWO WITH HERR DOCTOR KRACBAK

YOU SHOULD GO SEE A PODIATRIST FOR YOUR GIMPY LEG.

HELLO. DOWN THE HALL AND TO THE RIGHT.

HELLO.

...NOT REALLY ATHLETIC... RUN ANYWAY... PAIN IN MY KNEE...

MY SPECIALIST, A TEACHING-ORIENTED PODIATRIST, LAUNCHED INTO A DETAILED LESSON ON THE SUBTLETIES OF MY APPROACH.

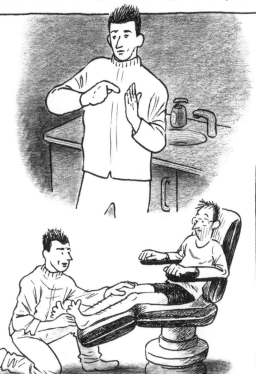

...COULDN'T DO SO WITHOUT HELP, APPARENTLY!

MY LEGS HAD BEEN SUPPORTING ME SINCE I WAS ONE, BUT NOW THAT I WAS POLITELY ASKING THEM TO RUN, THE MECHANISM WAS JAMMED. THESE LEGS THAT WERE SUPPOSED TO OBEY ME...

FLOTCH

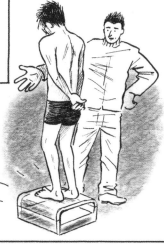

THINGS SHOULD BE BETTER WITH THESE SOLES.

AS IS OFTEN THE CASE WITH BIPEDS, YOUR LEGS AREN'T THE SAME EXACT LENGTH...

SPINE, HIPS, KNEES, FEET-THEY'RE ALL CONNECTED AND THEY ALL HAD TO COMPENSATE FOR THAT.

AT THE END OF THE ASSEMBLY LINE, YOUR FEET POINT TO THE OUTSIDE, ESPECIALLY THE RIGHT FOOT. ONE OF THE LINKS IN THE CHAIN IS NOT TAKING IT VERY WELL AND IT'S SHOWING. IT'S OFTEN THE KNEE.

MY KNEE IS MY ACHILLES' HEEL.

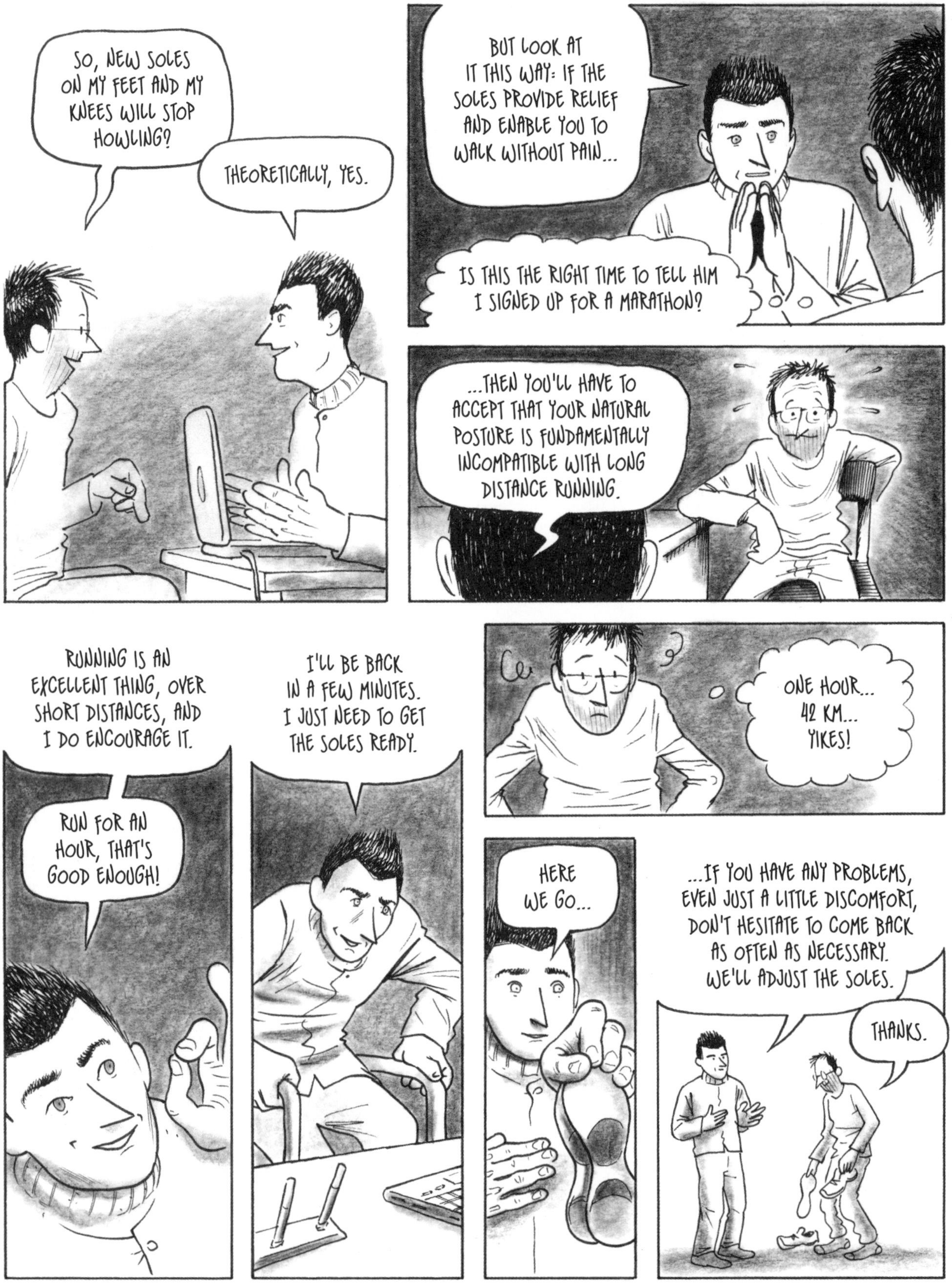
SO, NEW SOLES ON MY FEET AND MY KNEES WILL STOP HOWLING?
THEORETICALLY, YES.
BUT LOOK AT IT THIS WAY: IF THE SOLES PROVIDE RELIEF AND ENABLE YOU TO WALK WITHOUT PAIN...
IS THIS THE RIGHT TIME TO TELL HIM I SIGNED UP FOR A MARATHON?
...THEN YOU'LL HAVE TO ACCEPT THAT YOUR NATURAL POSTURE IS FUNDAMENTALLY INCOMPATIBLE WITH LONG DISTANCE RUNNING.
RUNNING IS AN EXCELLENT THING, OVER SHORT DISTANCES, AND I DO ENCOURAGE IT.
RUN FOR AN HOUR, THAT'S GOOD ENOUGH!
I'LL BE BACK IN A FEW MINUTES. I JUST NEED TO GET THE SOLES READY.
ONE HOUR... 42 KM... YIKES!
HERE WE GO...
...IF YOU HAVE ANY PROBLEMS, EVEN JUST A LITTLE DISCOMFORT, DON'T HESITATE TO COME BACK AS OFTEN AS NECESSARY. WE'LL ADJUST THE SOLES.
THANKS.

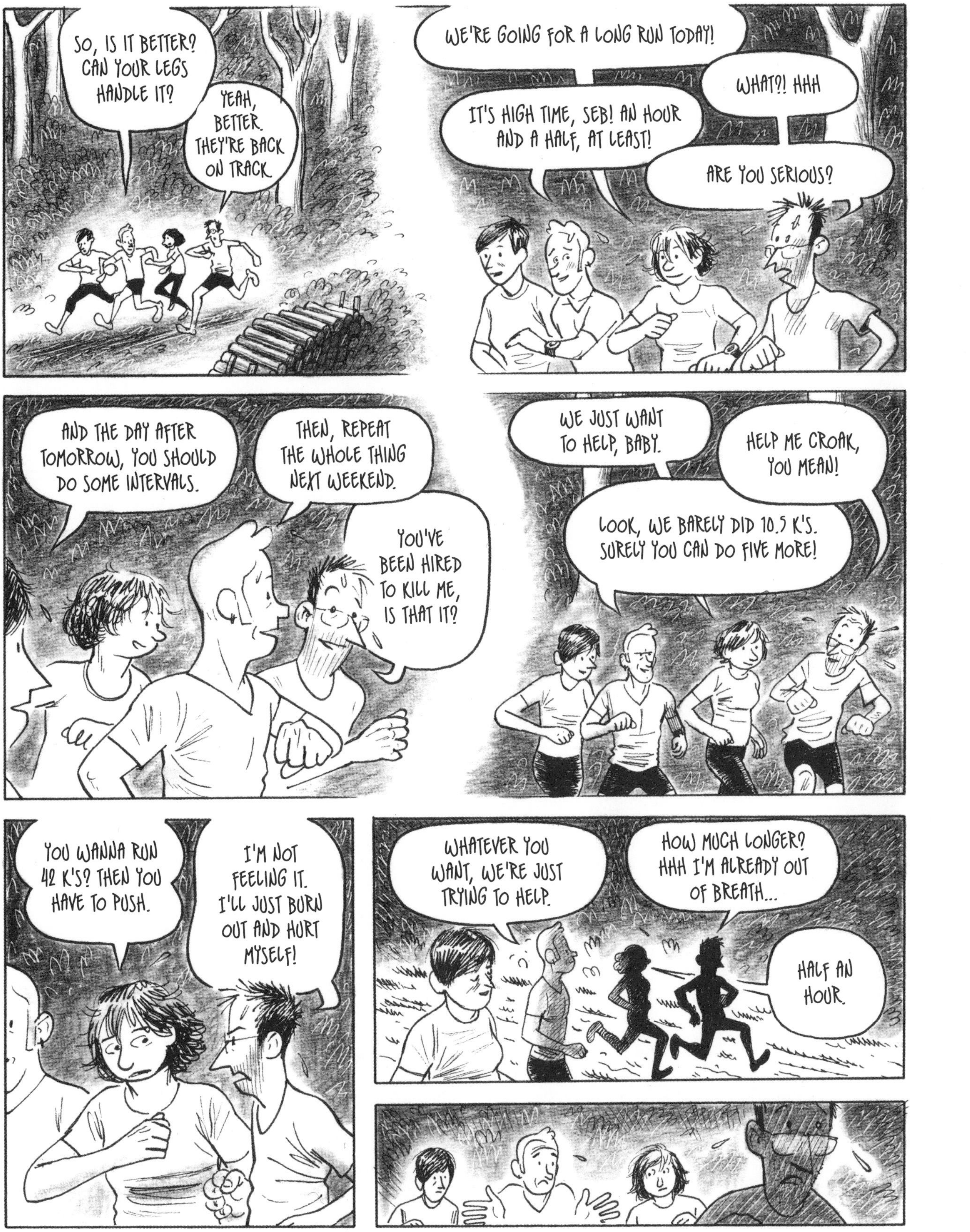
SO, IS IT BETTER? CAN YOUR LEGS HANDLE IT?
YEAH, BETTER. THEY'RE BACK ON TRACK.
WE'RE GOING FOR A LONG RUN TODAY!
IT'S HIGH TIME, SEB! AN HOUR AND A HALF, AT LEAST!
WHAT?! HHH
ARE YOU SERIOUS?
AND THE DAY AFTER TOMORROW, YOU SHOULD DO SOME INTERVALS.
THEN, REPEAT THE WHOLE THING NEXT WEEKEND.
YOU'VE BEEN HIRED TO KILL ME, IS THAT IT?
WE JUST WANT TO HELP, BABY.
HELP ME CROAK, YOU MEAN!
LOOK, WE BARELY DID 10.5 K'S. SURELY YOU CAN DO FIVE MORE!
YOU WANNA RUN 42 K'S? THEN YOU HAVE TO PUSH.
I'M NOT FEELING IT. I'LL JUST BURN OUT AND HURT MYSELF!
WHATEVER YOU WANT, WE'RE JUST TRYING TO HELP.
HOW MUCH LONGER? HHH I'M ALREADY OUT OF BREATH...
HALF AN HOUR.

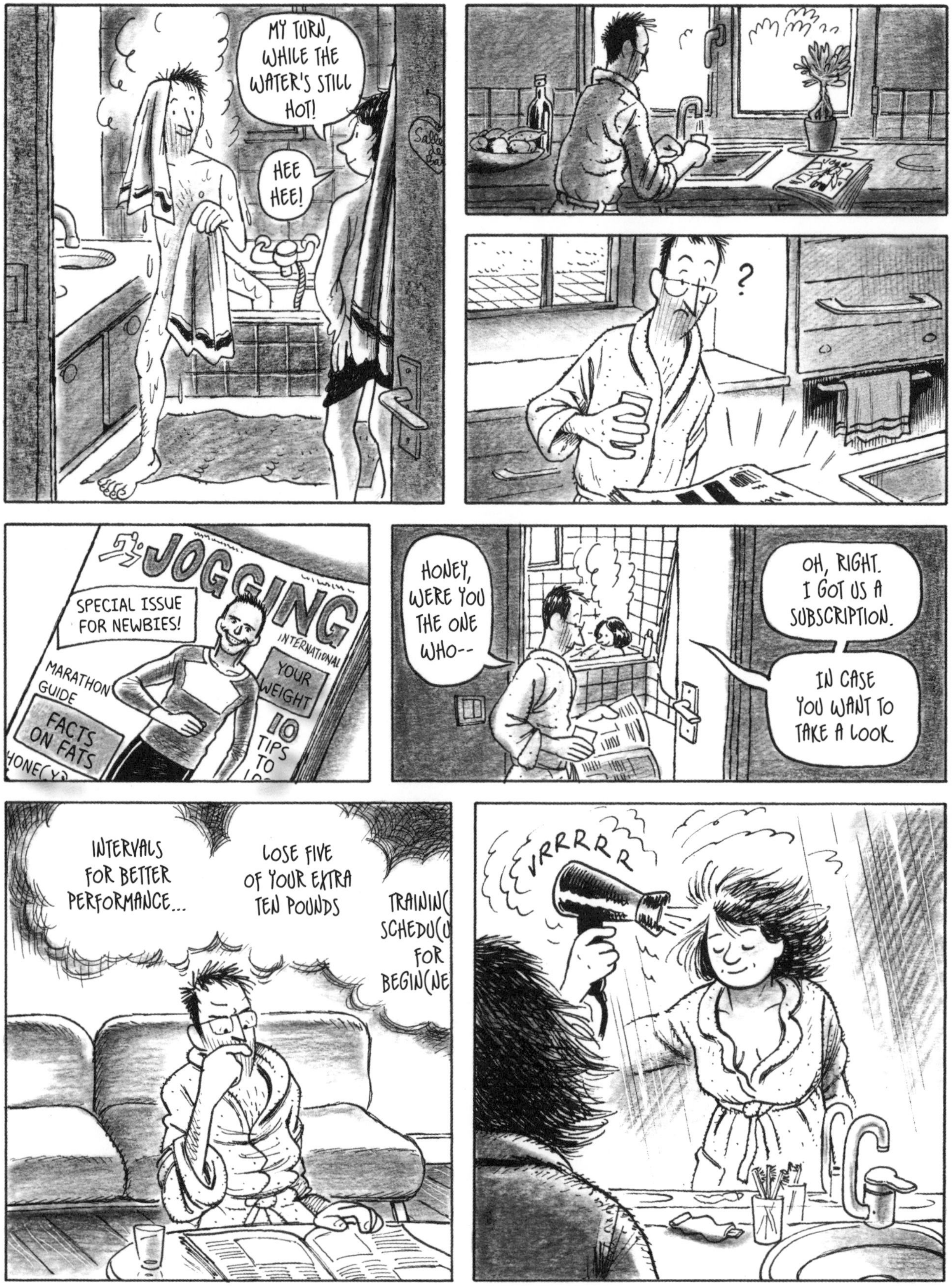

MY TURN, WHILE THE WATER'S STILL HOT!
HEE HEE!
?
JOGGING
INTERNATIONAL
SPECIAL ISSUE FOR NEWBIES!
MARATHON GUIDE
FACTS ON FATS
YOUR WEIGHT
10 TIPS TO
HONEY, WERE YOU THE ONE WHO--
OH, RIGHT. I GOT US A SUBSCRIPTION.
IN CASE YOU WANT TO TAKE A LOOK
INTERVALS FOR BETTER PERFORMANCE...
LOSE FIVE OF YOUR EXTRA TEN POUNDS
TRAININ SCHEDU FOR BEGIN
VRRRRRR

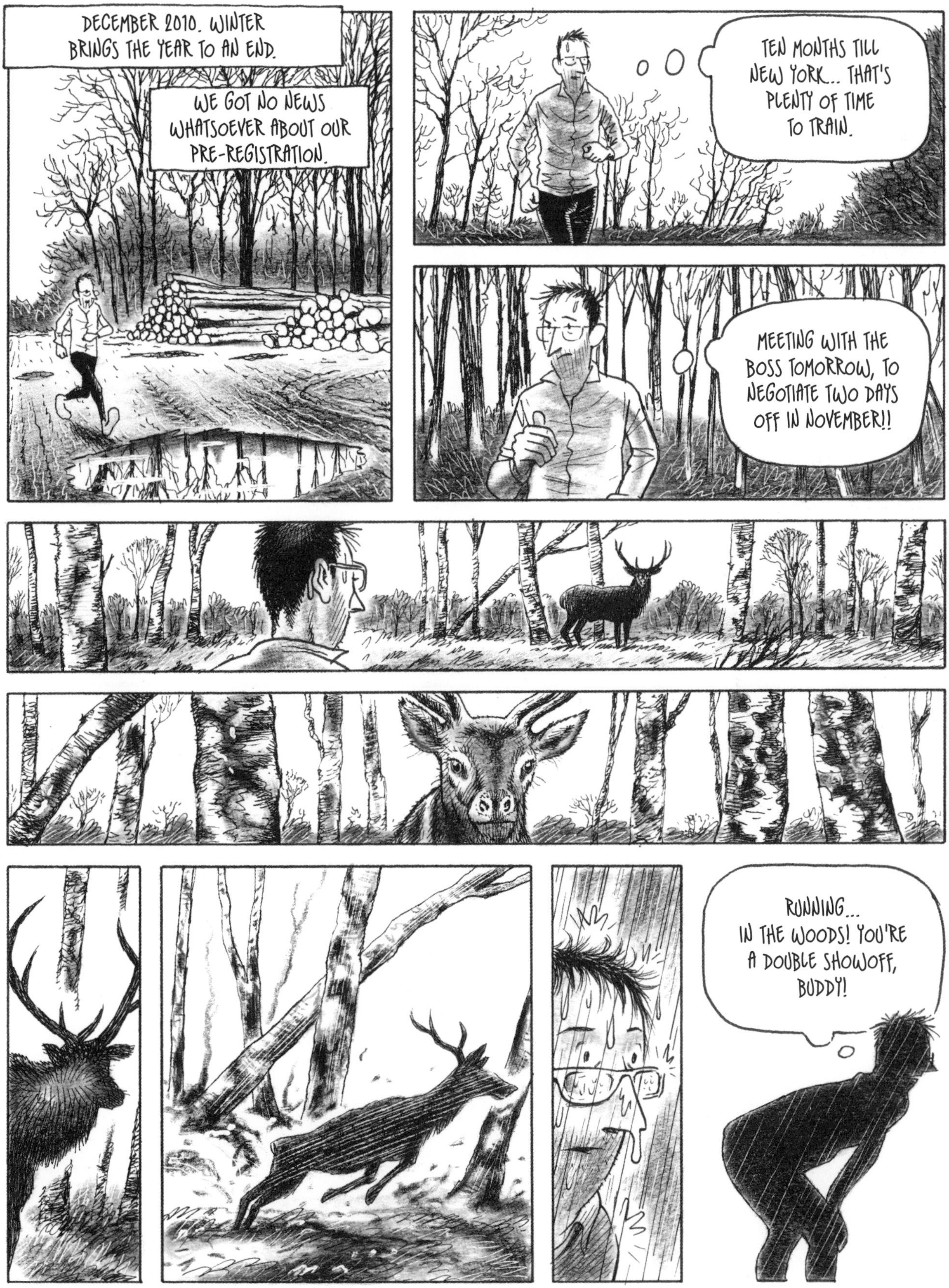

DECEMBER 2010. WINTER BRINGS THE YEAR TO AN END.
WE GOT NO NEWS WHATSOEVER ABOUT OUR PRE-REGISTRATION.
TEN MONTHS TILL NEW YORK... THAT'S PLENTY OF TIME TO TRAIN.
MEETING WITH THE BOSS TOMORROW, TO NEGOTIATE TWO DAYS OFF IN NOVEMBER!!
RUNNING... IN THE WOODS! YOU'RE A DOUBLE SHOWOFF, BUDDY!

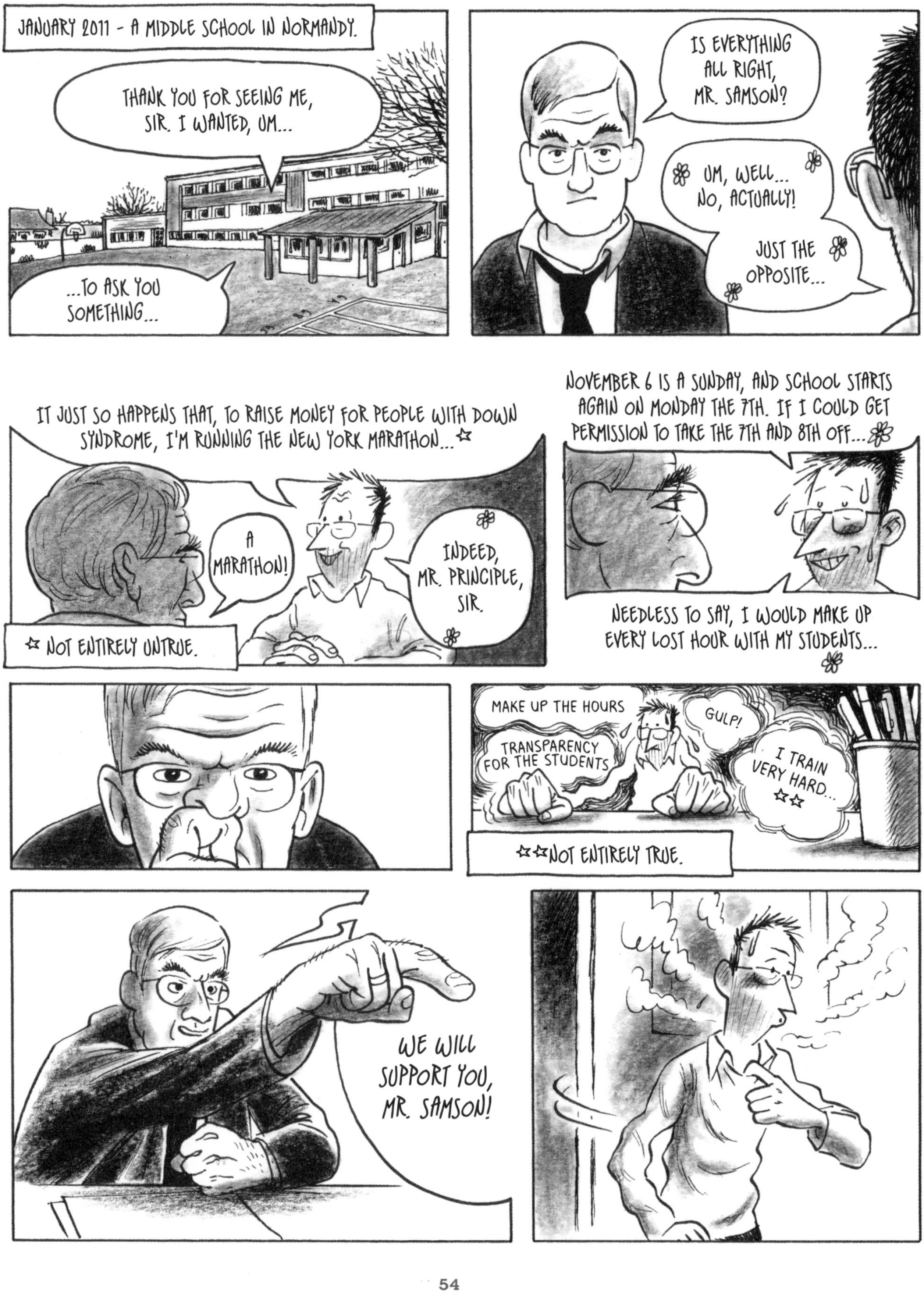

JANUARY 2011 - A MIDDLE SCHOOL IN NORMANDY.
THANK YOU FOR SEEING ME, SIR. I WANTED, UM...
...TO ASK YOU SOMETHING...
IS EVERYTHING ALL RIGHT, MR. SAMSON?
UM, WELL... NO, ACTUALLY!
JUST THE OPPOSITE...
IT JUST SO HAPPENS THAT, TO RAISE MONEY FOR PEOPLE WITH DOWN SYNDROME, I'M RUNNING THE NEW YORK MARATHON...☆
A MARATHON!
INDEED, MR. PRINCIPLE, SIR.
☆ NOT ENTIRELY UNTRUE.
NOVEMBER 6 IS A SUNDAY, AND SCHOOL STARTS AGAIN ON MONDAY THE 7TH. IF I COULD GET PERMISSION TO TAKE THE 7TH AND 8TH OFF...
NEEDLESS TO SAY, I WOULD MAKE UP EVERY LOST HOUR WITH MY STUDENTS...
MAKE UP THE HOURS
GULP!
TRANSPARENCY FOR THE STUDENTS
I TRAIN VERY HARD... ☆☆
☆☆NOT ENTIRELY TRUE.
WE WILL SUPPORT YOU, MR. SAMSON!

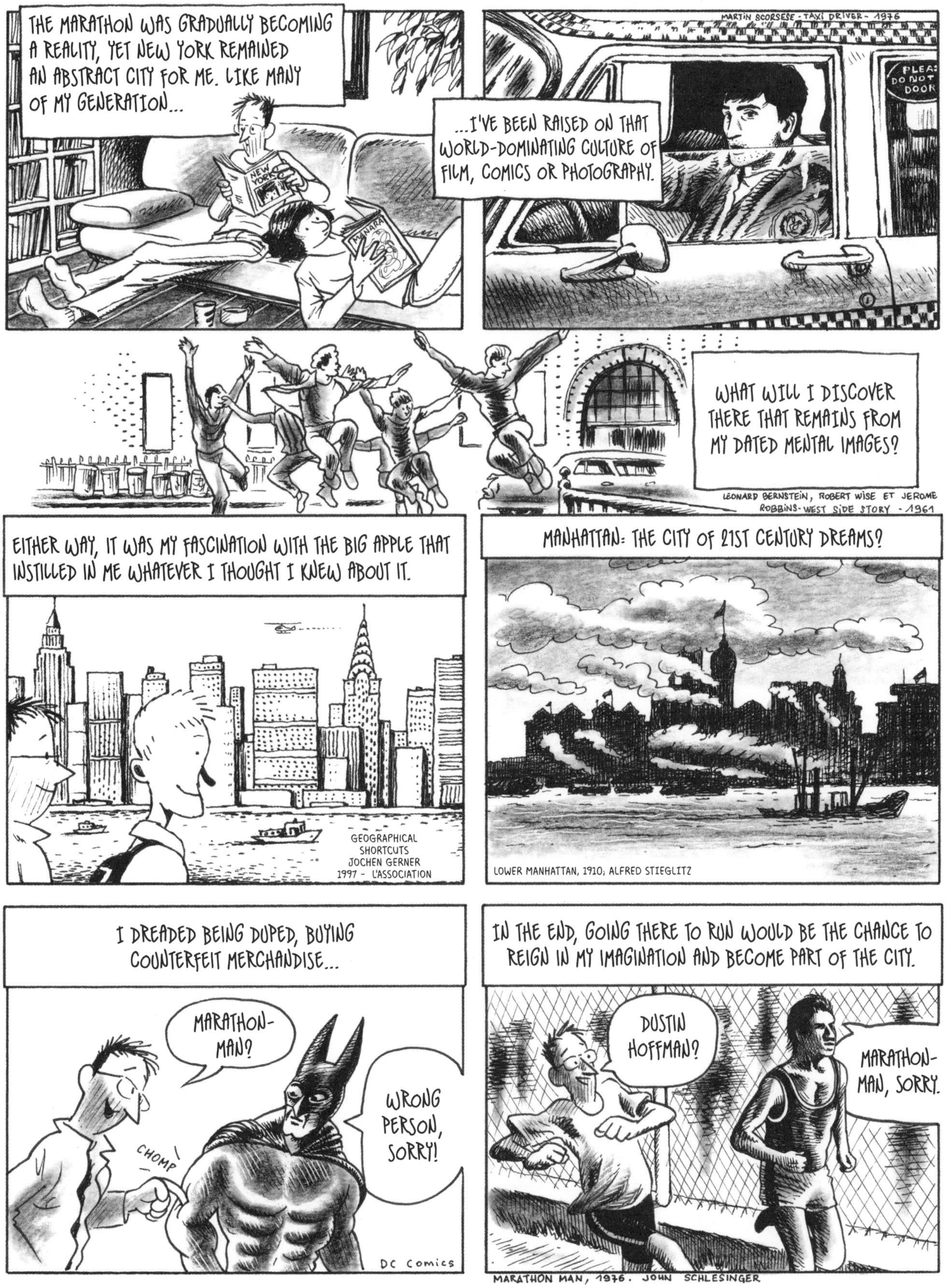
THE MARATHON WAS GRADUALLY BECOMING A REALITY, YET NEW YORK REMAINED AN ABSTRACT CITY FOR ME. LIKE MANY OF MY GENERATION...
NEW YORK
MANARA
MARTIN SCORSESE - TAXI DRIVER - 1976
...I'VE BEEN RAISED ON THAT WORLD-DOMINATING CULTURE OF FILM, COMICS OR PHOTOGRAPHY.
WHAT WILL I DISCOVER THERE THAT REMAINS FROM MY DATED MENTAL IMAGES?
LEONARD BERNSTEIN, ROBERT WISE ET JEROME ROBBINS - WEST SIDE STORY - 1961
EITHER WAY, IT WAS MY FASCINATION WITH THE BIG APPLE THAT INSTILLED IN ME WHATEVER I THOUGHT I KNEW ABOUT IT.
GEOGRAPHICAL SHORTCUTS JOCHEN GERNER 1997 - L'ASSOCIATION
MANHATTAN: THE CITY OF 21ST CENTURY DREAMS?
LOWER MANHATTAN, 1910; ALFRED STIEGLITZ
I DREADED BEING DUPED, BUYING COUNTERFEIT MERCHANDISE...
MARATHON-MAN?
CHOMP
WRONG PERSON, SORRY!
DC Comics
IN THE END, GOING THERE TO RUN WOULD BE THE CHANCE TO REIGN IN MY IMAGINATION AND BECOME PART OF THE CITY.
DUSTIN HOFFMAN?
MARATHON-MAN, SORRY.
MARATHON MAN, 1976. JOHN SCHLESINGER

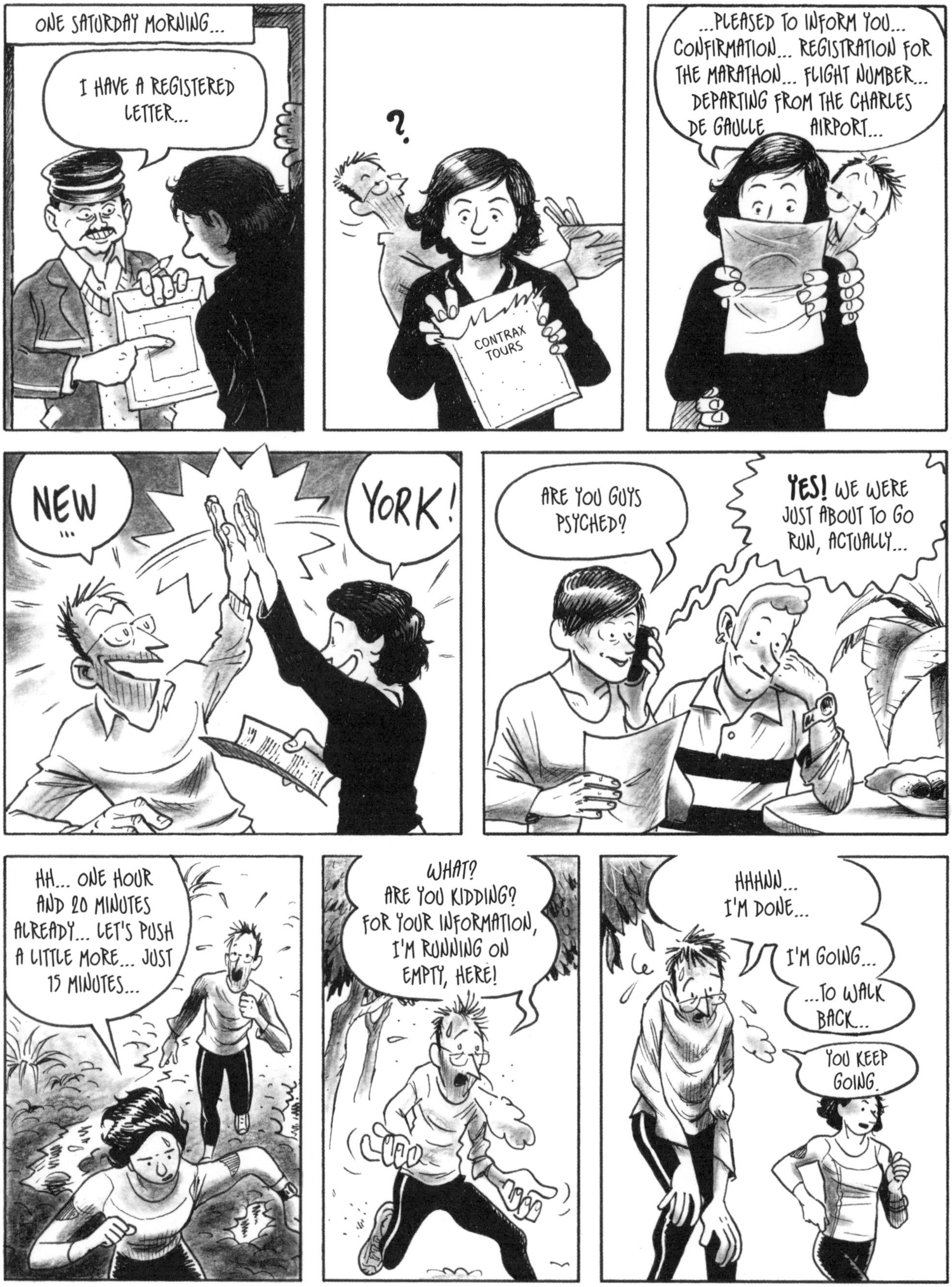

ONE SATURDAY MORNING...
I HAVE A REGISTERED LETTER...
?
CONTRAX TOURS
...PLEASED TO INFORM YOU... CONFIRMATION... REGISTRATION FOR THE MARATHON... FLIGHT NUMBER... DEPARTING FROM THE CHARLES DE GAULLE AIRPORT...
NEW...
YORK!
ARE YOU GUYS PSYCHED?
YES! WE WERE JUST ABOUT TO GO RUN, ACTUALLY...
HH... ONE HOUR AND 20 MINUTES ALREADY... LET'S PUSH A LITTLE MORE... JUST 15 MINUTES...
WHAT? ARE YOU KIDDING? FOR YOUR INFORMATION, I'M RUNNING ON EMPTY, HERE!
HHHNN... I'M DONE...
I'M GOING...
...TO WALK BACK...
YOU KEEP GOING.

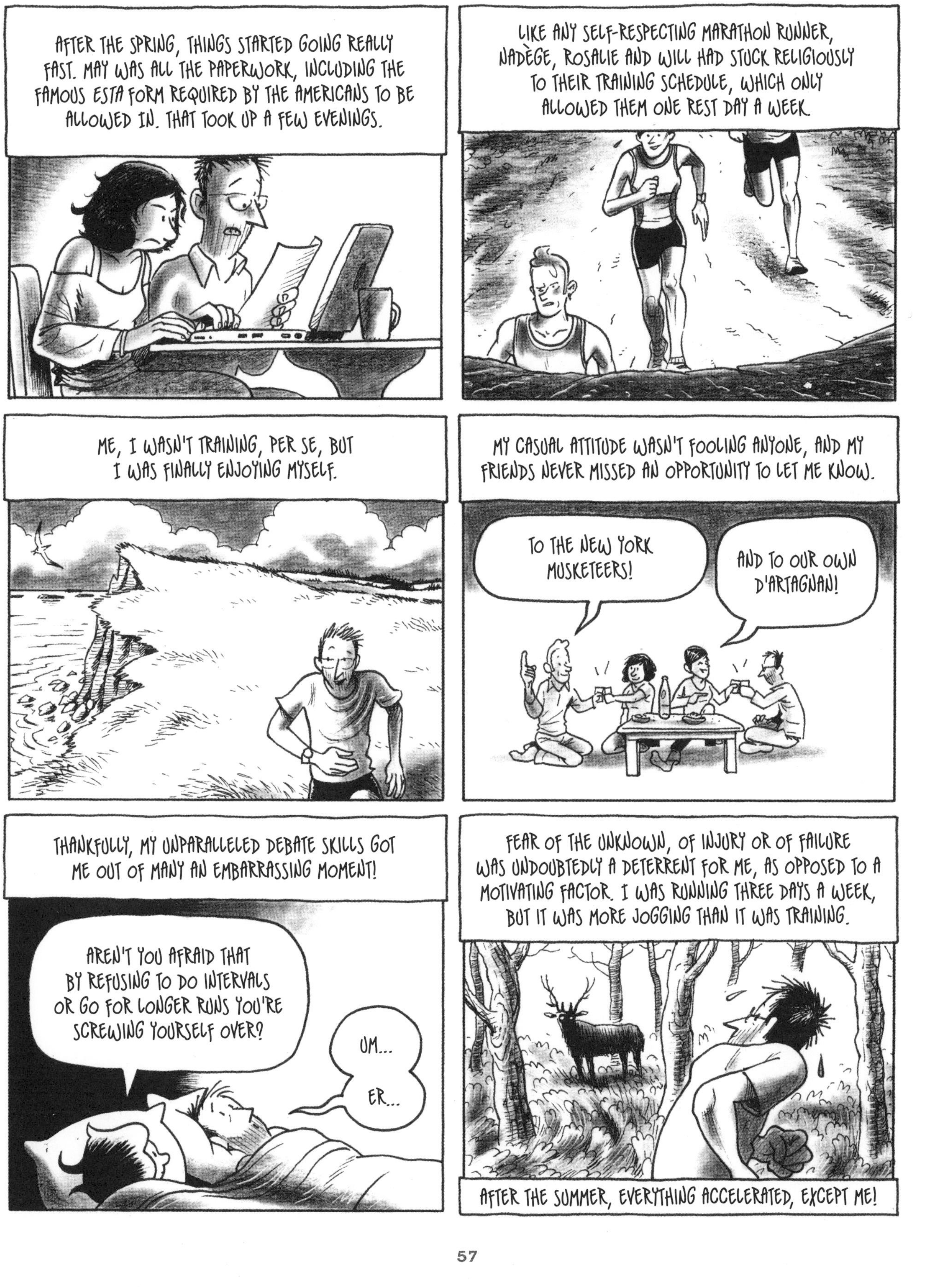
AFTER THE SPRING, THINGS STARTED GOING REALLY FAST. MAY WAS ALL THE PAPERWORK, INCLUDING THE FAMOUS ESTA FORM REQUIRED BY THE AMERICANS TO BE ALLOWED IN. THAT TOOK UP A FEW EVENINGS.
LIKE ANY SELF-RESPECTING MARATHON RUNNER, NADÈGE, ROSALIE AND WILL HAD STUCK RELIGIOUSLY TO THEIR TRAINING SCHEDULE, WHICH ONLY ALLOWED THEM ONE REST DAY A WEEK.
ME, I WASN'T TRAINING, PER SE, BUT I WAS FINALLY ENJOYING MYSELF.
MY CASUAL ATTITUDE WASN'T FOOLING ANYONE, AND MY FRIENDS NEVER MISSED AN OPPORTUNITY TO LET ME KNOW.
TO THE NEW YORK MUSKETEERS!
AND TO OUR OWN D'ARTAGNAN!
THANKFULLY, MY UNPARALLELED DEBATE SKILLS GOT ME OUT OF MANY AN EMBARRASSING MOMENT!
AREN'T YOU AFRAID THAT BY REFUSING TO DO INTERVALS OR GO FOR LONGER RUNS YOU'RE SCREWING YOURSELF OVER?
UM...
ER...
FEAR OF THE UNKNOWN, OF INJURY OR OF FAILURE WAS UNDOUBTEDLY A DETERRENT FOR ME, AS OPPOSED TO A MOTIVATING FACTOR. I WAS RUNNING THREE DAYS A WEEK, BUT IT WAS MORE JOGGING THAN IT WAS TRAINING.
AFTER THE SUMMER, EVERYTHING ACCELERATED, EXCEPT ME!

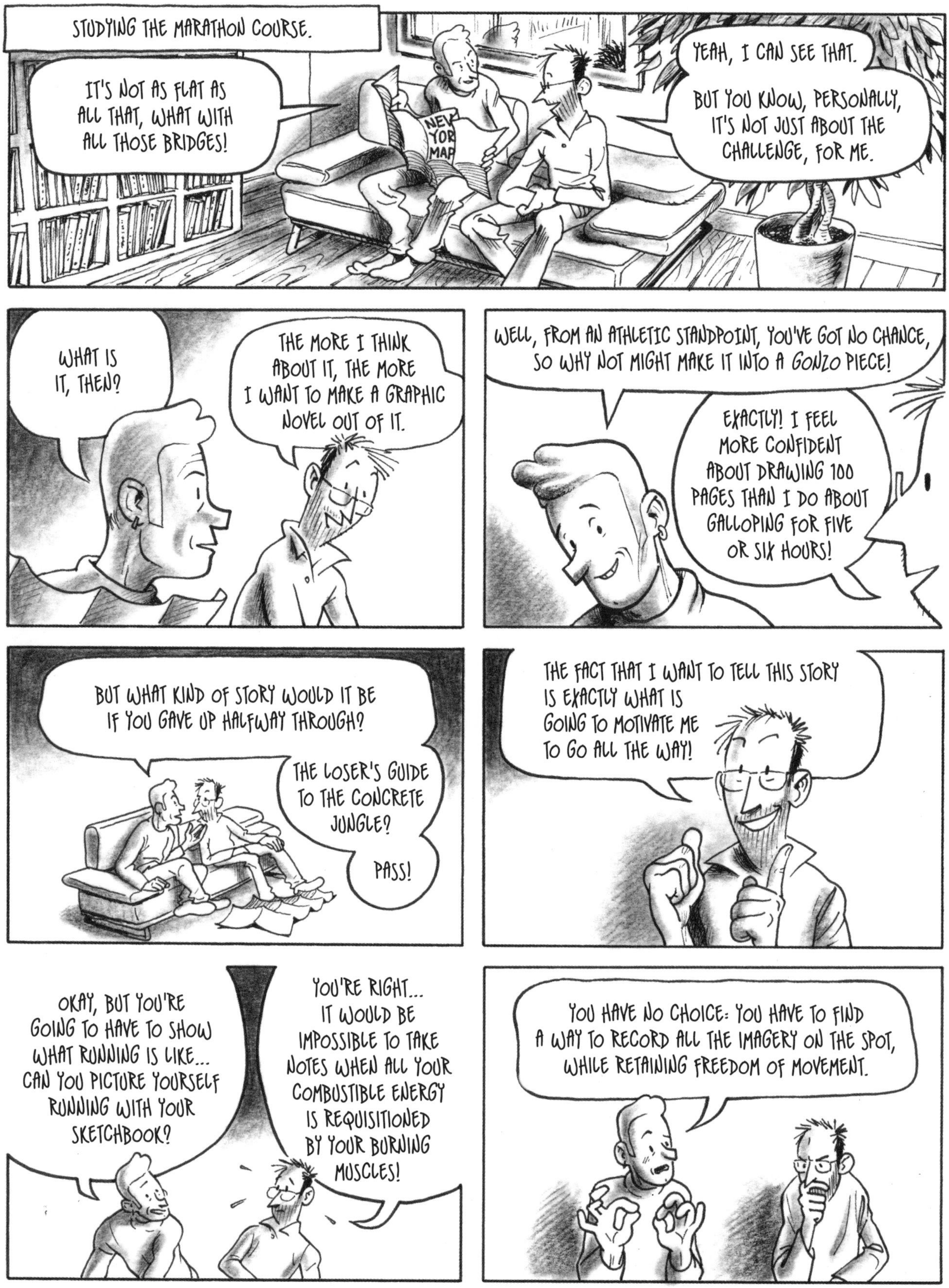
STUDYING THE MARATHON COURSE.
IT'S NOT AS FLAT AS ALL THAT, WHAT WITH ALL THOSE BRIDGES!
NEW YORK MAP
YEAH, I CAN SEE THAT.
BUT YOU KNOW, PERSONALLY, IT'S NOT JUST ABOUT THE CHALLENGE, FOR ME.
WHAT IS IT, THEN?
THE MORE I THINK ABOUT IT, THE MORE I WANT TO MAKE A GRAPHIC NOVEL OUT OF IT.
WELL, FROM AN ATHLETIC STANDPOINT, YOU'VE GOT NO CHANCE, SO WHY NOT MIGHT MAKE IT INTO A *GONZO* PIECE!
EXACTLY! I FEEL MORE CONFIDENT ABOUT DRAWING 100 PAGES THAN I DO ABOUT GALLOPING FOR FIVE OR SIX HOURS!
BUT WHAT KIND OF STORY WOULD IT BE IF YOU GAVE UP HALFWAY THROUGH?
THE LOSER'S GUIDE TO THE CONCRETE JUNGLE?
PASS!
THE FACT THAT I WANT TO TELL THIS STORY IS EXACTLY WHAT IS GOING TO MOTIVATE ME TO GO ALL THE WAY!
OKAY, BUT YOU'RE GOING TO HAVE TO SHOW WHAT RUNNING IS LIKE... CAN YOU PICTURE YOURSELF RUNNING WITH YOUR SKETCHBOOK?
YOU'RE RIGHT... IT WOULD BE IMPOSSIBLE TO TAKE NOTES WHEN ALL YOUR COMBUSTIBLE ENERGY IS REQUISITIONED BY YOUR BURNING MUSCLES!
YOU HAVE NO CHOICE: YOU HAVE TO FIND A WAY TO RECORD ALL THE IMAGERY ON THE SPOT, WHILE RETAINING FREEDOM OF MOVEMENT.

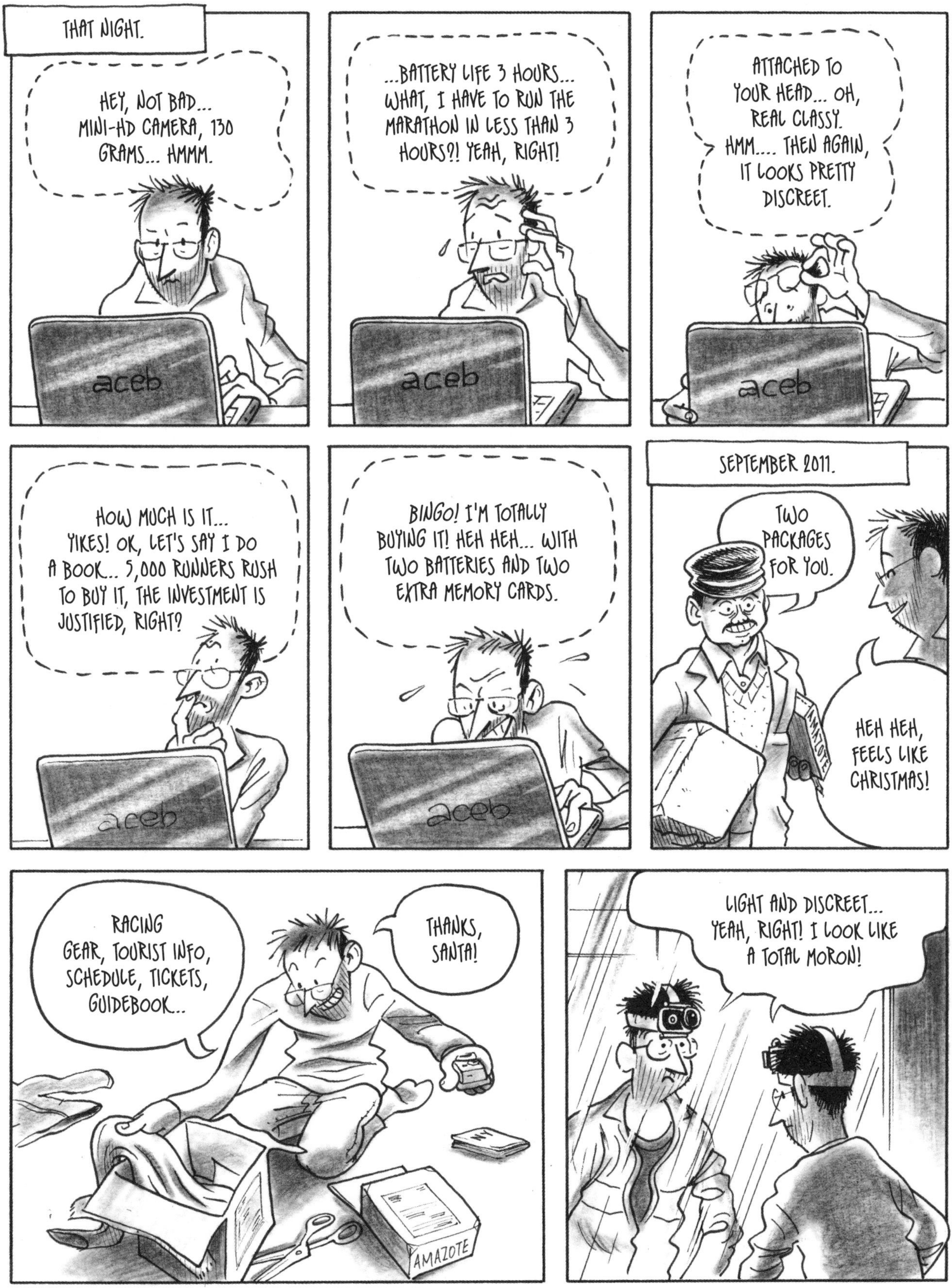
THAT NIGHT.
HEY, NOT BAD... MINI-HD CAMERA, 130 GRAMS... HMMM.
aceb
...BATTERY LIFE 3 HOURS... WHAT, I HAVE TO RUN THE MARATHON IN LESS THAN 3 HOURS?! YEAH, RIGHT!
aceb
ATTACHED TO YOUR HEAD... OH, REAL CLASSY. HMM.... THEN AGAIN, IT LOOKS PRETTY DISCREET.
aceb
HOW MUCH IS IT... YIKES! OK, LET'S SAY I DO A BOOK... 5,000 RUNNERS RUSH TO BUY IT, THE INVESTMENT IS JUSTIFIED, RIGHT?
aceb
BINGO! I'M TOTALLY BUYING IT! HEH HEH... WITH TWO BATTERIES AND TWO EXTRA MEMORY CARDS.
aceb
SEPTEMBER 2011.
TWO PACKAGES FOR YOU.
AMAZOTE
HEH HEH, FEELS LIKE CHRISTMAS!
RACING GEAR, TOURIST INFO, SCHEDULE, TICKETS, GUIDEBOOK...
THANKS, SANTA!
NY
AMAZOTE
LIGHT AND DISCREET... YEAH, RIGHT! I LOOK LIKE A TOTAL MORON!

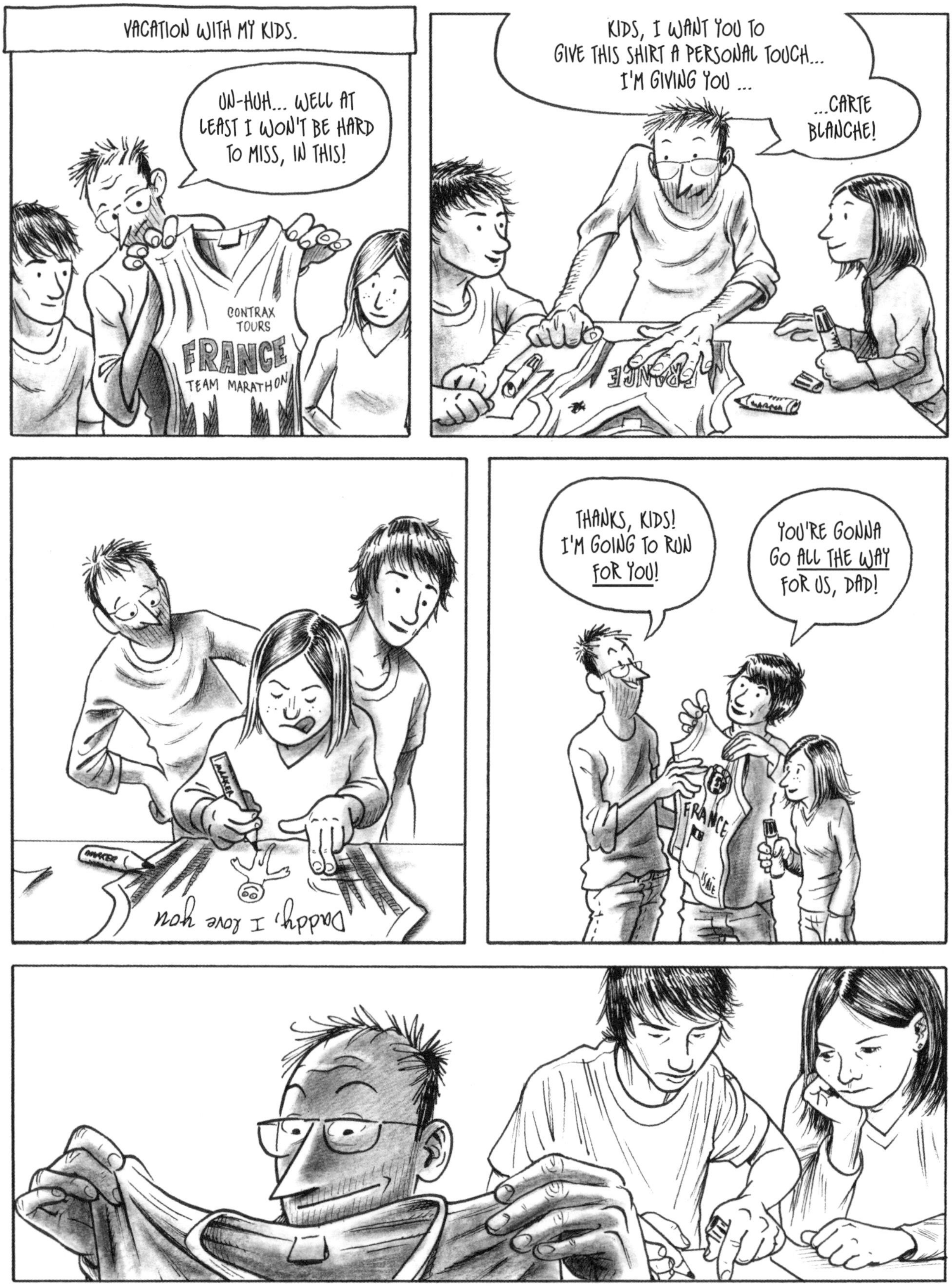
VACATION WITH MY KIDS.
UN-HUH... WELL AT LEAST I WON'T BE HARD TO MISS, IN THIS!
CONTRAX TOURS
FRANCE
TEAM MARATHON
KIDS, I WANT YOU TO GIVE THIS SHIRT A PERSONAL TOUCH... I'M GIVING YOU ...
...CARTE BLANCHE!
Daddy, I love you
THANKS, KIDS! I'M GOING TO RUN FOR YOU!
YOU'RE GONNA GO ALL THE WAY FOR US, DAD!
FRANCE

RAILROAD CROSSING 185. A DECOMMISSIONED RAIL LINE BETWEEN ARCAY AND NEUVILLE-DE-POITOU.

I'M STILL MISSING SOMETHING FOR THIS VOYAGE TO THE AMERICAS...

I HAD SPENT MY ENTIRE CHILDHOOD ON THAT RAILROAD LINE...

I NEEDED A PIECE OF THAT FAMILIAR "IN-BETWEEN-STATIONS" LINE FOR GOOD LUCK

WHAT ARE YOU GONNA DO WITH THAT, DAD?

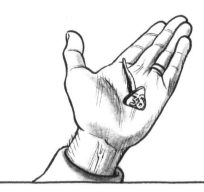

I WASN'T EXACTLY SURE WHY, BUT THAT RUSTY OLD NAIL FROM 1938 WAS COMING WITH ME TO NEW YORK

IN ONE MONTH, WE'LL BE ON A PLANE.

TIME TO START CARBO-LOADING ON PASTA.

OUR PASTA RICE

TO EVALUATE MY ODDS OF SUCCESS, I MADE OF LIST OF MY SKILLS.

A: ACQUIRED
ITP: IN THE PROCESS
NA: NON-ACQUIRED

RUNNING GEAR	A
REGISTRATION, FUNDING	A
MOTIVATION	ITP
(SERIOUS) TRAINING SCHEDULE	NA
VIDEO EQUIPMENT	ITP
TEAM SPIRIT	A

AMERICAN ENGLISH LANGUAGE SKILLS	ITP
FAMILIARITY WITH THE RACE COURSE	ITP
LOSING 12-17 POUNDS	ITP
RUNNING TWO HOURS WITHOUT A BREAK	NA
ACCEPTING THAT I WON'T WIN THE $200,000 FIRST PRIZE	A

GRR... DAMN STUFFY NOSE!

SNNNNNN

FRiiiT

ELIMINATION OF WASTEWATER... NON-ACQUIRED! ARGH!

FUDGE!

OVER THE FINAL DAYS OF OCTOBER, I DEALT WITH THE RISING PRESSURE BY DOWNPLAYING THE WHOLE THING.

...JUST COME BACK WITH BOTH LEGS AND A WHOLE HEART...

4.
I WANT TO BE
A Part Of It

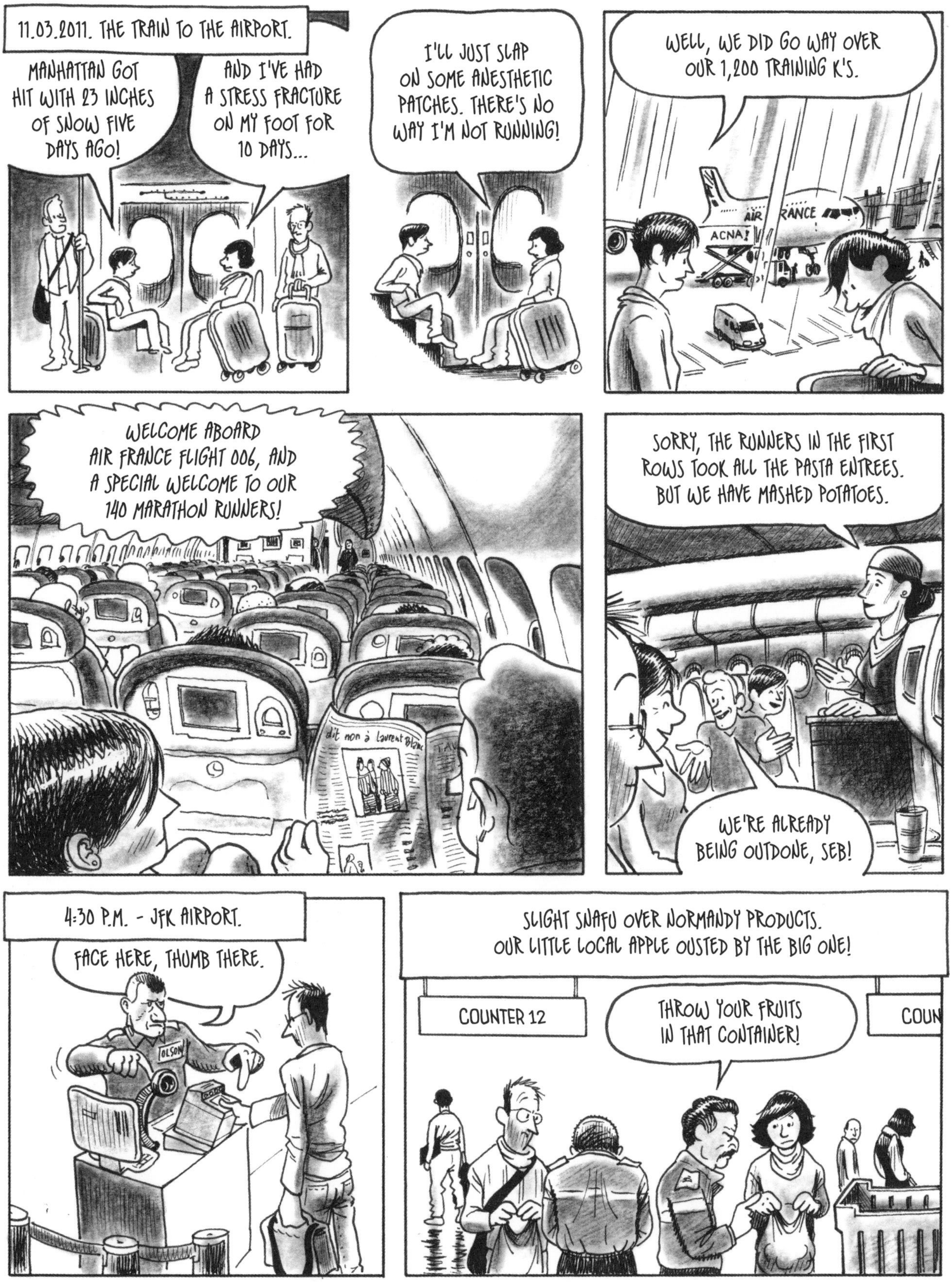
11.03.2011. THE TRAIN TO THE AIRPORT.
MANHATTAN GOT HIT WITH 23 INCHES OF SNOW FIVE DAYS AGO!
AND I'VE HAD A STRESS FRACTURE ON MY FOOT FOR 10 DAYS...
I'LL JUST SLAP ON SOME ANESTHETIC PATCHES. THERE'S NO WAY I'M NOT RUNNING!
WELL, WE DID GO WAY OVER OUR 1,200 TRAINING K'S.
WELCOME ABOARD AIR FRANCE FLIGHT 006, AND A SPECIAL WELCOME TO OUR 140 MARATHON RUNNERS!
SORRY, THE RUNNERS IN THE FIRST ROWS TOOK ALL THE PASTA ENTREES. BUT WE HAVE MASHED POTATOES.
WE'RE ALREADY BEING OUTDONE, SEB!
4:30 P.M. - JFK AIRPORT.
FACE HERE, THUMB THERE.
OLSON
SLIGHT SNAFU OVER NORMANDY PRODUCTS. OUR LITTLE LOCAL APPLE OUSTED BY THE BIG ONE!
COUNTER 12
THROW YOUR FRUITS IN THAT CONTAINER!

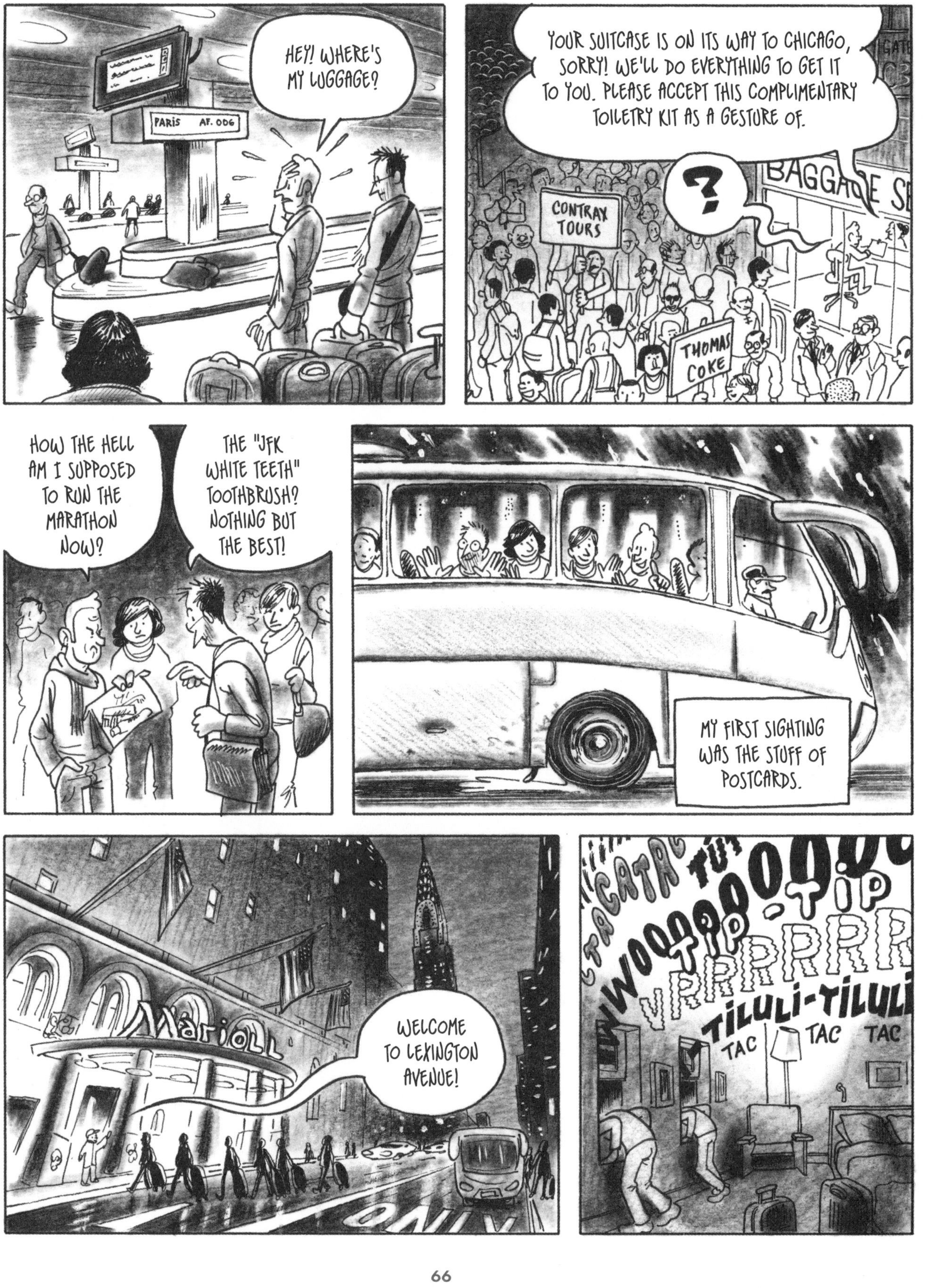
PARIS AF. 006
HEY! WHERE'S MY LUGGAGE?
YOUR SUITCASE IS ON ITS WAY TO CHICAGO, SORRY! WE'LL DO EVERYTHING TO GET IT TO YOU. PLEASE ACCEPT THIS COMPLIMENTARY TOILETRY KIT AS A GESTURE OF.
?
CONTRAX TOURS
THOMAS COKE
HOW THE HELL AM I SUPPOSED TO RUN THE MARATHON NOW?
THE "JFK WHITE TEETH" TOOTHBRUSH? NOTHING BUT THE BEST!
MY FIRST SIGHTING WAS THE STUFF OF POSTCARDS.
WELCOME TO LEXINGTON AVENUE!
TIP-TIP
TILULI-TILULI
TAC
TAC
TAC

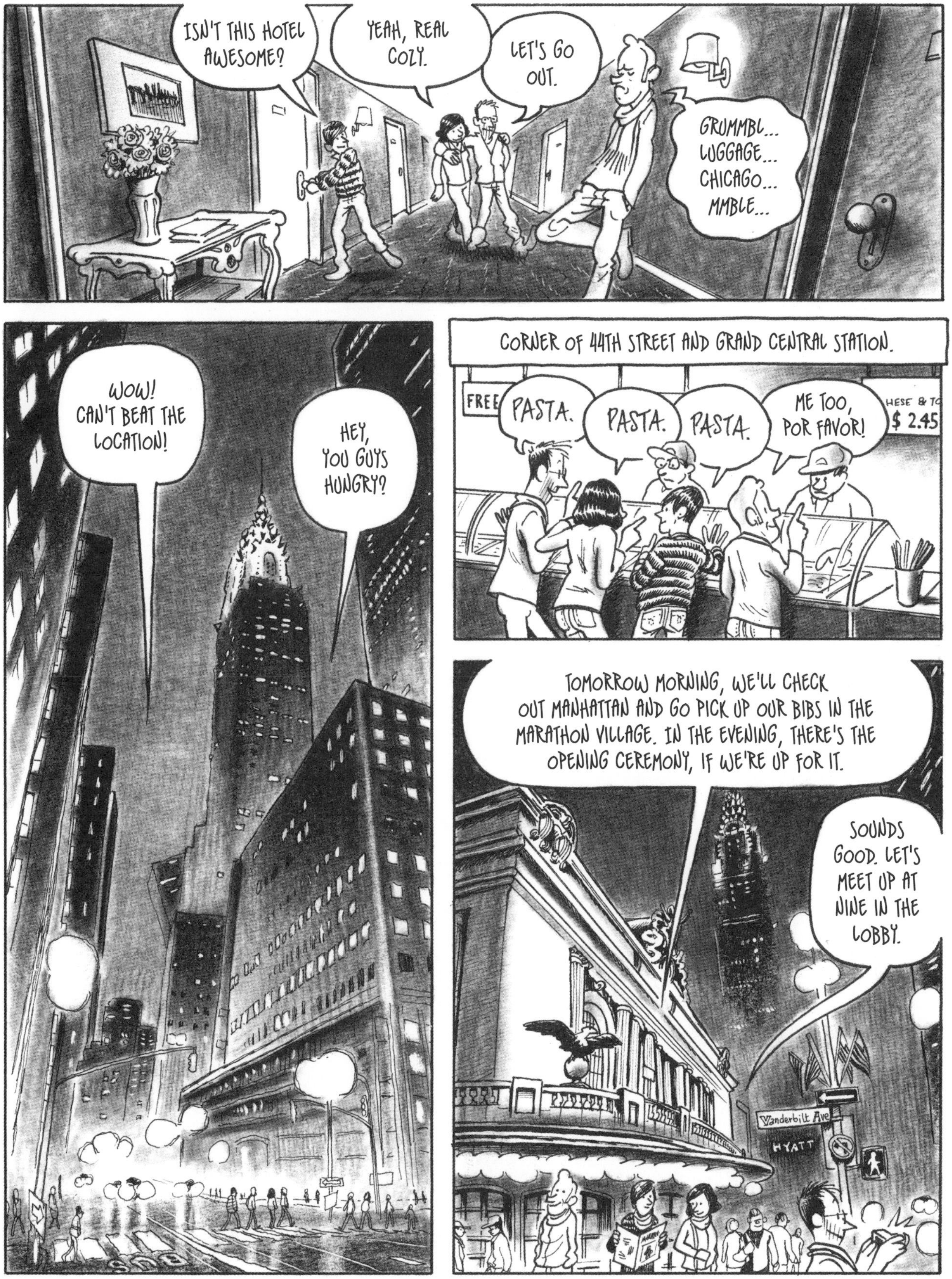
ISN'T THIS HOTEL AWESOME?
YEAH, REAL COZY.
LET'S GO OUT.
GRUMMBL... LUGGAGE... CHICAGO... MMBLE...
WOW! CAN'T BEAT THE LOCATION!
HEY, YOU GUYS HUNGRY?
CORNER OF 44TH STREET AND GRAND CENTRAL STATION.
FREE
PASTA.
PASTA.
PASTA.
ME TOO, POR FAVOR!
$ 2.45
TOMORROW MORNING, WE'LL CHECK OUT MANHATTAN AND GO PICK UP OUR BIBS IN THE MARATHON VILLAGE. IN THE EVENING, THERE'S THE OPENING CEREMONY, IF WE'RE UP FOR IT.
SOUNDS GOOD. LET'S MEET UP AT NINE IN THE LOBBY.
Vanderbilt Ave
HYATT

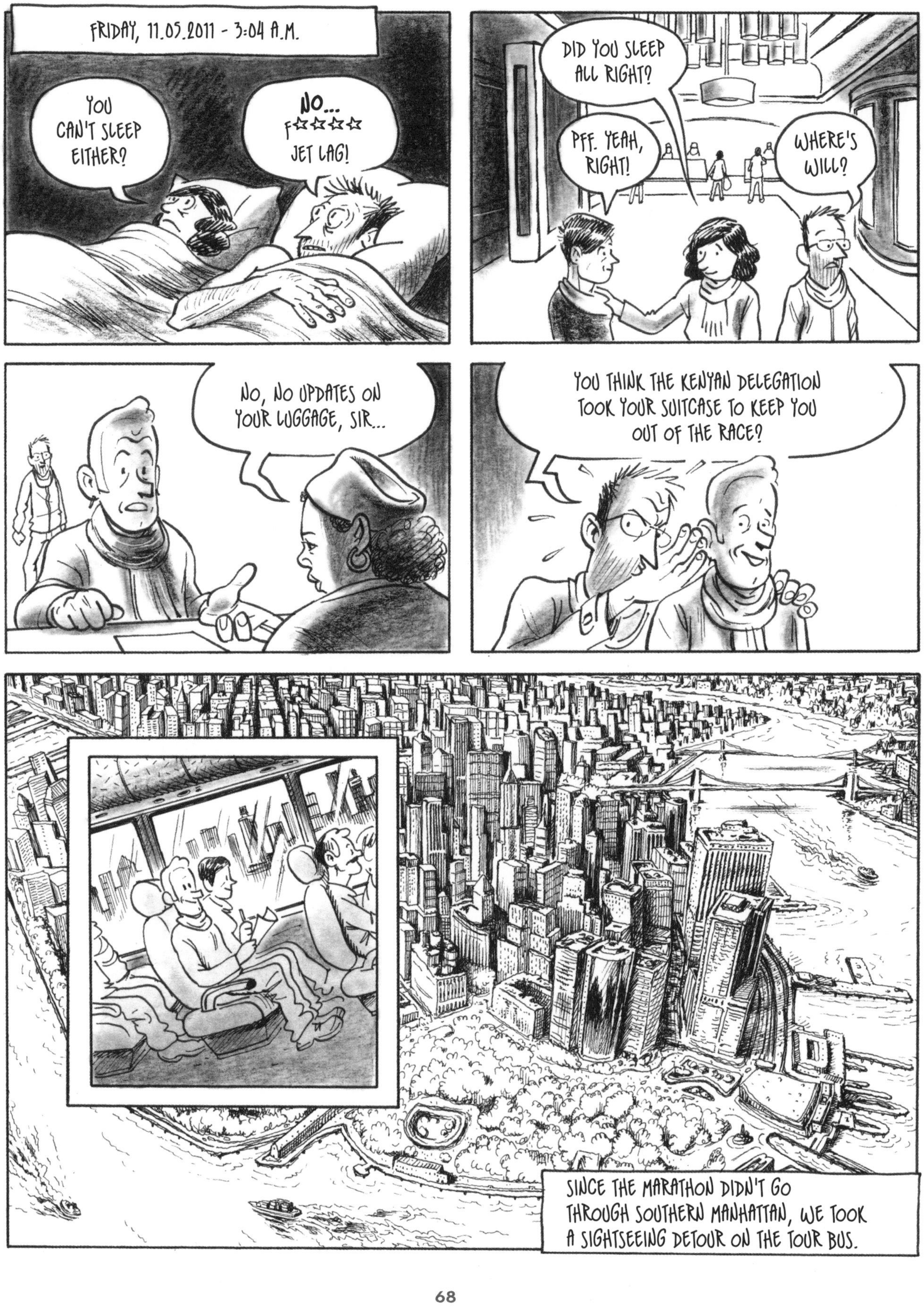
FRIDAY, 11.05.2011 - 3:04 A.M.
YOU CAN'T SLEEP EITHER?
NO... F☆☆☆☆☆ JET LAG!
DID YOU SLEEP ALL RIGHT?
PFF. YEAH, RIGHT!
WHERE'S WILL?
NO, NO UPDATES ON YOUR LUGGAGE, SIR...
YOU THINK THE KENYAN DELEGATION TOOK YOUR SUITCASE TO KEEP YOU OUT OF THE RACE?
SINCE THE MARATHON DIDN'T GO THROUGH SOUTHERN MANHATTAN, WE TOOK A SIGHTSEEING DETOUR ON THE TOUR BUS.

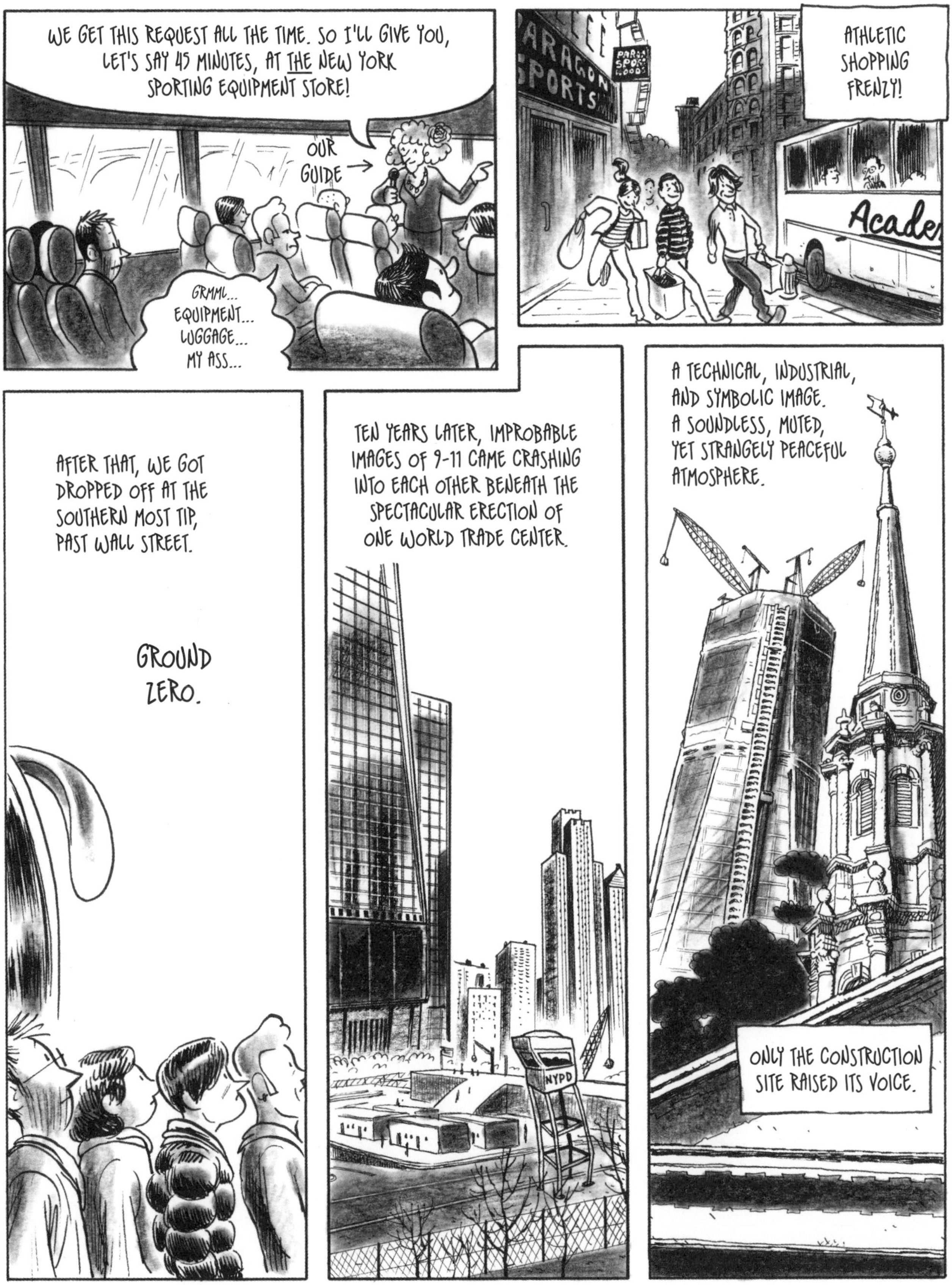
WE GET THIS REQUEST ALL THE TIME. SO I'LL GIVE YOU, LET'S SAY 45 MINUTES, AT THE NEW YORK SPORTING EQUIPMENT STORE!
OUR GUIDE
GRMML... EQUIPMENT... LUGGAGE... MY ASS...
ATHLETIC SHOPPING FRENZY!
PARAGON SPORTS
Acade
AFTER THAT, WE GOT DROPPED OFF AT THE SOUTHERN MOST TIP, PAST WALL STREET.
GROUND ZERO.
TEN YEARS LATER, IMPROBABLE IMAGES OF 9-11 CAME CRASHING INTO EACH OTHER BENEATH THE SPECTACULAR ERECTION OF ONE WORLD TRADE CENTER.
NYPD
A TECHNICAL, INDUSTRIAL, AND SYMBOLIC IMAGE. A SOUNDLESS, MUTED, YET STRANGELY PEACEFUL ATMOSPHERE.
ONLY THE CONSTRUCTION SITE RAISED ITS VOICE.

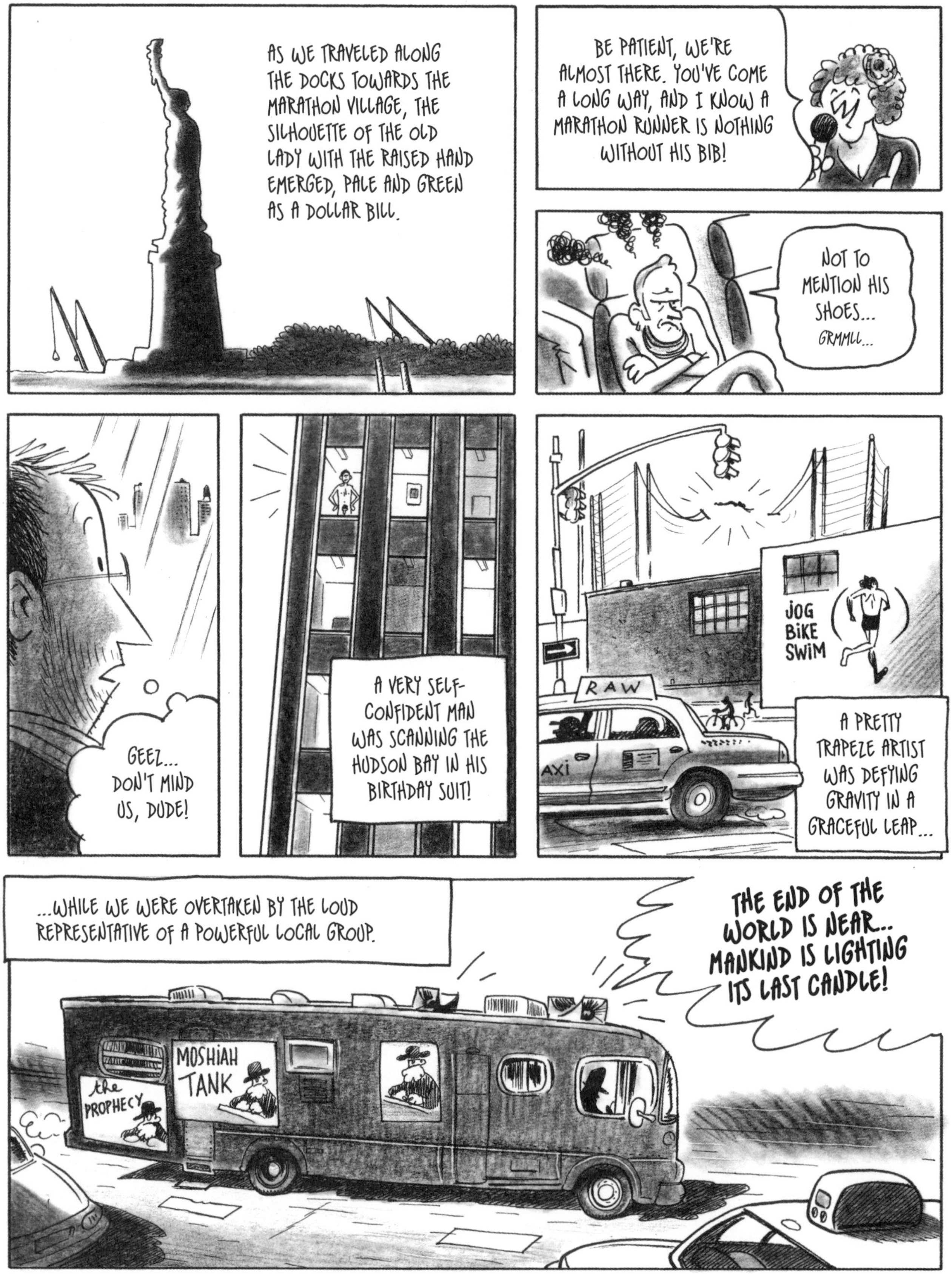
AS WE TRAVELED ALONG THE DOCKS TOWARDS THE MARATHON VILLAGE, THE SILHOUETTE OF THE OLD LADY WITH THE RAISED HAND EMERGED, PALE AND GREEN AS A DOLLAR BILL.
BE PATIENT, WE'RE ALMOST THERE. YOU'VE COME A LONG WAY, AND I KNOW A MARATHON RUNNER IS NOTHING WITHOUT HIS BIB!
NOT TO MENTION HIS SHOES... GRMMLL...
GEEZ... DON'T MIND US, DUDE!
A VERY SELF-CONFIDENT MAN WAS SCANNING THE HUDSON BAY IN HIS BIRTHDAY SUIT!
JOG BIKE SWIM
RAW
AXI
A PRETTY TRAPEZE ARTIST WAS DEFYING GRAVITY IN A GRACEFUL LEAP...
...WHILE WE WERE OVERTAKEN BY THE LOUD REPRESENTATIVE OF A POWERFUL LOCAL GROUP.
THE END OF THE WORLD IS NEAR... MANKIND IS LIGHTING ITS LAST CANDLE!
MOSHIAH TANK
the PROPHECY

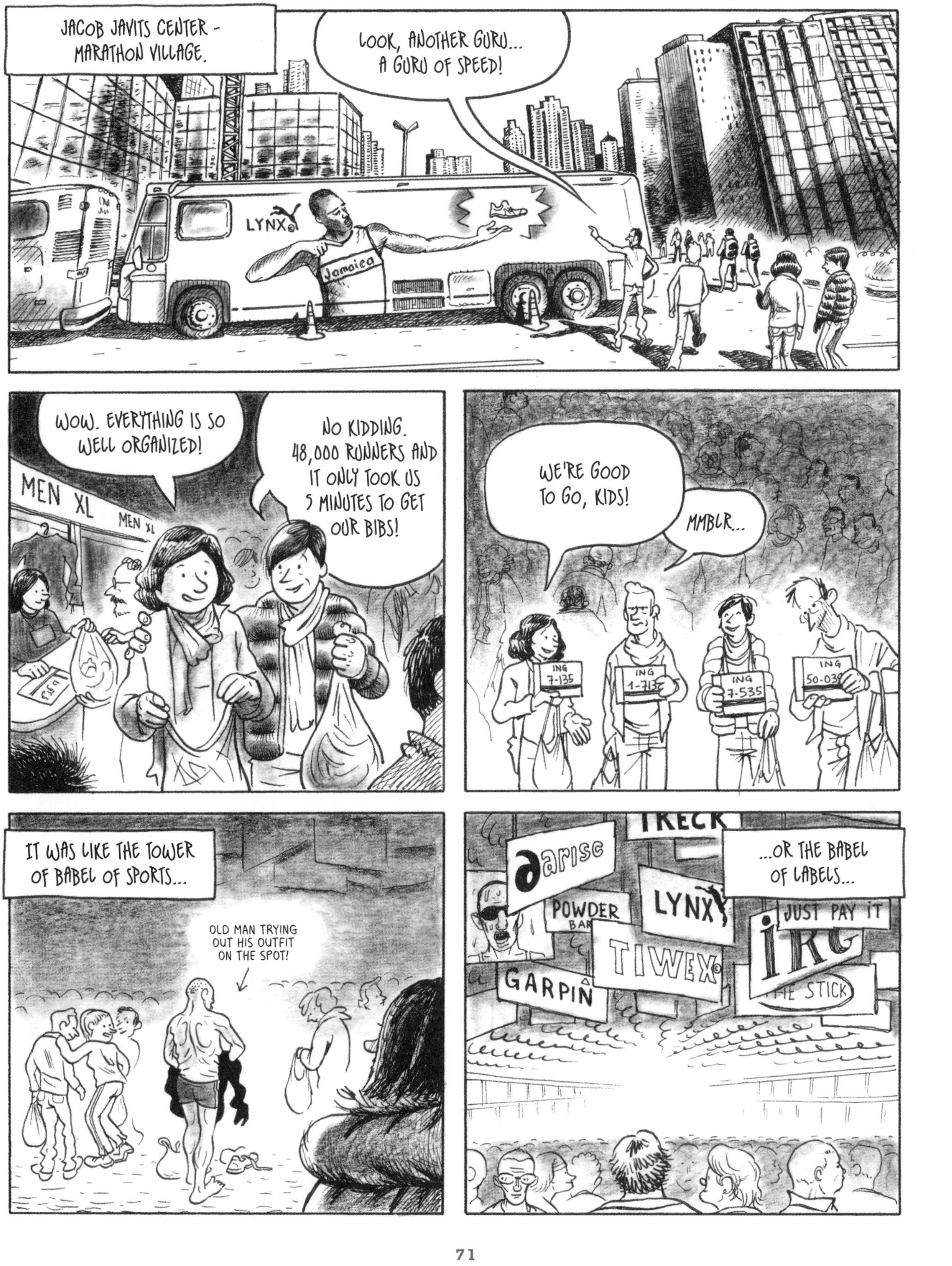
JACOB JAVITS CENTER - MARATHON VILLAGE.
LOOK, ANOTHER GURU... A GURU OF SPEED!
LYNX
Jamaica
WOW. EVERYTHING IS SO WELL ORGANIZED!
NO KIDDING. 48,000 RUNNERS AND IT ONLY TOOK US 5 MINUTES TO GET OUR BIBS!
MEN XL
MEN XL
WE'RE GOOD TO GO, KIDS!
MMBLR...
ING 7-135
ING 1-713
ING 7-535
ING 50-03
IT WAS LIKE THE TOWER OF BABEL OF SPORTS...
OLD MAN TRYING OUT HIS OUTFIT ON THE SPOT!
...OR THE BABEL OF LABELS...
TRECK
arise
POWDER BAR
LYNX
JUST PAY IT
TIWEX
GARPIN
THE STICK

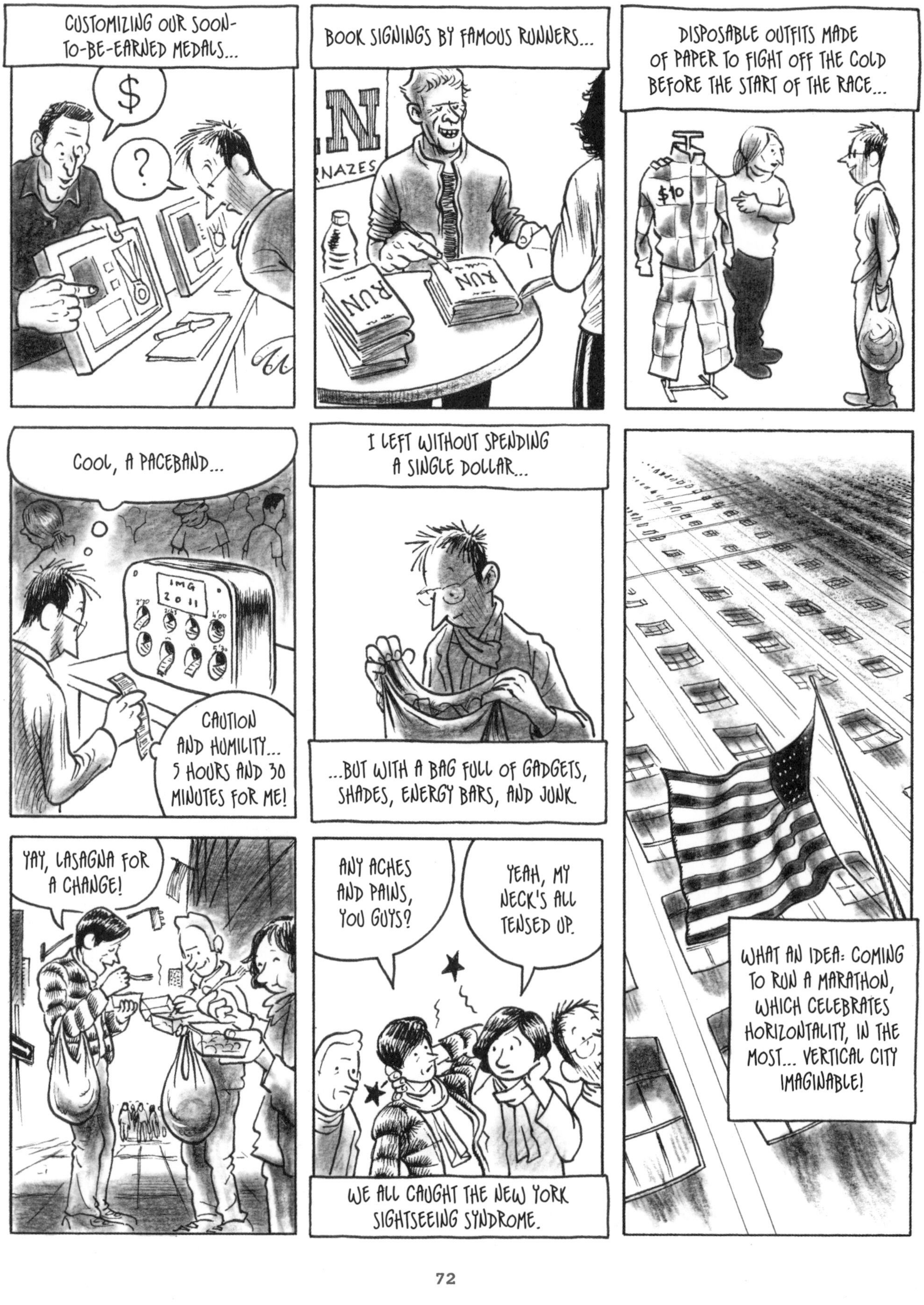
CUSTOMIZING OUR SOON-TO-BE-EARNED MEDALS...
$
?
BOOK SIGNINGS BY FAMOUS RUNNERS...
NAZES
RUN
RUN
DISPOSABLE OUTFITS MADE OF PAPER TO FIGHT OFF THE COLD BEFORE THE START OF THE RACE...
$10
COOL, A PACEBAND...
IMG 2011
CAUTION AND HUMILITY... 5 HOURS AND 30 MINUTES FOR ME!
I LEFT WITHOUT SPENDING A SINGLE DOLLAR...
...BUT WITH A BAG FULL OF GADGETS, SHADES, ENERGY BARS, AND JUNK.
YAY, LASAGNA FOR A CHANGE!
ANY ACHES AND PAINS, YOU GUYS?
YEAH, MY NECK'S ALL TENSED UP.
WE ALL CAUGHT THE NEW YORK SIGHTSEEING SYNDROME.
WHAT AN IDEA: COMING TO RUN A MARATHON, WHICH CELEBRATES HORIZONTALITY, IN THE MOST... VERTICAL CITY IMAGINABLE!

A GLACIAL, WINDY NIGHT FELL UPON CENTRAL PARK

WE CAN'T GO BACK TO THE HOTEL AT 8 P.M.! LET'S GO CHECK OUT THE OPENING NIGHT PARADE!

TIME TO LOCATE THE FINISH LINE, WHICH WE WERE ALL HOPING TO CROSS.

I'M IN

LOOK! FRENCHIES!

IT'S THE BRITTANY DELEGATION!

YEAH! WE'RE EVERYWHERE! YOU?

NORMANDY!

BAH! THAT'S OK!

THE KIWIS WERE ANNOYING.

YEP, IT WAS A CLOSE ONE, MATES. YOU'E WON BY ONE POINT.

RIGHT?

TWO MONTHS EARLIER, THE ALL BLACKS HAD WON THE RUGBY WORLD CUP ON THEIR HOME TURF.

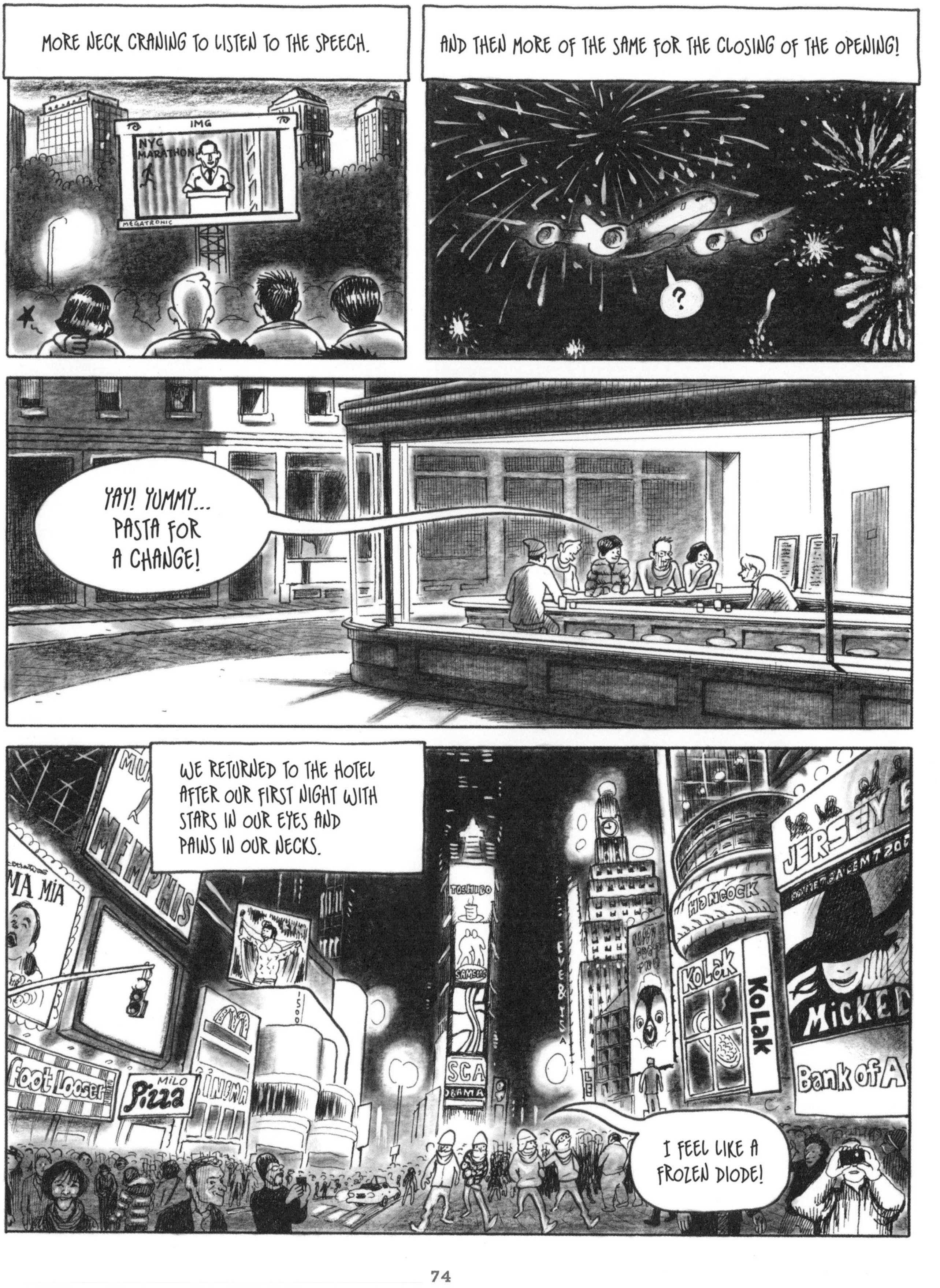
MORE NECK CRANING TO LISTEN TO THE SPEECH.
IMG
NYC MARATHON
MEGATRONIC
AND THEN MORE OF THE SAME FOR THE CLOSING OF THE OPENING!
?
YAY! YUMMY... PASTA FOR A CHANGE!
WE RETURNED TO THE HOTEL AFTER OUR FIRST NIGHT WITH STARS IN OUR EYES AND PAINS IN OUR NECKS.
MEMPHIS
MA MIA
Foot Looser
MILO Pizza
CINEMA
TOSHIBO
SCA
OBAMA
HANCOCK
KoLak
KoLak
JERSEY
MICKED
Bank of A
I FEEL LIKE A FROZEN DIODE!

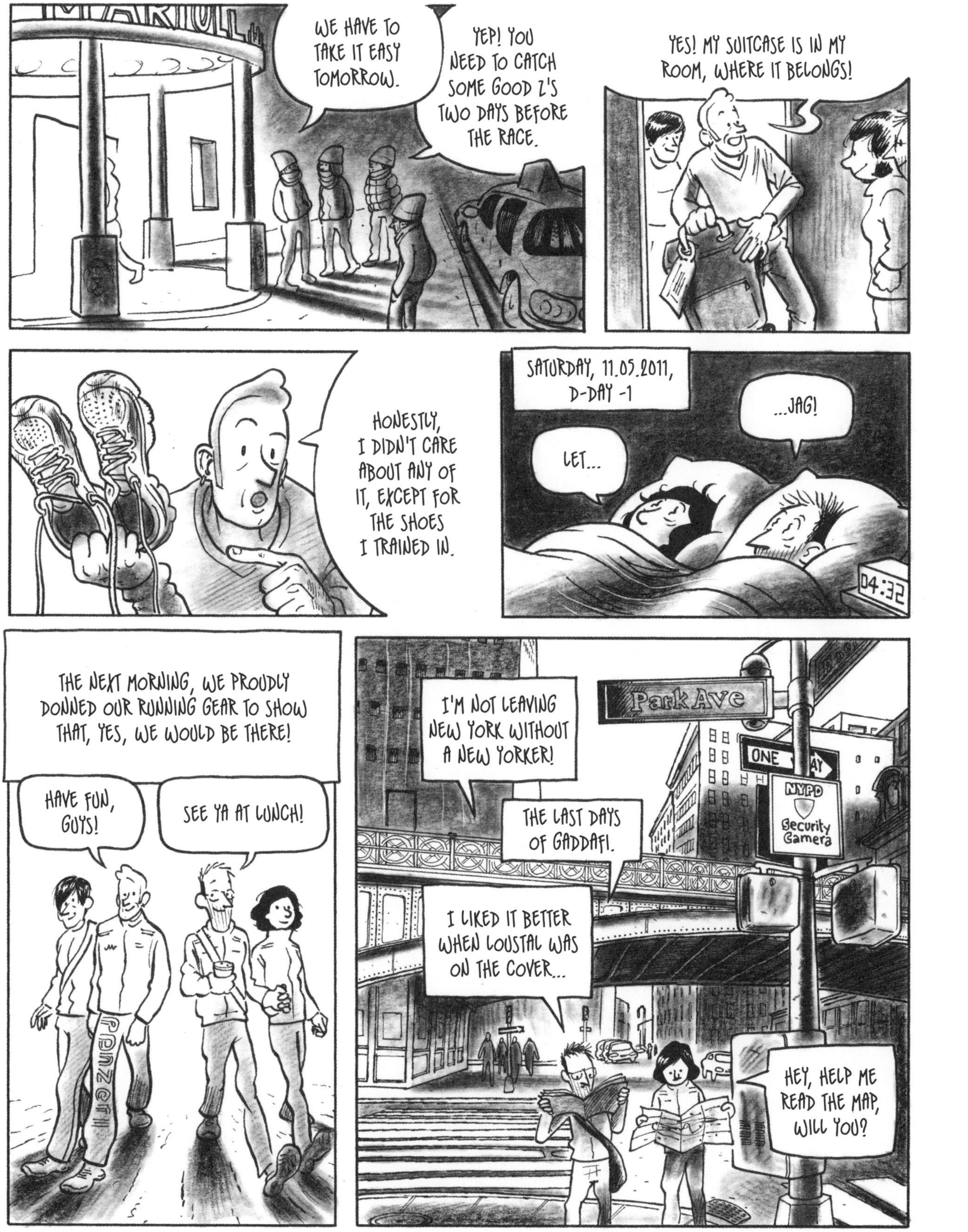
WE HAVE TO TAKE IT EASY TOMORROW.
YEP! YOU NEED TO CATCH SOME GOOD Z'S TWO DAYS BEFORE THE RACE.
YES! MY SUITCASE IS IN MY ROOM, WHERE IT BELONGS!
HONESTLY, I DIDN'T CARE ABOUT ANY OF IT, EXCEPT FOR THE SHOES I TRAINED IN.
SATURDAY, 11.05.2011, D-DAY -1
LET...
...JAG!
04:32
THE NEXT MORNING, WE PROUDLY DONNED OUR RUNNING GEAR TO SHOW THAT, YES, WE WOULD BE THERE!
HAVE FUN, GUYS!
SEE YA AT LUNCH!
Park Ave
ONE WAY
NYPD
Security Camera
I'M NOT LEAVING NEW YORK WITHOUT A NEW YORKER!
THE LAST DAYS OF GADDAFI.
I LIKED IT BETTER WHEN LOUSTAL WAS ON THE COVER...
HEY, HELP ME READ THE MAP, WILL YOU?

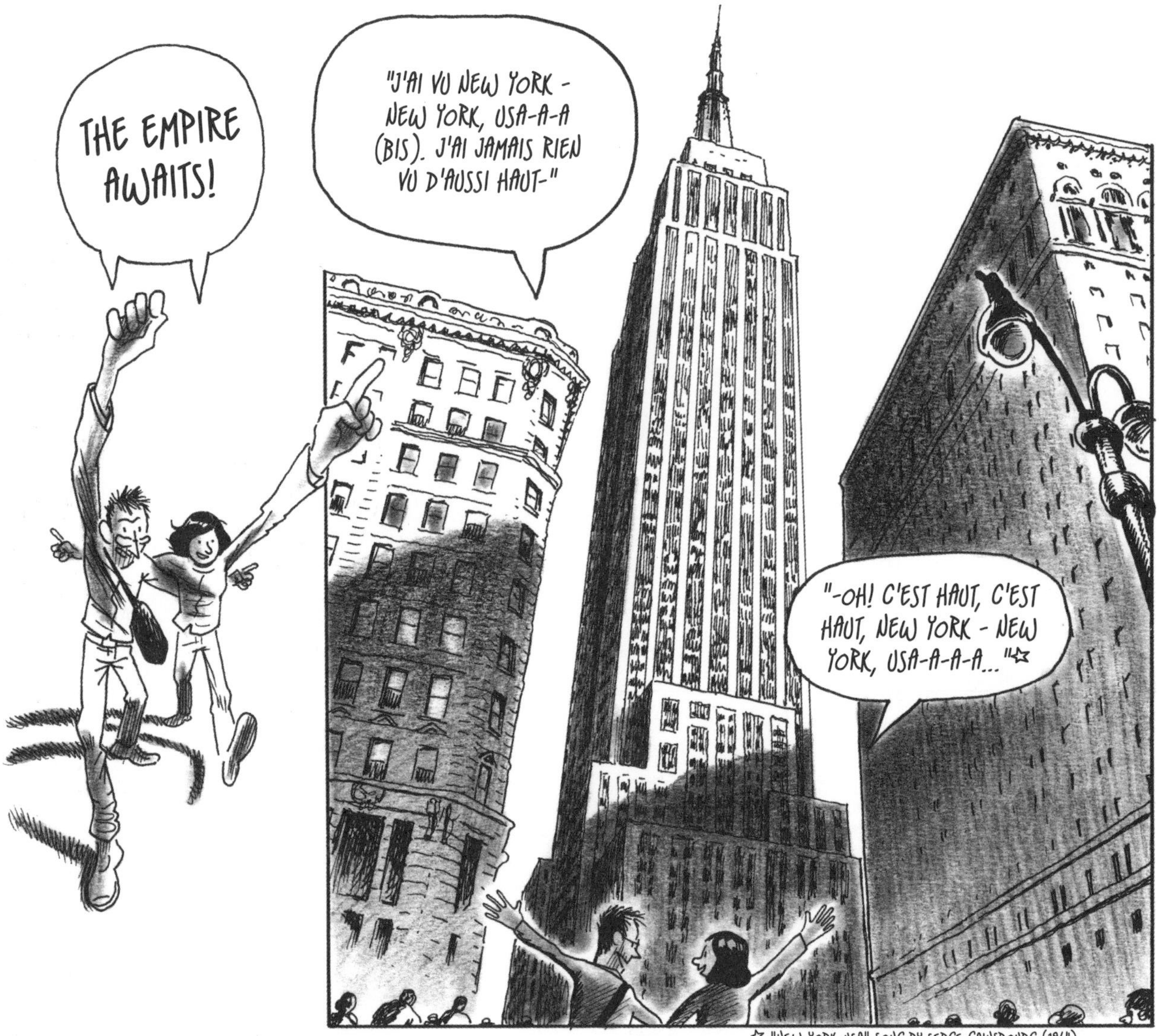
THE EMPIRE AWAITS!
"J'AI VU NEW YORK - NEW YORK, USA-A-A (BIS). J'AI JAMAIS RIEN VU D'AUSSI HAUT-"
"-OH! C'EST HAUT, C'EST HAUT, NEW YORK - NEW YORK, USA-A-A-A..."☆

☆ "NEW YORK-USA" SONG BY SERGE GAINSBOURG (1964)

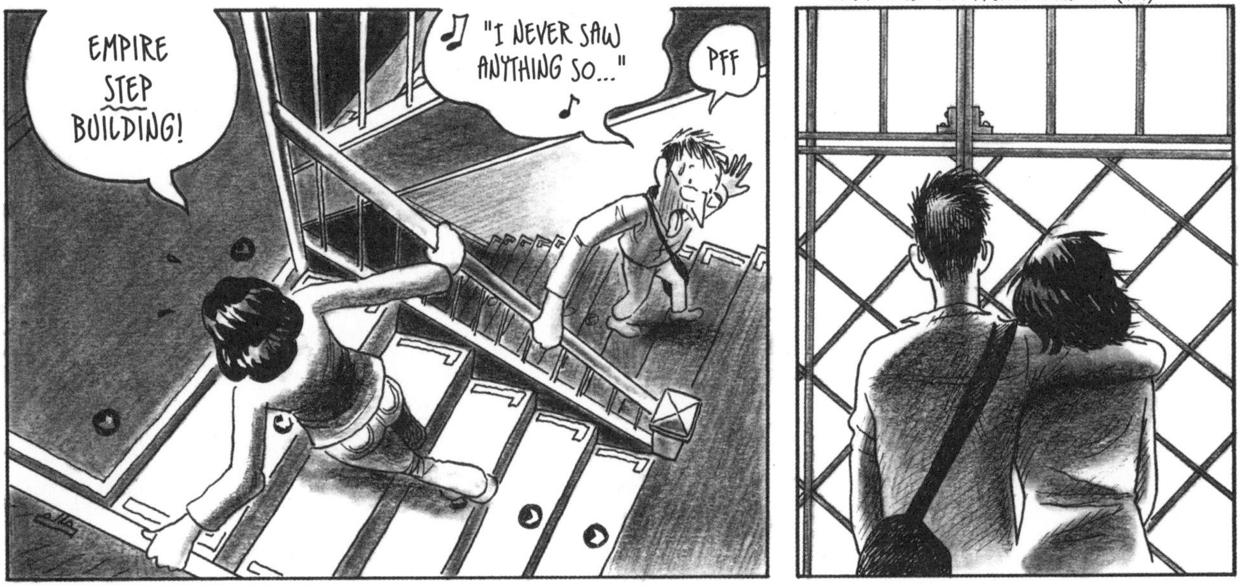
EMPIRE STEP BUILDING!
♫ "I NEVER SAW ANYTHING SO..." ♪
PFF

NORTHERN MANHATTAN, UPPER WEST AND EAST SIDES.

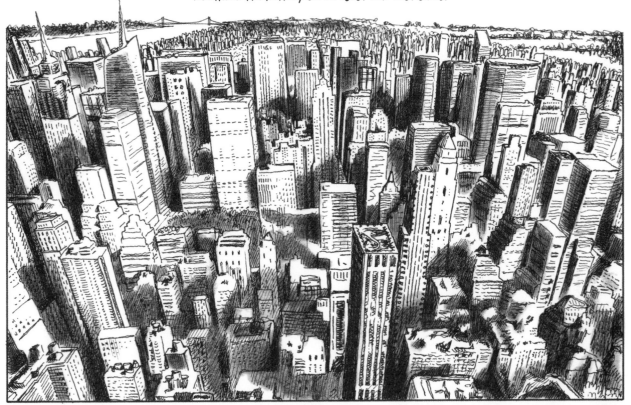

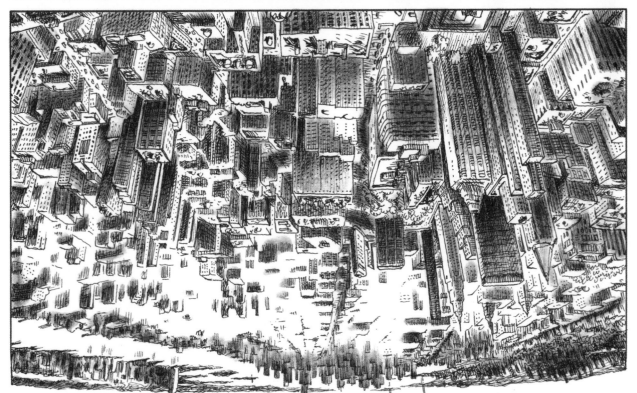

SOUTHERN MANHATTAN: GREENWICH VILLAGE, FINANCIAL DISTRICT, BROOKLYN AND NEW JERSEY IN THE DISTANCE.

STATEN ISLAND, BROOKLYN, QUEENS, THE BRONX AND MANHATTAN: OUR EYES TRAVELED ACROSS THE CITY'S FIVE BOROUGHS FASTER THAN OUR FEET WOULD THE NEXT DAY.

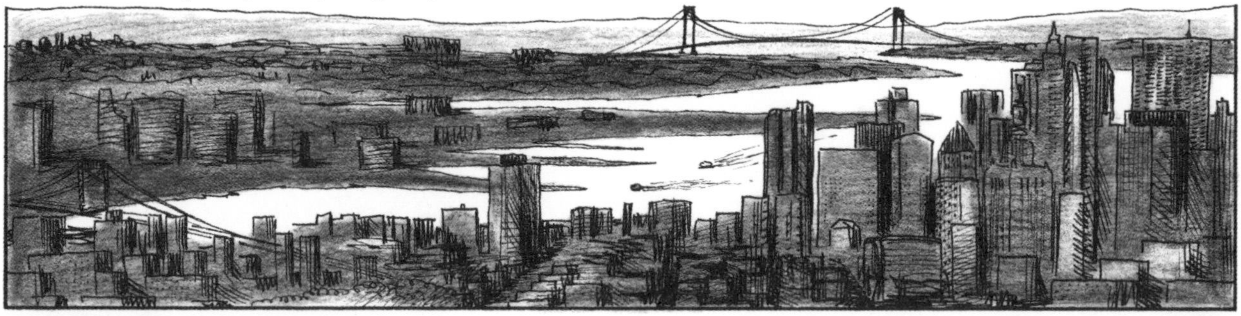

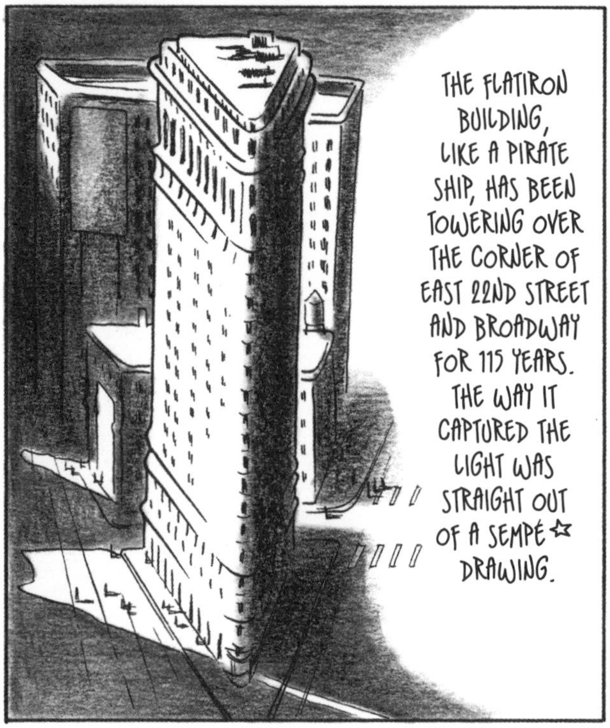
THE FLATIRON BUILDING, LIKE A PIRATE SHIP, HAS BEEN TOWERING OVER THE CORNER OF EAST 22ND STREET AND BROADWAY FOR 115 YEARS. THE WAY IT CAPTURED THE LIGHT WAS STRAIGHT OUT OF A SEMPÉ☆ DRAWING.

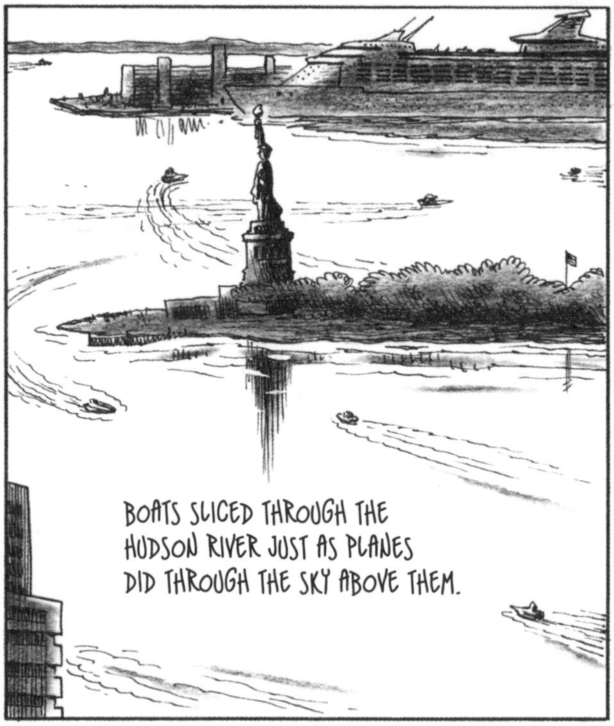
BOATS SLICED THROUGH THE HUDSON RIVER JUST AS PLANES DID THROUGH THE SKY ABOVE THEM.

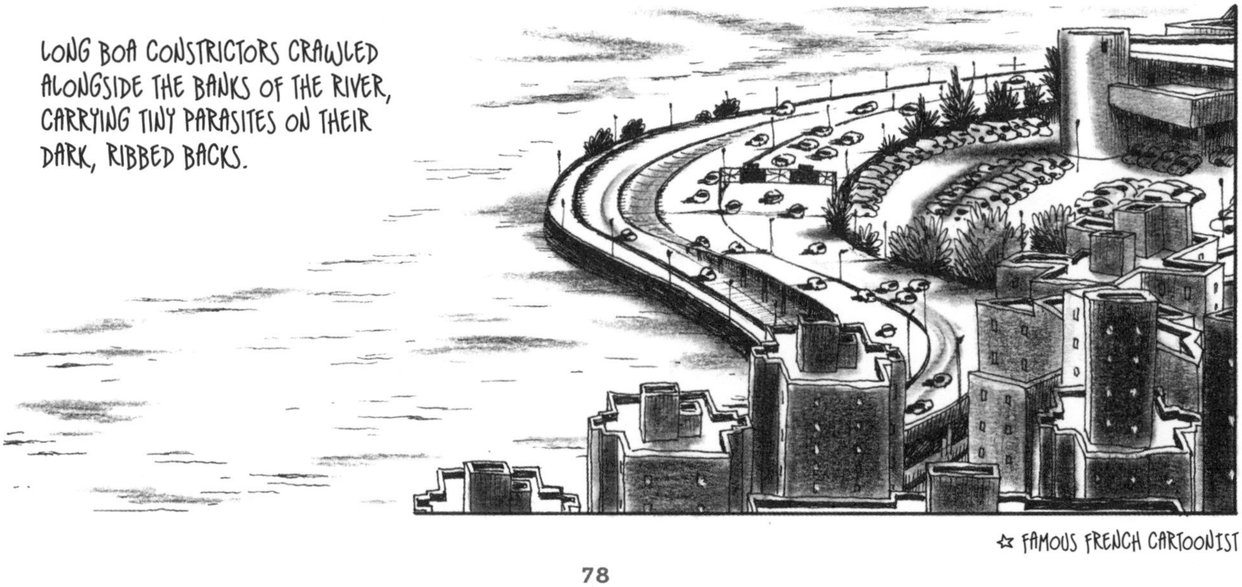
LONG BOA CONSTRICTORS CRAWLED ALONGSIDE THE BANKS OF THE RIVER, CARRYING TINY PARASITES ON THEIR DARK, RIBBED BACKS.

☆ FAMOUS FRENCH CARTOONIST

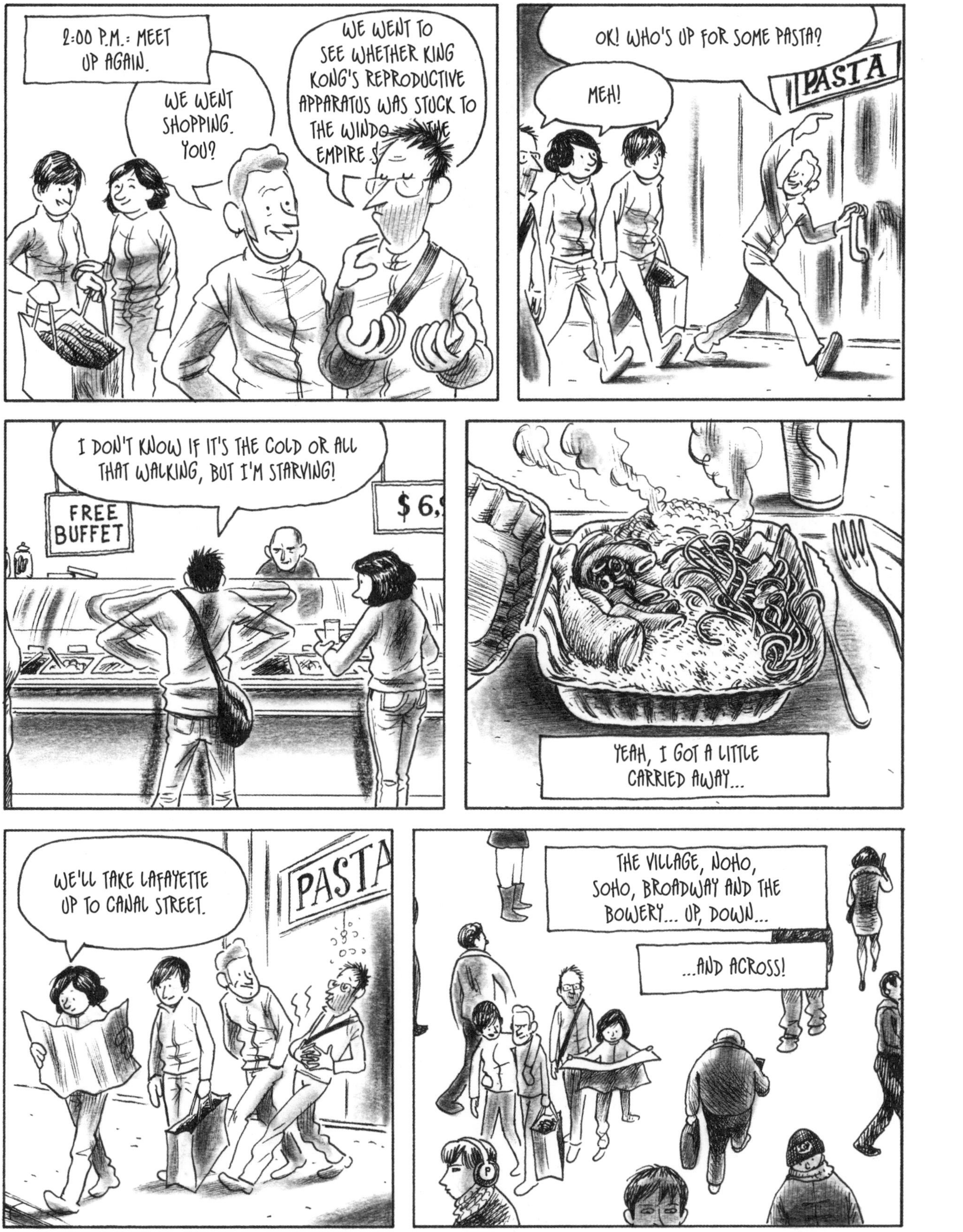

2:00 P.M.: MEET UP AGAIN.
WE WENT SHOPPING. YOU?
WE WENT TO SEE WHETHER KING KONG'S REPRODUCTIVE APPARATUS WAS STUCK TO THE WINDO THE EMPIRE S
OK! WHO'S UP FOR SOME PASTA?
MEH!
PASTA
I DON'T KNOW IF IT'S THE COLD OR ALL THAT WALKING, BUT I'M STARVING!
FREE BUFFET
$ 6,9
YEAH, I GOT A LITTLE CARRIED AWAY...
WE'LL TAKE LAFAYETTE UP TO CANAL STREET.
PASTA
THE VILLAGE, NOHO, SOHO, BROADWAY AND THE BOWERY... UP, DOWN...
...AND ACROSS!

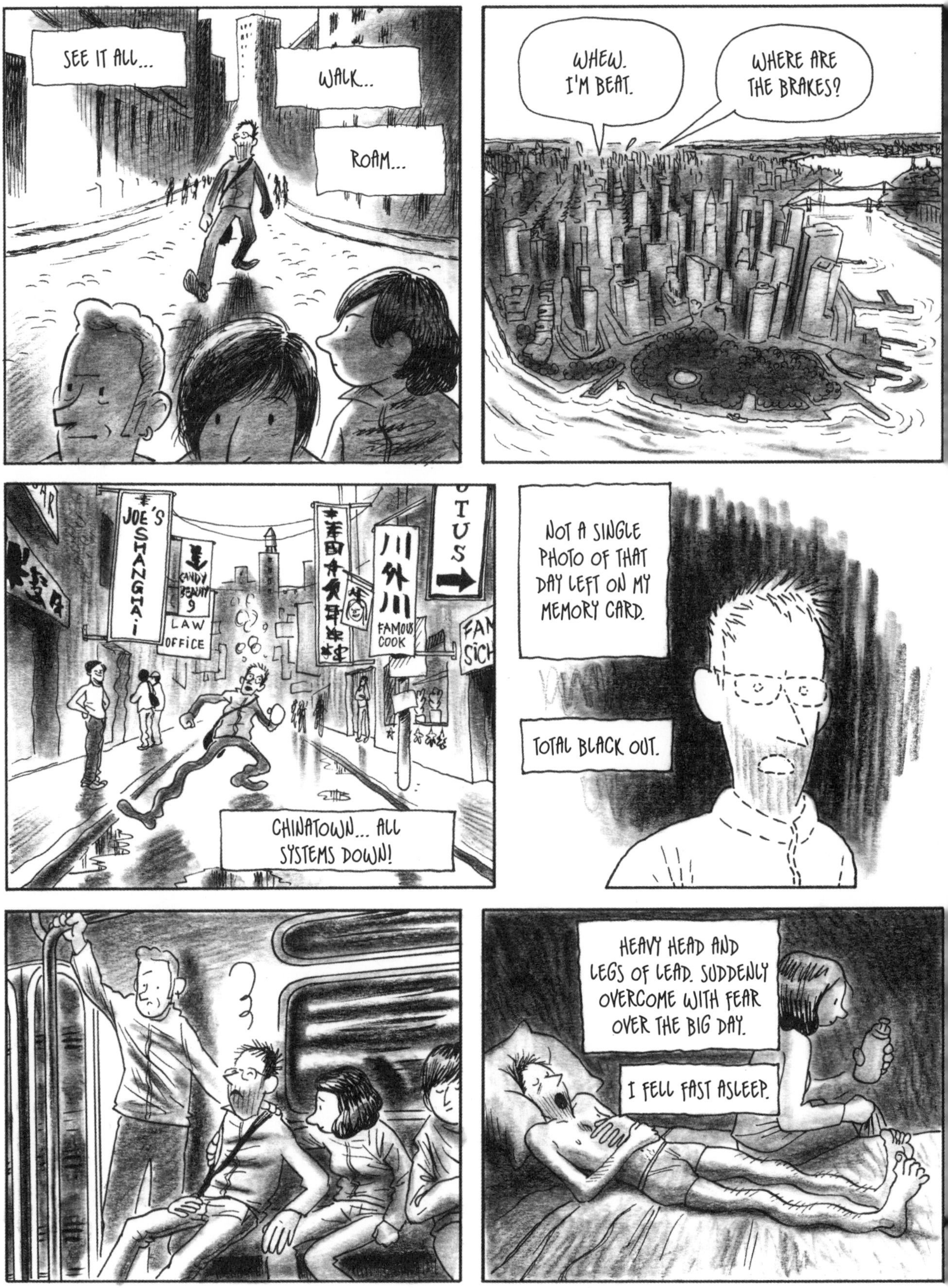
SEE IT ALL...
WALK...
ROAM...
WHEW. I'M BEAT.
WHERE ARE THE BRAKES?
JOE'S SHANGHAI
CANDY BEAUTY 9
LAW OFFICE
FAMOUS COOK
CHINATOWN... ALL SYSTEMS DOWN!
NOT A SINGLE PHOTO OF THAT DAY LEFT ON MY MEMORY CARD.
TOTAL BLACK OUT.
HEAVY HEAD AND LEGS OF LEAD. SUDDENLY OVERCOME WITH FEAR OVER THE BIG DAY.
I FELL FAST ASLEEP.

5.
NOVEMBER
6th

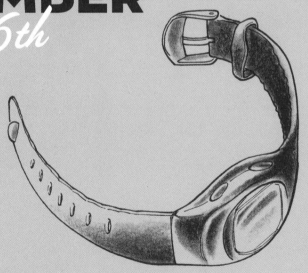

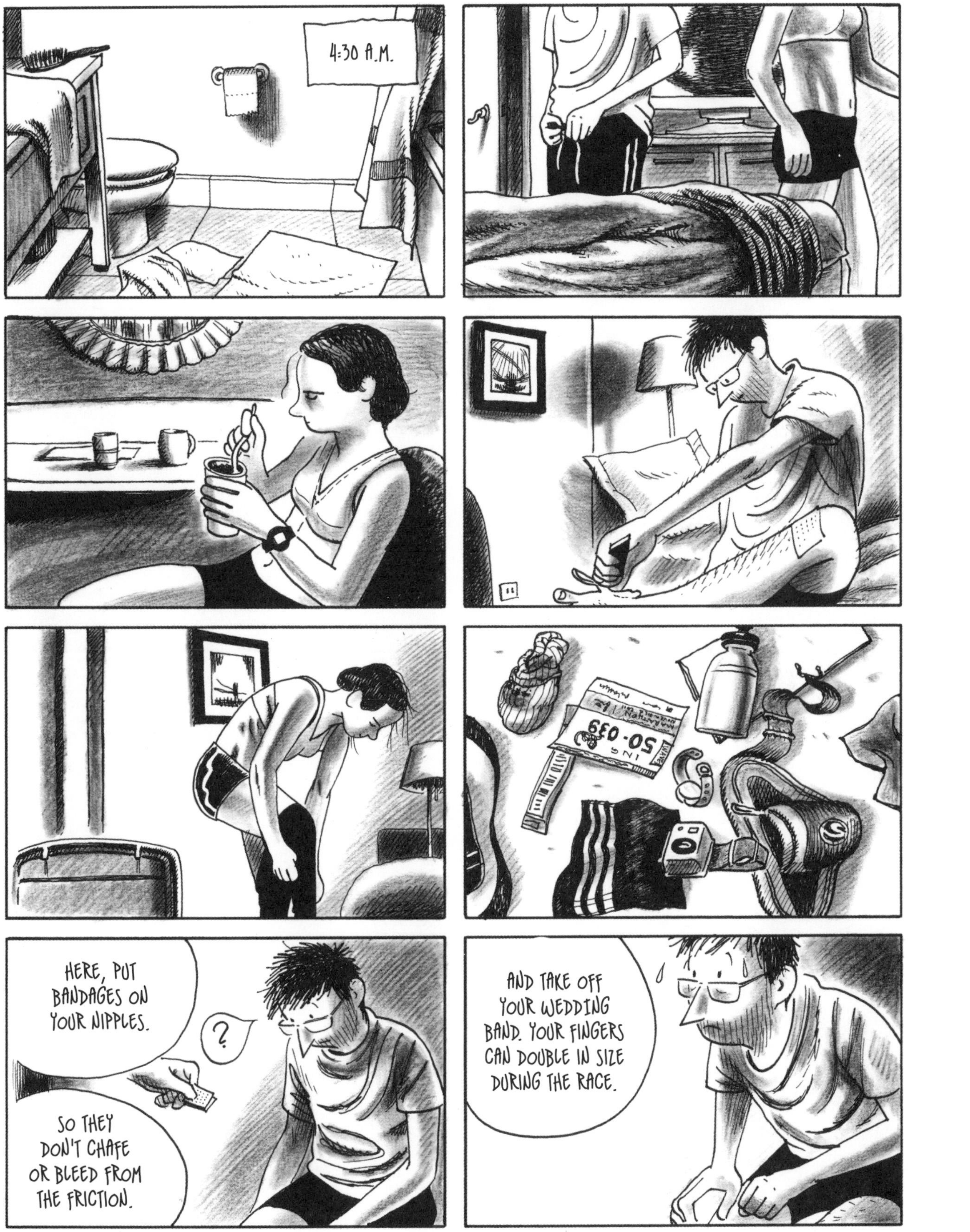
4:30 A.M.
HERE, PUT BANDAGES ON YOUR NIPPLES.
?
SO THEY DON'T CHAFE OR BLEED FROM THE FRICTION.
AND TAKE OFF YOUR WEDDING BAND. YOUR FINGERS CAN DOUBLE IN SIZE DURING THE RACE.

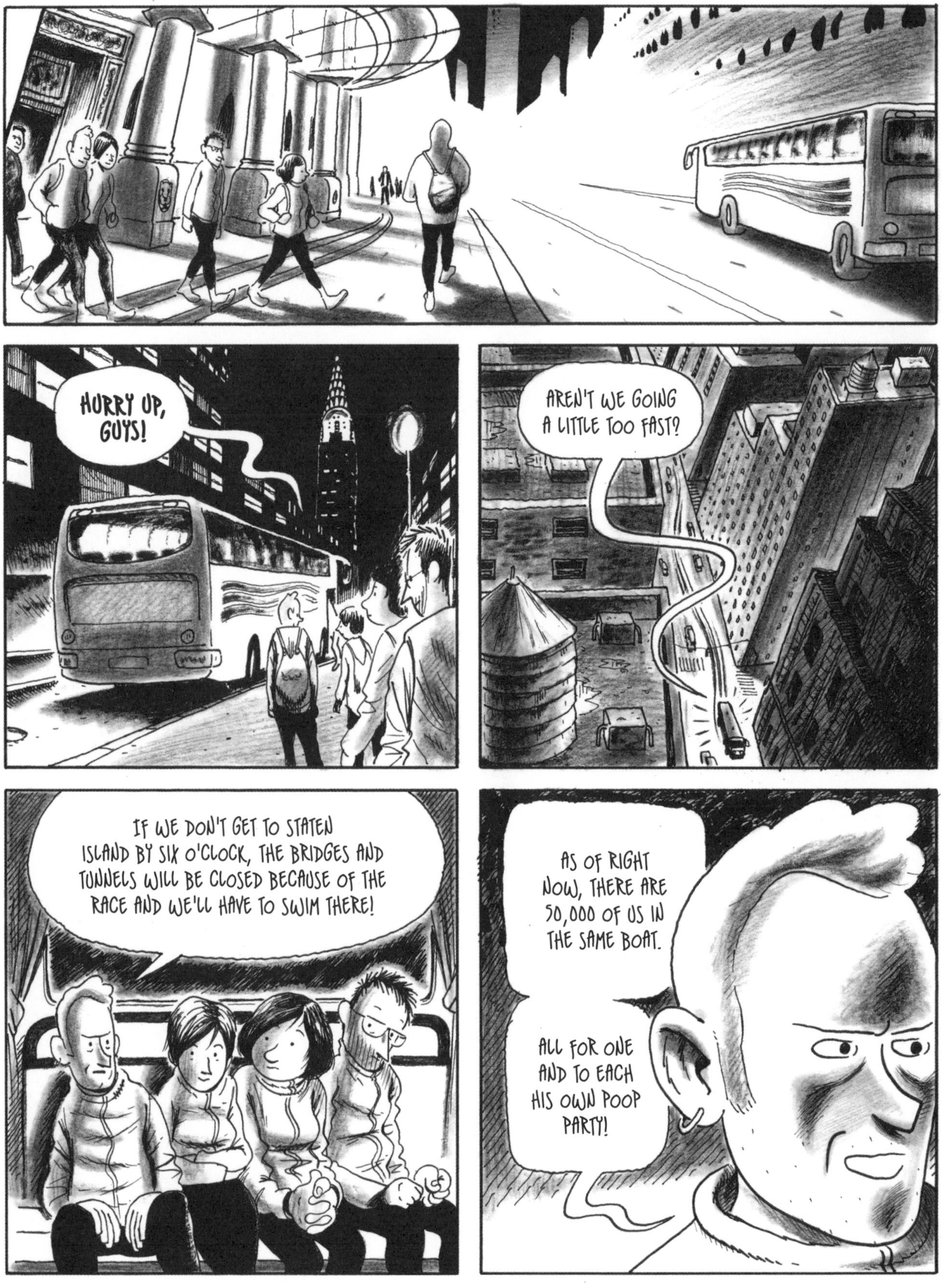
HURRY UP, GUYS!
AREN'T WE GOING A LITTLE TOO FAST?
IF WE DON'T GET TO STATEN ISLAND BY SIX O'CLOCK, THE BRIDGES AND TUNNELS WILL BE CLOSED BECAUSE OF THE RACE AND WE'LL HAVE TO SWIM THERE!
AS OF RIGHT NOW, THERE ARE 50,000 OF US IN THE SAME BOAT.
ALL FOR ONE AND TO EACH HIS OWN POOP PARTY!

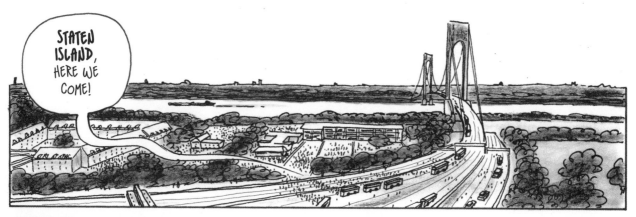

STATEN ISLAND, HERE WE COME!

Start 2011

OPEN... THANK YOU.

THIS IS IT, GUYS! IT'S SHOWTIME!

SECURITY

IS YOUR CAMERA ROLLING?

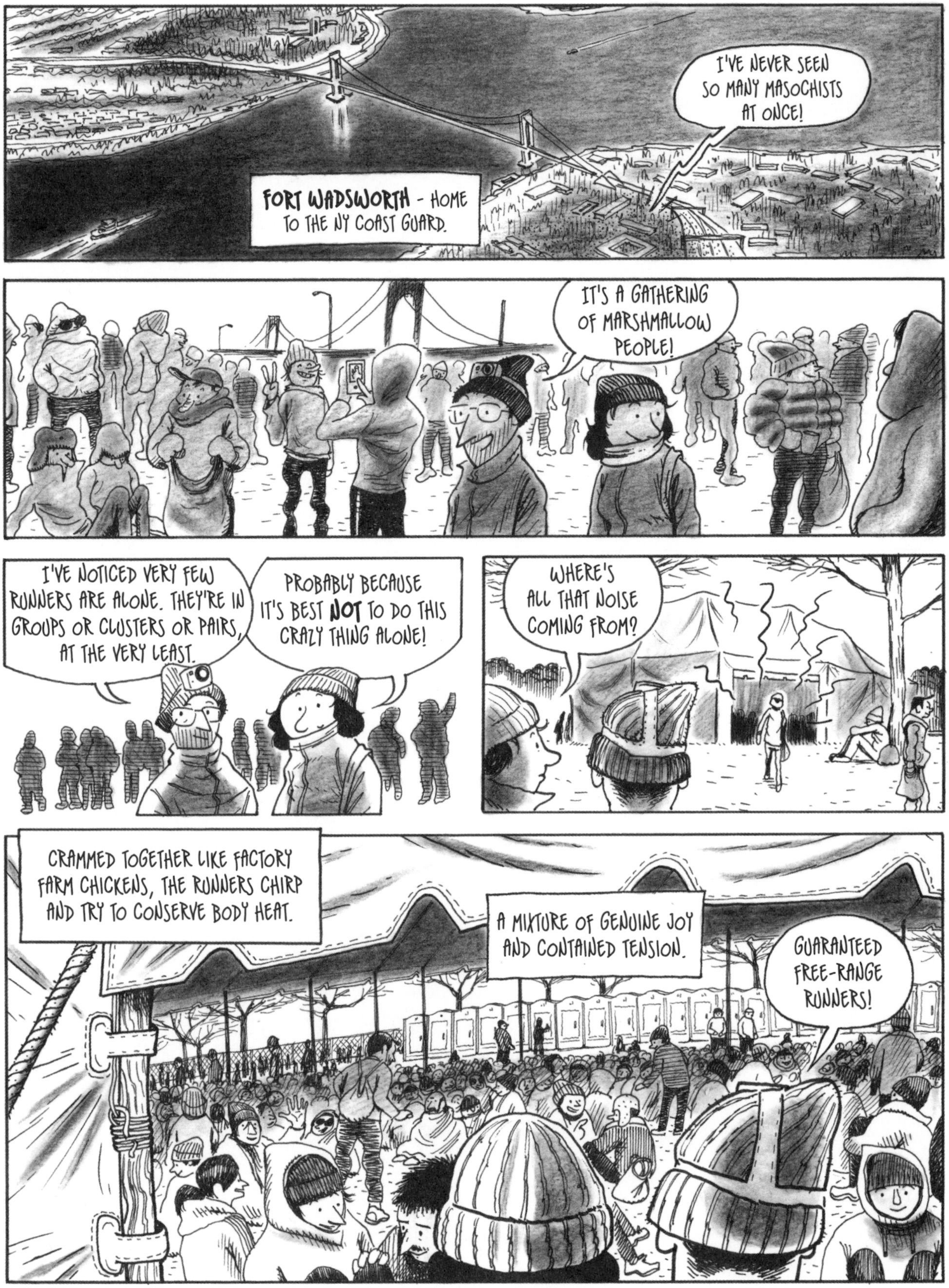
FORT WADSWORTH - HOME TO THE NY COAST GUARD.
I'VE NEVER SEEN SO MANY MASOCHISTS AT ONCE!
IT'S A GATHERING OF MARSHMALLOW PEOPLE!
I'VE NOTICED VERY FEW RUNNERS ARE ALONE. THEY'RE IN GROUPS OR CLUSTERS OR PAIRS, AT THE VERY LEAST.
PROBABLY BECAUSE IT'S BEST **NOT** TO DO THIS CRAZY THING ALONE!
WHERE'S ALL THAT NOISE COMING FROM?
CRAMMED TOGETHER LIKE FACTORY FARM CHICKENS, THE RUNNERS CHIRP AND TRY TO CONSERVE BODY HEAT.
A MIXTURE OF GENUINE JOY AND CONTAINED TENSION.
GUARANTEED FREE-RANGE RUNNERS!

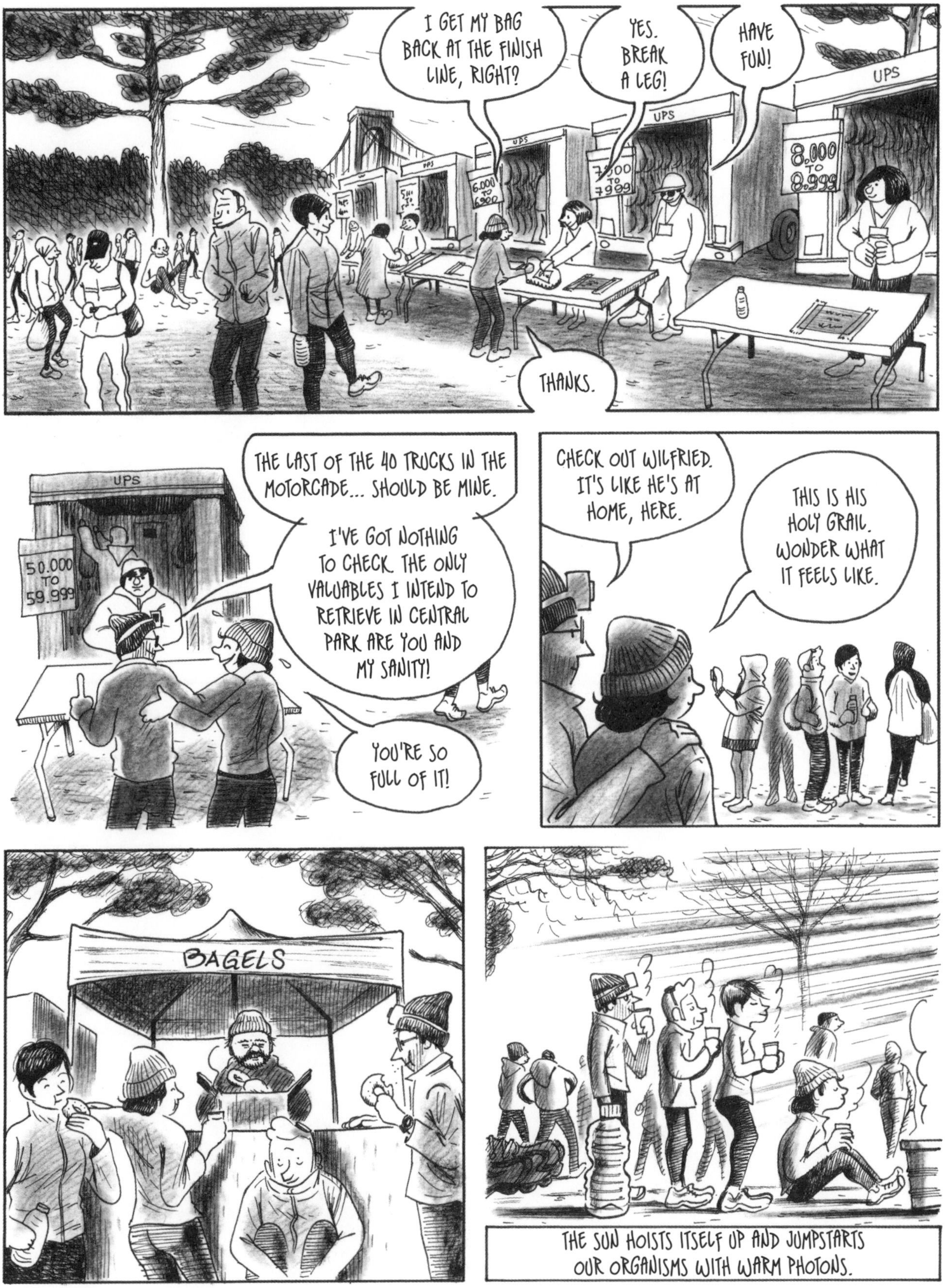
I GET MY BAG BACK AT THE FINISH LINE, RIGHT?
YES. BREAK A LEG!
HAVE FUN!
UPS
6.000 TO 6.999
7.000 TO 7.999
8.000 TO 8.999
THANKS.
UPS
50.000 TO 59.999
THE LAST OF THE 40 TRUCKS IN THE MOTORCADE... SHOULD BE MINE.
I'VE GOT NOTHING TO CHECK. THE ONLY VALUABLES I INTEND TO RETRIEVE IN CENTRAL PARK ARE YOU AND MY SANITY!
YOU'RE SO FULL OF IT!
CHECK OUT WILFRIED. IT'S LIKE HE'S AT HOME, HERE.
THIS IS HIS HOLY GRAIL. WONDER WHAT IT FEELS LIKE.
BAGELS
THE SUN HOISTS ITSELF UP AND JUMPSTARTS OUR ORGANISMS WITH WARM PHOTONS.

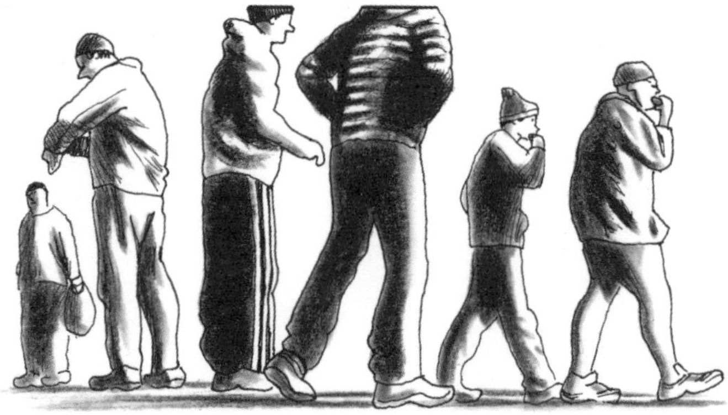

LIKE A CHOREOGRAPHED DANCE, THE PRE-RACE PROCESSION OF RUNNERS SLOWLY MOVES INTO POSITION.

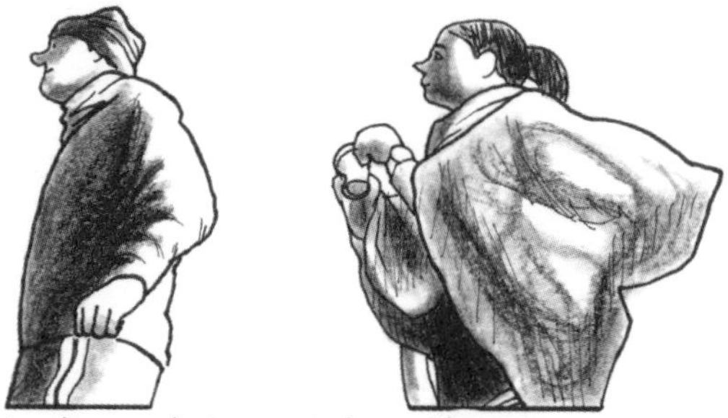

THE INFO I ENTERED WHEN I SIGNED UP PUTS ME IN THE THIRD WAVE START.

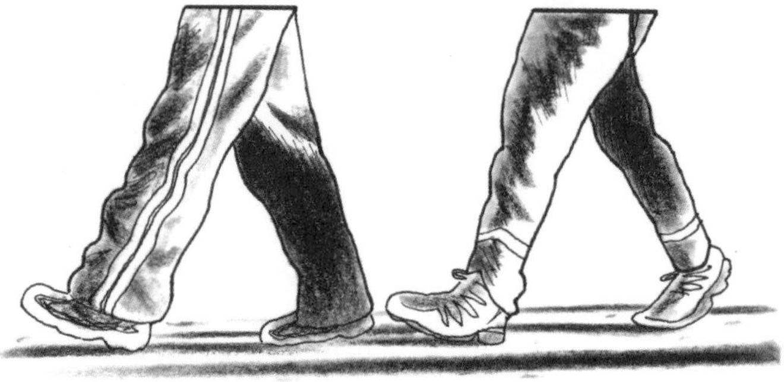

MY FRIENDS LEAVE ME TO GET TO THE FIRST WAVE START, ONE HOUR BEFORE MINE.

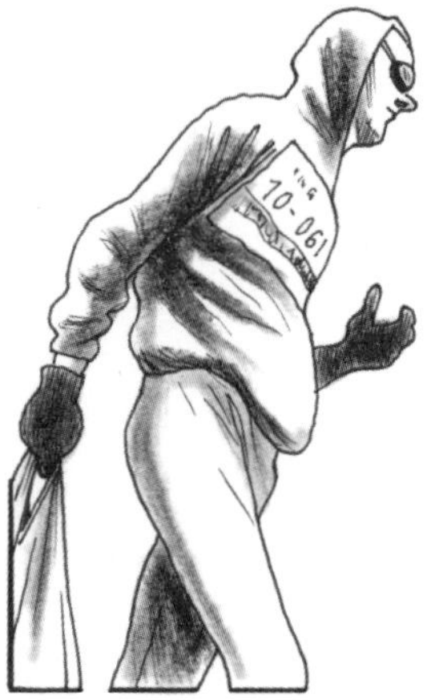

WHILE I WISH WE COULD ALL FOUR SHARE THIS MOMENT, I TELL MYSELF IT'S A FAIR AND NECESSARY WAY OF DOING THINGS.

WHEN DONE RIGHT, IT ALLOWS THE MOST AMBITIOUS RUNNERS NOT TO STUMBLE INTO THE SLOWER ONES AND TO KEEP THE RACE MOVING ALONG.

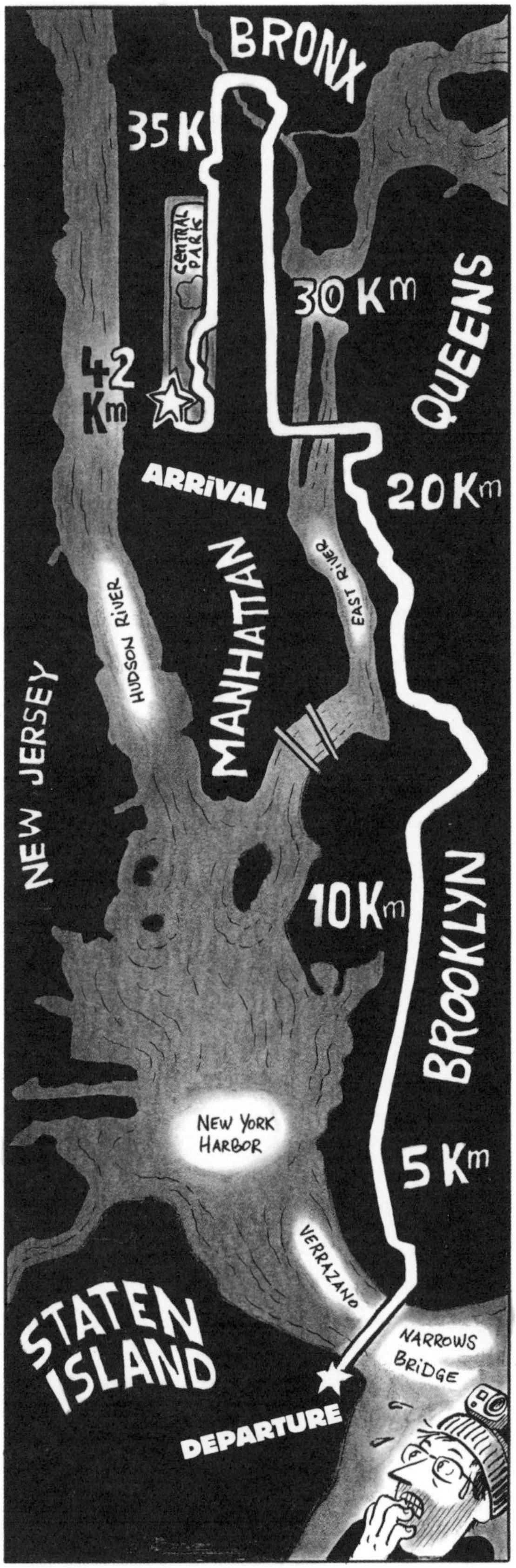
BRONX
35K
CENTRAL PARK
30Km
QUEENS
42 Km
ARRIVAL
20Km
MANHATTAN
EAST RIVER
HUDSON RIVER
NEW JERSEY
10Km
BROOKLYN
NEW YORK HARBOR
5Km
VERRAZANO
NARROWS BRIDGE
STATEN ISLAND
DEPARTURE

THIS IS YOUR BIG MOMENT, GUYS! HAVE A BLAST!

SEE YOU AT THE FINISH...

...OR AT THE AIRPORT IN 3 DAYS, IF YOU'RE TOO SLOW!

ONE HOUR!

OK! LET'S WALK TO PASS THE TIME.

A GROUP OF INDONESIAN RUNNERS TAKE OFF THEIR SHOES TO PRAY IN A MAKESHIFT PLACE OF WORSHIP.

THE ORGANIZERS PASS OUT CONES OF VASELINE TO PUT ON ANY SPOTS THAT MIGHT CHAFE.

GOOD, MY BANDAGES SEEM TO BE HOLDING UP.

PANG

YEEEEEEAHH!!

THEY'RE OFF!

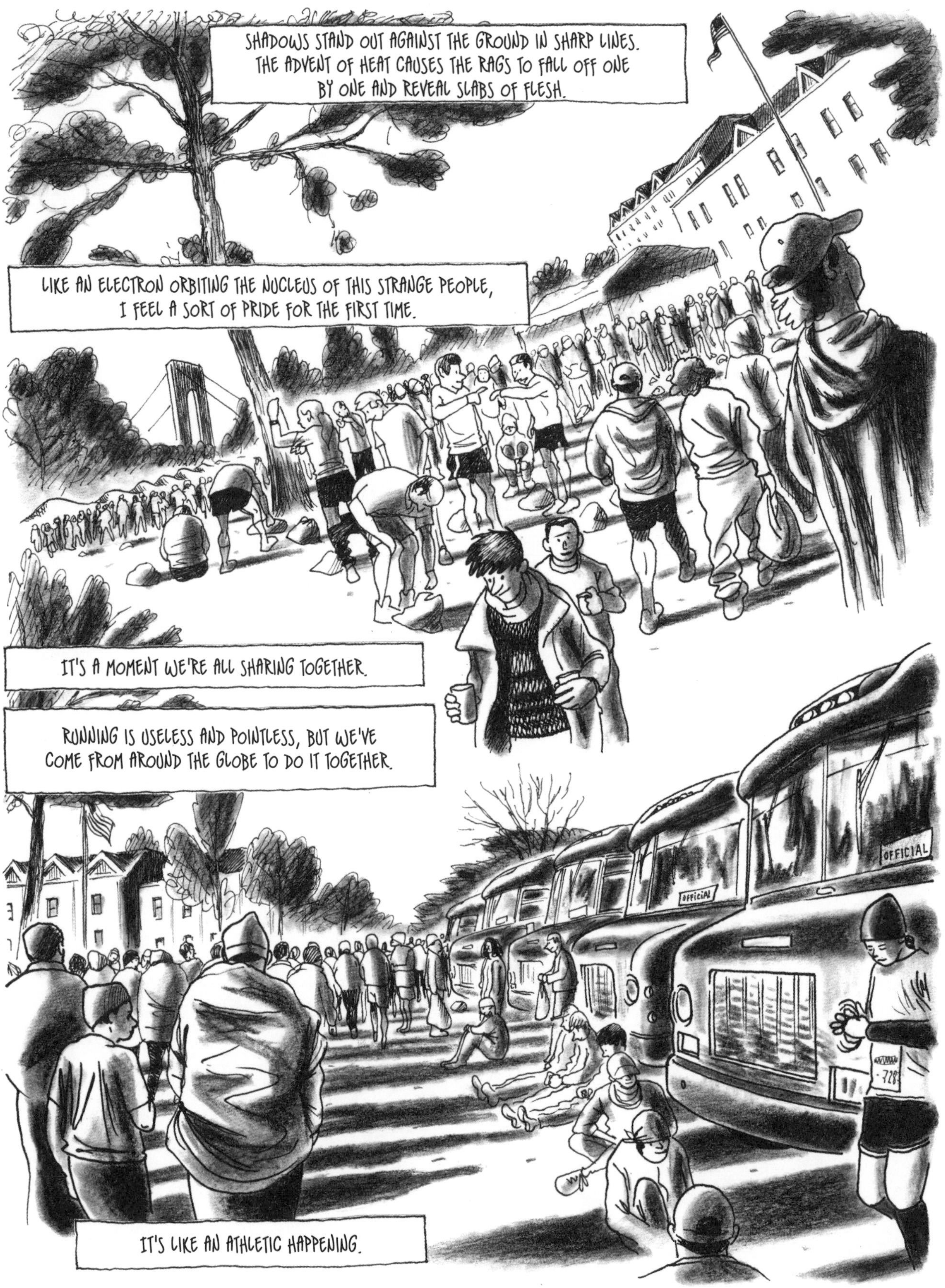
SHADOWS STAND OUT AGAINST THE GROUND IN SHARP LINES. THE ADVENT OF HEAT CAUSES THE RAGS TO FALL OFF ONE BY ONE AND REVEAL SLABS OF FLESH.
LIKE AN ELECTRON ORBITING THE NUCLEUS OF THIS STRANGE PEOPLE, I FEEL A SORT OF PRIDE FOR THE FIRST TIME.
IT'S A MOMENT WE'RE ALL SHARING TOGETHER.
RUNNING IS USELESS AND POINTLESS, BUT WE'VE COME FROM AROUND THE GLOBE TO DO IT TOGETHER.
OFFICIAL
OFFICIAL
IT'S LIKE AN ATHLETIC HAPPENING.

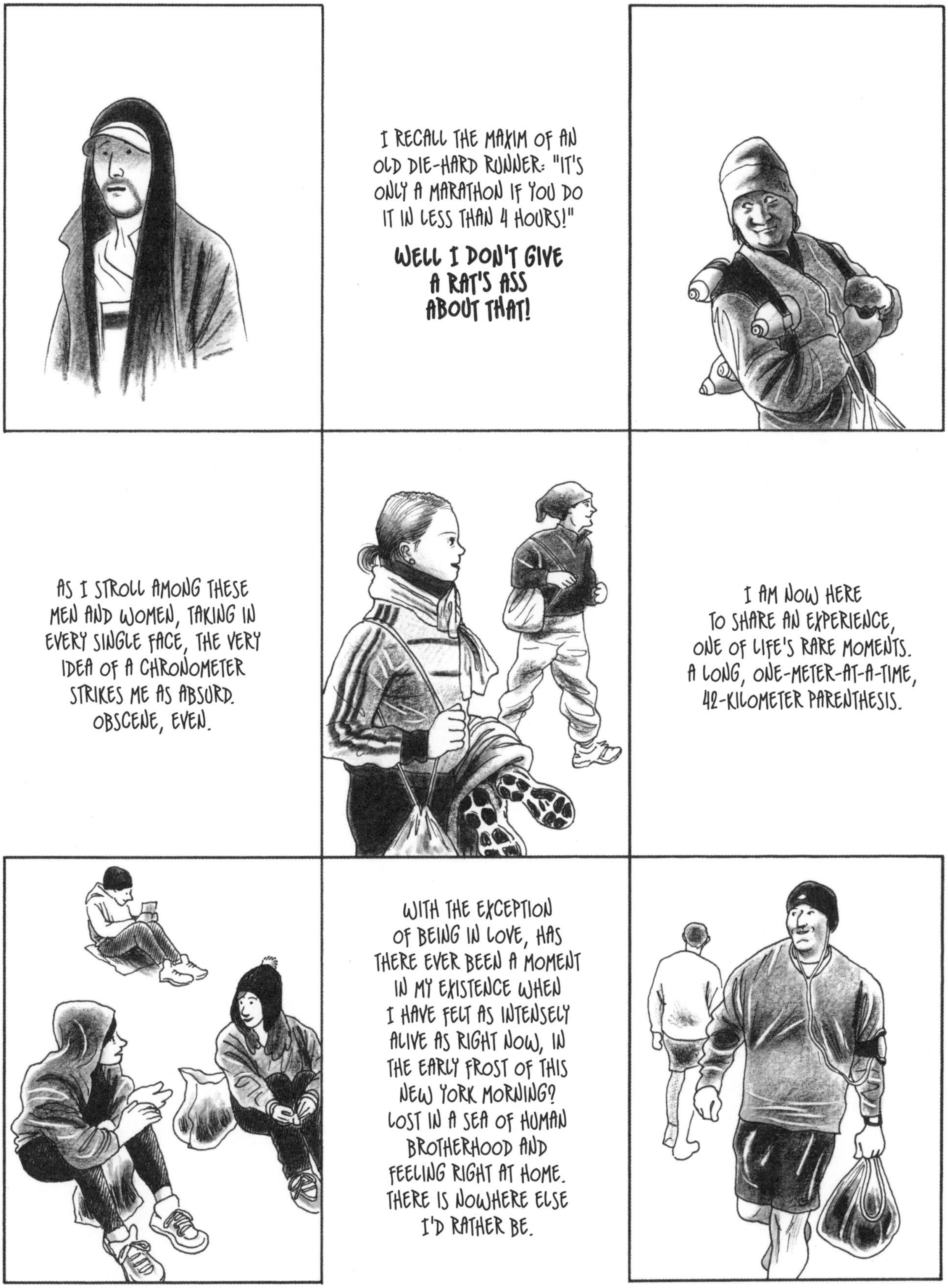
I RECALL THE MAXIM OF AN OLD DIE-HARD RUNNER: "IT'S ONLY A MARATHON IF YOU DO IT IN LESS THAN 4 HOURS!"
WELL I DON'T GIVE A RAT'S ASS ABOUT THAT!
AS I STROLL AMONG THESE MEN AND WOMEN, TAKING IN EVERY SINGLE FACE, THE VERY IDEA OF A CHRONOMETER STRIKES ME AS ABSURD. OBSCENE, EVEN.
I AM NOW HERE TO SHARE AN EXPERIENCE, ONE OF LIFE'S RARE MOMENTS. A LONG, ONE-METER-AT-A-TIME, 42-KILOMETER PARENTHESIS.
WITH THE EXCEPTION OF BEING IN LOVE, HAS THERE EVER BEEN A MOMENT IN MY EXISTENCE WHEN I HAVE FELT AS INTENSELY ALIVE AS RIGHT NOW, IN THE EARLY FROST OF THIS NEW YORK MORNING? LOST IN A SEA OF HUMAN BROTHERHOOD AND FEELING RIGHT AT HOME. THERE IS NOWHERE ELSE I'D RATHER BE.

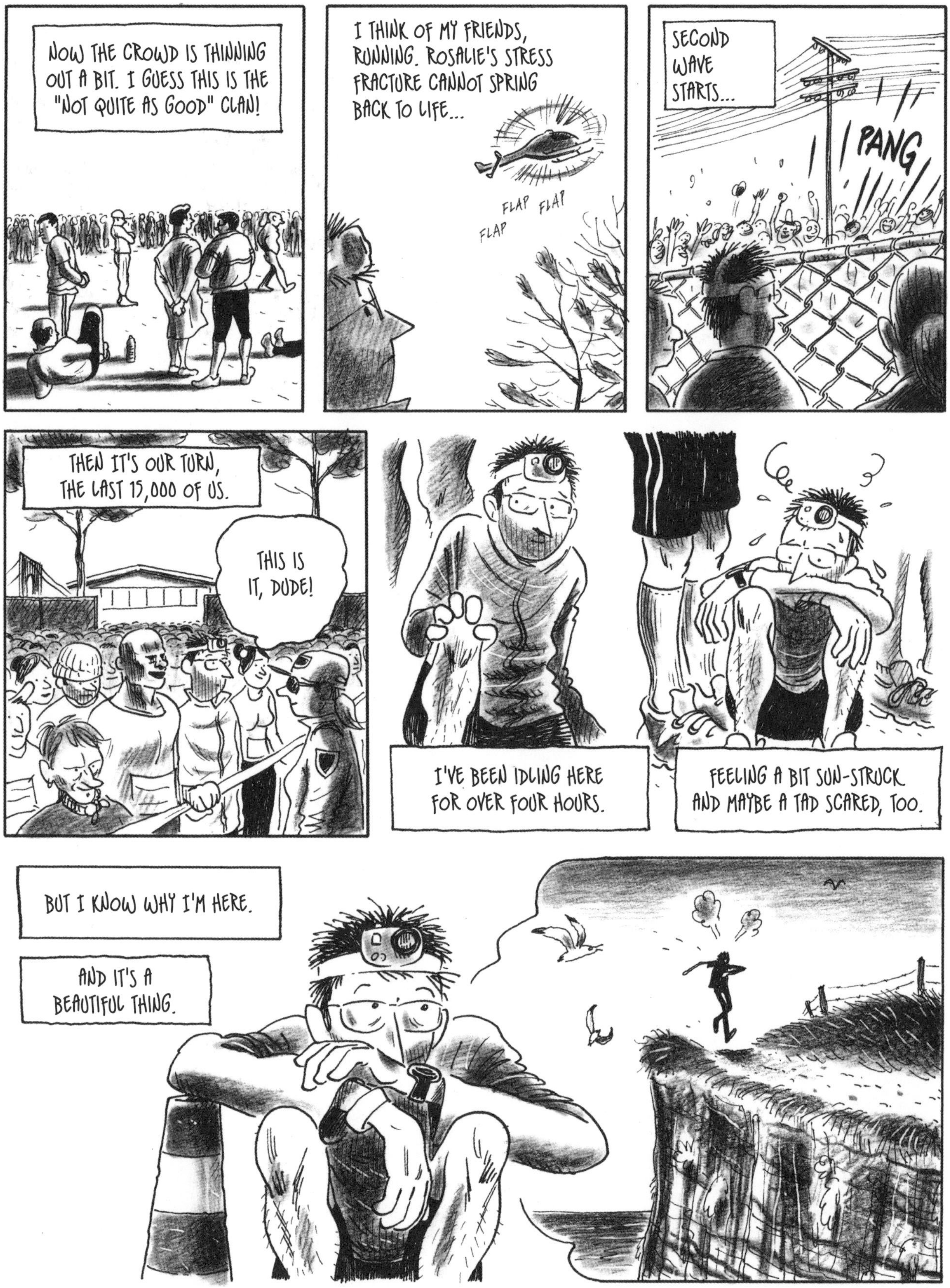
NOW THE CROWD IS THINNING OUT A BIT. I GUESS THIS IS THE "NOT QUITE AS GOOD" CLAN!
I THINK OF MY FRIENDS, RUNNING. ROSALIE'S STRESS FRACTURE CANNOT SPRING BACK TO LIFE...
FLAP FLAP FLAP
SECOND WAVE STARTS...
PANG
THEN IT'S OUR TURN, THE LAST 15,000 OF US.
THIS IS IT, DUDE!
I'VE BEEN IDLING HERE FOR OVER FOUR HOURS.
FEELING A BIT SUN-STRUCK. AND MAYBE A TAD SCARED, TOO.
BUT I KNOW WHY I'M HERE.
AND IT'S A BEAUTIFUL THING.

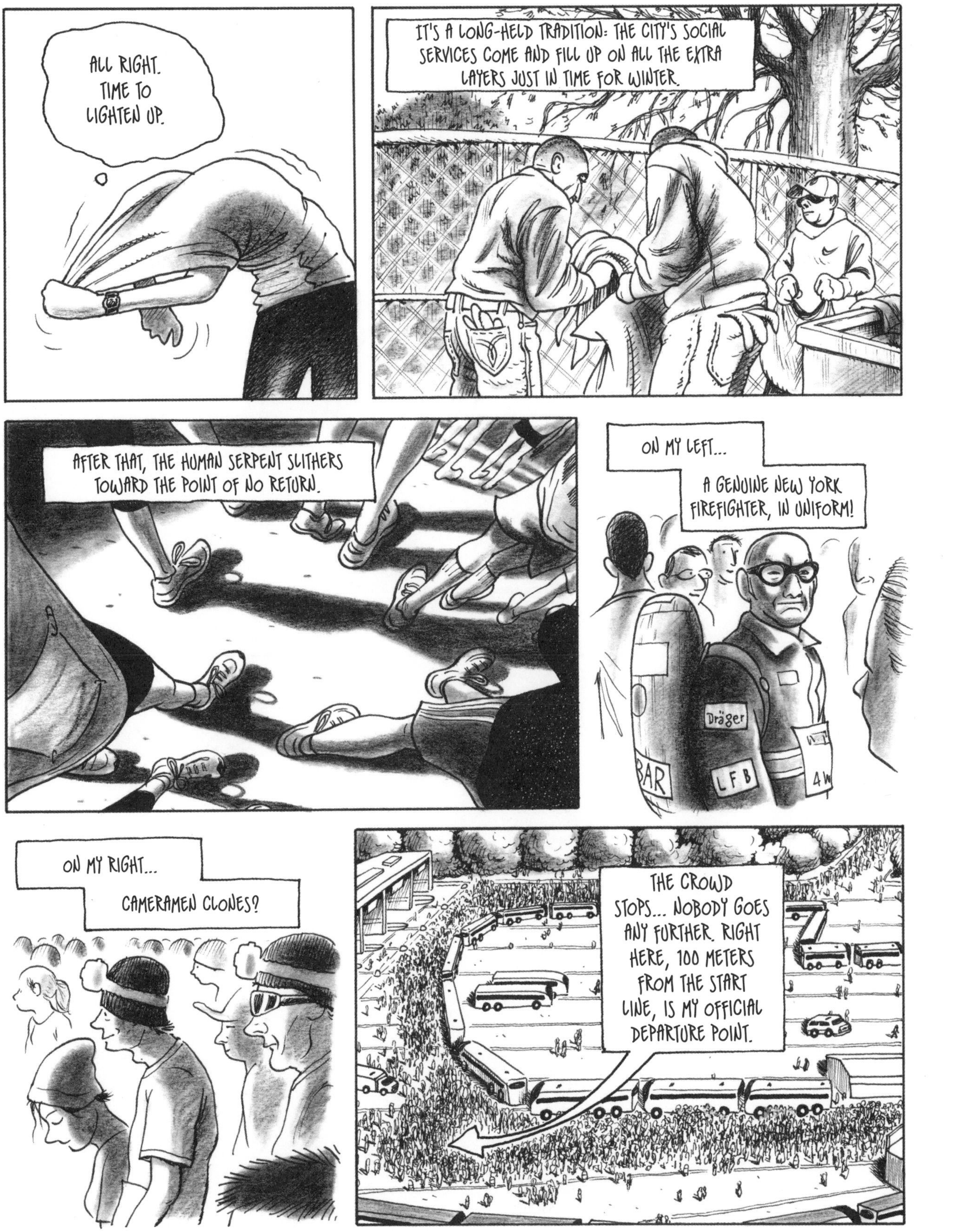
ALL RIGHT. TIME TO LIGHTEN UP.
IT'S A LONG-HELD TRADITION: THE CITY'S SOCIAL SERVICES COME AND FILL UP ON ALL THE EXTRA LAYERS JUST IN TIME FOR WINTER.
AFTER THAT, THE HUMAN SERPENT SLITHERS TOWARD THE POINT OF NO RETURN.
ON MY LEFT...
A GENUINE NEW YORK FIREFIGHTER, IN UNIFORM!
Dräger
BAR
LFB
ON MY RIGHT...
CAMERAMEN CLONES?
THE CROWD STOPS... NOBODY GOES ANY FURTHER. RIGHT HERE, 100 METERS FROM THE START LINE, IS MY OFFICIAL DEPARTURE POINT.

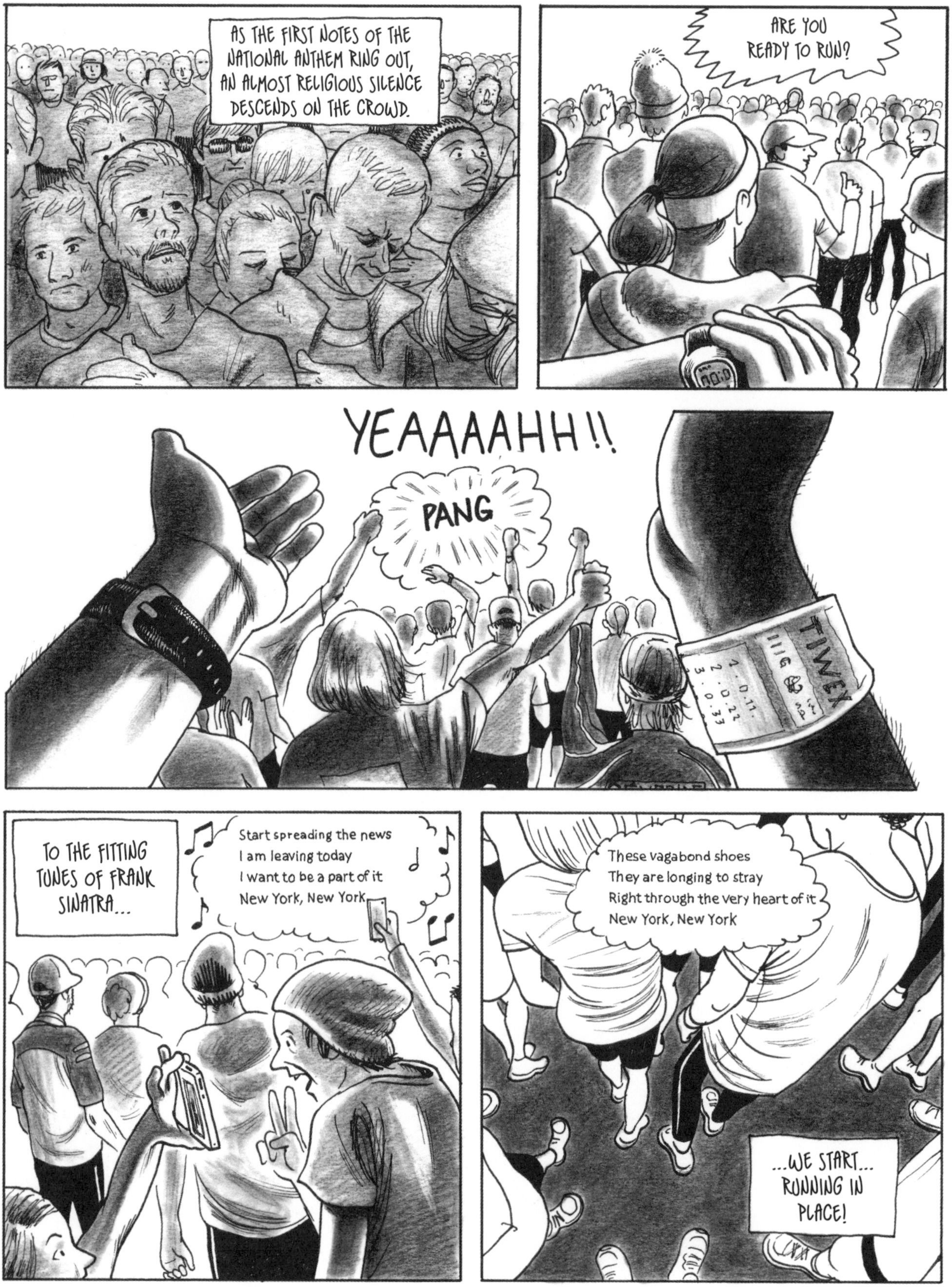
AS THE FIRST NOTES OF THE NATIONAL ANTHEM RING OUT, AN ALMOST RELIGIOUS SILENCE DESCENDS ON THE CROWD.
ARE YOU READY TO RUN?
YEAAAAHH!!
PANG
TIMEX
TO THE FITTING TUNES OF FRANK SINATRA...
Start spreading the news
I am leaving today
I want to be a part of it
New York, New York
These vagabond shoes
They are longing to stray
Right through the very heart of it
New York, New York
...WE START... RUNNING IN PLACE!

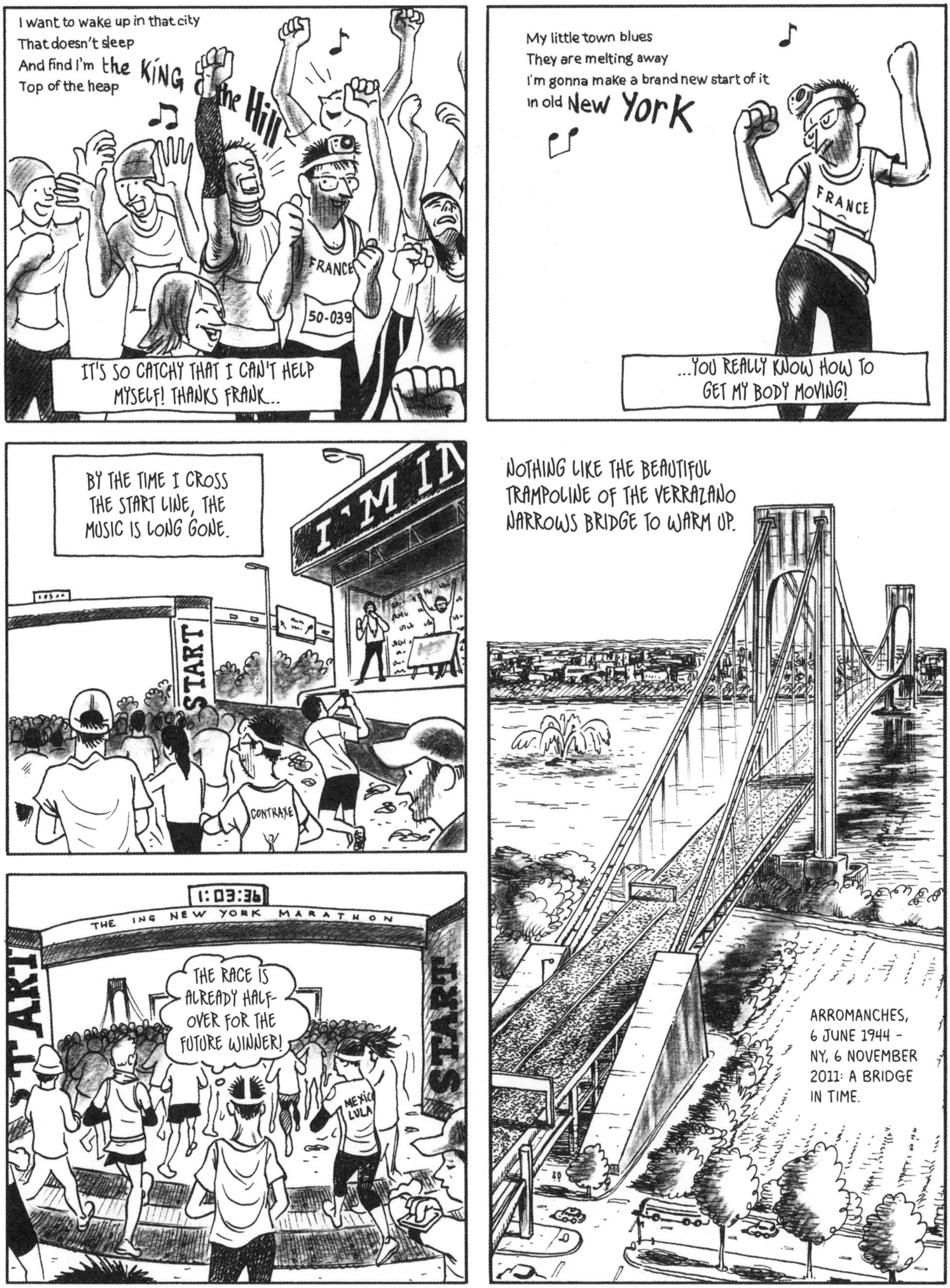
I want to wake up in that city
That doesn't sleep
And find I'm the KING the Hill
Top of the heap
FRANCE
50-039
IT'S SO CATCHY THAT I CAN'T HELP MYSELF! THANKS FRANK...
My little town blues
They are melting away
I'm gonna make a brand new start of it
in old New York
FRANCE
...YOU REALLY KNOW HOW TO GET MY BODY MOVING!
BY THE TIME I CROSS THE START LINE, THE MUSIC IS LONG GONE.
I'M IN
START
CONTRAXE
1:03:36
THE ING NEW YORK MARATHON
START
START
THE RACE IS ALREADY HALF-OVER FOR THE FUTURE WINNER!
MEXICO LULA
NOTHING LIKE THE BEAUTIFUL TRAMPOLINE OF THE VERRAZANO NARROWS BRIDGE TO WARM UP.
ARROMANCHES, 6 JUNE 1944 – NY, 6 NOVEMBER 2011: A BRIDGE IN TIME.

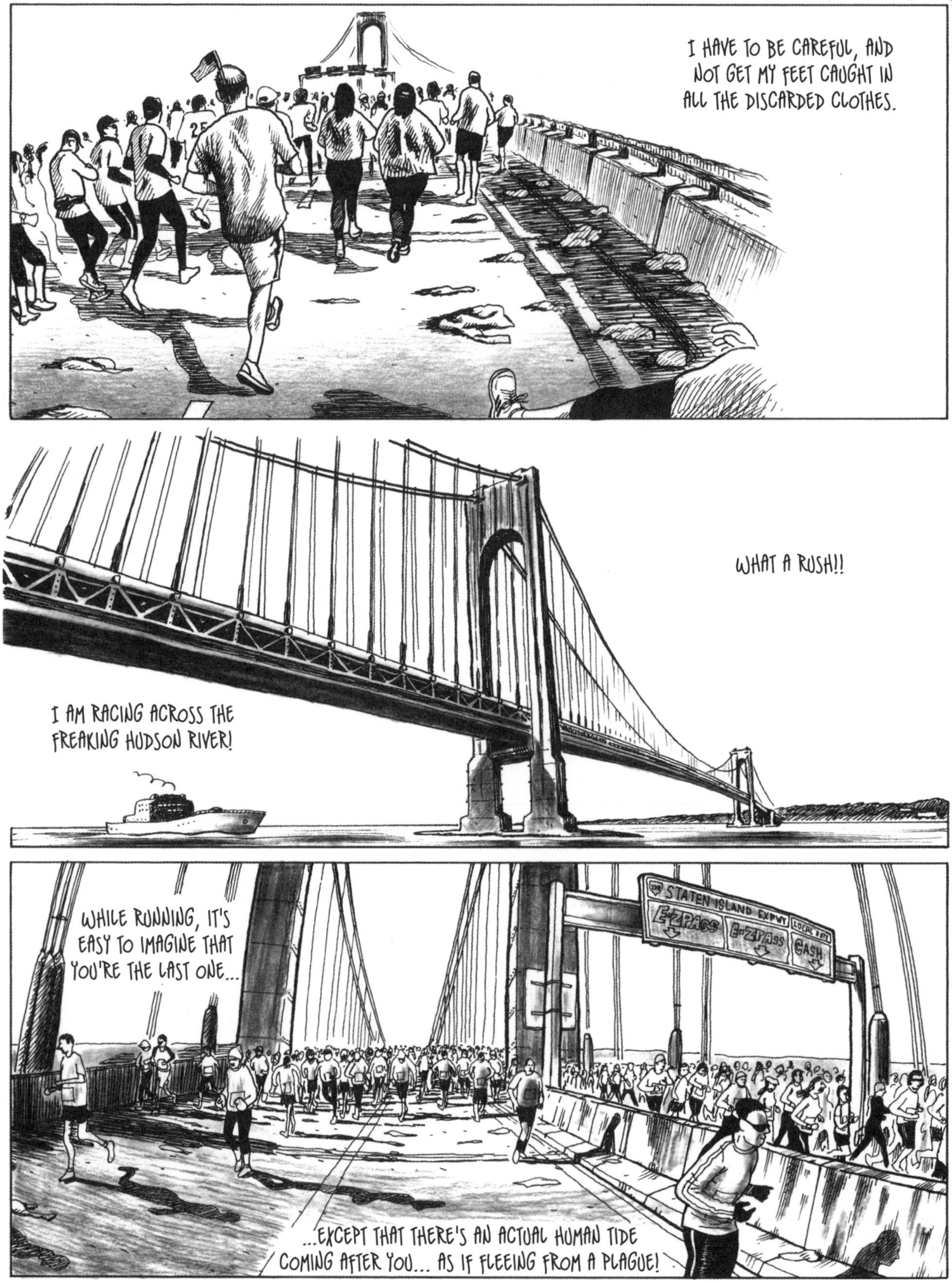
I HAVE TO BE CAREFUL, AND NOT GET MY FEET CAUGHT IN ALL THE DISCARDED CLOTHES.
WHAT A RUSH!!
I AM RACING ACROSS THE FREAKING HUDSON RIVER!
WHILE RUNNING, IT'S EASY TO IMAGINE THAT YOU'RE THE LAST ONE...
STATEN ISLAND EXPWY
E-ZPASS
E-ZPASS
CASH
...EXCEPT THAT THERE'S AN ACTUAL HUMAN TIDE COMING AFTER YOU... AS IF FLEEING FROM A PLAGUE!

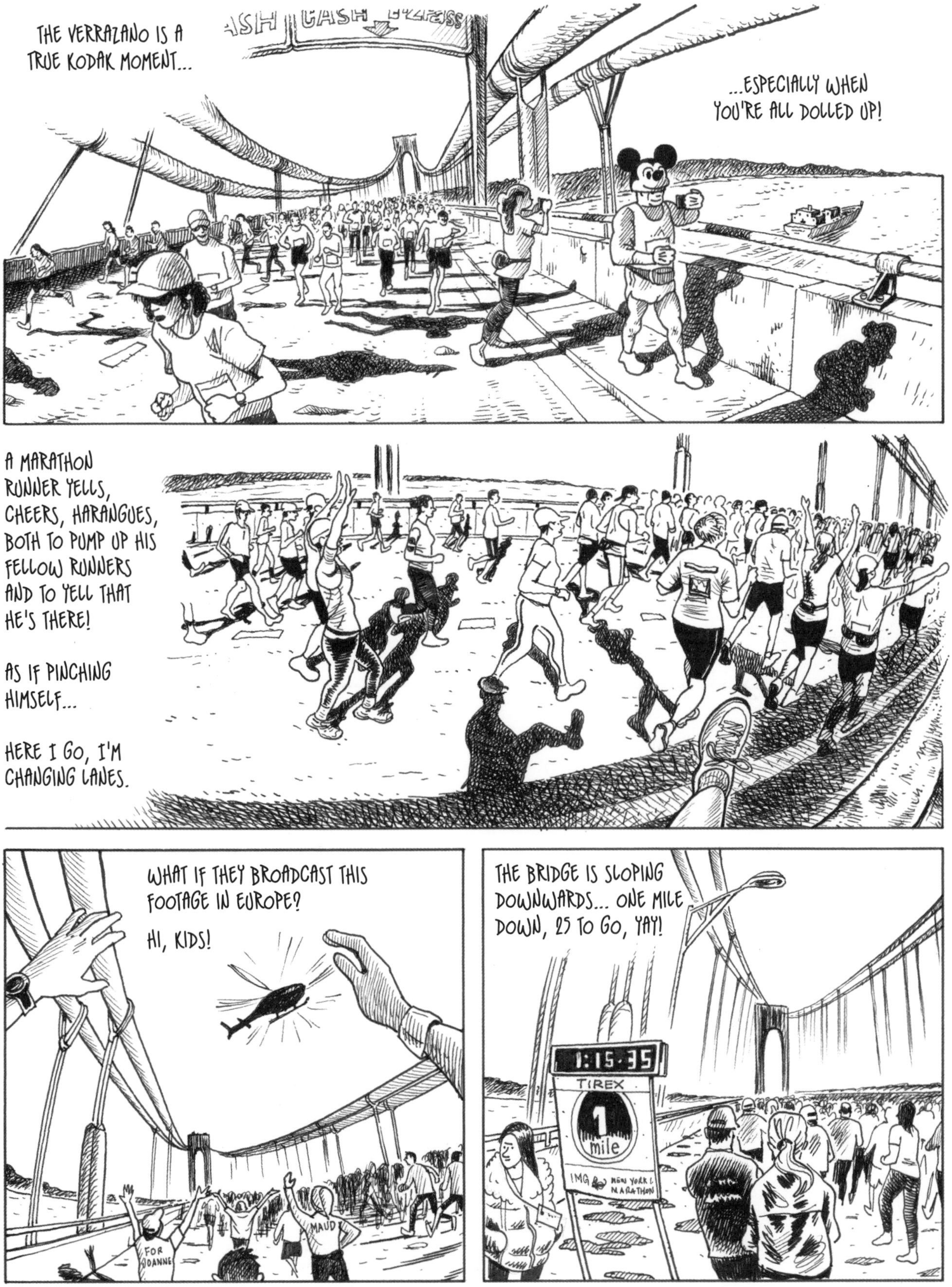
THE VERRAZANO IS A TRUE KODAK MOMENT...
...ESPECIALLY WHEN YOU'RE ALL DOLLED UP!
A MARATHON RUNNER YELLS, CHEERS, HARANGUES, BOTH TO PUMP UP HIS FELLOW RUNNERS AND TO YELL THAT HE'S THERE!
AS IF PINCHING HIMSELF...
HERE I GO, I'M CHANGING LANES.
WHAT IF THEY BROADCAST THIS FOOTAGE IN EUROPE?
HI, KIDS!
MAUD
THE BRIDGE IS SLOPING DOWNWARDS... ONE MILE DOWN, 25 TO GO, YAY!
1:15:35
TIREX
1
mile

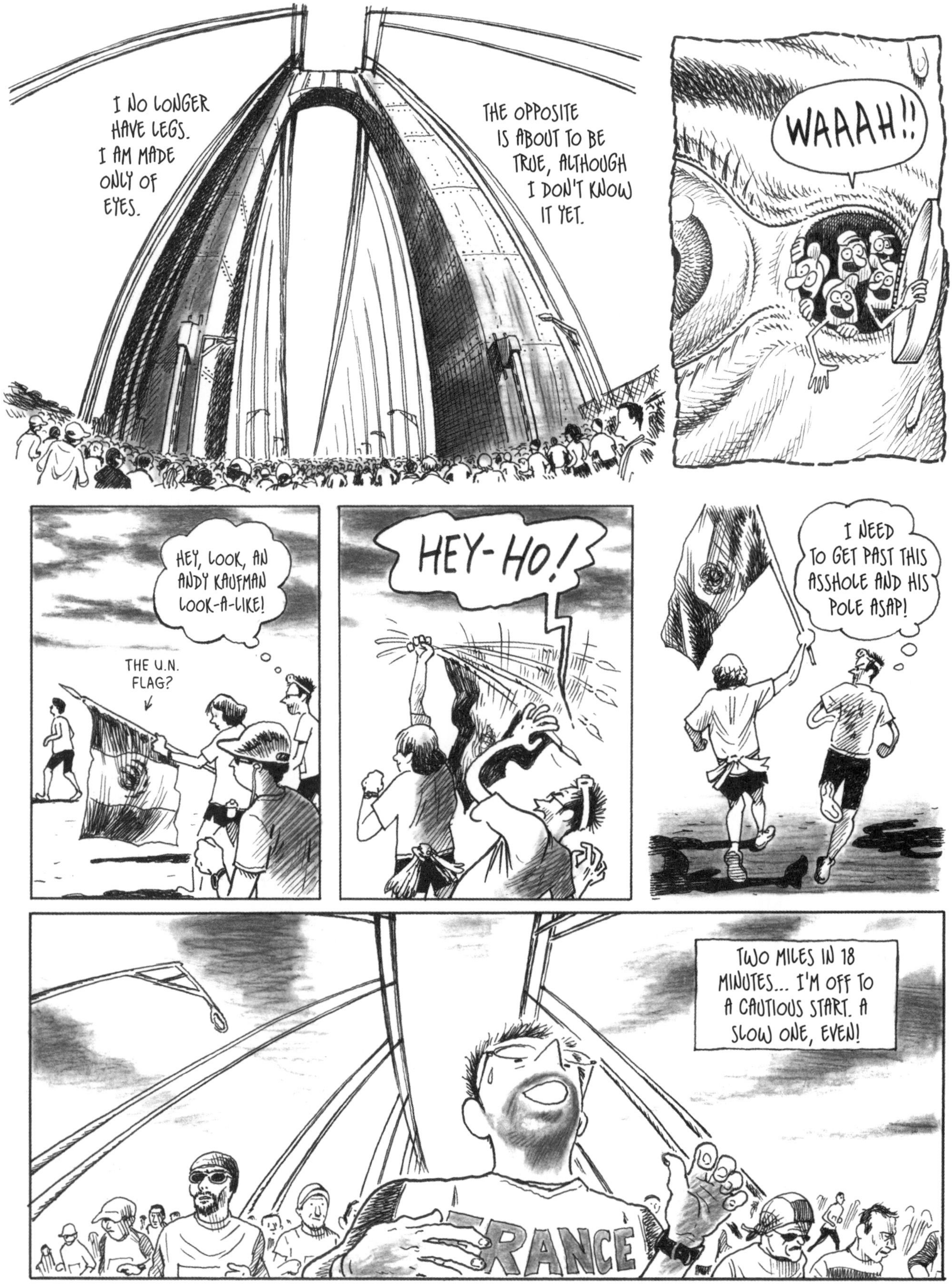
I NO LONGER HAVE LEGS. I AM MADE ONLY OF EYES.
THE OPPOSITE IS ABOUT TO BE TRUE, ALTHOUGH I DON'T KNOW IT YET.
WAAAH!!
HEY, LOOK, AN ANDY KAUFMAN LOOK-A-LIKE!
THE U.N. FLAG?
HEY-HO!
I NEED TO GET PAST THIS ASSHOLE AND HIS POLE ASAP!
TWO MILES IN 18 MINUTES... I'M OFF TO A CAUTIOUS START. A SLOW ONE, EVEN!
RANCE

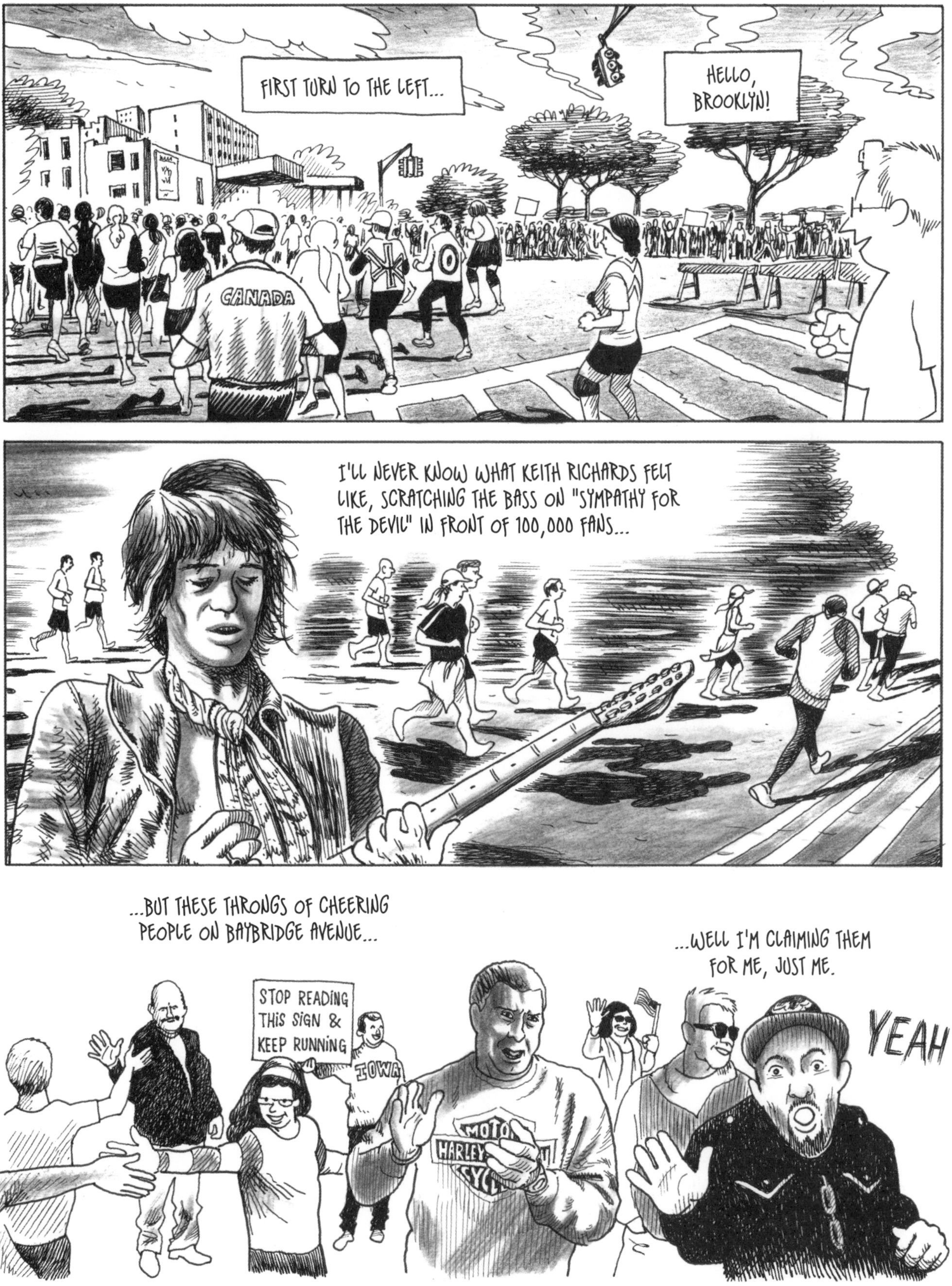

FIRST TURN TO THE LEFT...
HELLO, BROOKLYN!
CANADA
I'LL NEVER KNOW WHAT KEITH RICHARDS FELT LIKE, SCRATCHING THE BASS ON "SYMPATHY FOR THE DEVIL" IN FRONT OF 100,000 FANS...
...BUT THESE THRONGS OF CHEERING PEOPLE ON BAYBRIDGE AVENUE...
...WELL I'M CLAIMING THEM FOR ME, JUST ME.
STOP READING THIS SIGN & KEEP RUNNING
IOWA
YEAH

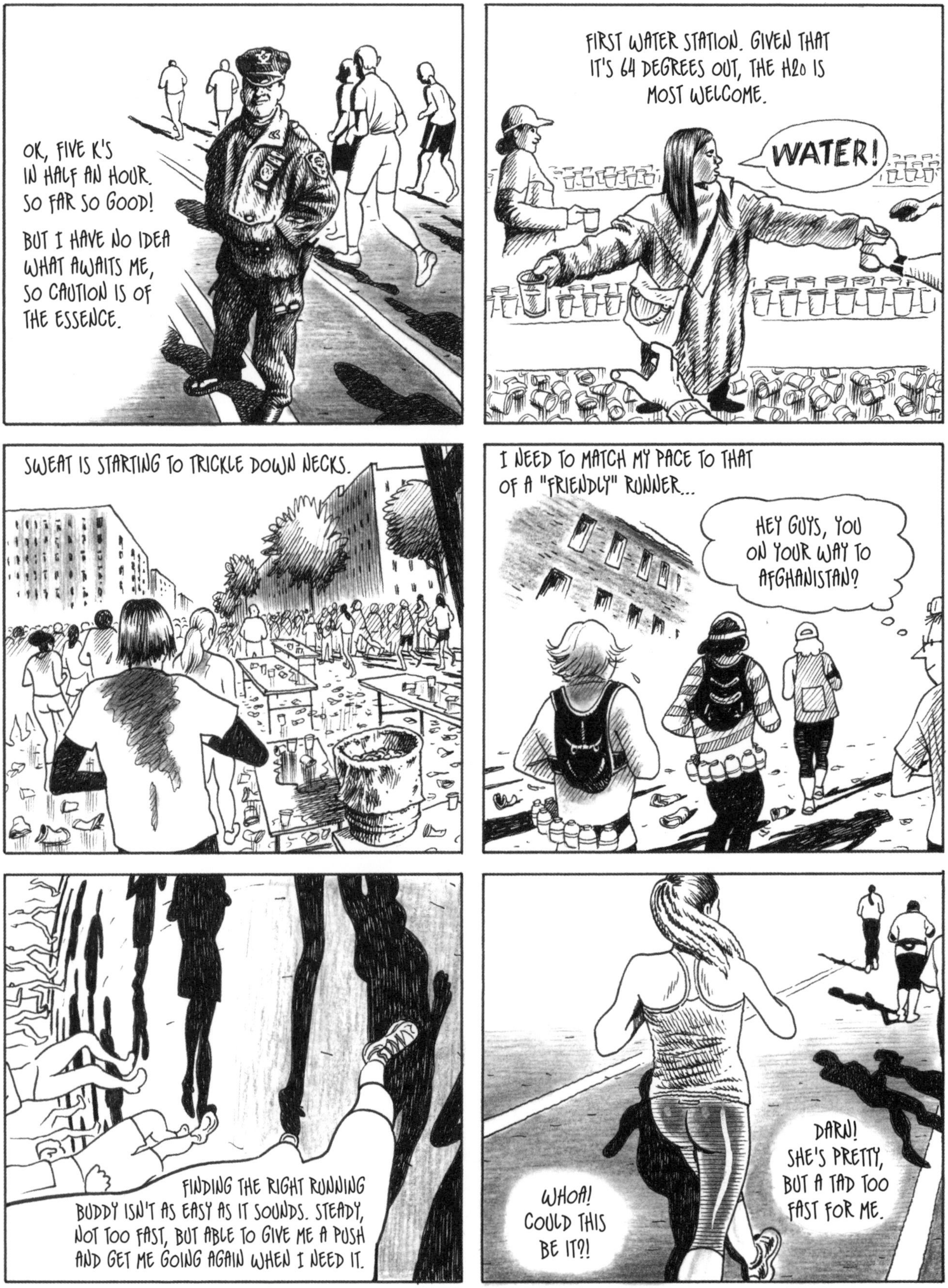
OK, FIVE K'S IN HALF AN HOUR. SO FAR SO GOOD!
BUT I HAVE NO IDEA WHAT AWAITS ME, SO CAUTION IS OF THE ESSENCE.
FIRST WATER STATION. GIVEN THAT IT'S 64 DEGREES OUT, THE H2O IS MOST WELCOME.
WATER!
SWEAT IS STARTING TO TRICKLE DOWN NECKS.
I NEED TO MATCH MY PACE TO THAT OF A "FRIENDLY" RUNNER...
HEY GUYS, YOU ON YOUR WAY TO AFGHANISTAN?
FINDING THE RIGHT RUNNING BUDDY ISN'T AS EASY AS IT SOUNDS. STEADY, NOT TOO FAST, BUT ABLE TO GIVE ME A PUSH AND GET ME GOING AGAIN WHEN I NEED IT.
WHOA! COULD THIS BE IT?!
DARN! SHE'S PRETTY, BUT A TAD TOO FAST FOR ME.

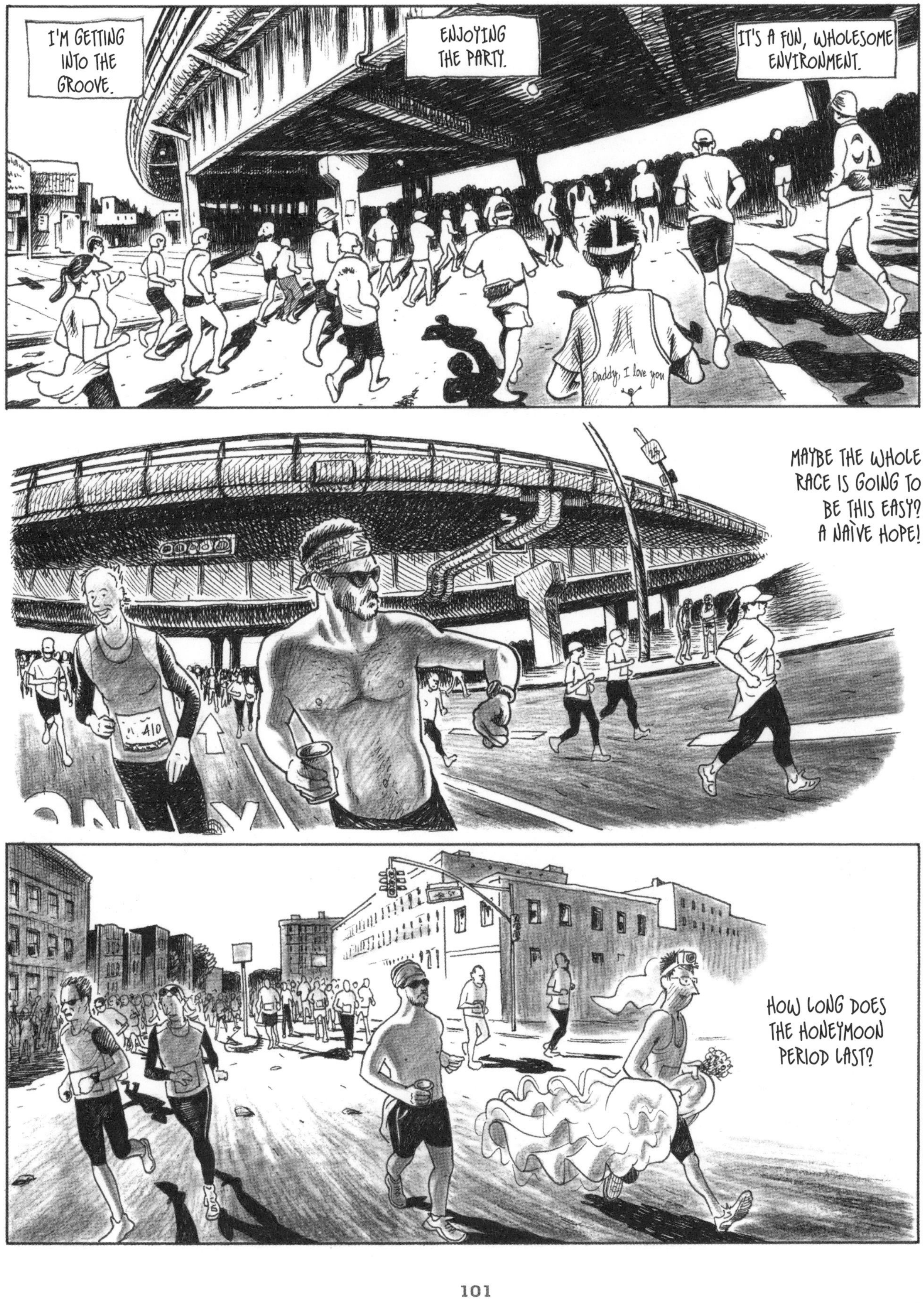
I'M GETTING INTO THE GROOVE.
ENJOYING THE PARTY.
IT'S A FUN, WHOLESOME ENVIRONMENT.
Daddy, I love you
MAYBE THE WHOLE RACE IS GOING TO BE THIS EASY? A NAÏVE HOPE!
HOW LONG DOES THE HONEYMOON PERIOD LAST?

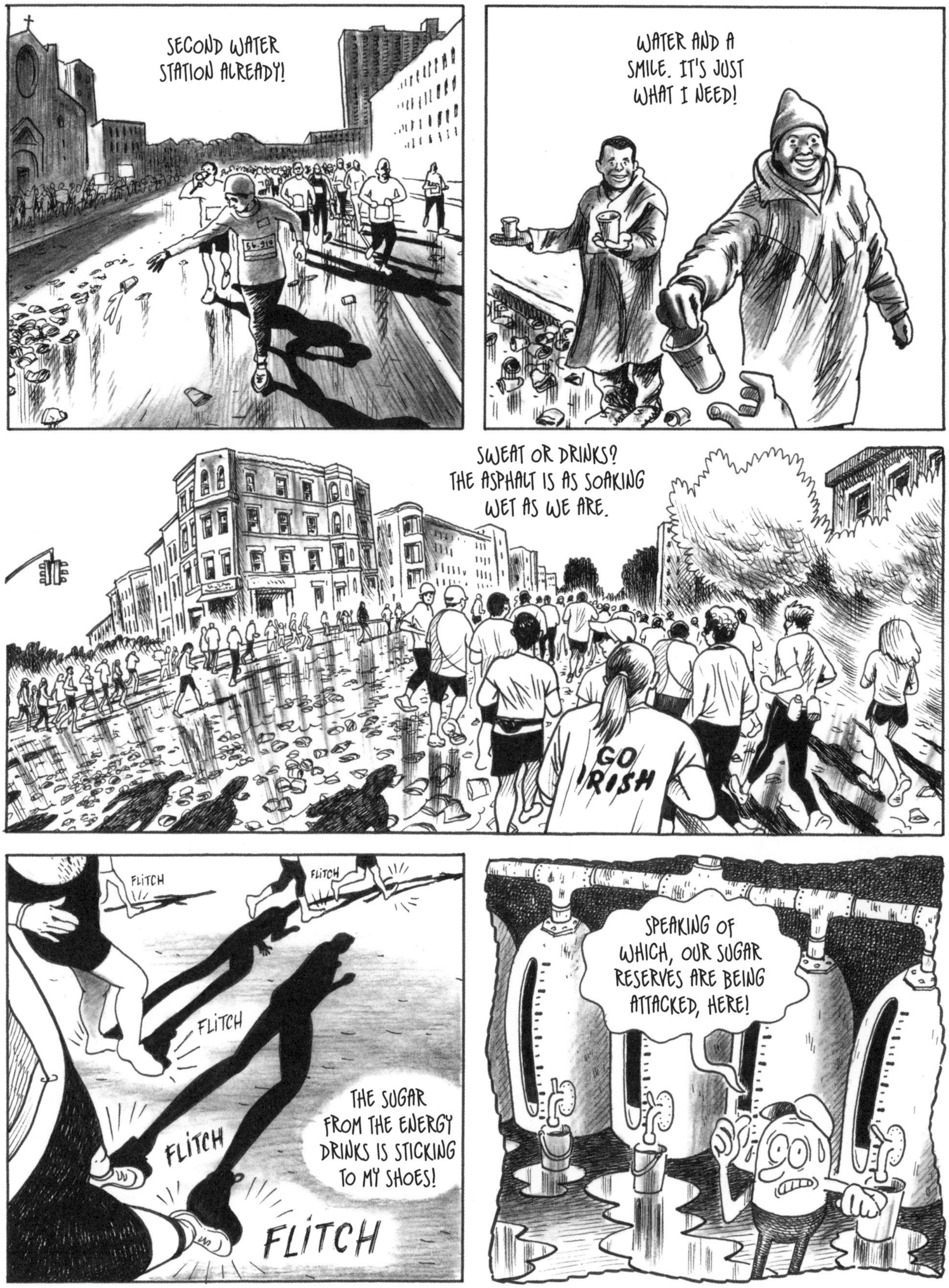
SECOND WATER STATION ALREADY!
WATER AND A SMILE. IT'S JUST WHAT I NEED!
SWEAT OR DRINKS? THE ASPHALT IS AS SOAKING WET AS WE ARE.
GO IRISH
FLITCH
FLITCH
FLITCH
FLITCH
FLITCH
THE SUGAR FROM THE ENERGY DRINKS IS STICKING TO MY SHOES!
SPEAKING OF WHICH, OUR SUGAR RESERVES ARE BEING ATTACKED, HERE!

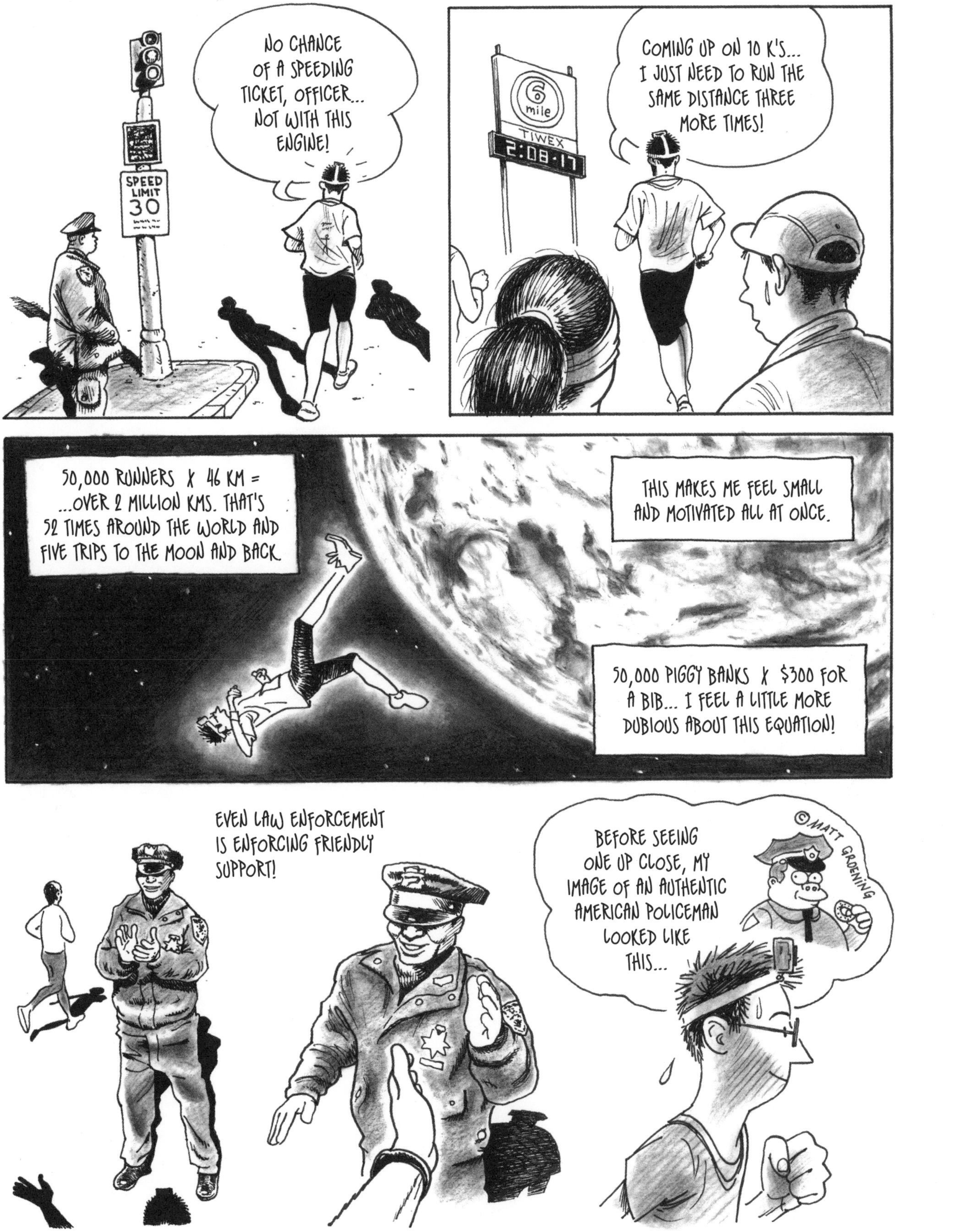

SPEED LIMIT 30
NO CHANCE OF A SPEEDING TICKET, OFFICER... NOT WITH THIS ENGINE!
6 mile
TIWEX
2:08:17
COMING UP ON 10 K'S... I JUST NEED TO RUN THE SAME DISTANCE THREE MORE TIMES!
50,000 RUNNERS X 46 KM = ...OVER 2 MILLION KMS. THAT'S 52 TIMES AROUND THE WORLD AND FIVE TRIPS TO THE MOON AND BACK.
THIS MAKES ME FEEL SMALL AND MOTIVATED ALL AT ONCE.
50,000 PIGGY BANKS X $300 FOR A BIB... I FEEL A LITTLE MORE DUBIOUS ABOUT THIS EQUATION!
EVEN LAW ENFORCEMENT IS ENFORCING FRIENDLY SUPPORT!
BEFORE SEEING ONE UP CLOSE, MY IMAGE OF AN AUTHENTIC AMERICAN POLICEMAN LOOKED LIKE THIS...
©MATT GROENING

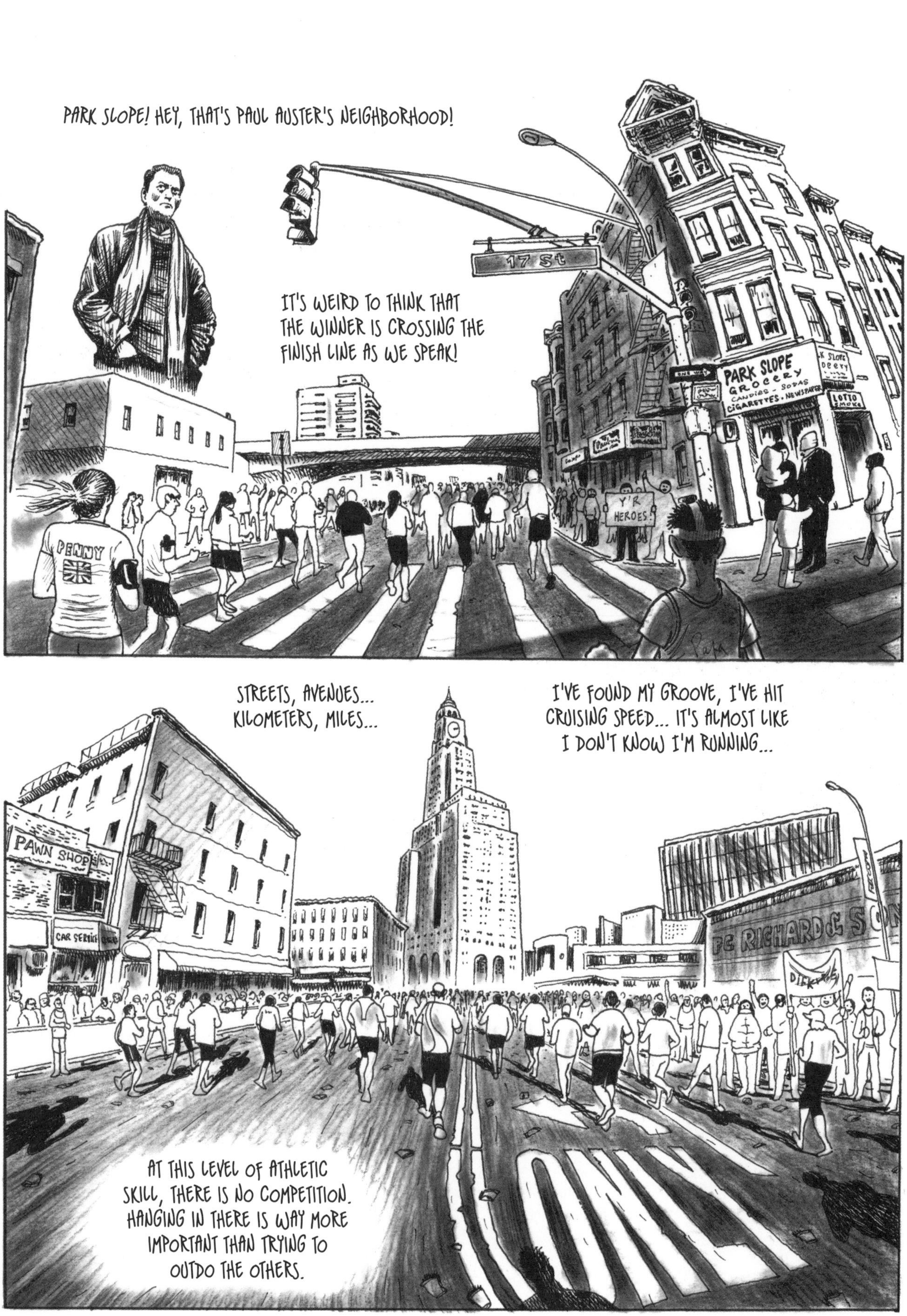
PARK SLOPE! HEY, THAT'S PAUL AUSTER'S NEIGHBORHOOD!
IT'S WEIRD TO THINK THAT THE WINNER IS CROSSING THE FINISH LINE AS WE SPEAK!
17 St
PARK SLOPE GROCERY
CIGARETTES - NEWSPAPER
LOTTO
Y'R HEROES
PENNY
STREETS, AVENUES... KILOMETERS, MILES...
I'VE FOUND MY GROOVE, I'VE HIT CRUISING SPEED... IT'S ALMOST LIKE I DON'T KNOW I'M RUNNING...
PAWN SHOP
AT THIS LEVEL OF ATHLETIC SKILL, THERE IS NO COMPETITION. HANGING IN THERE IS WAY MORE IMPORTANT THAN TRYING TO OUTDO THE OTHERS.
ONLY

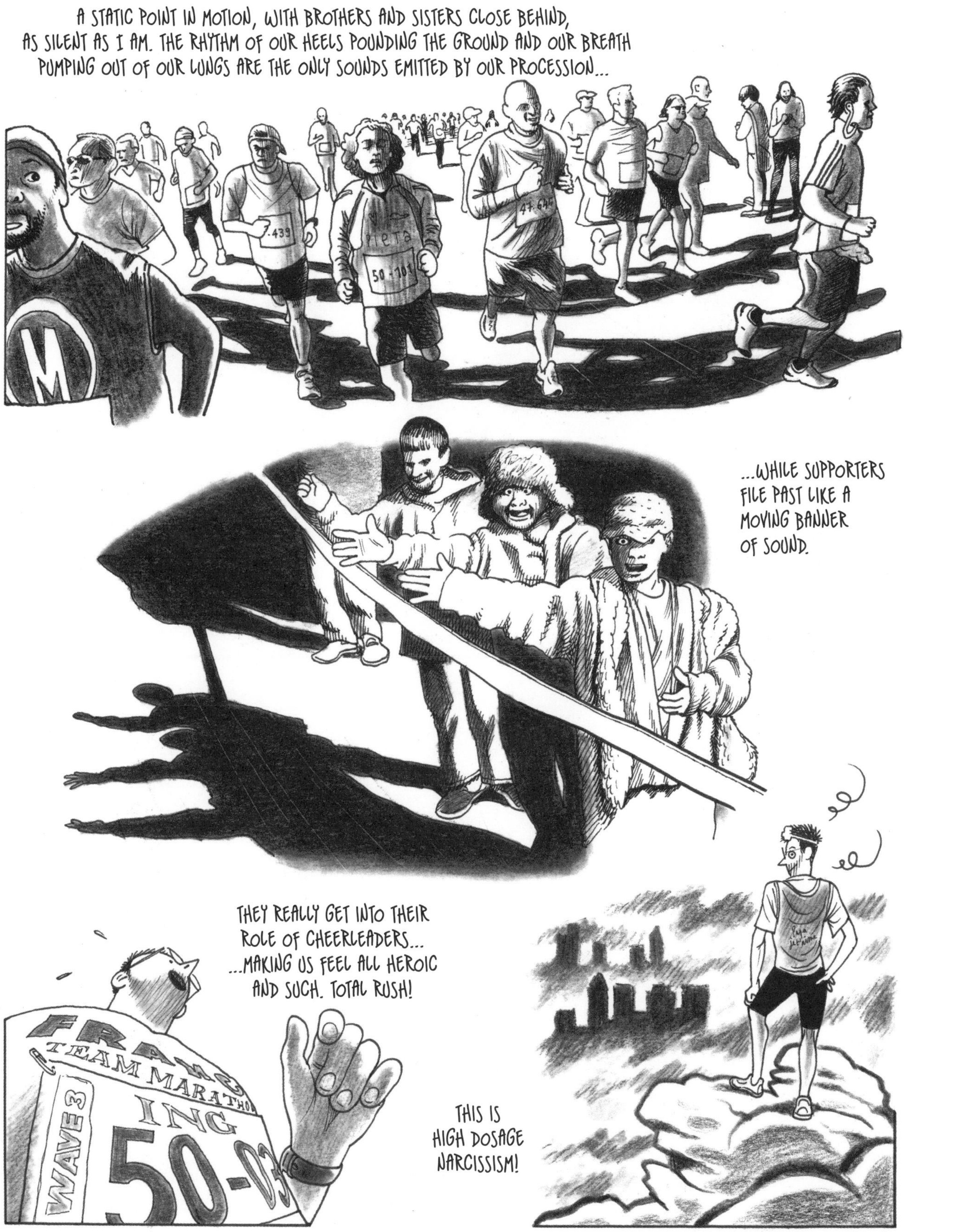
A STATIC POINT IN MOTION, WITH BROTHERS AND SISTERS CLOSE BEHIND, AS SILENT AS I AM. THE RHYTHM OF OUR HEELS POUNDING THE GROUND AND OUR BREATH PUMPING OUT OF OUR LUNGS ARE THE ONLY SOUNDS EMITTED BY OUR PROCESSION...
...WHILE SUPPORTERS FILE PAST LIKE A MOVING BANNER OF SOUND.
THEY REALLY GET INTO THEIR ROLE OF CHEERLEADERS... ...MAKING US FEEL ALL HEROIC AND SUCH. TOTAL RUSH!
THIS IS HIGH DOSAGE NARCISSISM!

AND WHEN THEY CHEER IN WRITING,
THIS IS WHAT YOU GET...

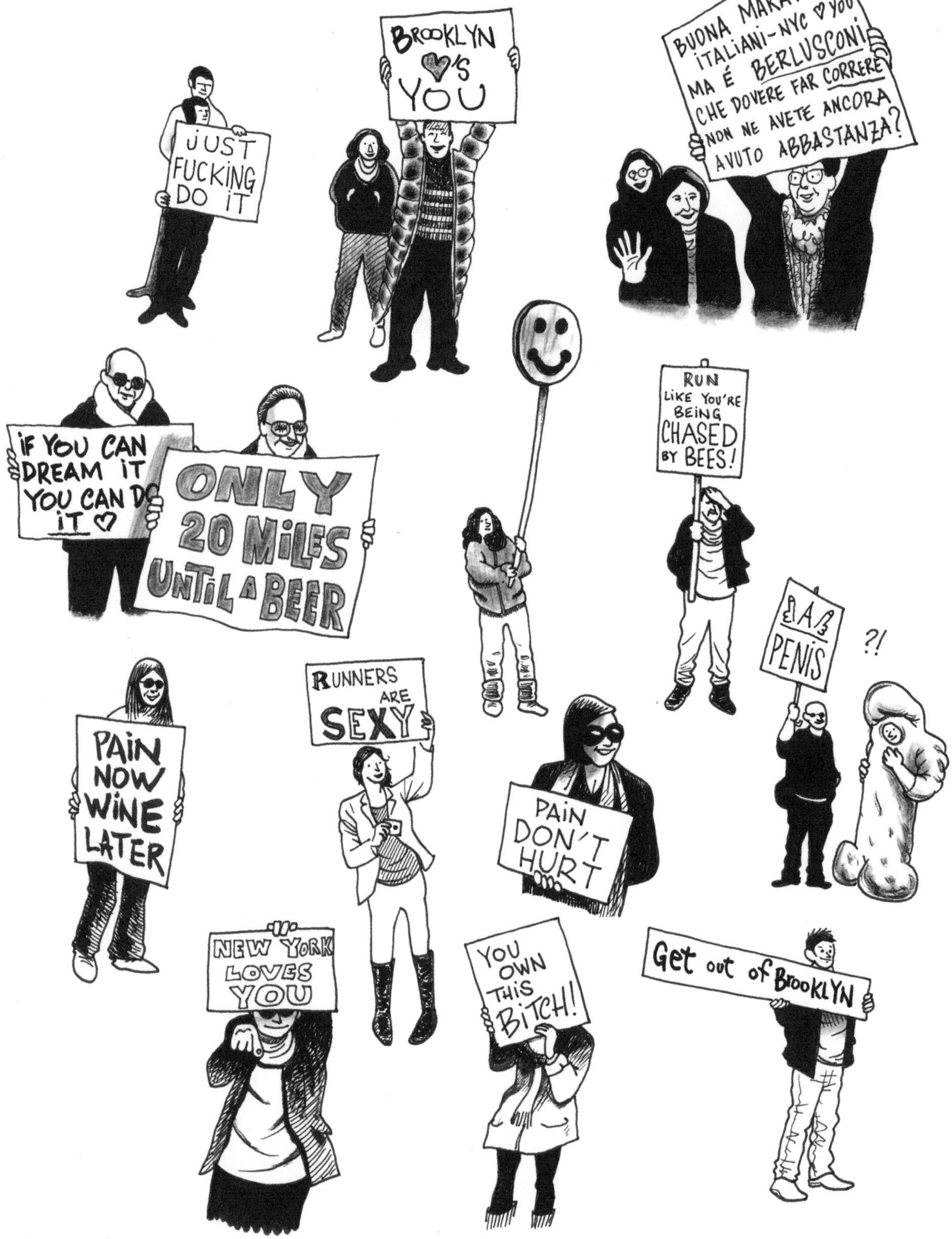
JUST FUCKING DO IT
BROOKLYN ♡'S YOU
BUONA MARATONA ITALIANI-NYC ♡ YOU MA É BERLUSCONI CHE DOVERE FAR CORRERE NON NE AVETE ANCORA AVUTO ABBASTANZA?
IF YOU CAN DREAM IT YOU CAN DO IT ♡
ONLY 20 MILES UNTIL A BEER
RUN LIKE YOU'RE BEING CHASED BY BEES!
A PENIS
?!
PAIN NOW WINE LATER
RUNNERS ARE SEXY
PAIN DON'T HURT
NEW YORK LOVES YOU
YOU OWN THIS BITCH!
Get out of BROOKLYN

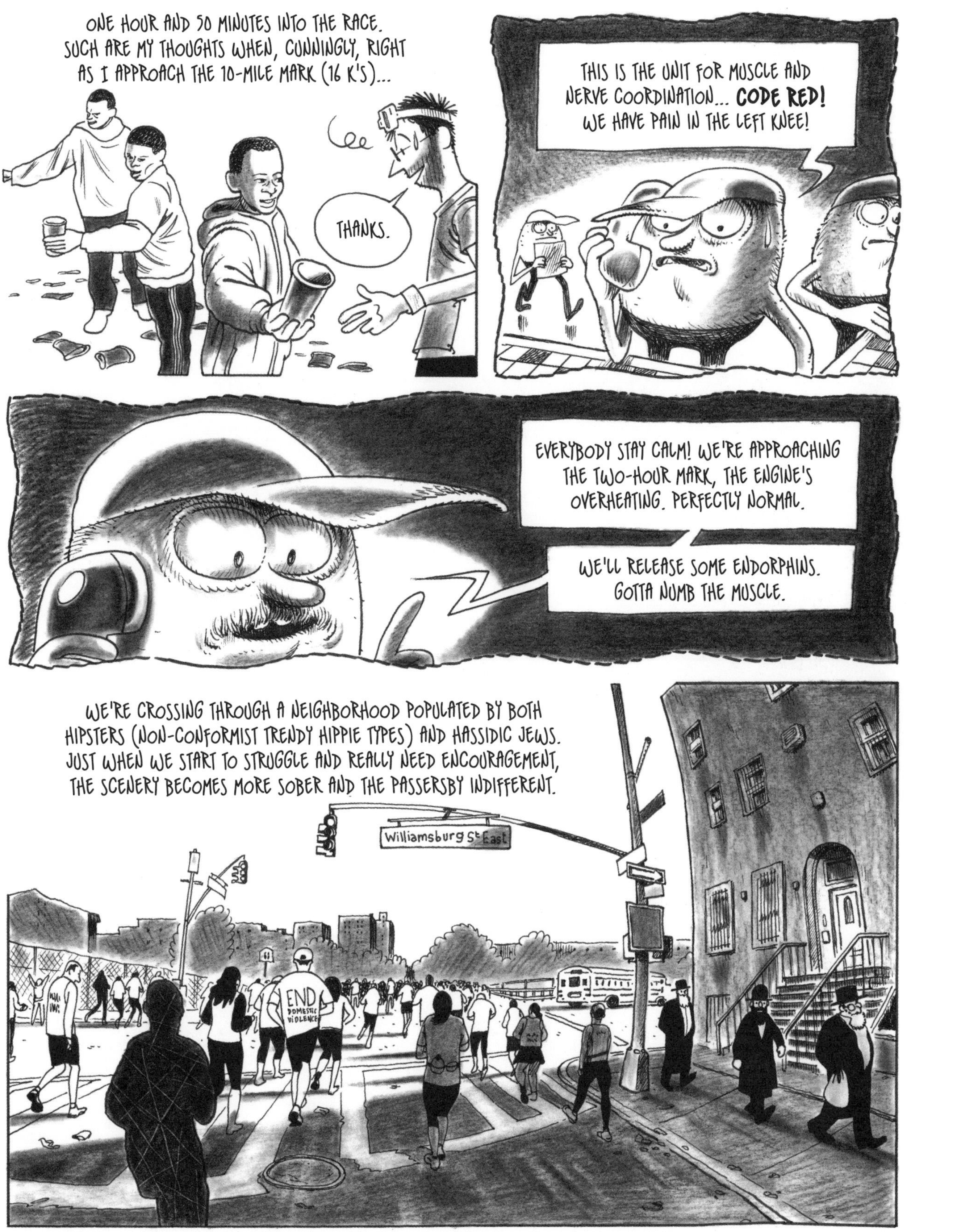
ONE HOUR AND 50 MINUTES INTO THE RACE. SUCH ARE MY THOUGHTS WHEN, CUNNINGLY, RIGHT AS I APPROACH THE 10-MILE MARK (16 K'S)...
THANKS.
THIS IS THE UNIT FOR MUSCLE AND NERVE COORDINATION... **CODE RED!** WE HAVE PAIN IN THE LEFT KNEE!
EVERYBODY STAY CALM! WE'RE APPROACHING THE TWO-HOUR MARK, THE ENGINE'S OVERHEATING. PERFECTLY NORMAL.
WE'LL RELEASE SOME ENDORPHINS. GOTTA NUMB THE MUSCLE.
WE'RE CROSSING THROUGH A NEIGHBORHOOD POPULATED BY BOTH HIPSTERS (NON-CONFORMIST TRENDY HIPPIE TYPES) AND HASSIDIC JEWS. JUST WHEN WE START TO STRUGGLE AND REALLY NEED ENCOURAGEMENT, THE SCENERY BECOMES MORE SOBER AND THE PASSERSBY INDIFFERENT.
Williamsburg St East
END DOMESTIC VIOLENCE

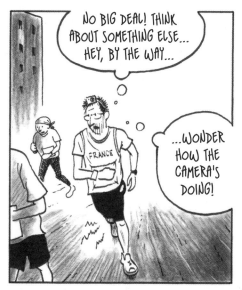

NO BIG DEAL! THINK ABOUT SOMETHING ELSE... HEY, BY THE WAY...
...WONDER HOW THE CAMERA'S DOING!
FRANCE
YOU'RE HURTING. NO SURPRISE HERE: YOU'VE NEVER RUN THAT LONG BEFORE, NOT EVEN WHILE TRAINING.
LOOK, YOU'RE NOT THE ONLY ONE STRUGGLING!
051
5
HERO
THE BATTERY'S RUNNING OUT OF STEAM TOO! GOOD THING I'VE GOT TWO OF 'EM.
AND TOO BAD THE RUNNER'S ONLY GOT ONE...
ALRIGHTY! YOU CAME TO RUN A MARATHON, DUDE, NOT WHINE. STEP UP OR GO HOME!
I MEAN, WOULD ANY OF US EVEN BE HERE IF IT WERE **EASY**?
OPEN 24 H
BROOKLYN

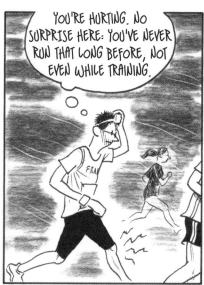

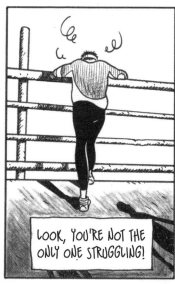

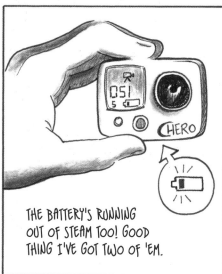

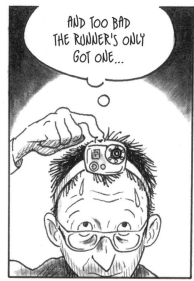

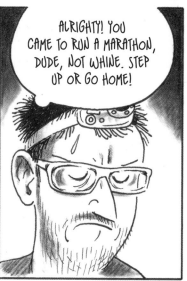

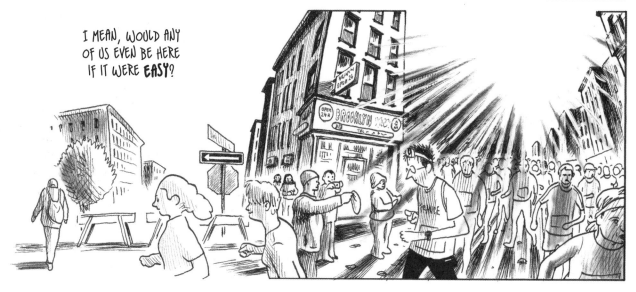

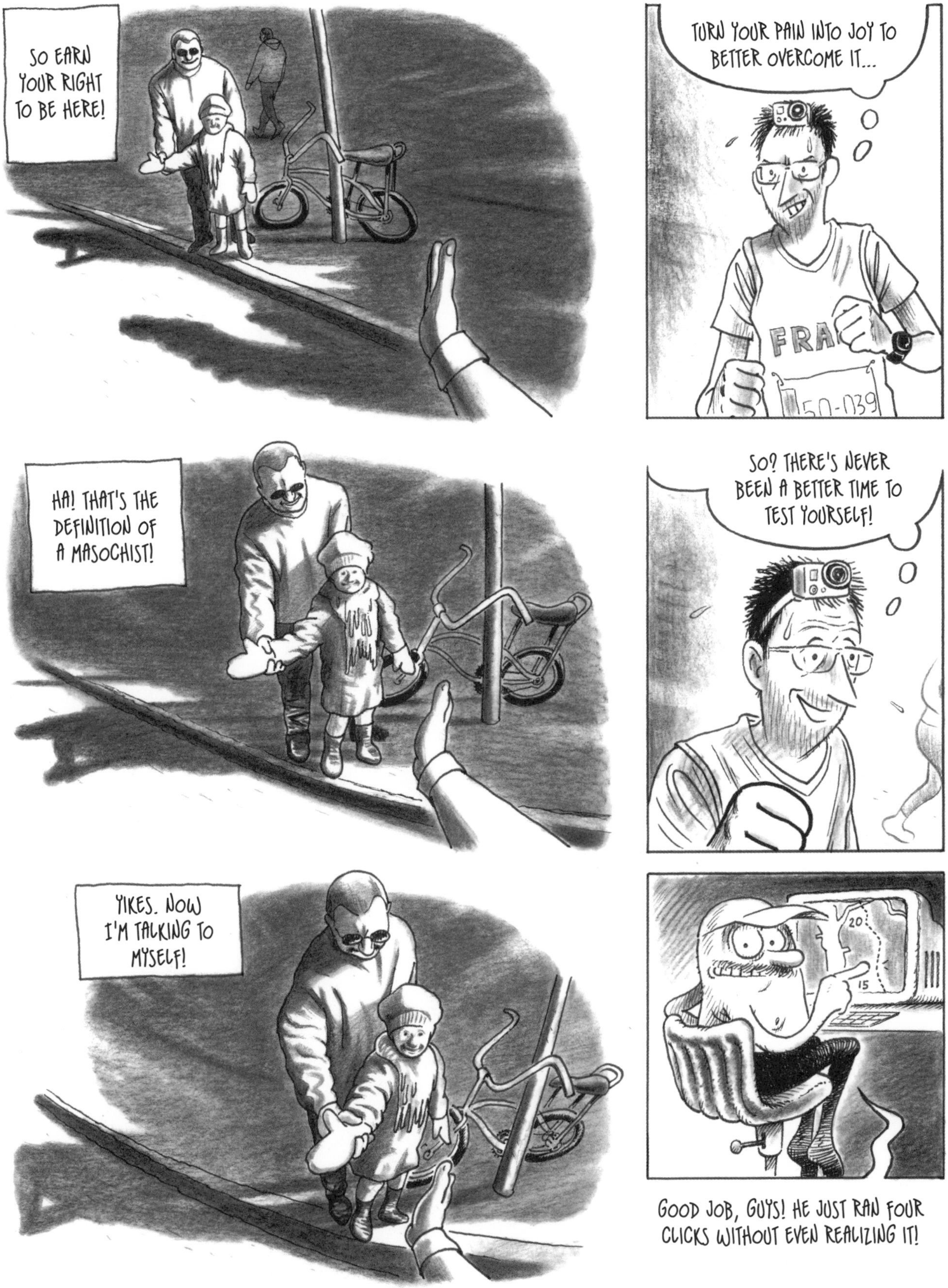
SO EARN YOUR RIGHT TO BE HERE!
HA! THAT'S THE DEFINITION OF A MASOCHIST!
YIKES. NOW I'M TALKING TO MYSELF!
TURN YOUR PAIN INTO JOY TO BETTER OVERCOME IT...
FRA
50-039
SO? THERE'S NEVER BEEN A BETTER TIME TO TEST YOURSELF!
20
15
GOOD JOB, GUYS! HE JUST RAN FOUR CLICKS WITHOUT EVEN REALIZING IT!

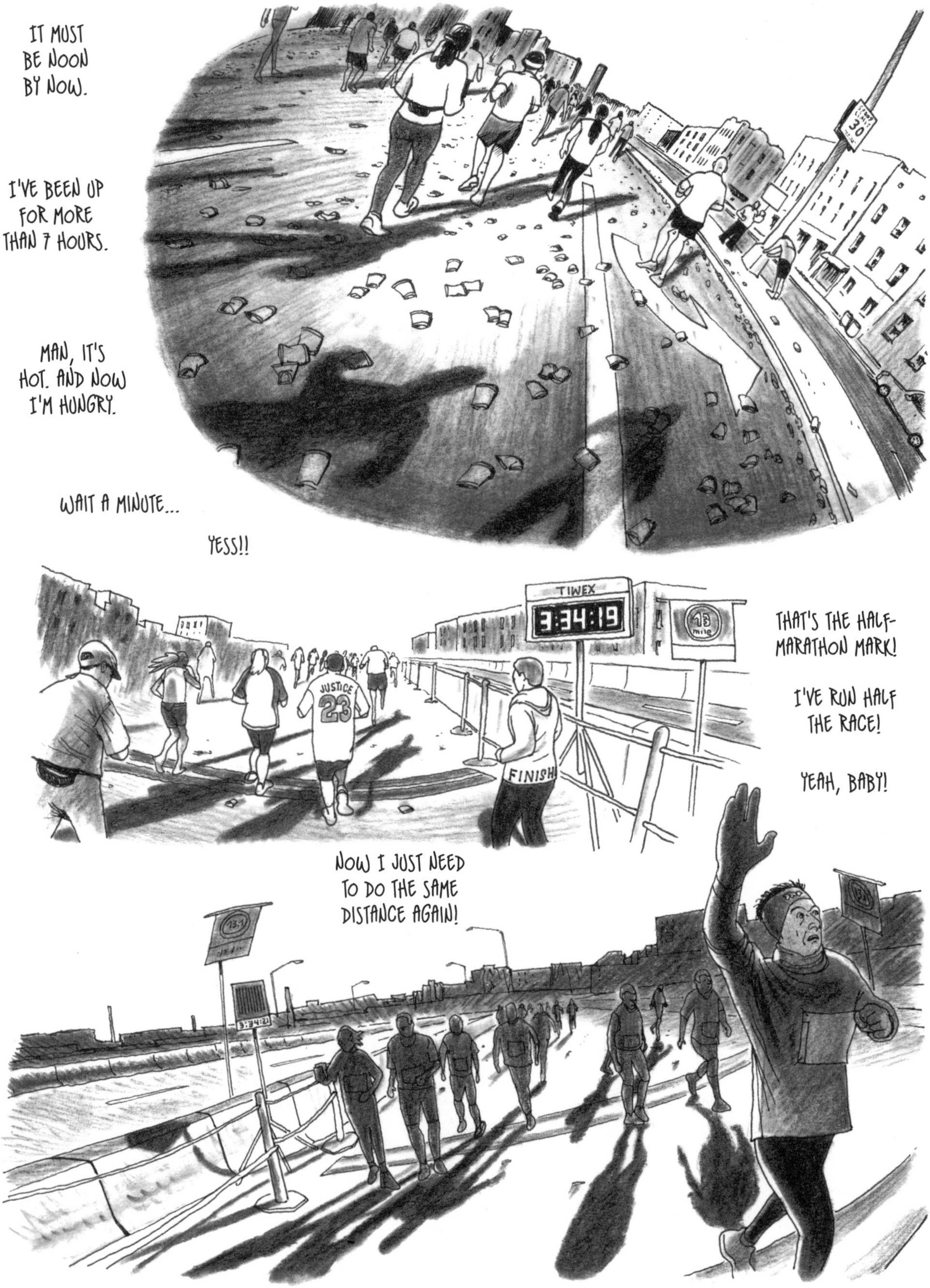
IT MUST BE NOON BY NOW.
I'VE BEEN UP FOR MORE THAN 7 HOURS.
MAN, IT'S HOT. AND NOW I'M HUNGRY.
WAIT A MINUTE...
YESS!!
TIWEX
3:34:19
JUSTICE
23
FINISH
THAT'S THE HALF-MARATHON MARK!
I'VE RUN HALF THE RACE!
YEAH, BABY!
NOW I JUST NEED TO DO THE SAME DISTANCE AGAIN!

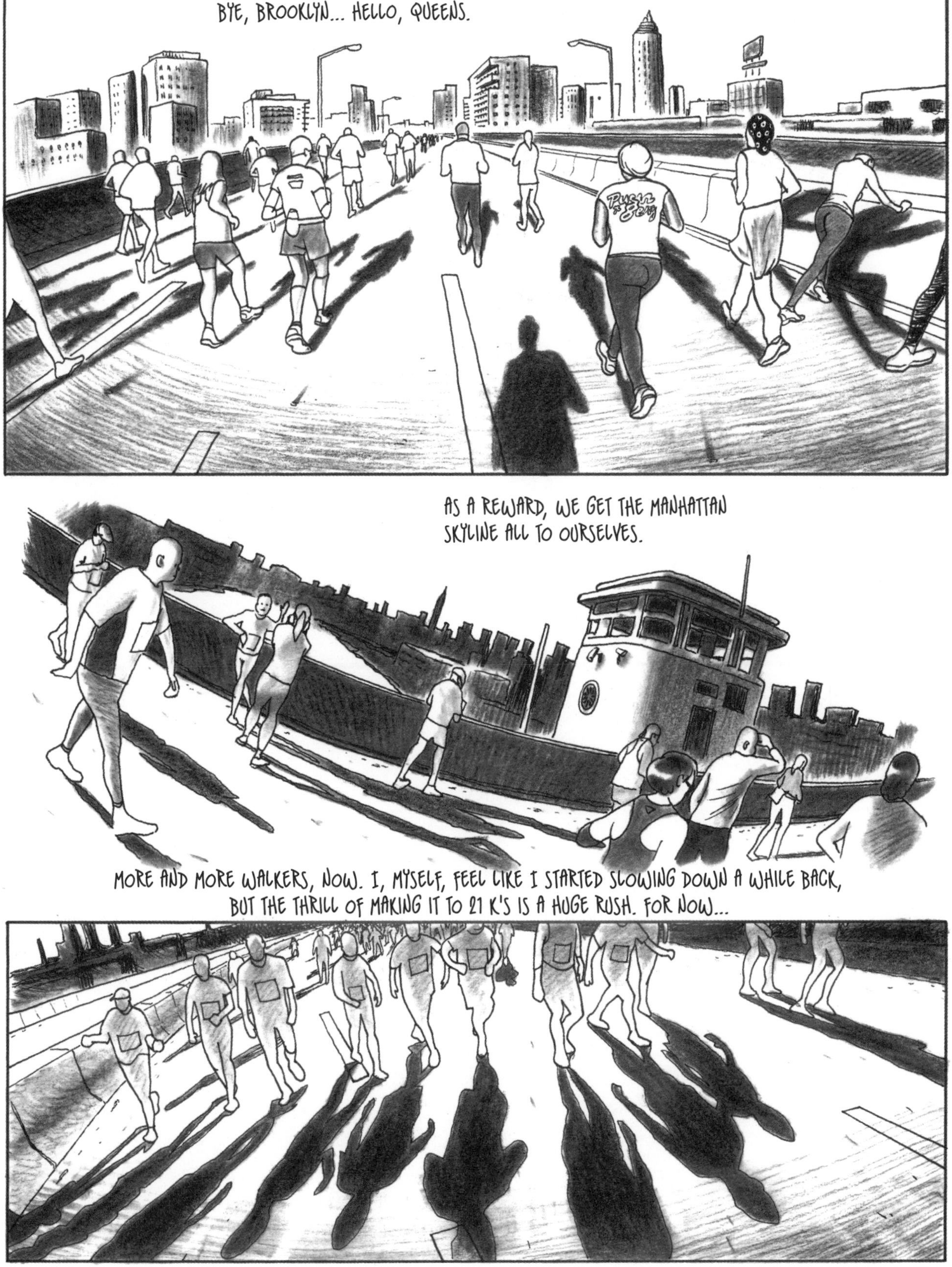
BYE, BROOKLYN... HELLO, QUEENS.
AS A REWARD, WE GET THE MANHATTAN SKYLINE ALL TO OURSELVES.
MORE AND MORE WALKERS, NOW. I, MYSELF, FEEL LIKE I STARTED SLOWING DOWN A WHILE BACK, BUT THE THRILL OF MAKING IT TO 21 K'S IS A HUGE RUSH. FOR NOW...

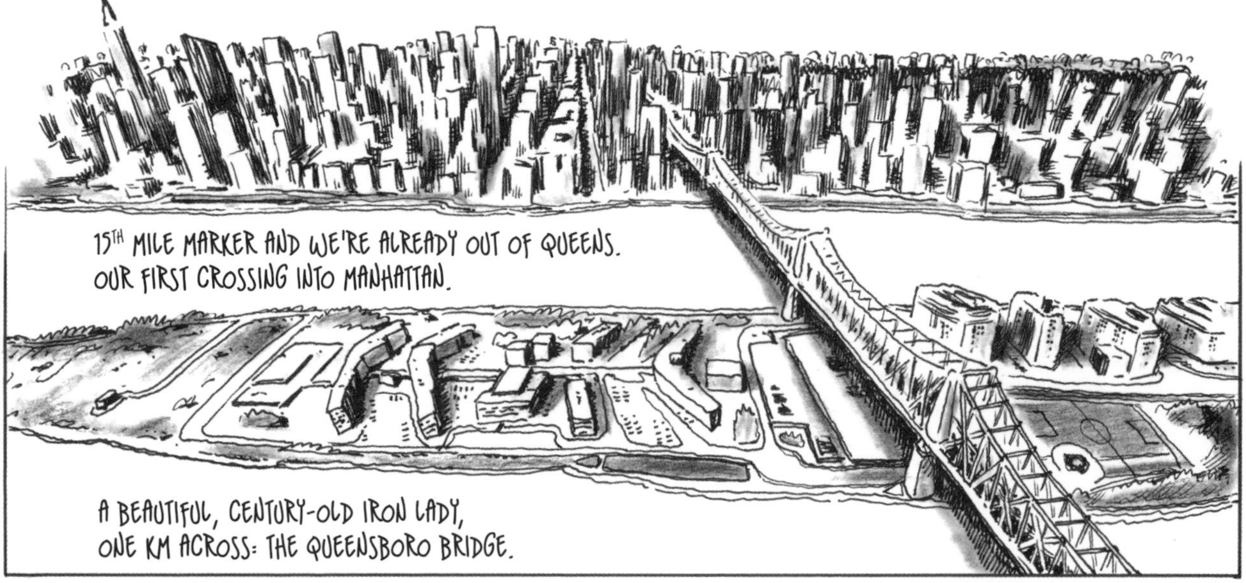
15TH MILE MARKER AND WE'RE ALREADY OUT OF QUEENS.
OUR FIRST CROSSING INTO MANHATTAN.
A BEAUTIFUL, CENTURY-OLD IRON LADY,
ONE KM ACROSS: THE QUEENSBORO BRIDGE.

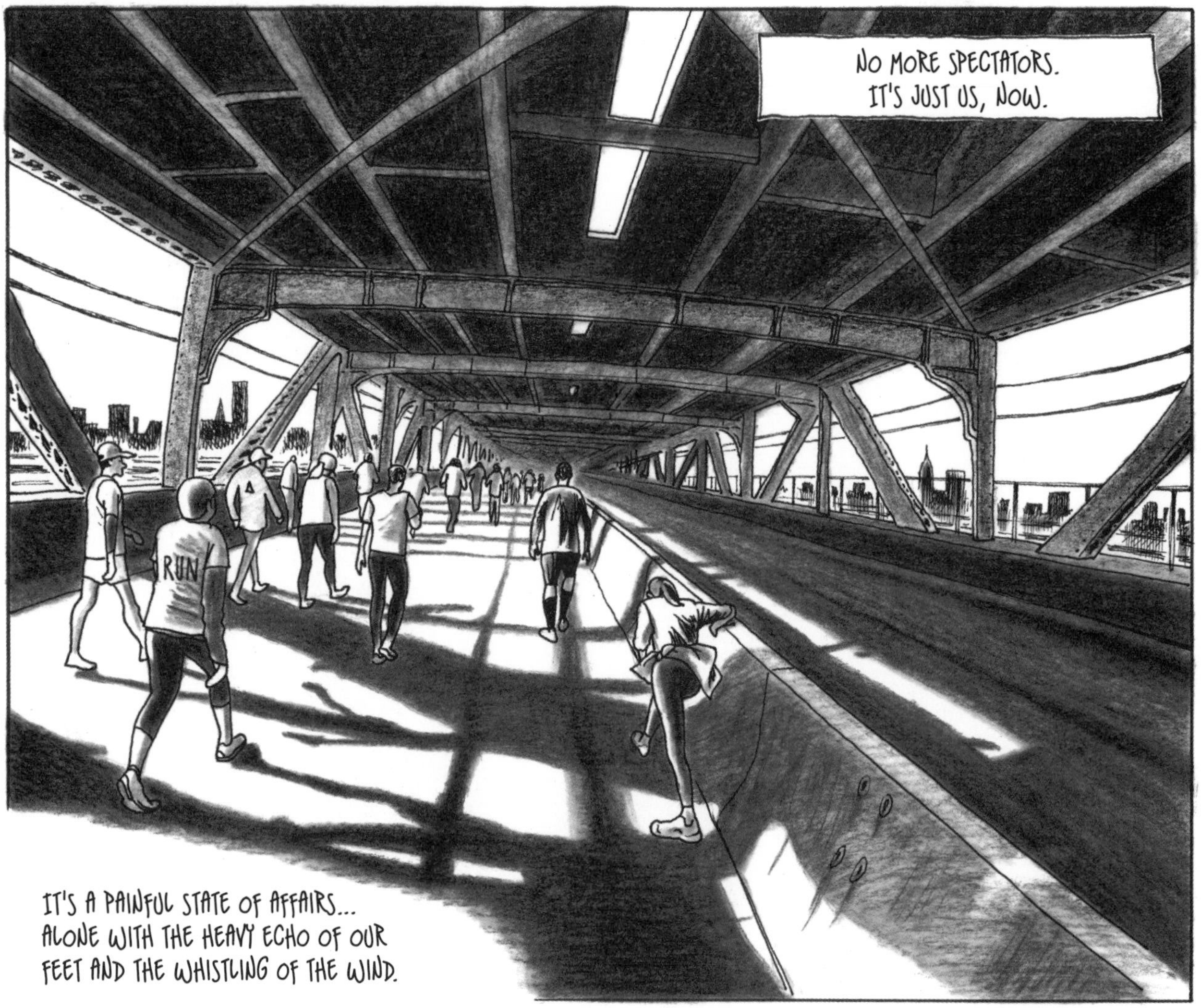
NO MORE SPECTATORS.
IT'S JUST US, NOW.
RUN
IT'S A PAINFUL STATE OF AFFAIRS...
ALONE WITH THE HEAVY ECHO OF OUR
FEET AND THE WHISTLING OF THE WIND.

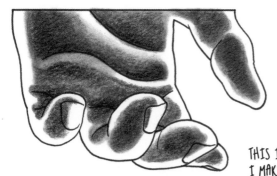

THIS IS WHEN
I MAKE A DEADLY MISTAKE...

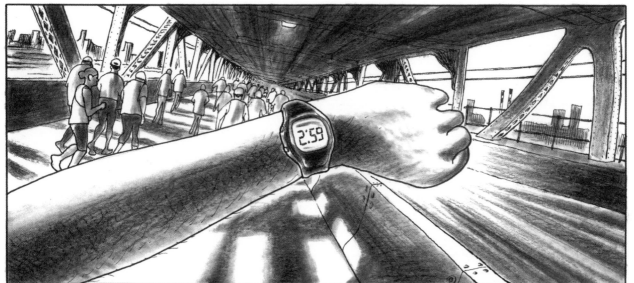

...I CHECK MY WATCH!

THREE HOURS IS A HUGE MENTAL
BLOW FOR ME.

MY MIND GOES BLANK

MY LEGS DEMAND A BREAK

AND NOT JUST THE
LEGS, ALAS!

MY HIPS, MY BACK,
MY SHOULDERS...

THEY ALL REFUSE
TO MOVE.

FORTUNATELY, THE TRIUMPHANT
WELCOME ON FIRST AVENUE
CHEERS ME UP!

THE ACCLAMATION GETS ME
ALL CHOKED UP.

COME ON...

RUN...

YEAH!

NONE OF THOSE PEOPLE CAME
HERE TO SEE SOME DUDE WALK!

AND I DIDN'T CROSS THE POND
TO GO FOR A STROLL!

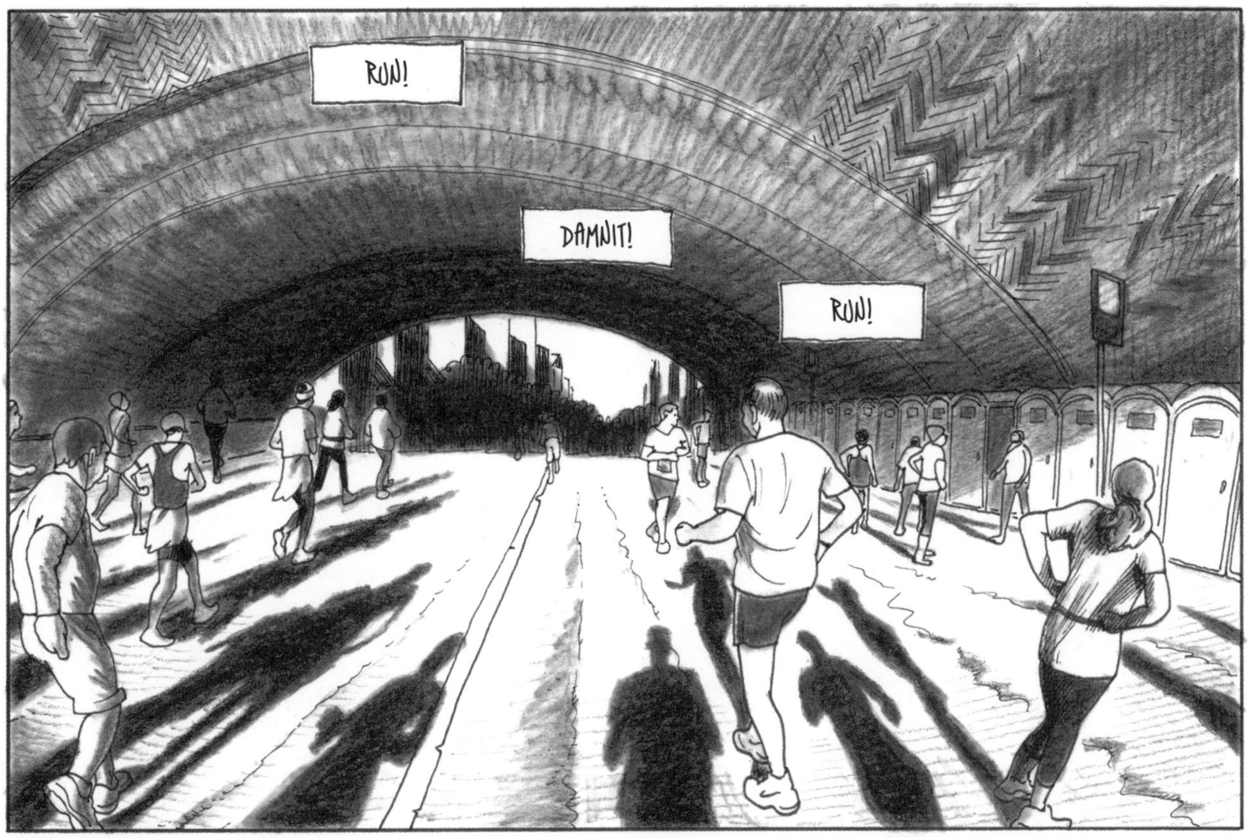
RUN!
DAMNIT!
RUN!

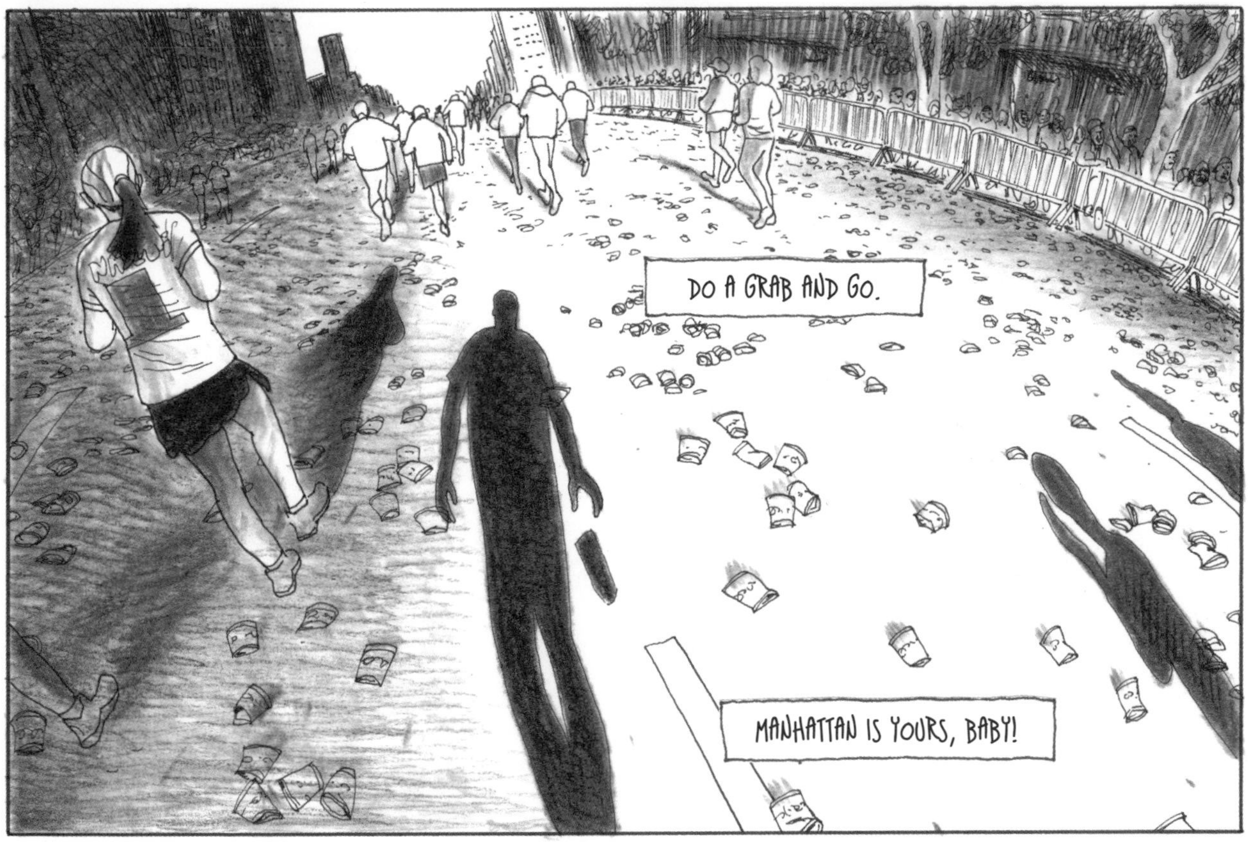
DO A GRAB AND GO.
MANHATTAN IS YOURS, BABY!

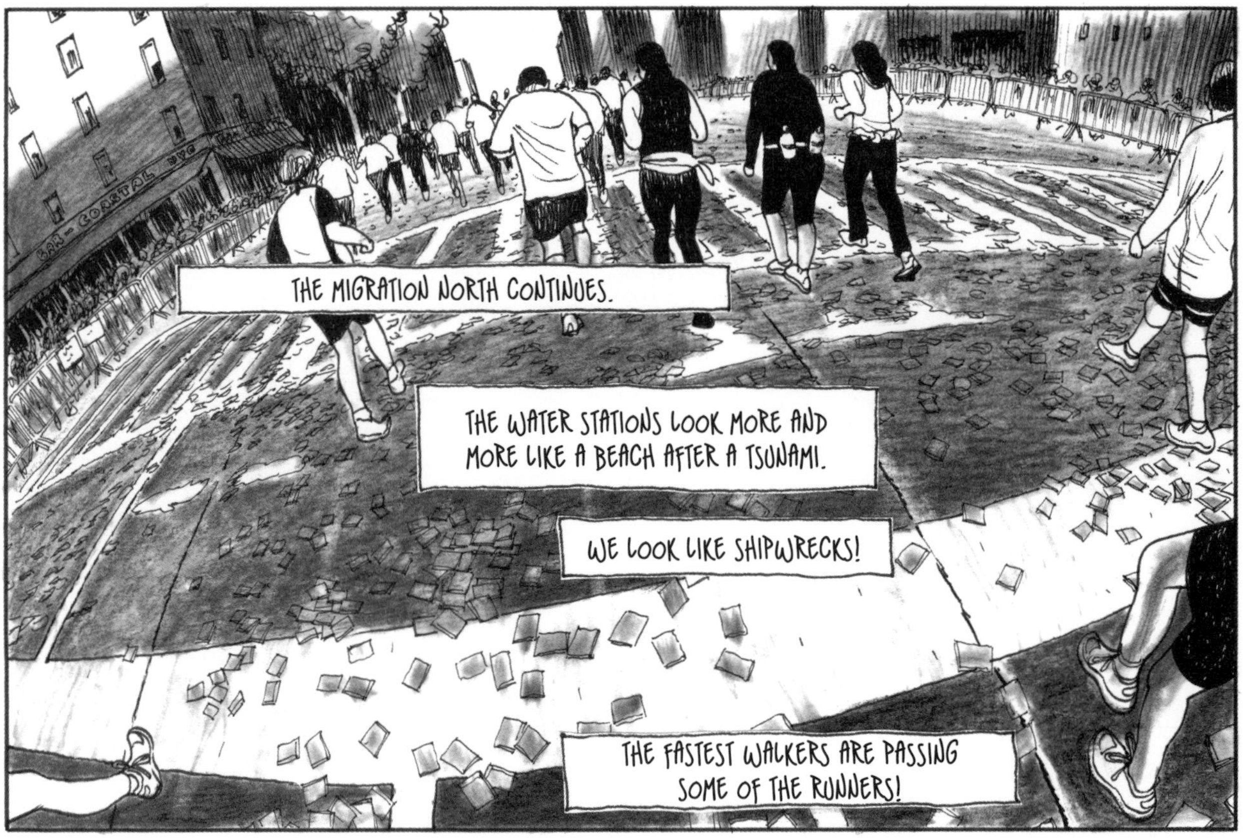
THE MIGRATION NORTH CONTINUES.
THE WATER STATIONS LOOK MORE AND MORE LIKE A BEACH AFTER A TSUNAMI.
WE LOOK LIKE SHIPWRECKS!
THE FASTEST WALKERS ARE PASSING SOME OF THE RUNNERS!

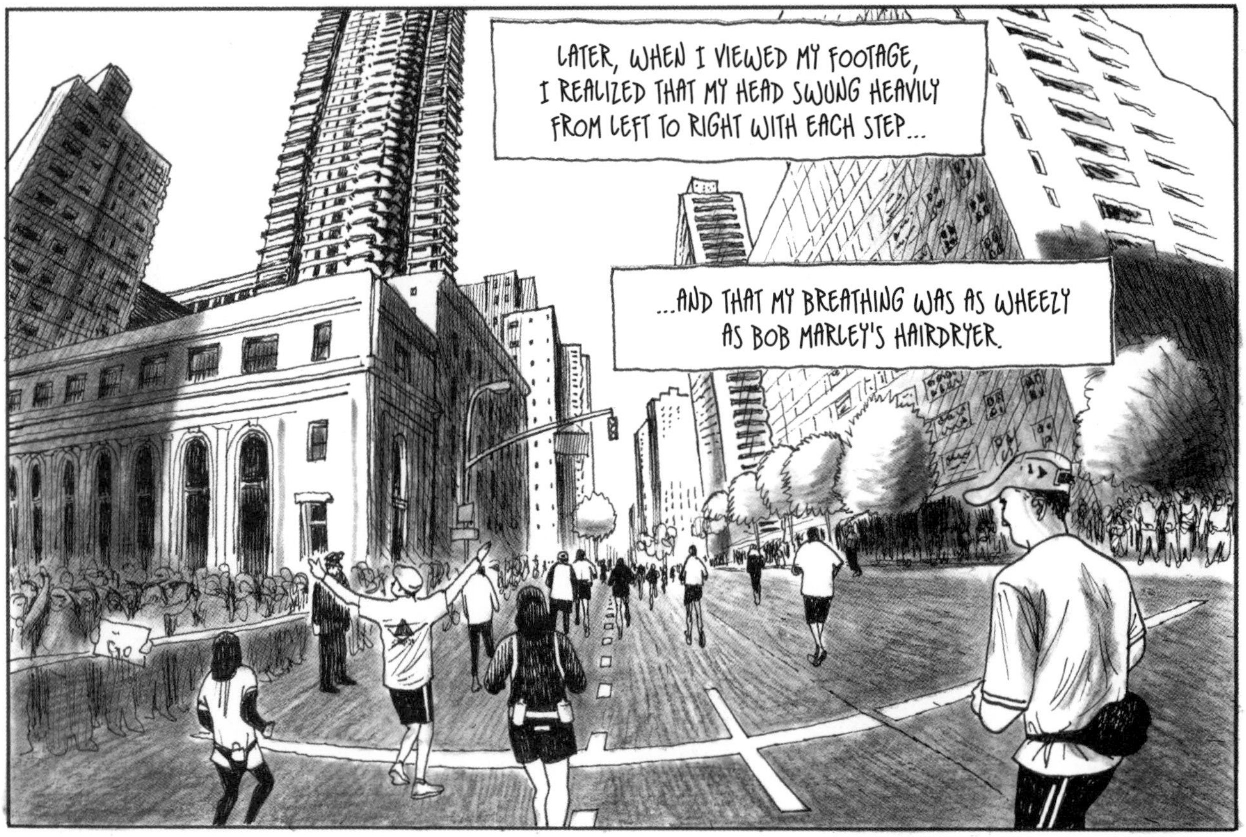
LATER, WHEN I VIEWED MY FOOTAGE, I REALIZED THAT MY HEAD SWUNG HEAVILY FROM LEFT TO RIGHT WITH EACH STEP...
...AND THAT MY BREATHING WAS AS WHEEZY AS BOB MARLEY'S HAIRDRYER.

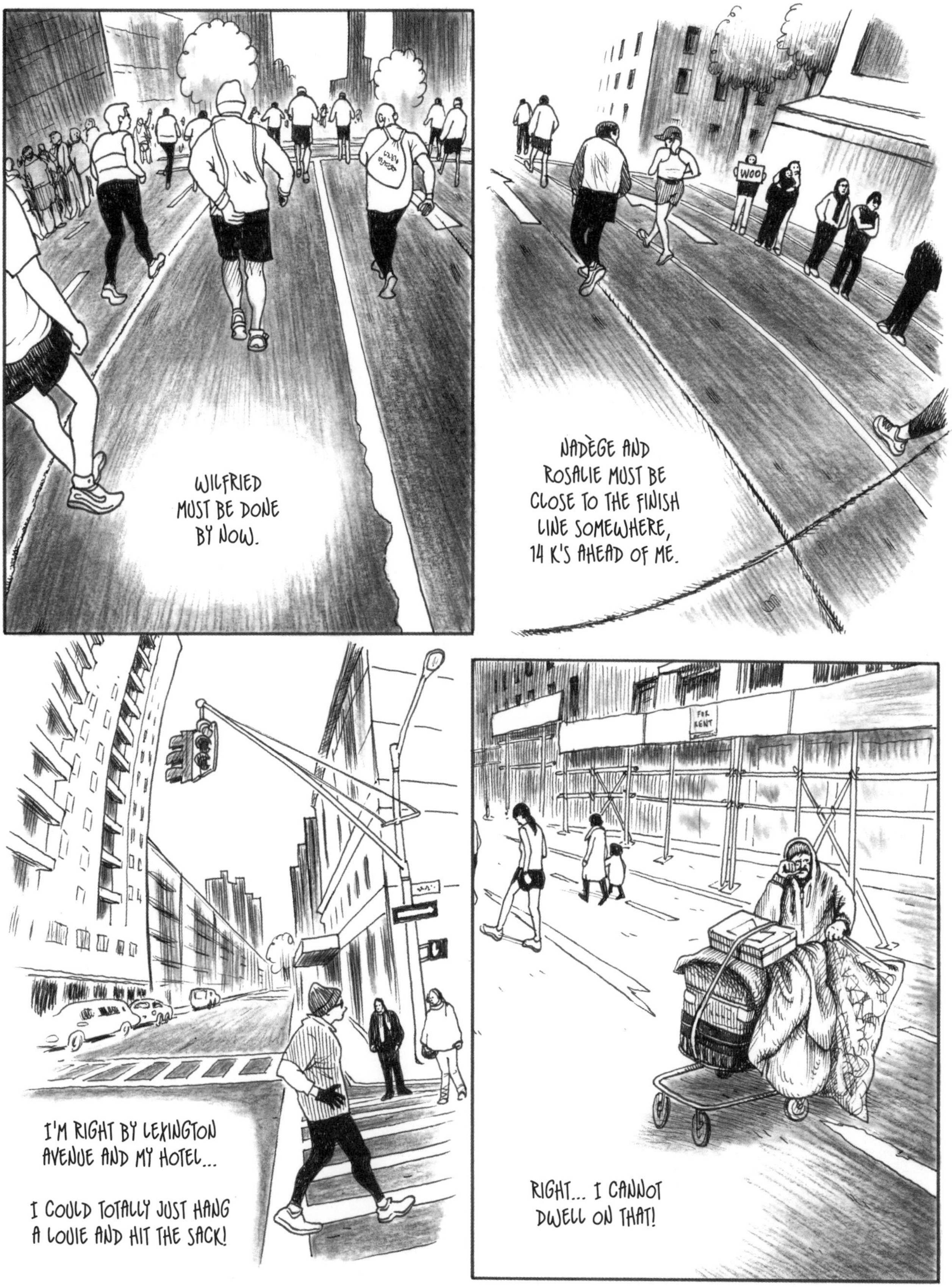
WILFRIED MUST BE DONE BY NOW.
WOO
NADÈGE AND ROSALIE MUST BE CLOSE TO THE FINISH LINE SOMEWHERE, 14 K'S AHEAD OF ME.
I'M RIGHT BY LEXINGTON AVENUE AND MY HOTEL...
I COULD TOTALLY JUST HANG A LOUIE AND HIT THE SACK!
FOR RENT
RIGHT... I CANNOT DWELL ON THAT!

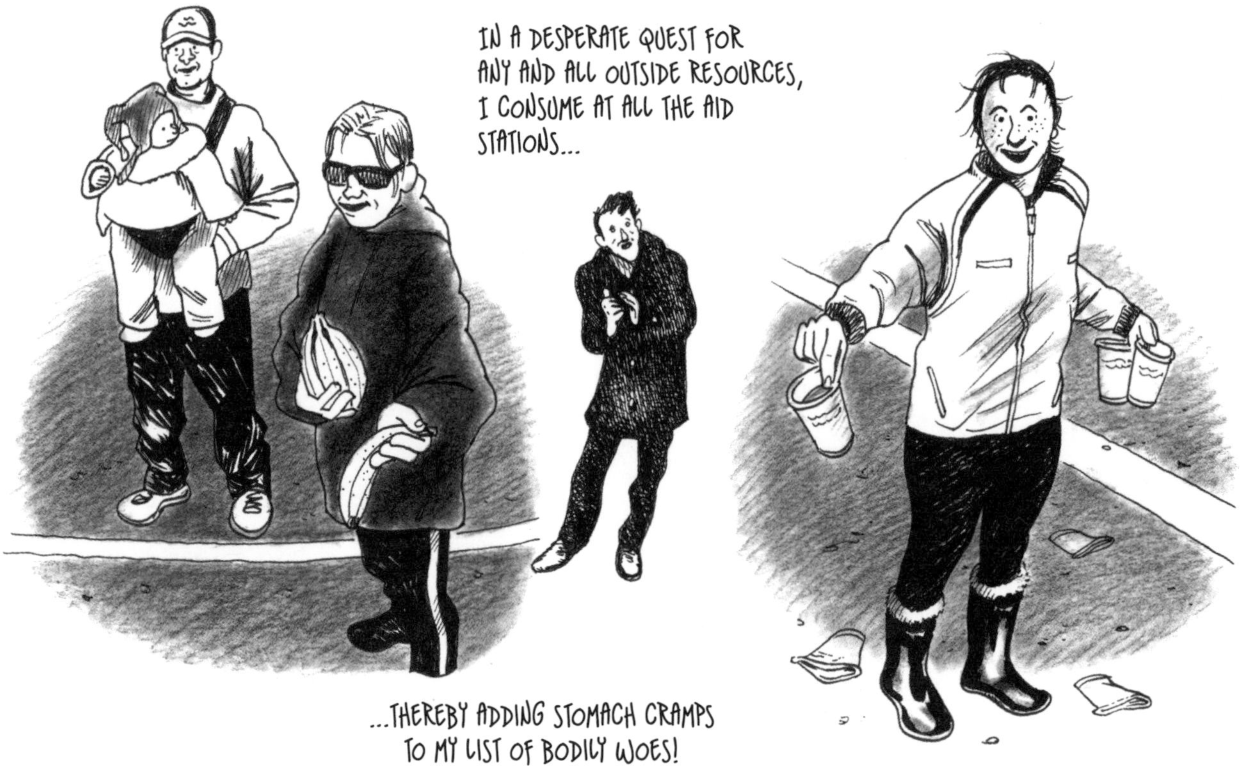
IN A DESPERATE QUEST FOR ANY AND ALL OUTSIDE RESOURCES, I CONSUME AT ALL THE AID STATIONS...
...THEREBY ADDING STOMACH CRAMPS TO MY LIST OF BODILY WOES!

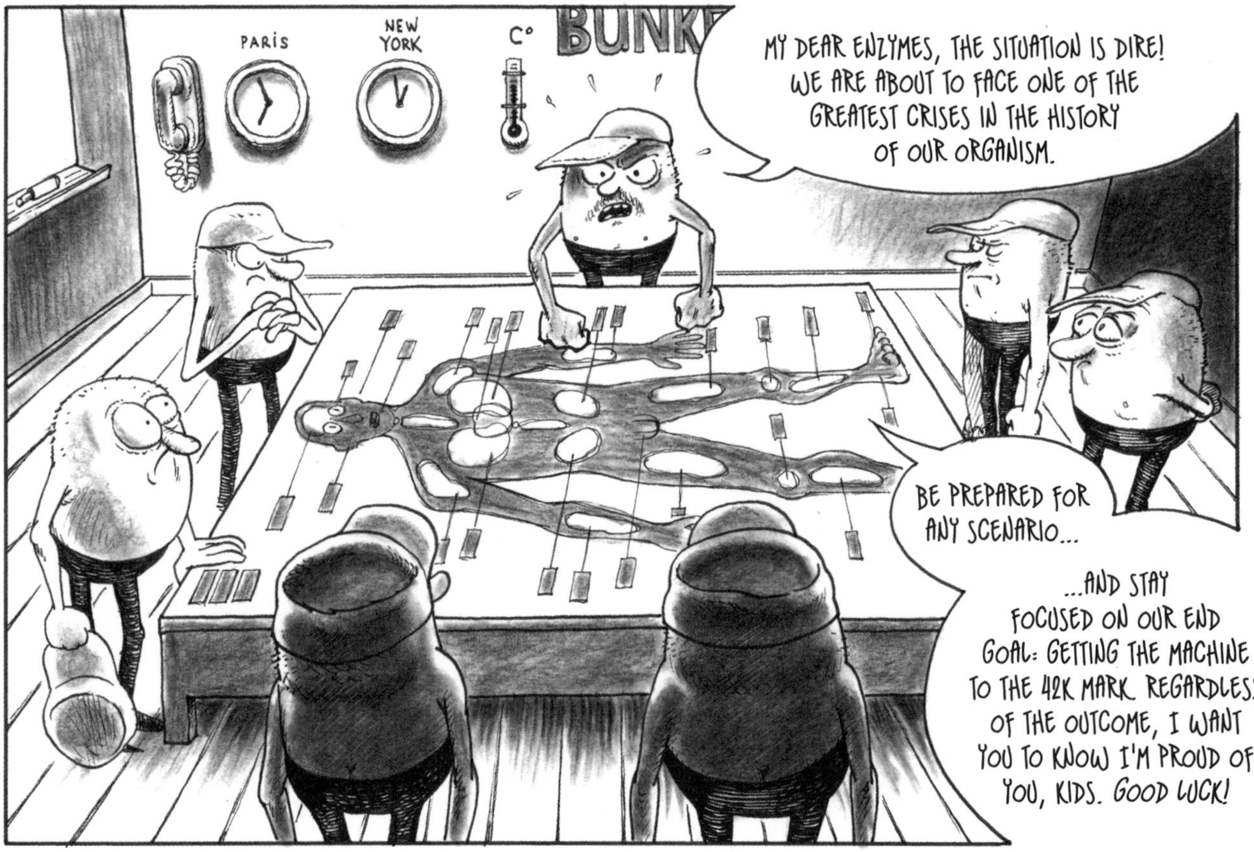
PARIS
NEW YORK
C°
BUNK
MY DEAR ENZYMES, THE SITUATION IS DIRE! WE ARE ABOUT TO FACE ONE OF THE GREATEST CRISES IN THE HISTORY OF OUR ORGANISM.
BE PREPARED FOR ANY SCENARIO...
...AND STAY FOCUSED ON OUR END GOAL: GETTING THE MACHINE TO THE 42K MARK. REGARDLESS OF THE OUTCOME, I WANT YOU TO KNOW I'M PROUD OF YOU, KIDS. GOOD LUCK!

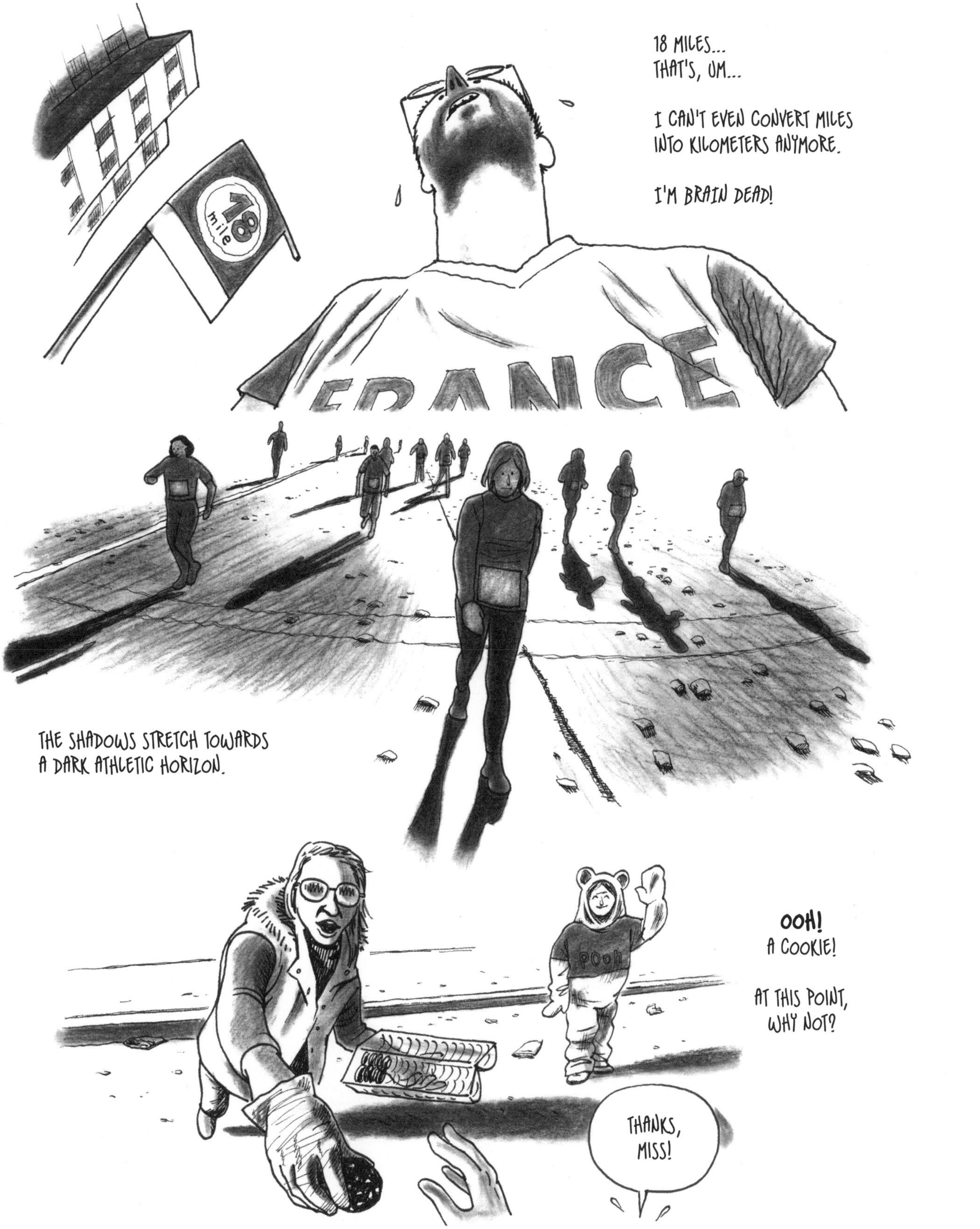

18 mile
18 MILES...
THAT'S, UM...
I CAN'T EVEN CONVERT MILES INTO KILOMETERS ANYMORE.
I'M BRAIN DEAD!
THE SHADOWS STRETCH TOWARDS A DARK ATHLETIC HORIZON.
OOH!
A COOKIE!
AT THIS POINT, WHY NOT?
Pooh
THANKS, MISS!

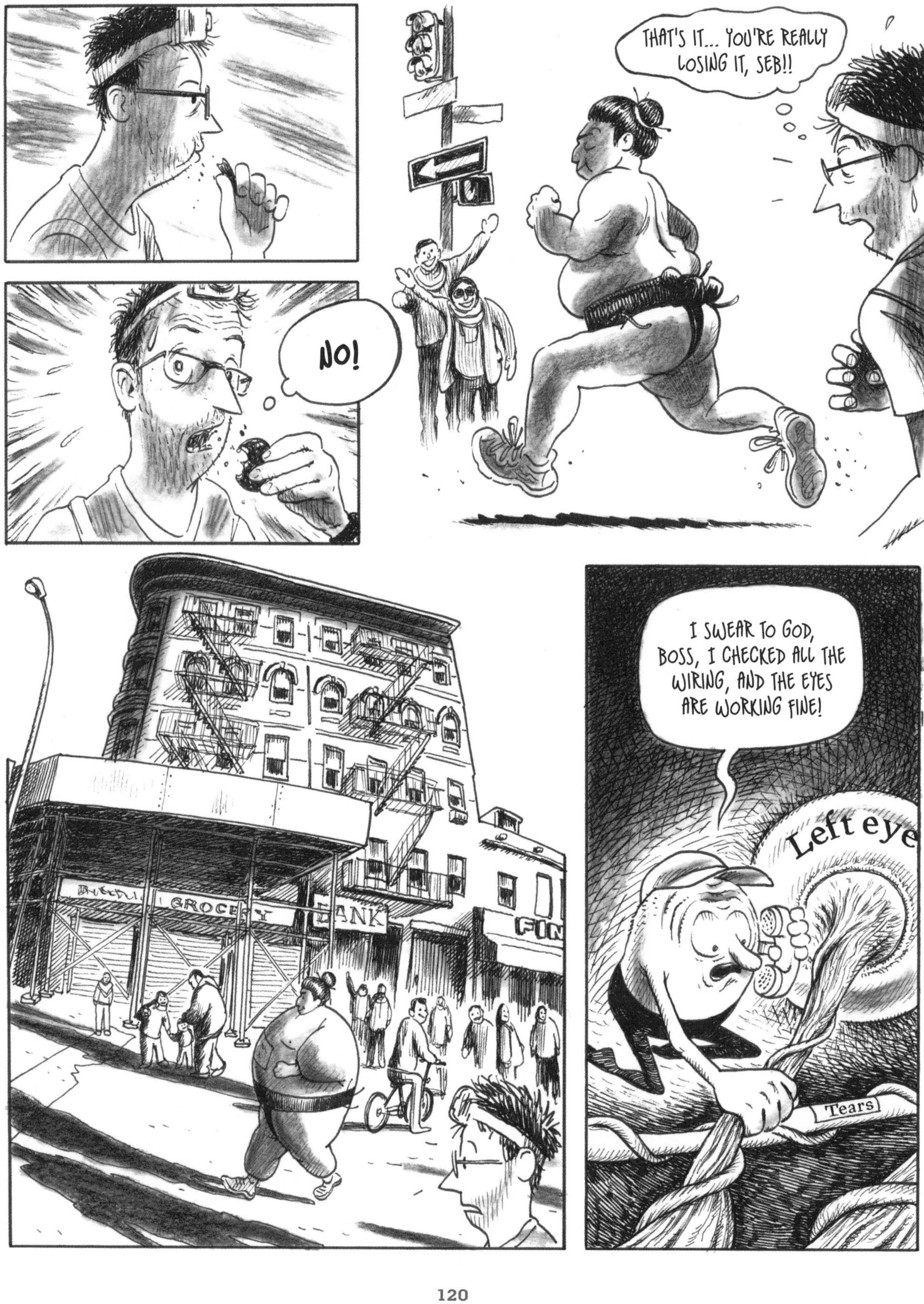

NO!
THAT'S IT... YOU'RE REALLY LOSING IT, SEB!!
GROCERY
BANK
I SWEAR TO GOD, BOSS, I CHECKED ALL THE WIRING, AND THE EYES ARE WORKING FINE!
Left eye
Tears

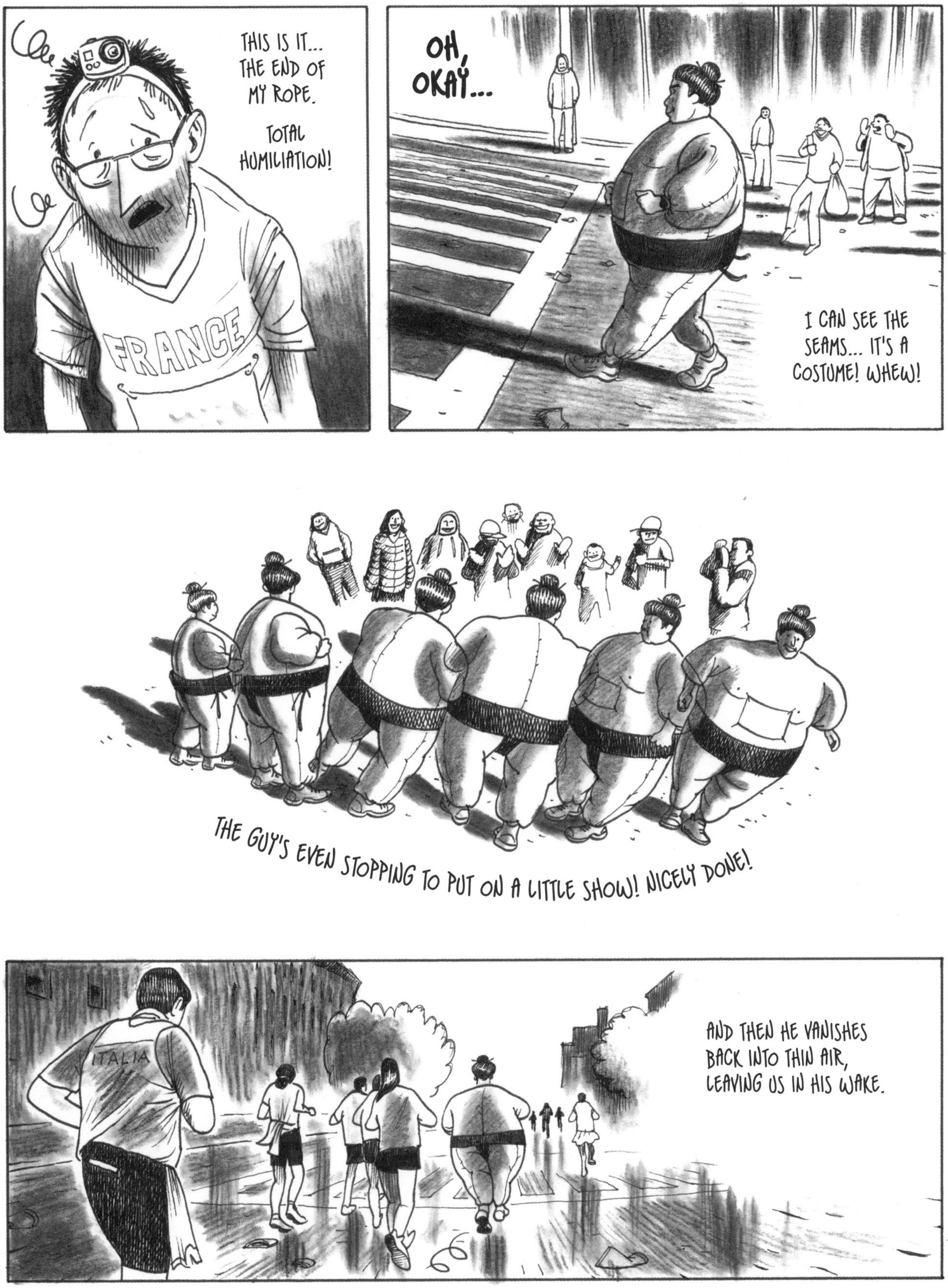
THIS IS IT... THE END OF MY ROPE.
TOTAL HUMILIATION!
OH, OKAY...
I CAN SEE THE SEAMS... IT'S A COSTUME! WHEW!
THE GUY'S EVEN STOPPING TO PUT ON A LITTLE SHOW! NICELY DONE!
ITALIA
AND THEN HE VANISHES BACK INTO THIN AIR, LEAVING US IN HIS WAKE.

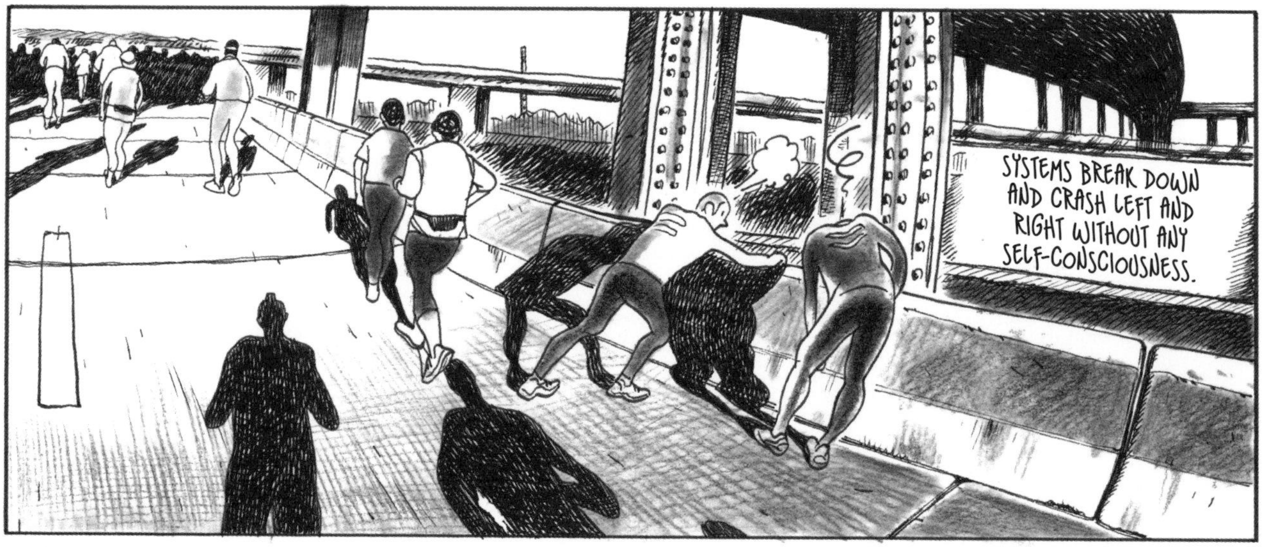
SYSTEMS BREAK DOWN AND CRASH LEFT AND RIGHT WITHOUT ANY SELF-CONSCIOUSNESS.

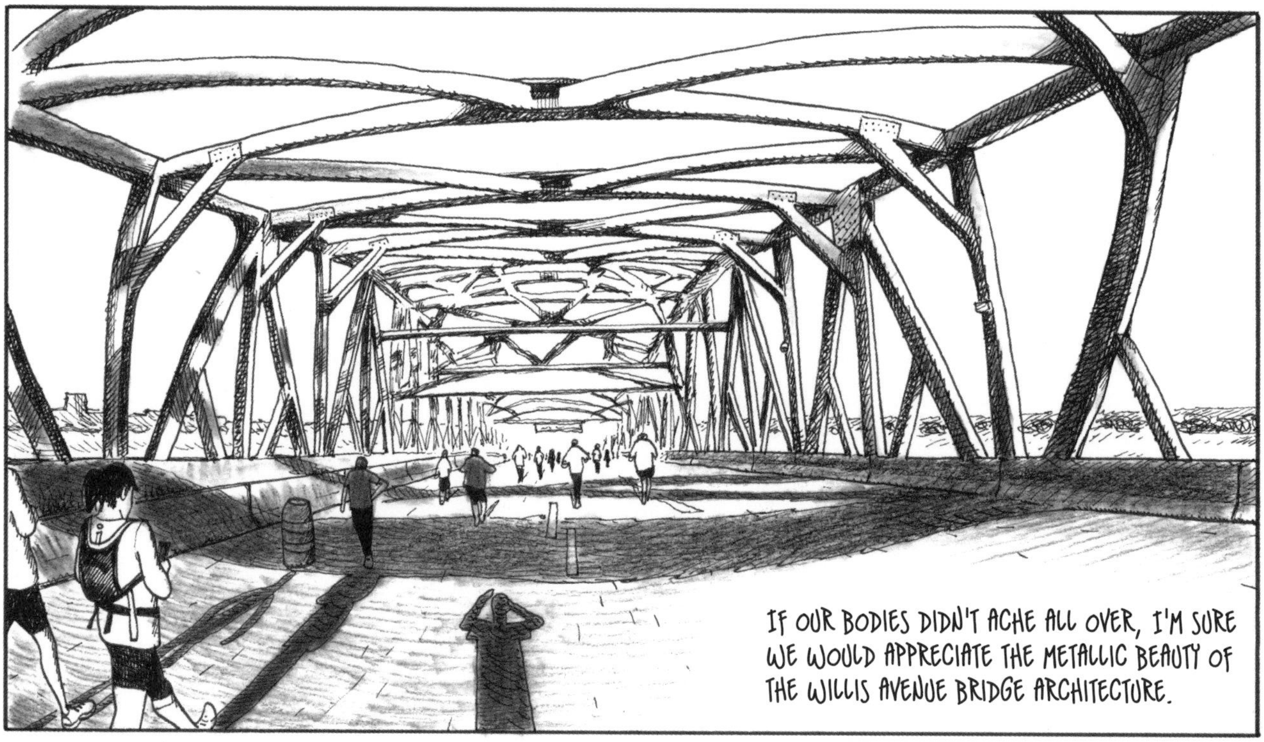
IF OUR BODIES DIDN'T ACHE ALL OVER, I'M SURE WE WOULD APPRECIATE THE METALLIC BEAUTY OF THE WILLIS AVENUE BRIDGE ARCHITECTURE.

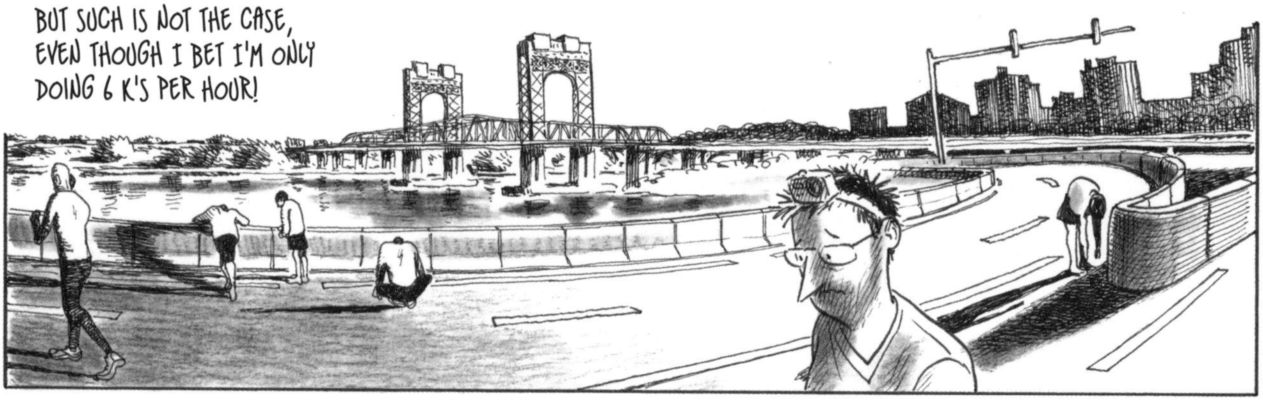
BUT SUCH IS NOT THE CASE, EVEN THOUGH I BET I'M ONLY DOING 6 K'S PER HOUR!

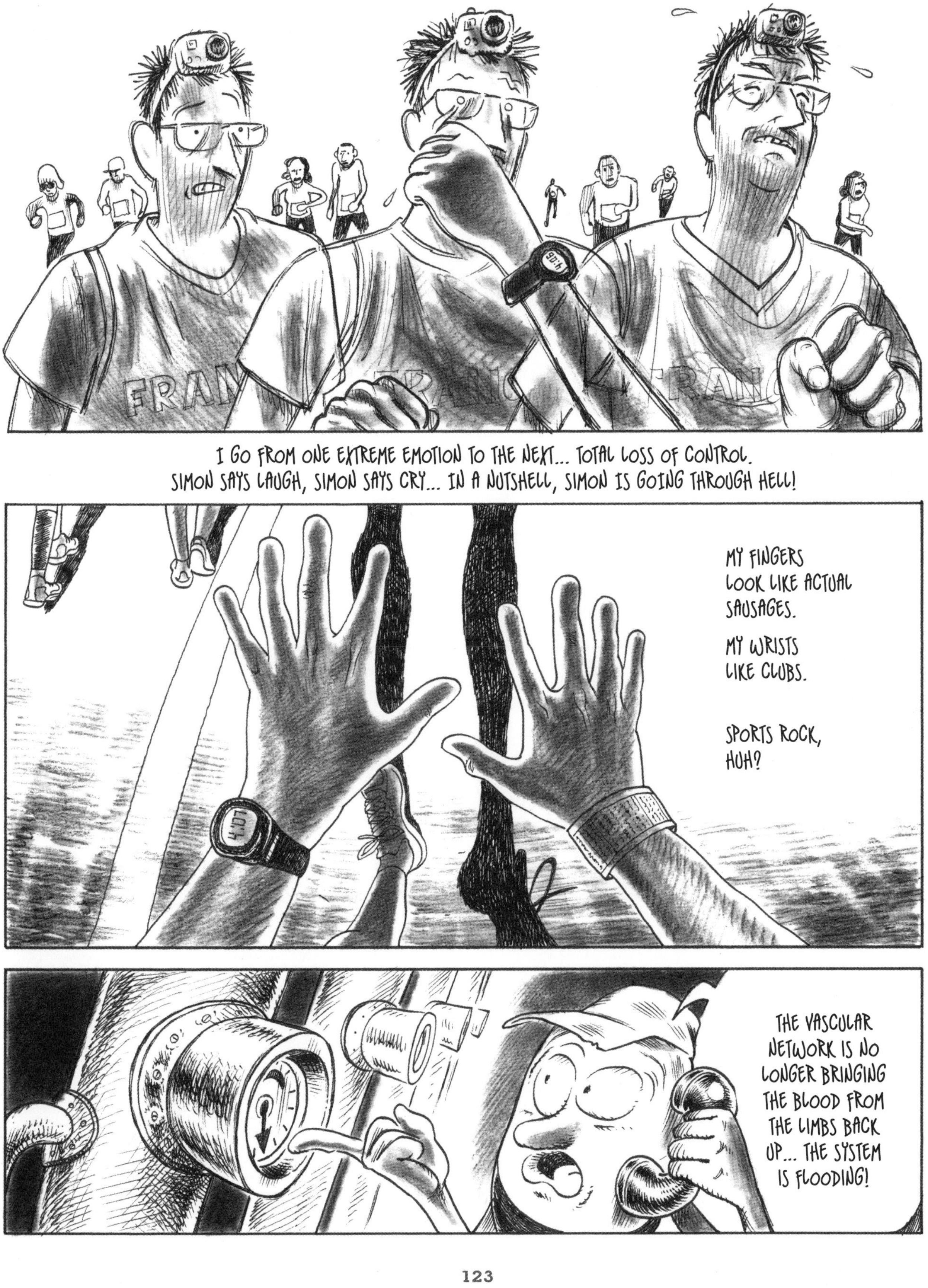
I GO FROM ONE EXTREME EMOTION TO THE NEXT... TOTAL LOSS OF CONTROL.
SIMON SAYS LAUGH, SIMON SAYS CRY... IN A NUTSHELL, SIMON IS GOING THROUGH HELL!
MY FINGERS LOOK LIKE ACTUAL SAUSAGES.
MY WRISTS LIKE CLUBS.
SPORTS ROCK, HUH?
THE VASCULAR NETWORK IS NO LONGER BRINGING THE BLOOD FROM THE LIMBS BACK UP... THE SYSTEM IS FLOODING!

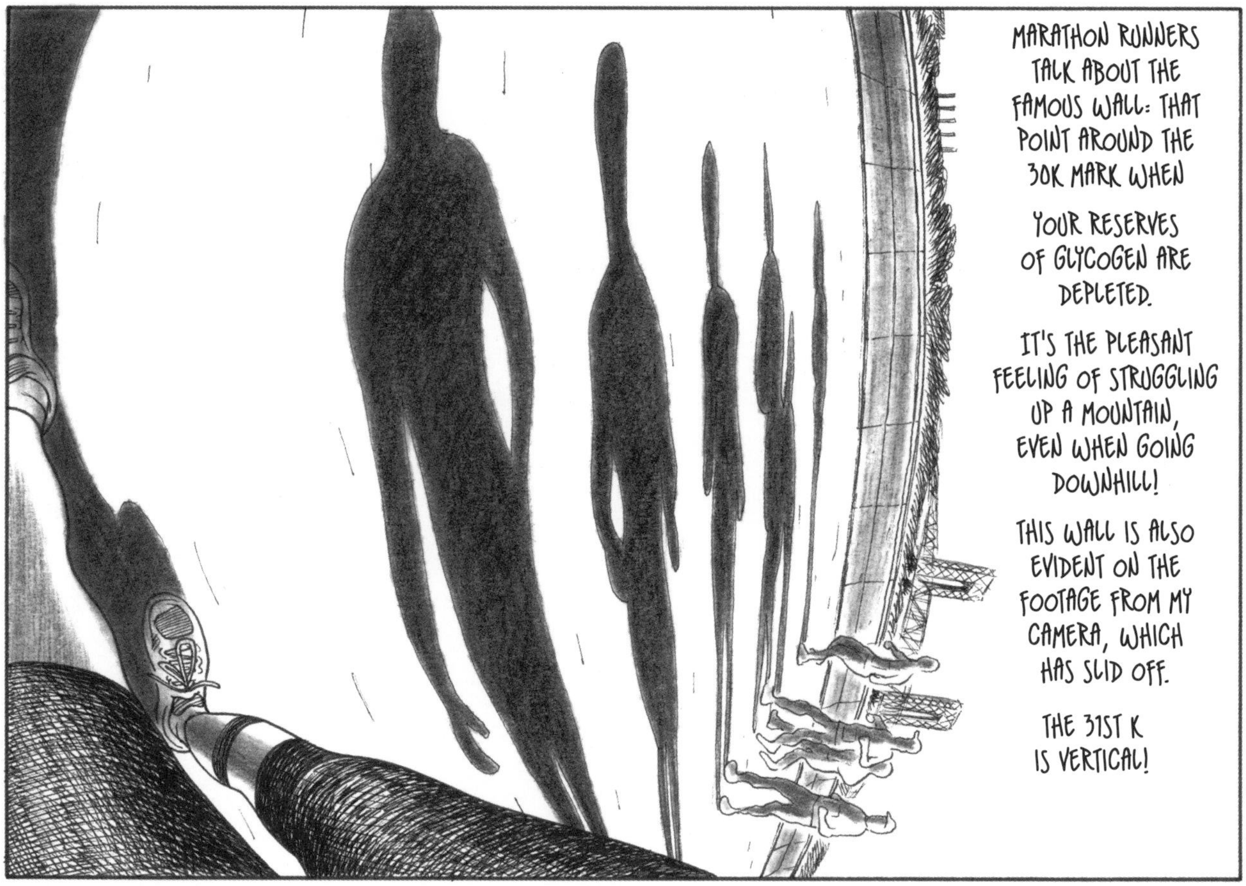
MARATHON RUNNERS TALK ABOUT THE FAMOUS WALL: THAT POINT AROUND THE 30K MARK WHEN
YOUR RESERVES OF GLYCOGEN ARE DEPLETED.
IT'S THE PLEASANT FEELING OF STRUGGLING UP A MOUNTAIN, EVEN WHEN GOING DOWNHILL!
THIS WALL IS ALSO EVIDENT ON THE FOOTAGE FROM MY CAMERA, WHICH HAS SLID OFF.
THE 31ST K IS VERTICAL!

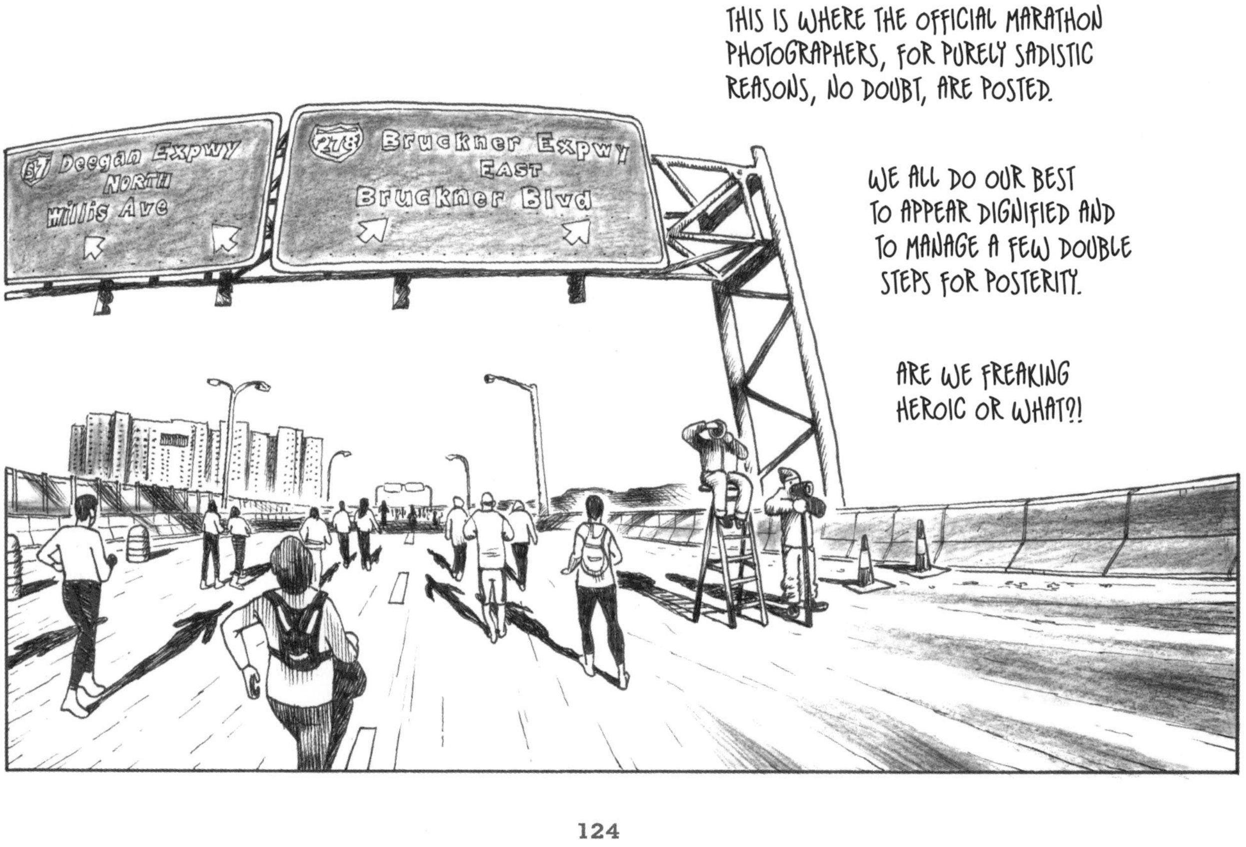
THIS IS WHERE THE OFFICIAL MARATHON PHOTOGRAPHERS, FOR PURELY SADISTIC REASONS, NO DOUBT, ARE POSTED.
87 Deegan Expwy NORTH Willis Ave
278 Bruckner Expwy EAST Bruckner Blvd
WE ALL DO OUR BEST TO APPEAR DIGNIFIED AND TO MANAGE A FEW DOUBLE STEPS FOR POSTERITY.
ARE WE FREAKING HEROIC OR WHAT?!

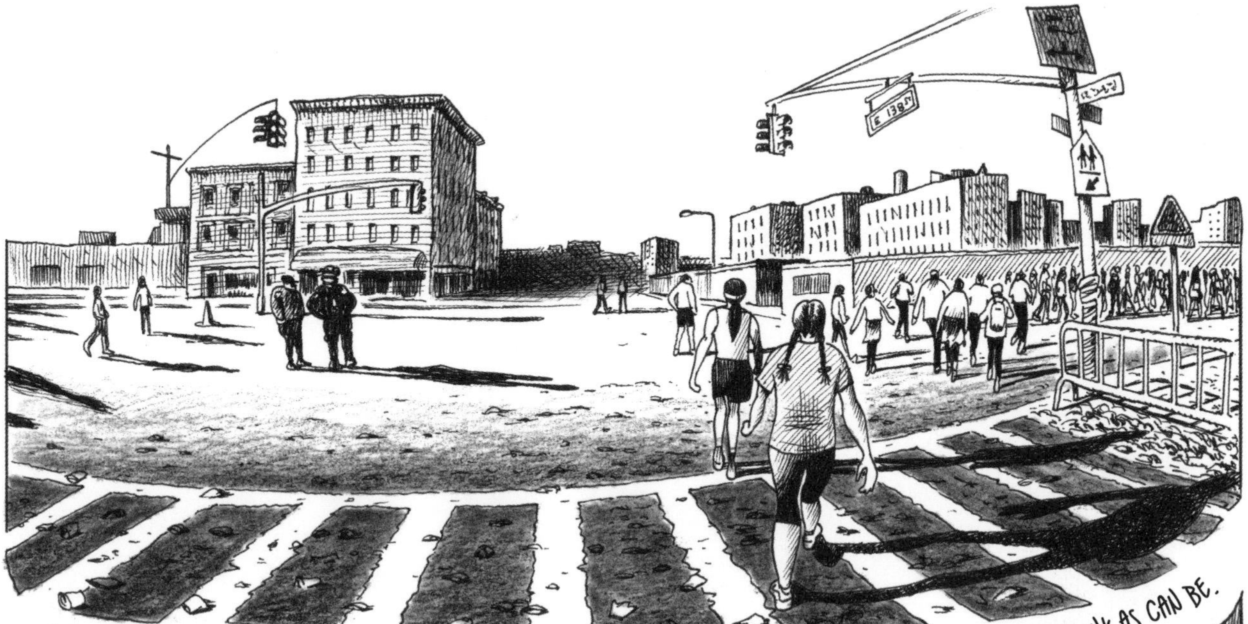

Ten kilometers from the finish line, the fifth and last city borough welcomes us: the Bronx, as Bronx as can be.

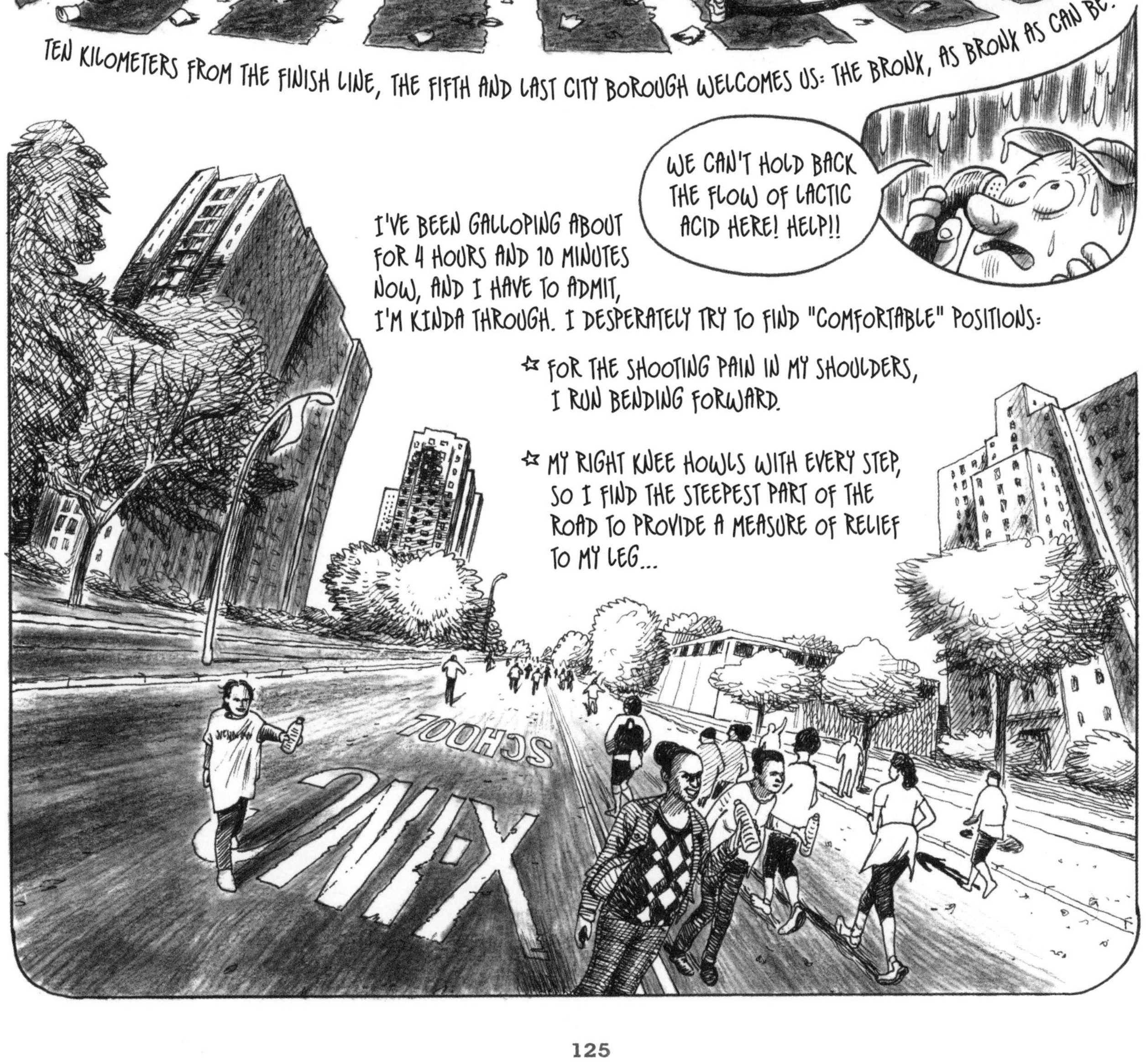

We can't hold back the flow of lactic acid here! Help!!
I've been galloping about for 4 hours and 10 minutes now, and I have to admit, I'm kinda through. I desperately try to find "comfortable" positions:
☆ For the shooting pain in my shoulders, I run bending forward.
☆ My right knee howls with every step, so I find the steepest part of the road to provide a measure of relief to my leg...

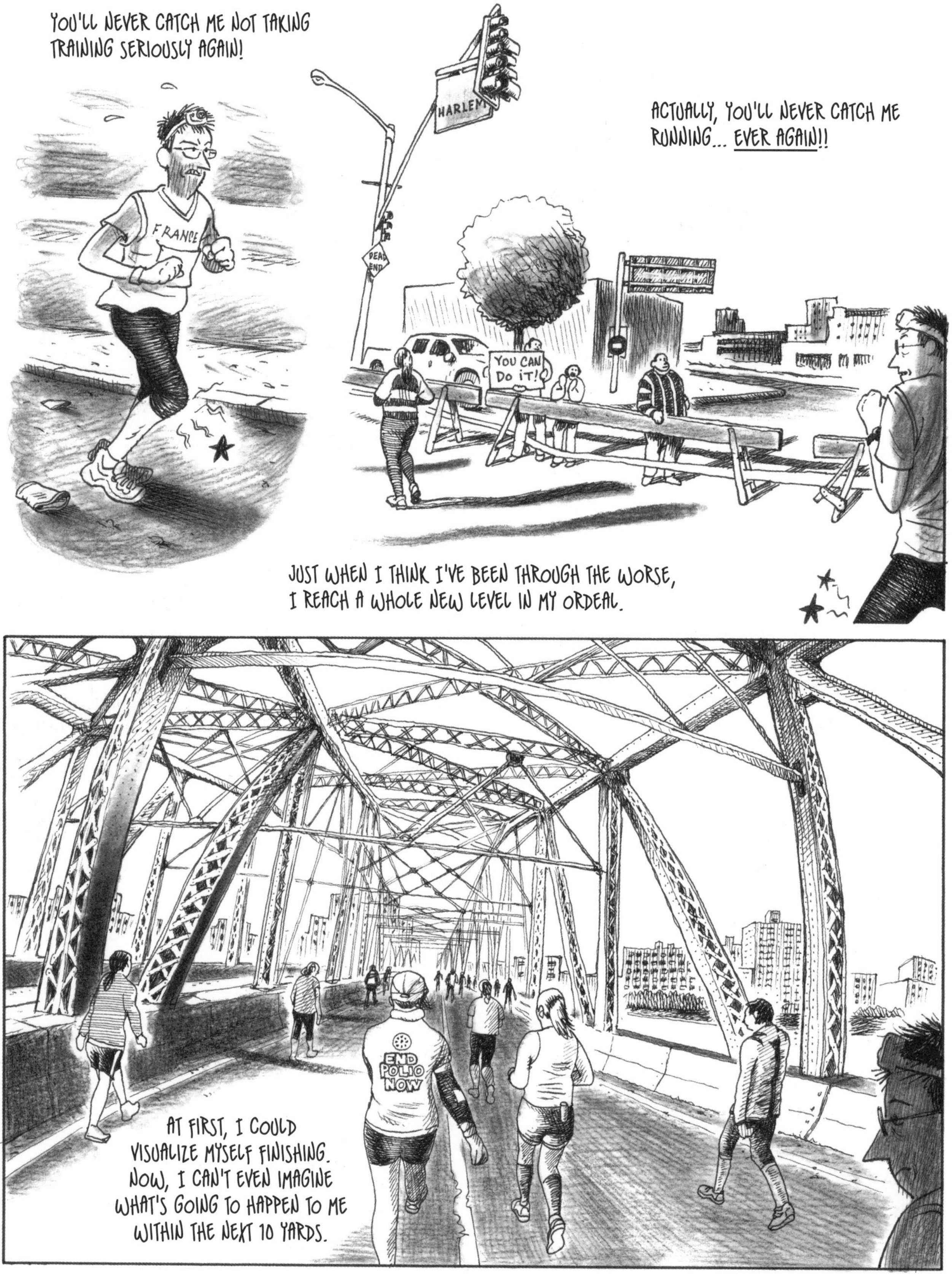
YOU'LL NEVER CATCH ME NOT TAKING TRAINING SERIOUSLY AGAIN!
FRANCE
HARLEM
ACTUALLY, YOU'LL NEVER CATCH ME RUNNING... EVER AGAIN!!
YOU CAN DO IT!
JUST WHEN I THINK I'VE BEEN THROUGH THE WORSE, I REACH A WHOLE NEW LEVEL IN MY ORDEAL.
END POLIO NOW
AT FIRST, I COULD VISUALIZE MYSELF FINISHING. NOW, I CAN'T EVEN IMAGINE WHAT'S GOING TO HAPPEN TO ME WITHIN THE NEXT 10 YARDS.

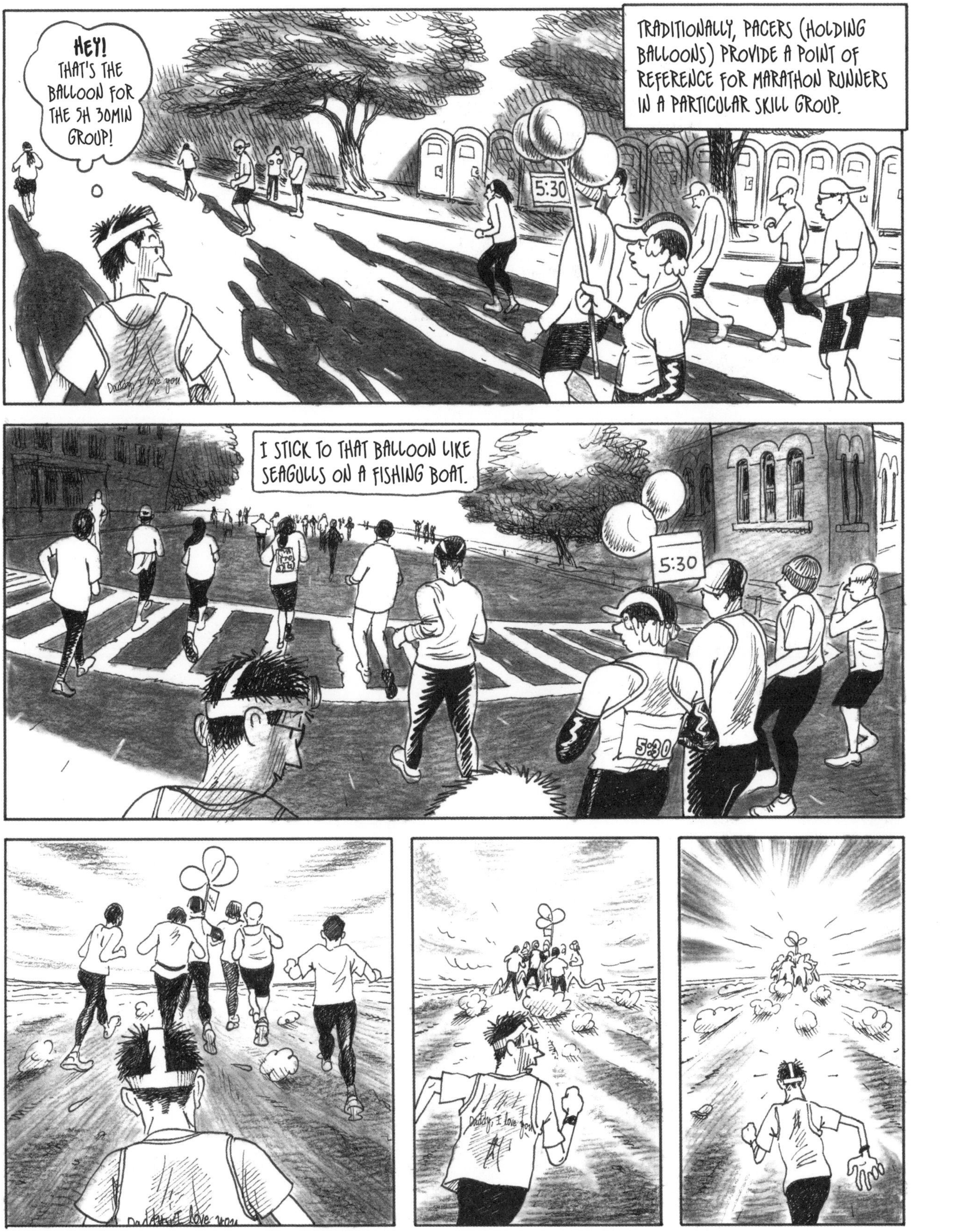
HEY! THAT'S THE BALLOON FOR THE 5H 30MIN GROUP!
TRADITIONALLY, PACERS (HOLDING BALLOONS) PROVIDE A POINT OF REFERENCE FOR MARATHON RUNNERS IN A PARTICULAR SKILL GROUP.
5:30
Daddy, I love you
I STICK TO THAT BALLOON LIKE SEAGULLS ON A FISHING BOAT.
5:30
5:30
Daddy, I love you

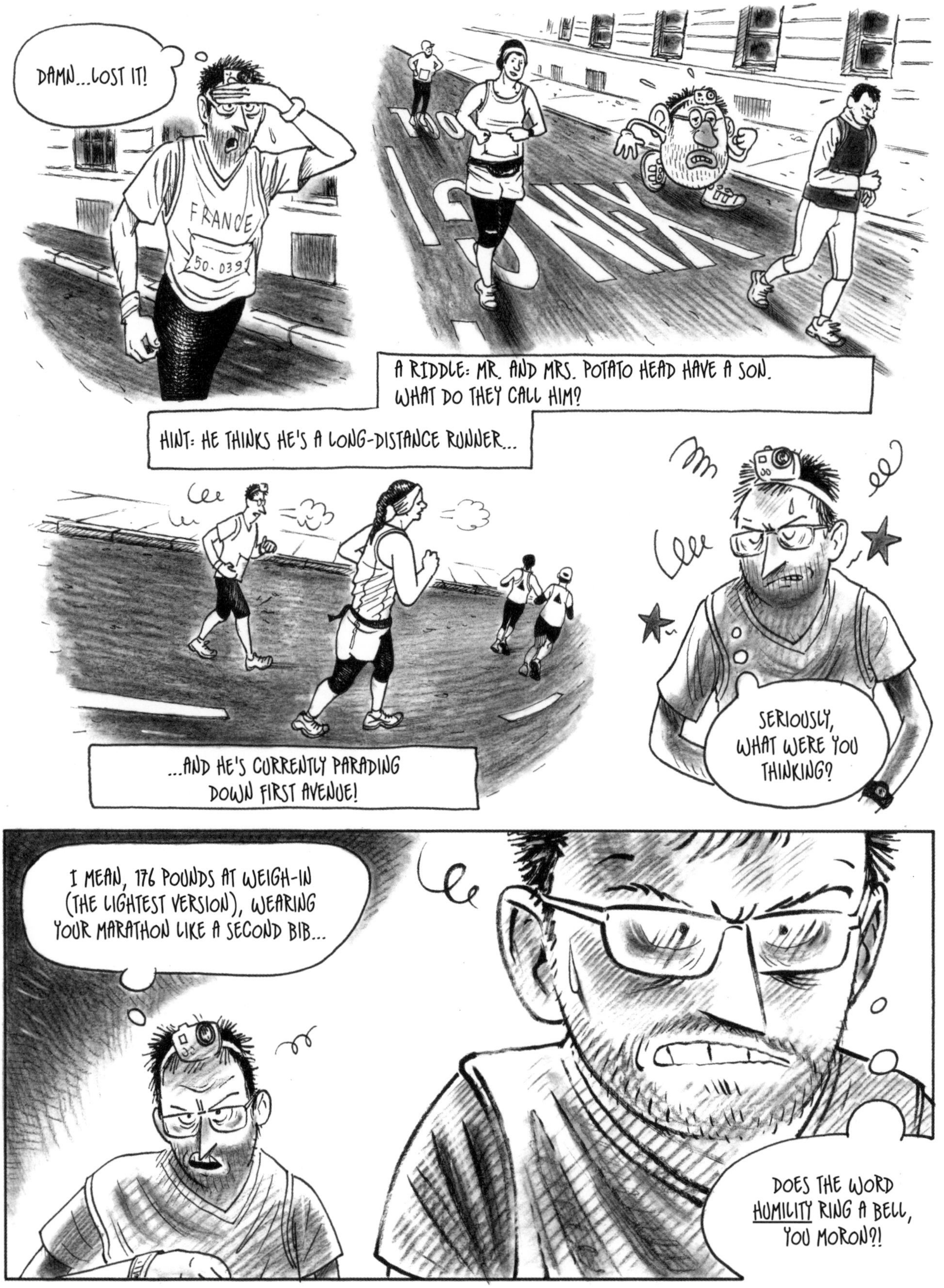
DAMN...LOST IT!
FRANCE
50.039
A RIDDLE: MR. AND MRS. POTATO HEAD HAVE A SON. WHAT DO THEY CALL HIM?
HINT: HE THINKS HE'S A LONG-DISTANCE RUNNER...
...AND HE'S CURRENTLY PARADING DOWN FIRST AVENUE!
SERIOUSLY, WHAT WERE YOU THINKING?
I MEAN, 176 POUNDS AT WEIGH-IN (THE LIGHTEST VERSION), WEARING YOUR MARATHON LIKE A SECOND BIB...
DOES THE WORD HUMILITY RING A BELL, YOU MORON?!

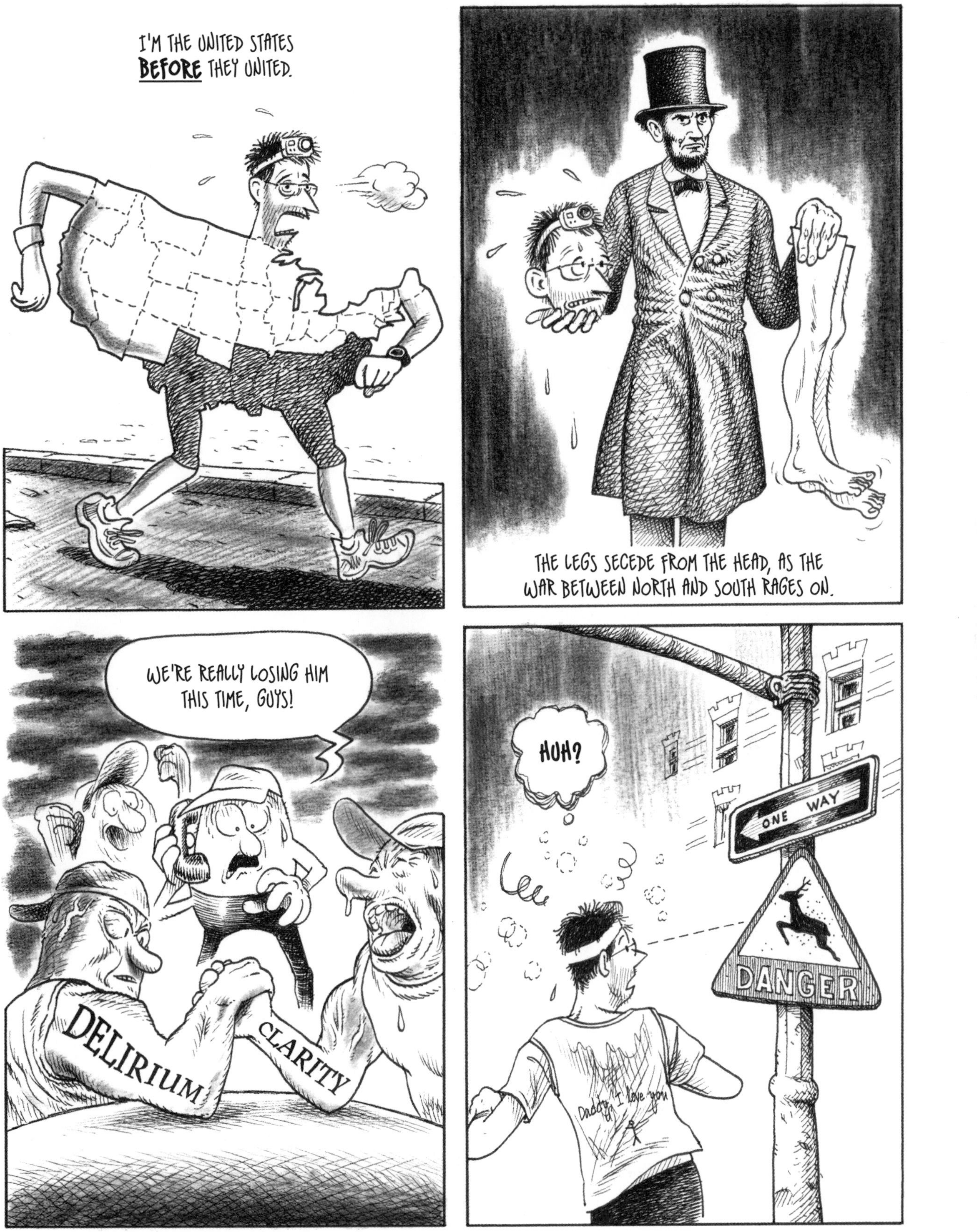
I'M THE UNITED STATES BEFORE THEY UNITED.
THE LEGS SECEDE FROM THE HEAD, AS THE WAR BETWEEN NORTH AND SOUTH RAGES ON.
WE'RE REALLY LOSING HIM THIS TIME, GUYS!
DELIRIUM
CLARITY
HUH?
ONE WAY
DANGER
Daddy I love you

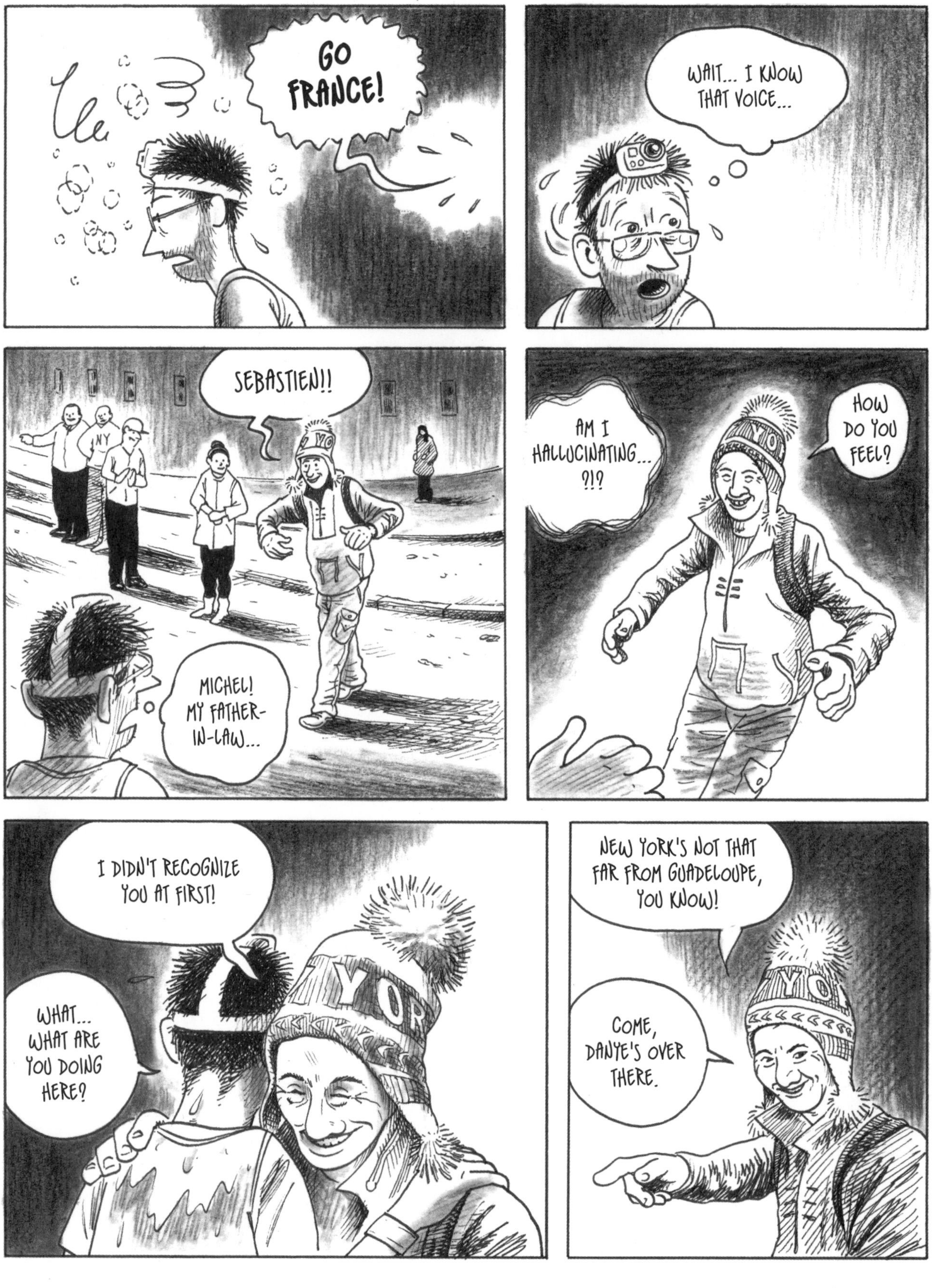
GO FRANCE!
WAIT... I KNOW THAT VOICE...
SEBASTIEN!!
MICHEL! MY FATHER-IN-LAW...
AM I HALLUCINATING... ?!?
HOW DO YOU FEEL?
I DIDN'T RECOGNIZE YOU AT FIRST!
WHAT... WHAT ARE YOU DOING HERE?
NEW YORK'S NOT THAT FAR FROM GUADELOUPE, YOU KNOW!
COME, DANYE'S OVER THERE.

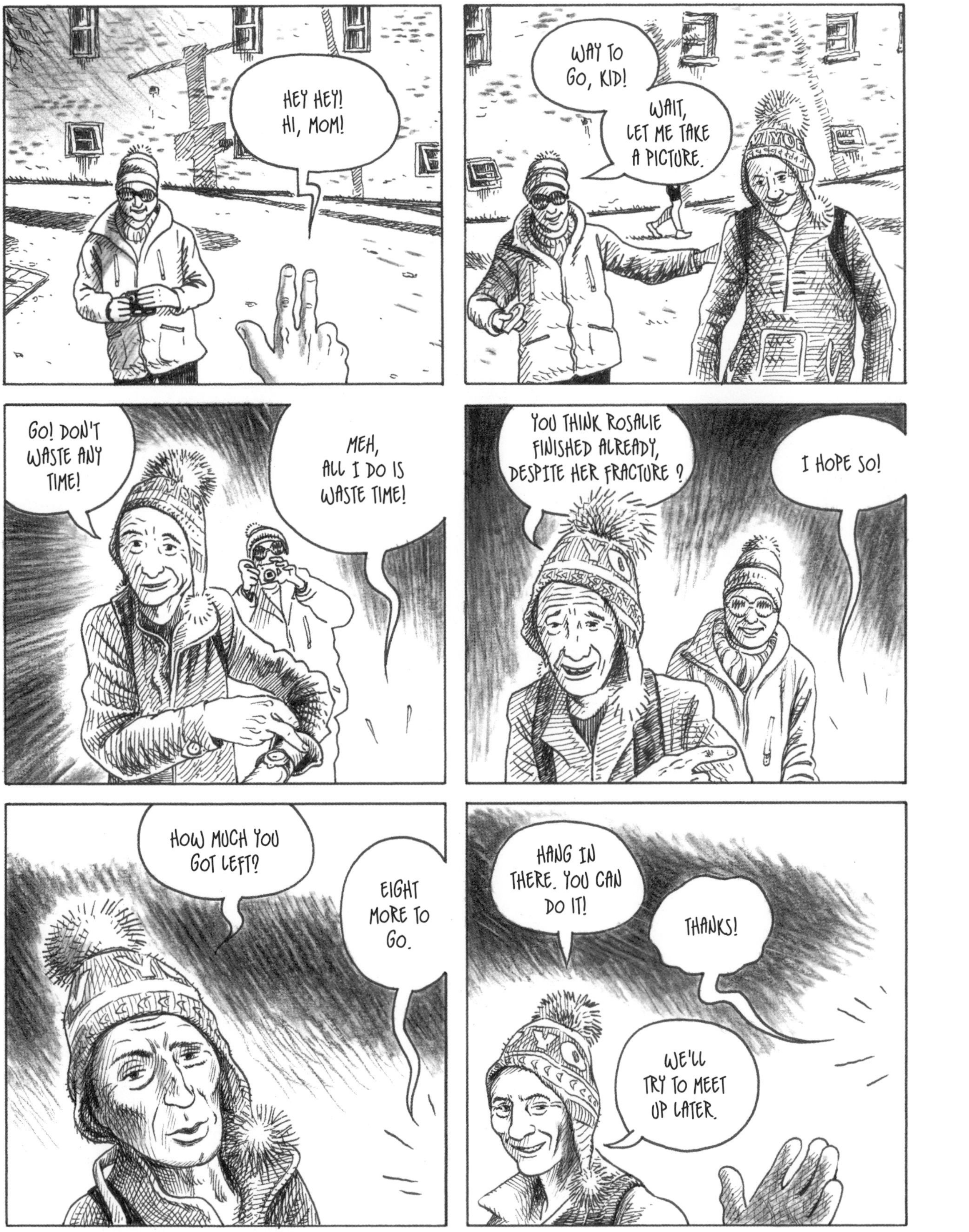
HEY HEY! HI, MOM!
WAY TO GO, KID!
WAIT, LET ME TAKE A PICTURE.
GO! DON'T WASTE ANY TIME!
MEH, ALL I DO IS WASTE TIME!
YOU THINK ROSALIE FINISHED ALREADY, DESPITE HER FRACTURE ?
I HOPE SO!
HOW MUCH YOU GOT LEFT?
EIGHT MORE TO GO.
HANG IN THERE. YOU CAN DO IT!
THANKS!
WE'LL TRY TO MEET UP LATER.

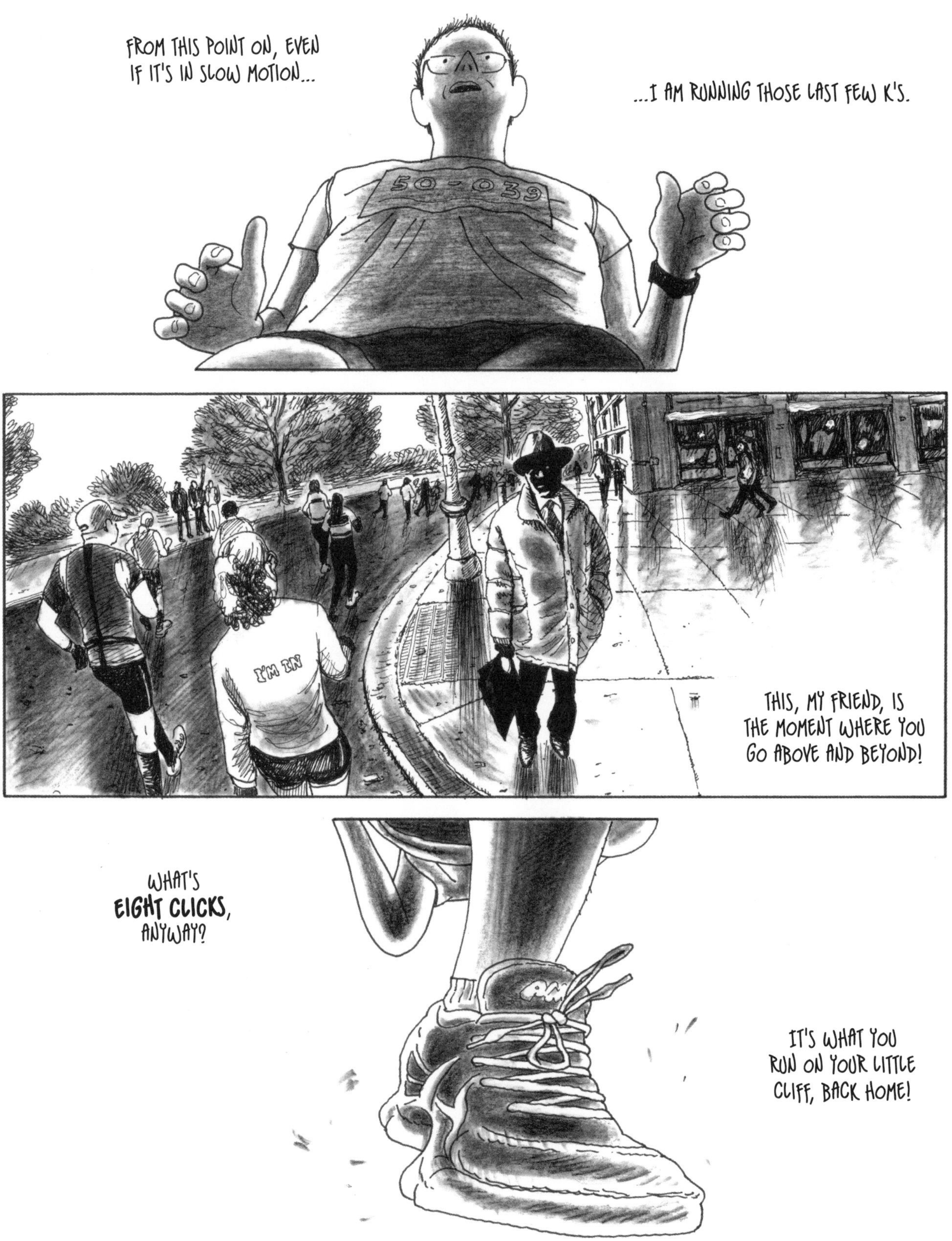
FROM THIS POINT ON, EVEN IF IT'S IN SLOW MOTION...
...I AM RUNNING THOSE LAST FEW K'S.
50-039
I'M IN
THIS, MY FRIEND, IS THE MOMENT WHERE YOU GO ABOVE AND BEYOND!
WHAT'S **EIGHT CLICKS,** ANYWAY?
IT'S WHAT YOU RUN ON YOUR LITTLE CLIFF, BACK HOME!

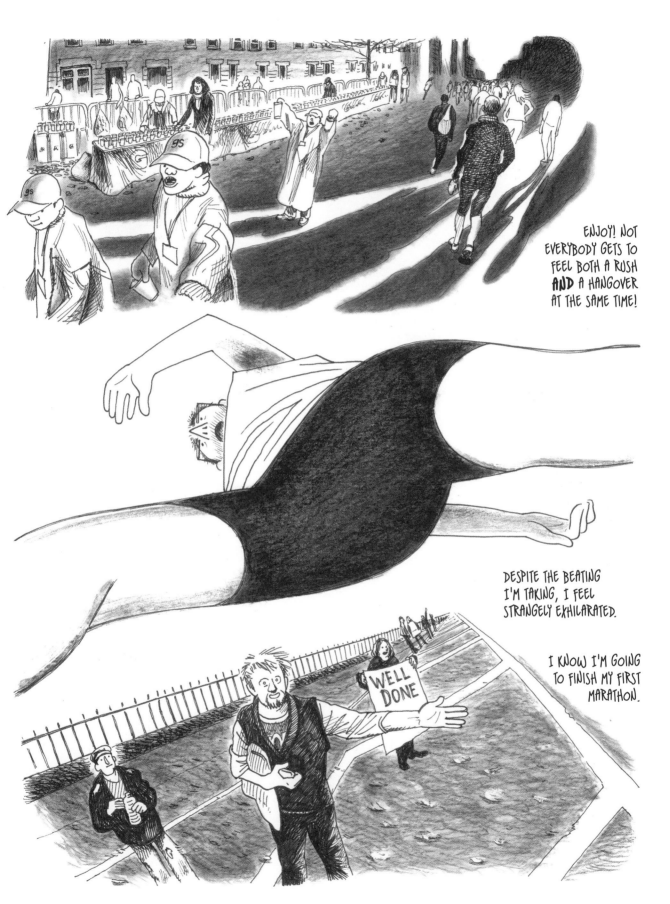

ENJOY! NOT EVERYBODY GETS TO FEEL BOTH A RUSH **AND** A HANGOVER AT THE SAME TIME!

DESPITE THE BEATING I'M TAKING, I FEEL STRANGELY EXHILARATED.

I KNOW I'M GOING TO FINISH MY FIRST MARATHON.

WELL DONE

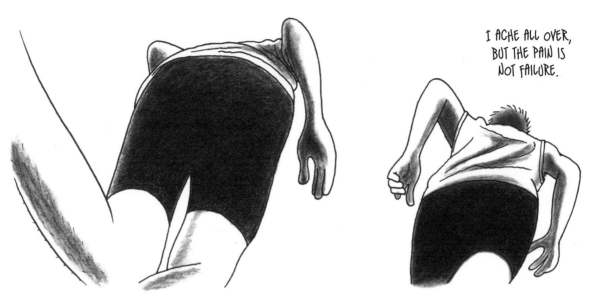

I ACHE ALL OVER, BUT THE PAIN IS NOT FAILURE.

THE EXHAUSTION WILL VANISH IN A FEW DAYS, AND ONLY THE KNOWLEDGE THAT I SUCCEEDED IN MY MAD ENTERPRISE WILL REMAIN.

I RUN PAST EACH MILE MARKER LIKE AN ENDING AND A NEW BEGINNING.

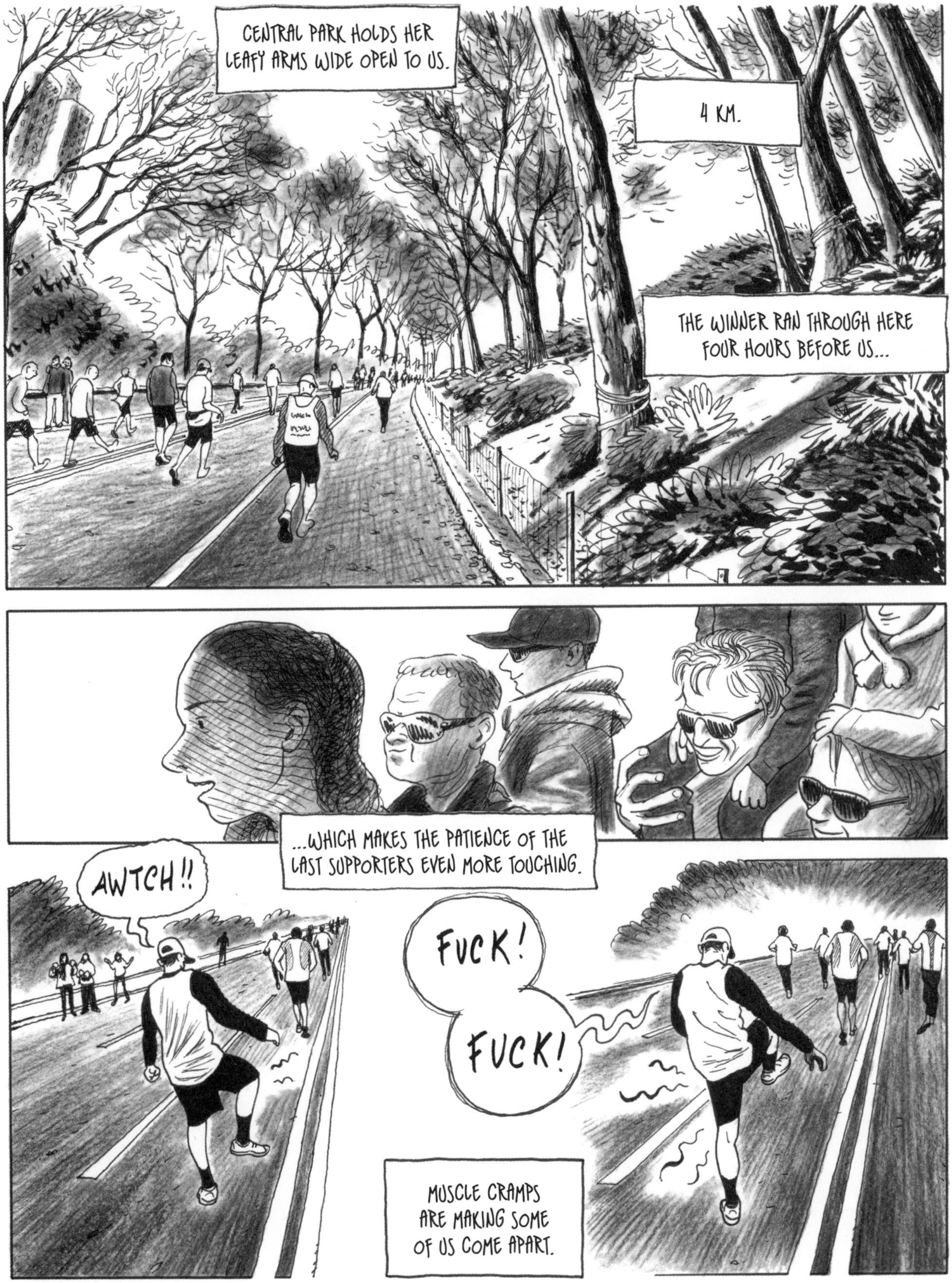
CENTRAL PARK HOLDS HER LEAFY ARMS WIDE OPEN TO US.
4 KM.
THE WINNER RAN THROUGH HERE FOUR HOURS BEFORE US...
...WHICH MAKES THE PATIENCE OF THE LAST SUPPORTERS EVEN MORE TOUCHING.
AWTCH!!
FUCK!
FUCK!
MUSCLE CRAMPS ARE MAKING SOME OF US COME APART.

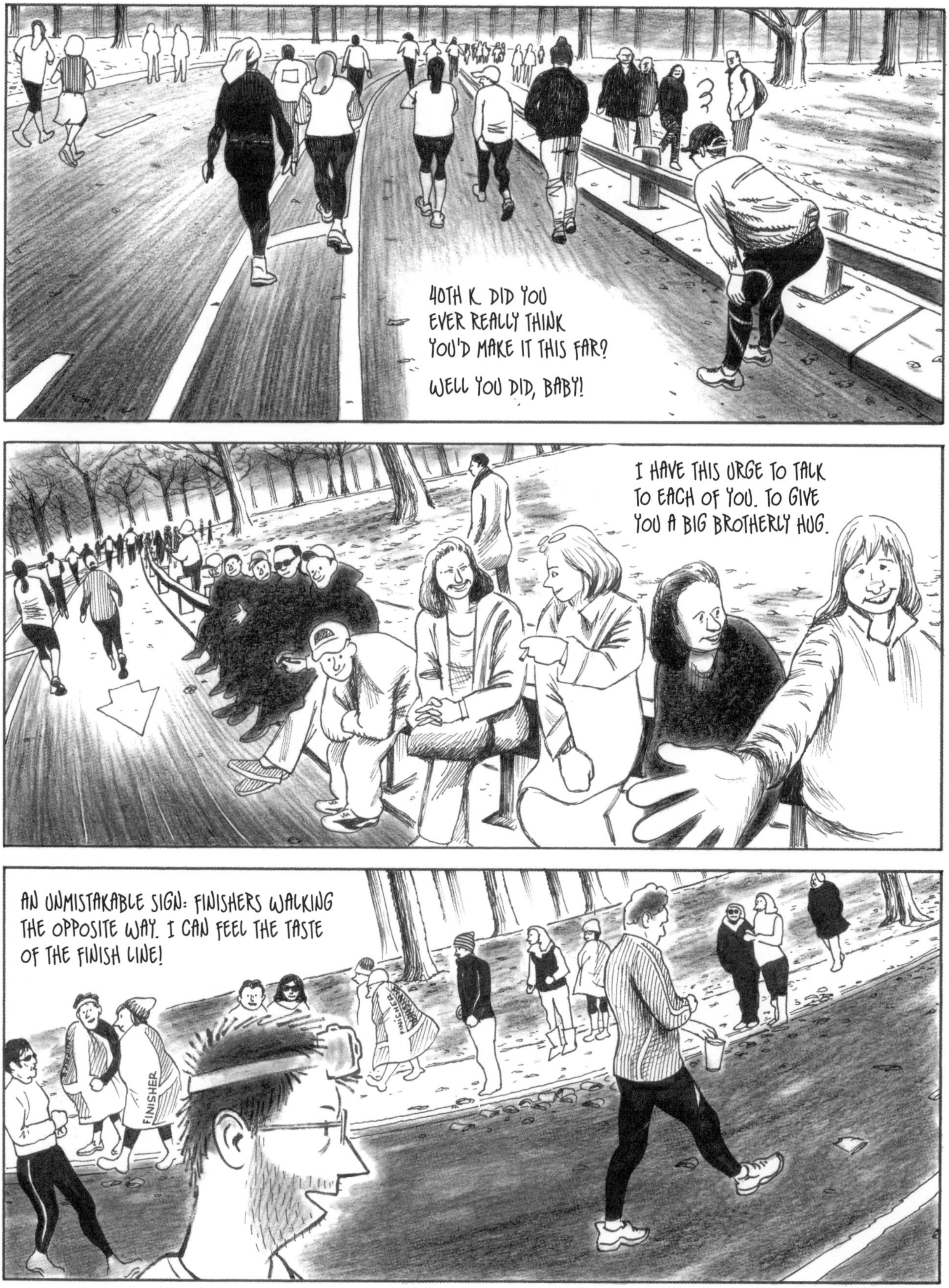
40TH K. DID YOU EVER REALLY THINK YOU'D MAKE IT THIS FAR?
WELL YOU DID, BABY!
I HAVE THIS URGE TO TALK TO EACH OF YOU. TO GIVE YOU A BIG BROTHERLY HUG.
AN UNMISTAKABLE SIGN: FINISHERS WALKING THE OPPOSITE WAY. I CAN FEEL THE TASTE OF THE FINISH LINE!
FINISHER
FINISHER

PAIN IS TEMPORARY PRIDE IS PERMANENT

RUN

YOU'RE ABSOLUTELY RIGHT, MAN. PAIN IS TEMPORARY... MY HEAD BELIEVES YOU, BUT THE REST OF ME, NOT SO MUCH!

ONE MORE MILE AND I WILL BE LIBERATED...

MY RUN TIME MATTERS LESS THAN EVER.

LIVING THE INTENSITY OF THE MOMENT IS THE ONLY THING THAT DOES.

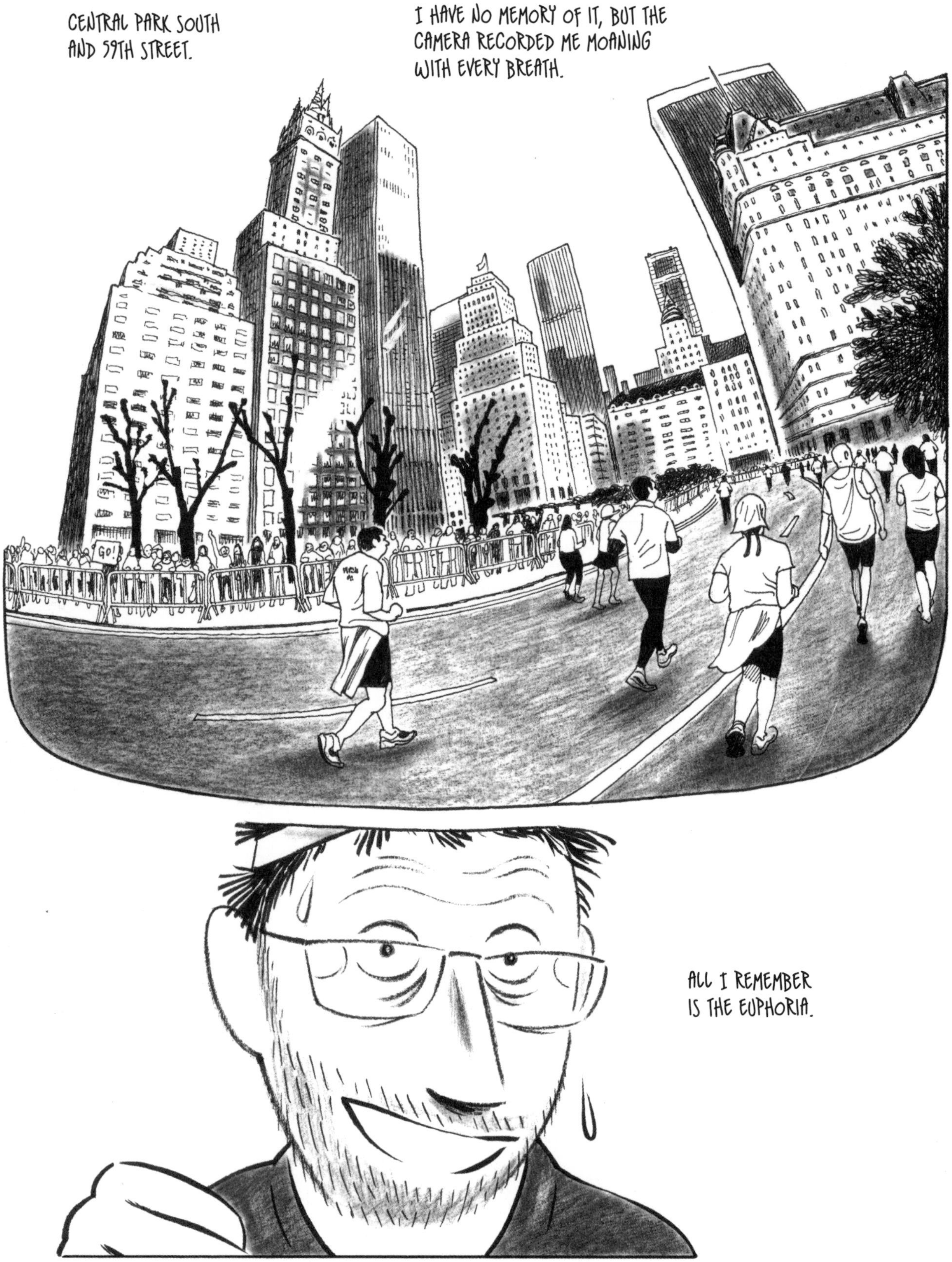
CENTRAL PARK SOUTH AND 59TH STREET.
I HAVE NO MEMORY OF IT, BUT THE CAMERA RECORDED ME MOANING WITH EVERY BREATH.
GO!
ALL I REMEMBER IS THE EUPHORIA.

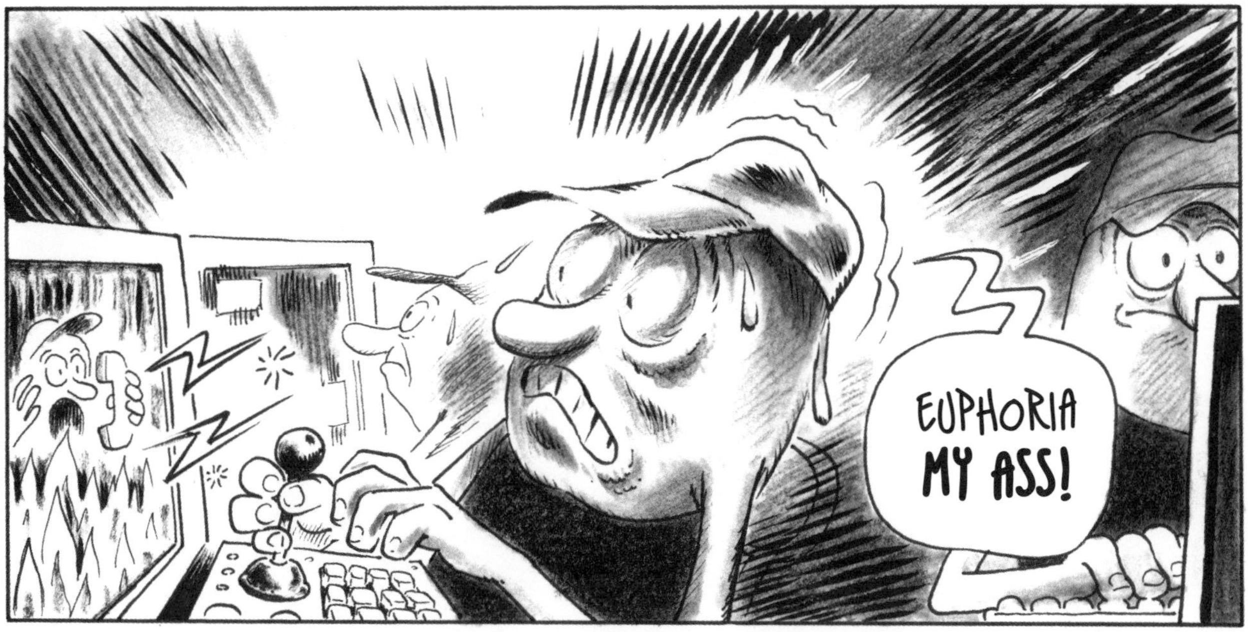
EUPHORIA MY ASS!

I NOW UNDERSTAND THE REASON FOR THOSE LAST TWO K'S PAST THE 40-K MARK...
THAT'S PAYDAY FOR THE MARATHON RUNNER. THE PART WHEN CHALLENGE TURNS INTO VICTORY.

EVERY STEP HURTS, EVERY STEP COUNTS.

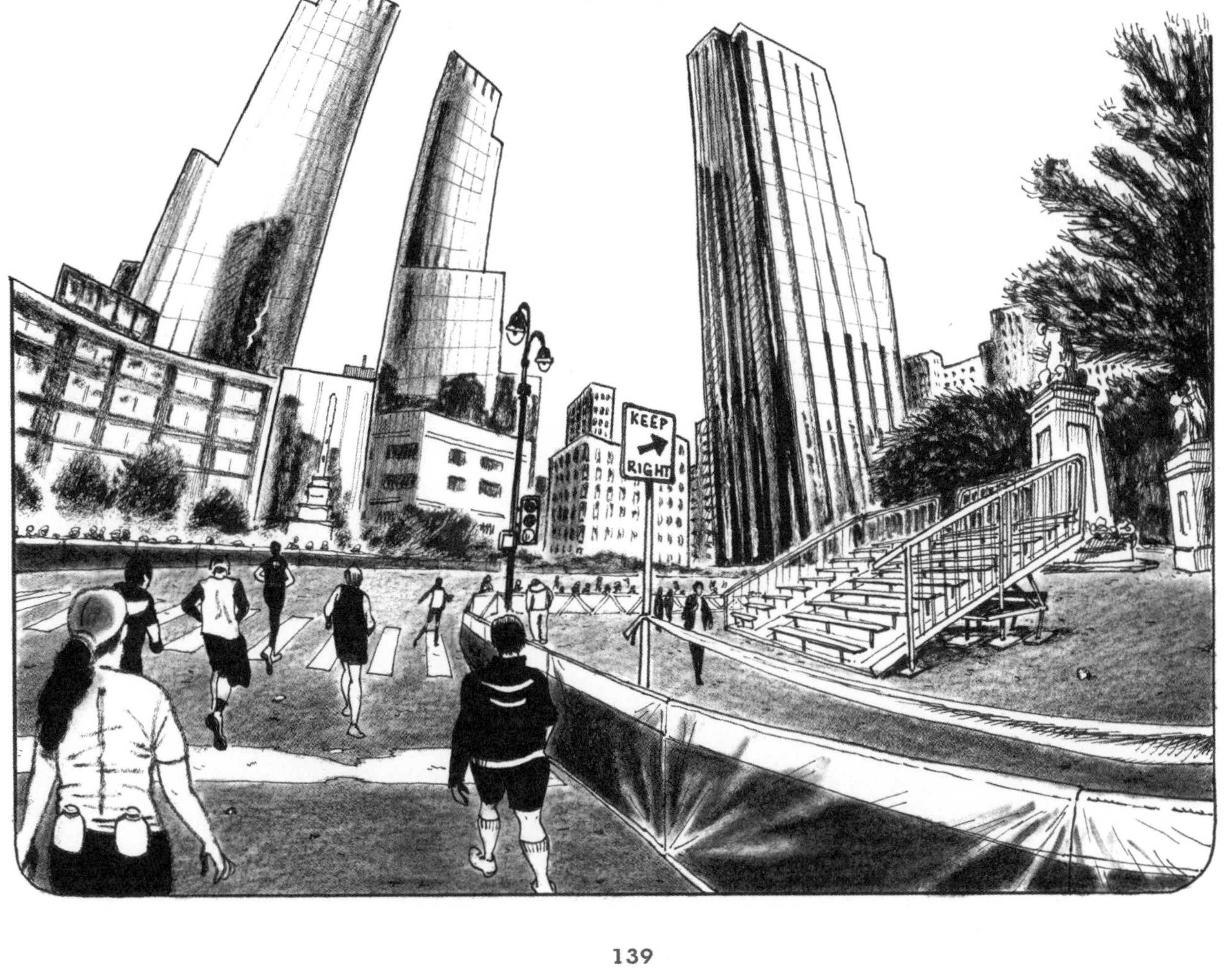
KEEP
RIGHT

400
meters to GO
NYRR
MARATHON
I SEE YOU DARLING
THE NEW YORK MARATHON
I'M SO PROUD OF YOU, KEEP GOING, YOU'RE ALMOST THERE!
...
ROSALIE!

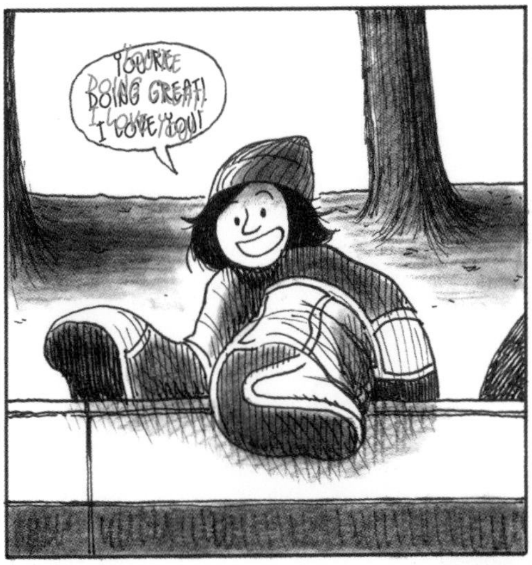
YOU'RE DOING GREAT! I LOVE YOU!

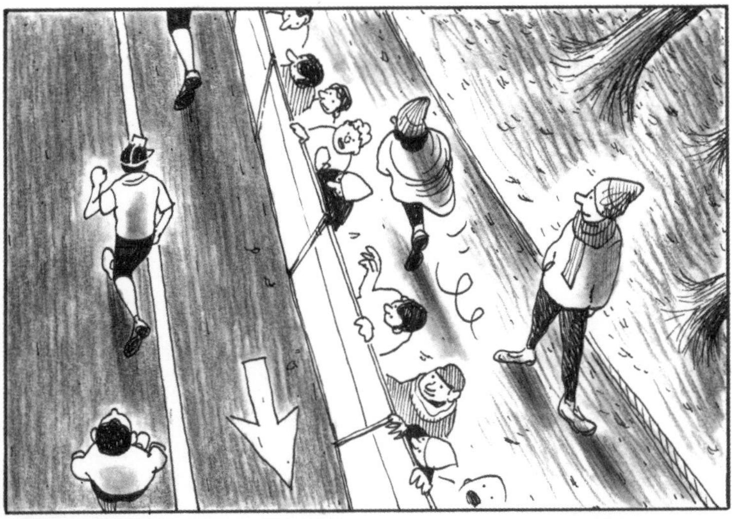

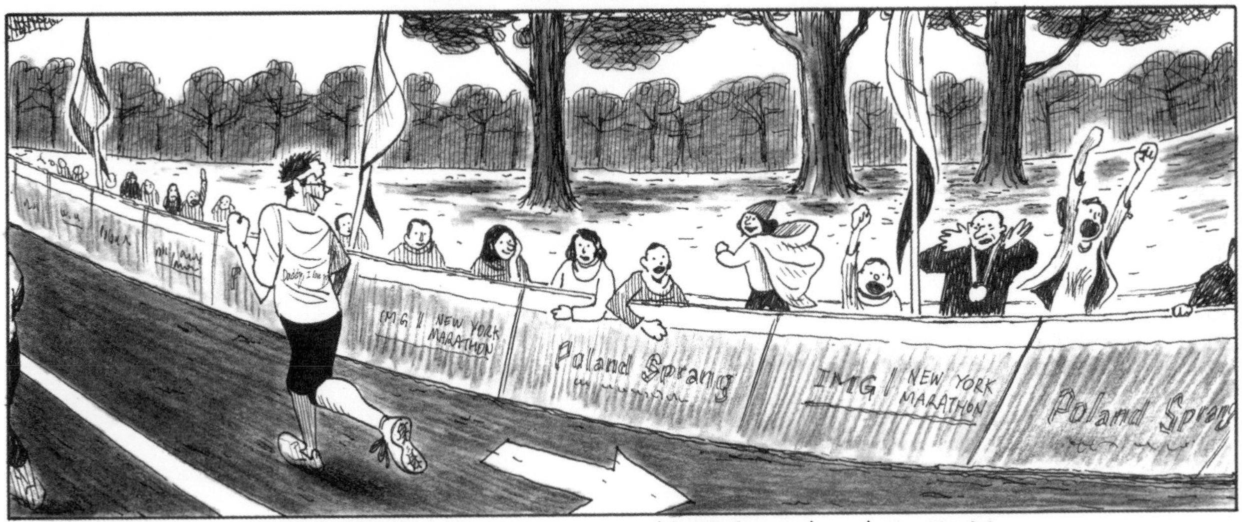
IMG NEW YORK MARATHON
Poland Spring
IMG NEW YORK MARATHON
Poland Spring

I DON'T REMEMBER THE WORDS WE EXCHANGED RIGHT THEN... ON THE CAMERA, ALL YOU CAN HEAR IS THE SOUND OF THE WIND AND THE CHEERS OF THE CROWD.

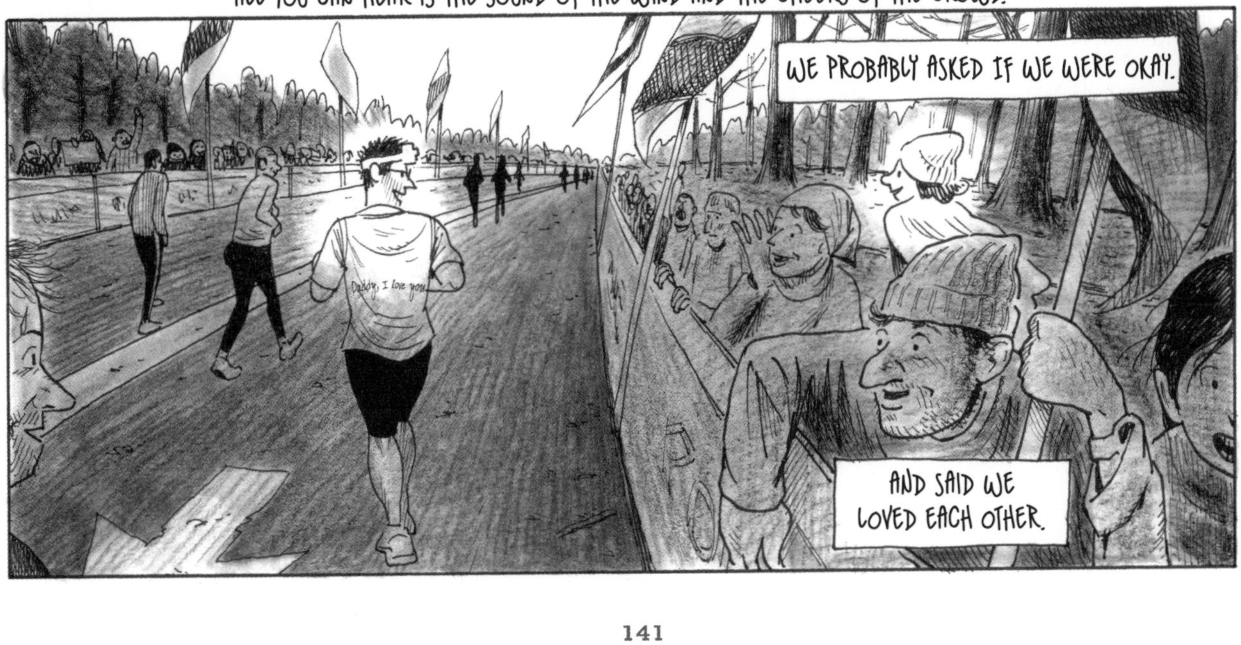
WE PROBABLY ASKED IF WE WERE OKAY.
AND SAID WE LOVED EACH OTHER.

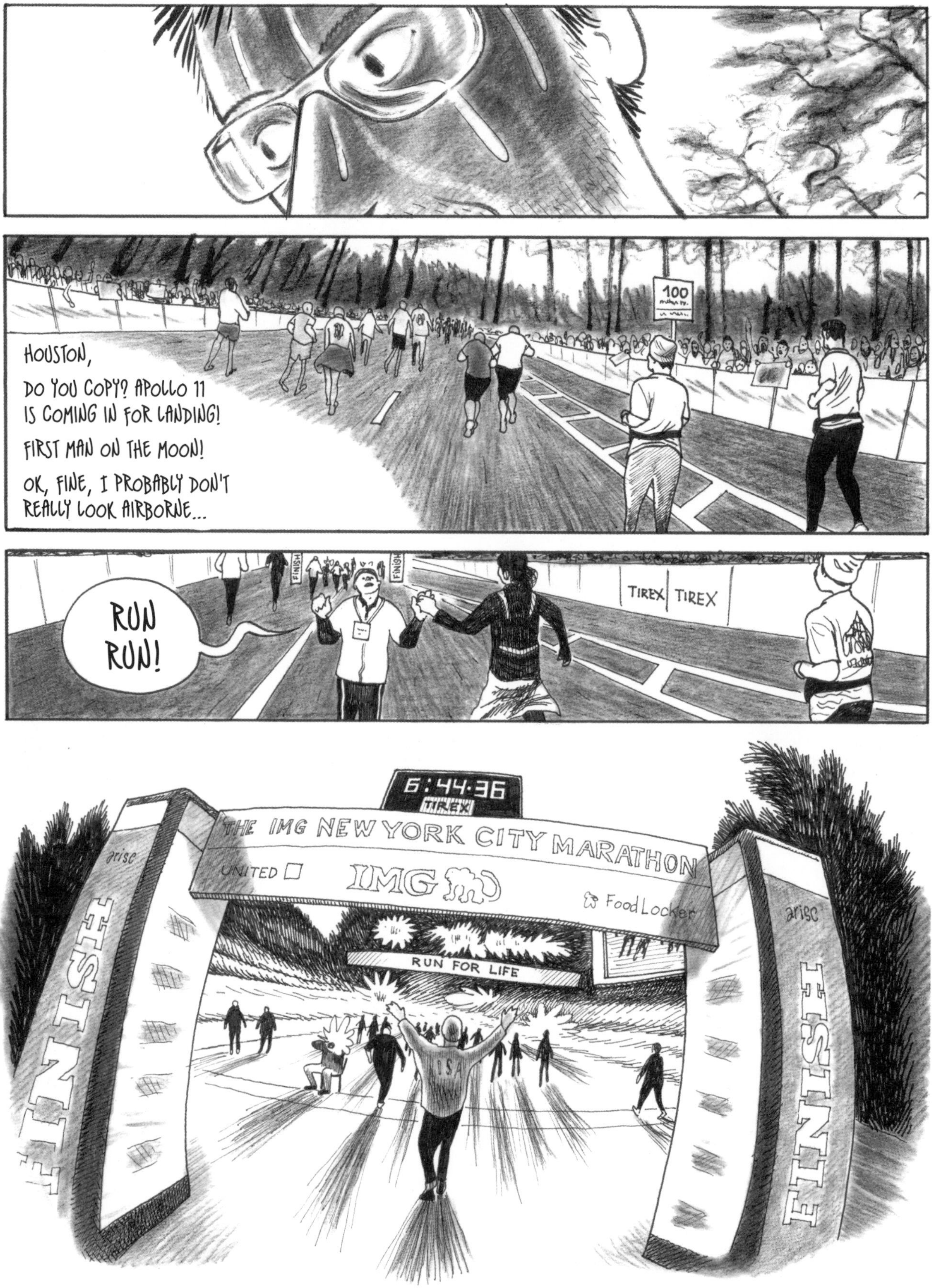
100
HOUSTON,
DO YOU COPY? APOLLO 11 IS COMING IN FOR LANDING!
FIRST MAN ON THE MOON!
OK, FINE, I PROBABLY DON'T REALLY LOOK AIRBORNE...
FINISH
TIREX TIREX
RUN RUN!
6:44:36
TIREX
THE IMG NEW YORK CITY MARATHON
UNITED
IMG
FoodLocker
RUN FOR LIFE
arise
FINISH
arise
FINISH
USA

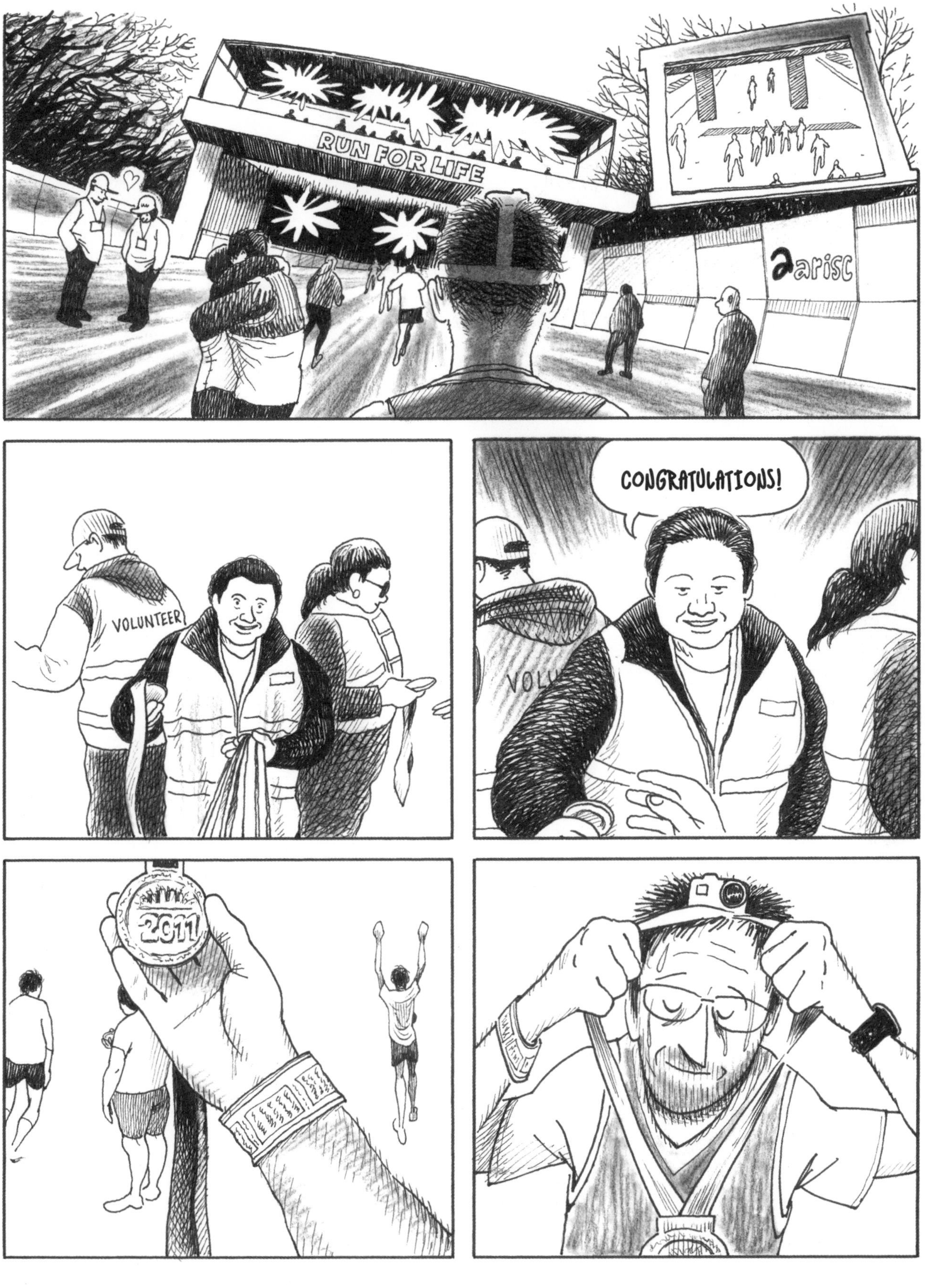
RUN FOR LIFE
arisc
VOLUNTEER
CONGRATULATIONS!
2011

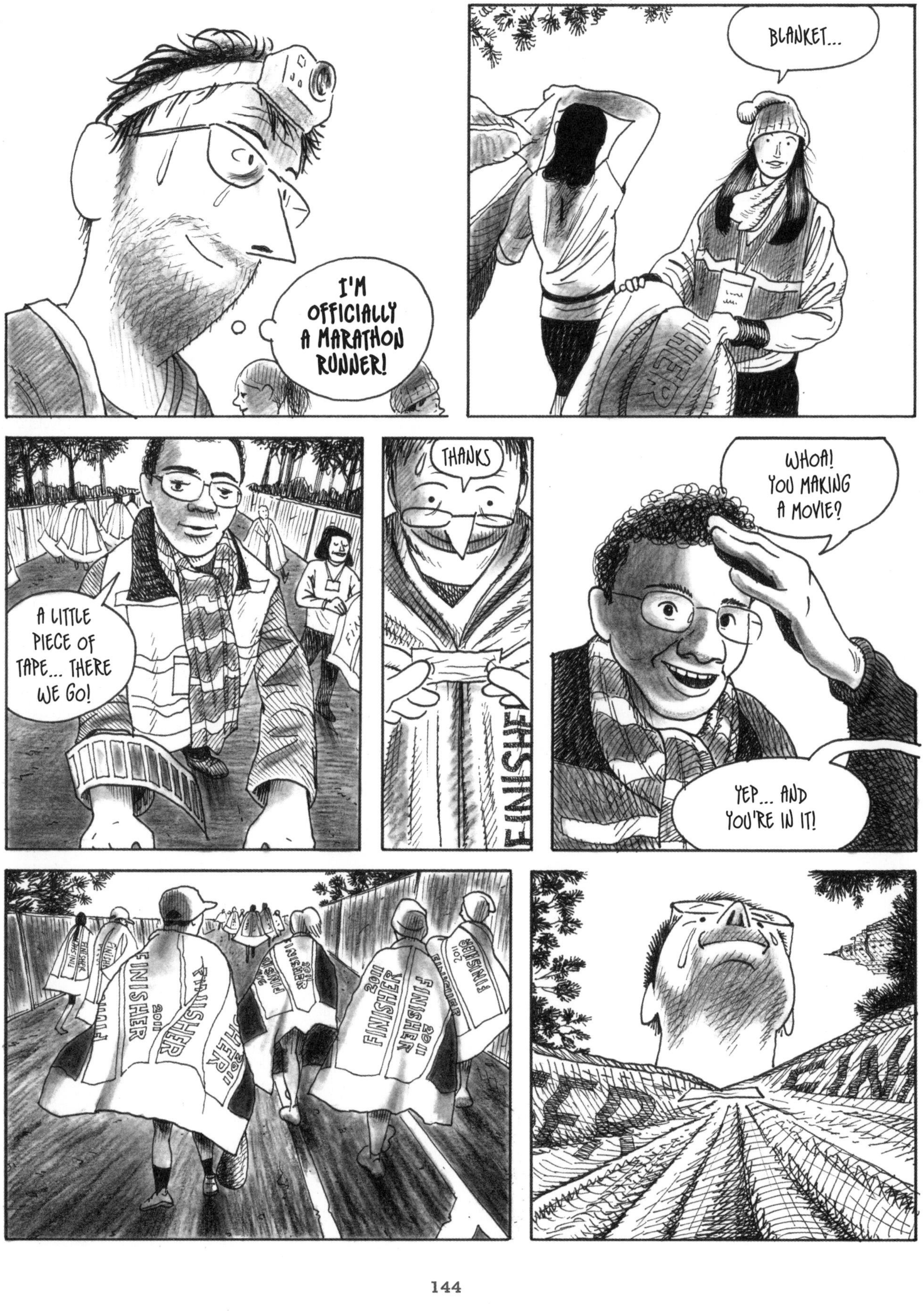
I'M OFFICIALLY A MARATHON RUNNER!
BLANKET...
A LITTLE PIECE OF TAPE... THERE WE GO!
THANKS
FINISHER
WHOA! YOU MAKING A MOVIE?
YEP... AND YOU'RE IN IT!
FINISHER 2011

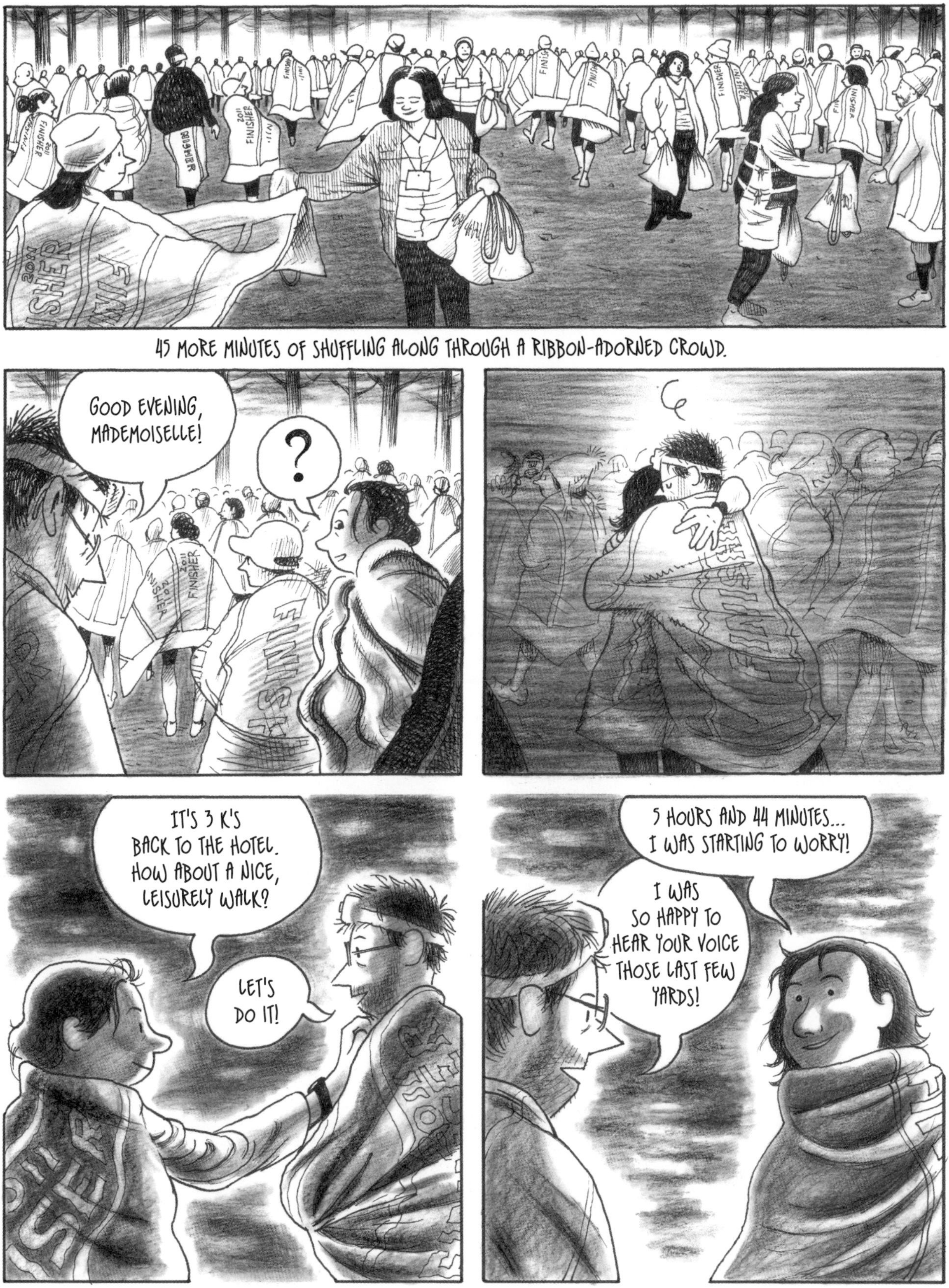
FINISHER
2011 FINISHER
45 MORE MINUTES OF SHUFFLING ALONG THROUGH A RIBBON-ADORNED CROWD.
GOOD EVENING, MADEMOISELLE!
?
IT'S 3 K'S BACK TO THE HOTEL. HOW ABOUT A NICE, LEISURELY WALK?
LET'S DO IT!
5 HOURS AND 44 MINUTES... I WAS STARTING TO WORRY!
I WAS SO HAPPY TO HEAR YOUR VOICE THOSE LAST FEW YARDS!

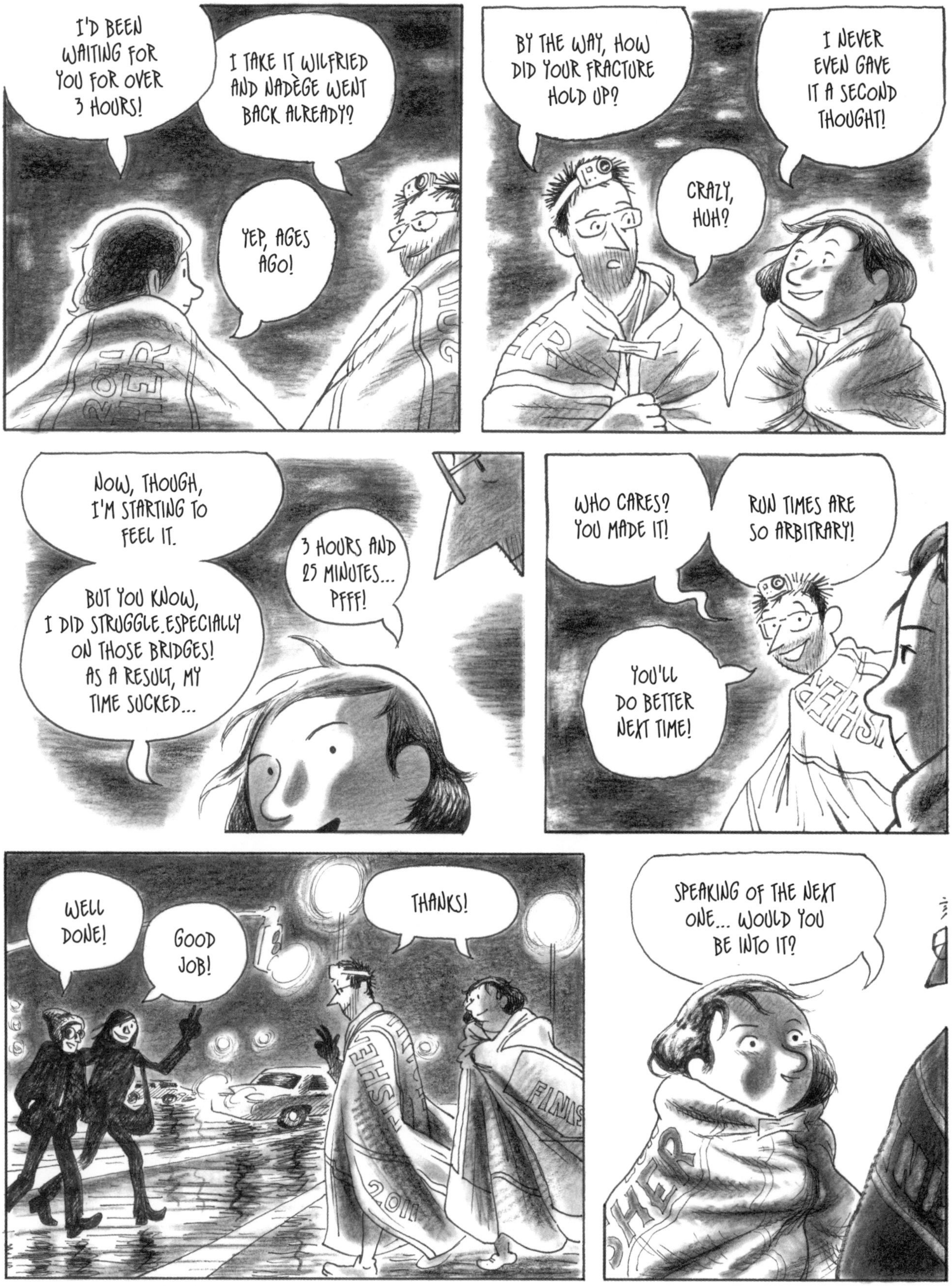
I'D BEEN WAITING FOR YOU FOR OVER 3 HOURS!
I TAKE IT WILFRIED AND NADÈGE WENT BACK ALREADY?
YEP, AGES AGO!
BY THE WAY, HOW DID YOUR FRACTURE HOLD UP?
CRAZY, HUH?
I NEVER EVEN GAVE IT A SECOND THOUGHT!
NOW, THOUGH, I'M STARTING TO FEEL IT.
BUT YOU KNOW, I DID STRUGGLE. ESPECIALLY ON THOSE BRIDGES! AS A RESULT, MY TIME SUCKED...
3 HOURS AND 25 MINUTES... PFFF!
WHO CARES? YOU MADE IT!
RUN TIMES ARE SO ARBITRARY!
YOU'LL DO BETTER NEXT TIME!
WELL DONE!
GOOD JOB!
THANKS!
SPEAKING OF THE NEXT ONE... WOULD YOU BE INTO IT?

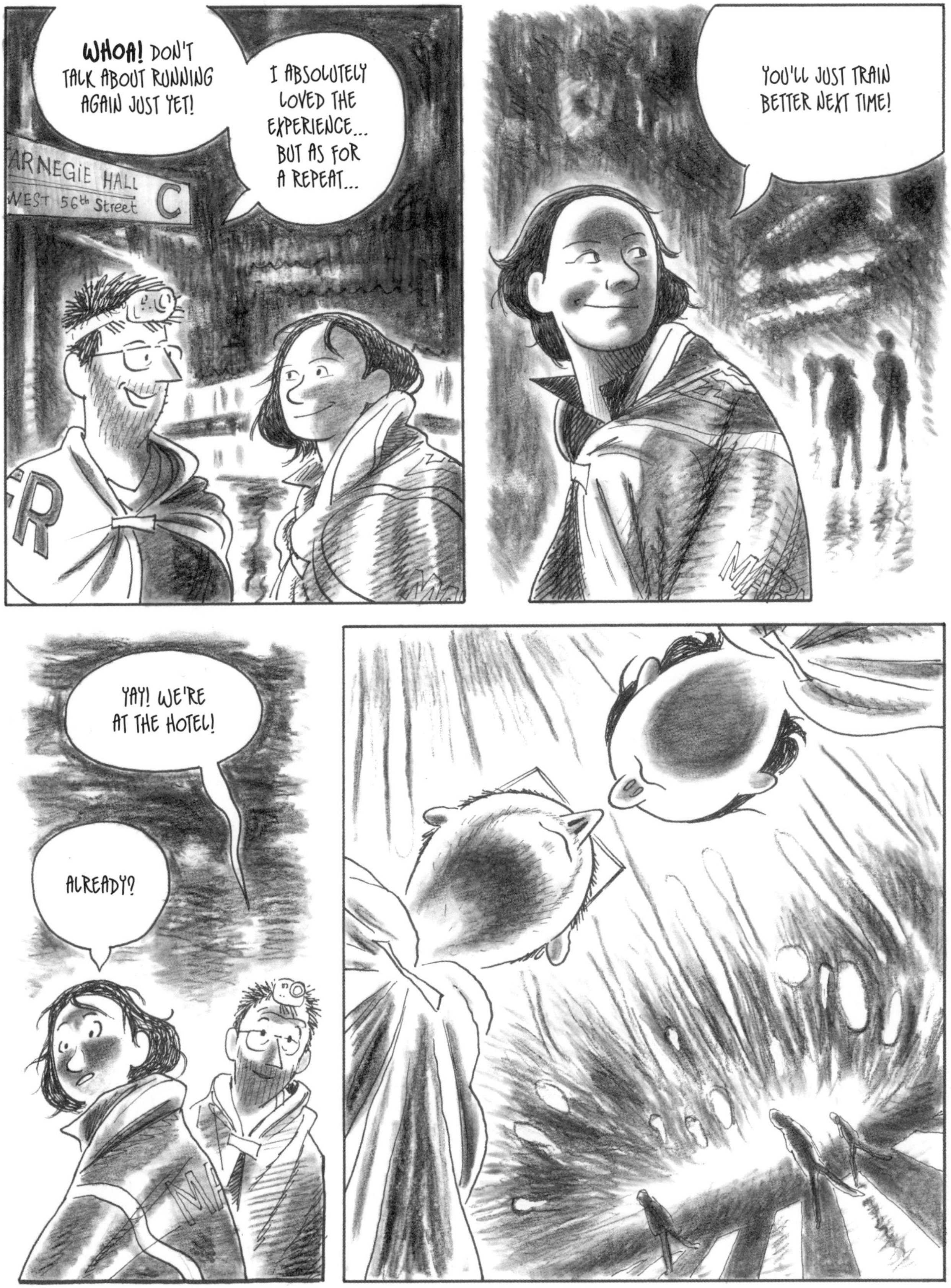
WHOA! DON'T TALK ABOUT RUNNING AGAIN JUST YET!
I ABSOLUTELY LOVED THE EXPERIENCE... BUT AS FOR A REPEAT...
CARNEGIE HALL
WEST 56th Street
C
YOU'LL JUST TRAIN BETTER NEXT TIME!
YAY! WE'RE AT THE HOTEL!
ALREADY?

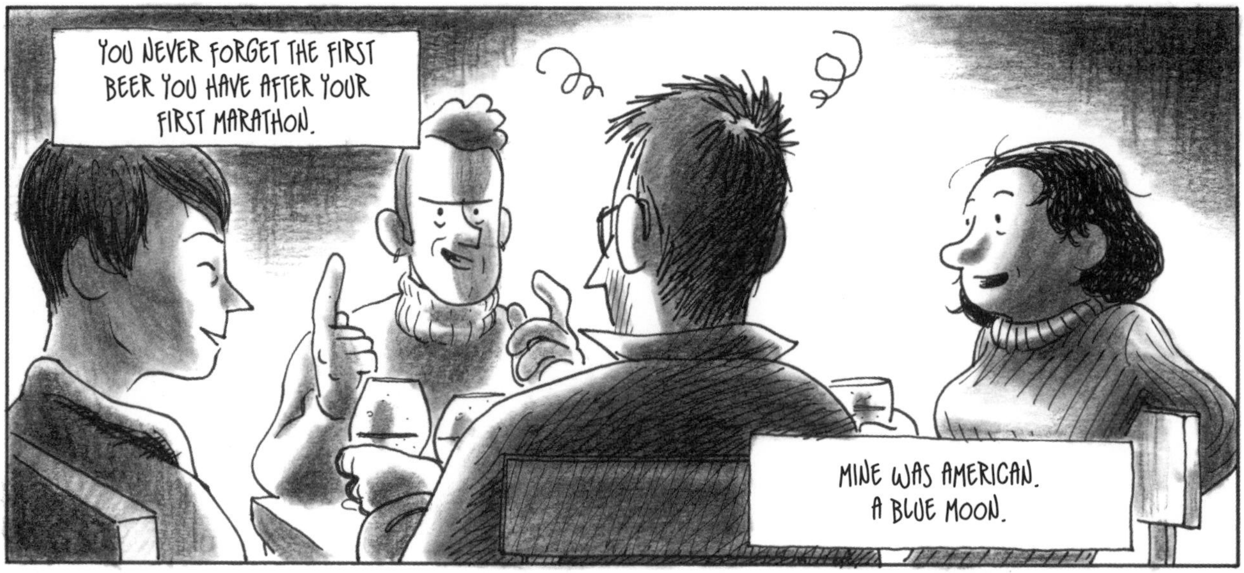
YOU NEVER FORGET THE FIRST BEER YOU HAVE AFTER YOUR FIRST MARATHON.
MINE WAS AMERICAN. A BLUE MOON.

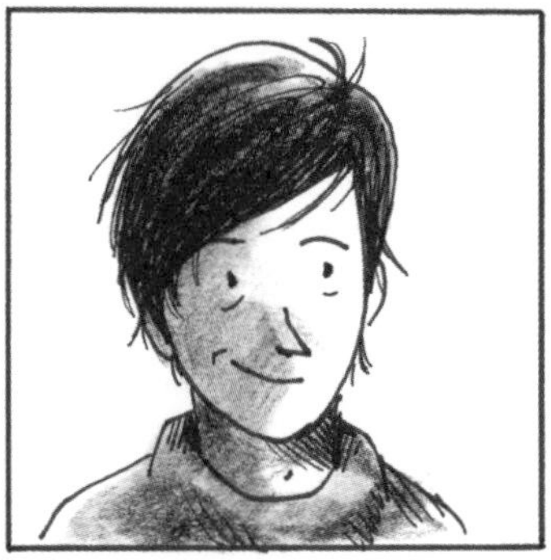

NADÈGE NEVER REALLY FOUND HER GROOVE DURING THE RACE BUT FINISHED IN 3 HOURS AND 46 MINUTES NONETHELESS.

WILL WALKED FOR THE FIRST TIME IN A RUNNING RACE. HE'S A BIT DISAPPOINTED WITH HIS 3 HOUR AND 3 MINUTES RUN TIME.

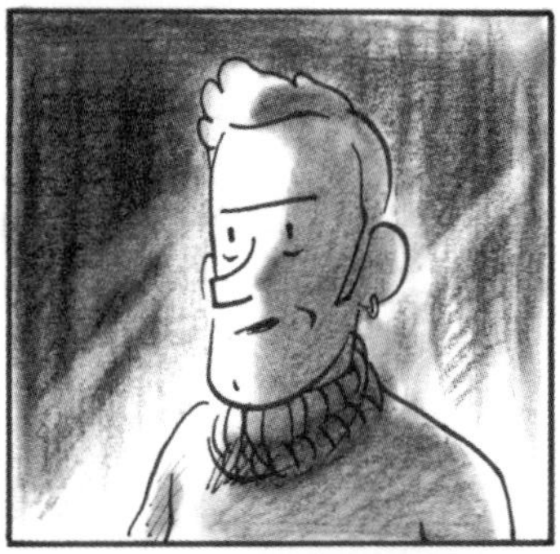

AS FOR THE ANNALS OF HISTORY, GEOFFREY MUTAI FROM KENYA BLEW AWAY THE NY MARATHON RECORD IN 2 HOURS, 5 MINUTES AND 6 SECONDS.

HIS FELLOW KENYAN FIREHIWOT DADO CAME IN FIRST IN THE WOMEN'S CATEGORY, IN JUST 2 HOURS AND 23 MINUTES.

47,180 RUNNERS CROSSED THE FINISH LINE. ONLY 4,000 OF THEM WERE BEHIND ME!

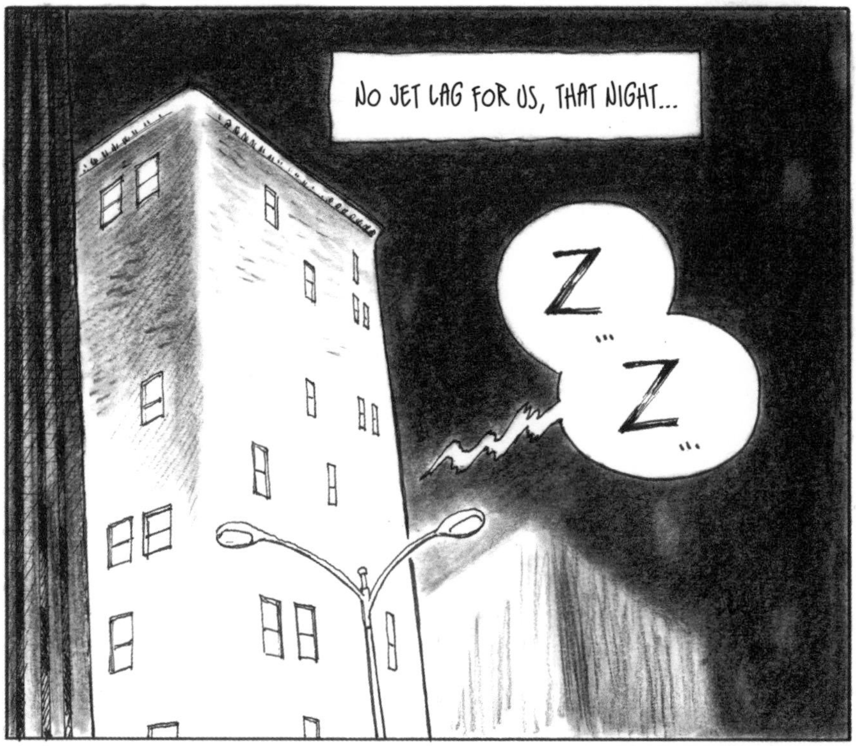
NO JET LAG FOR US, THAT NIGHT...
Z... Z...

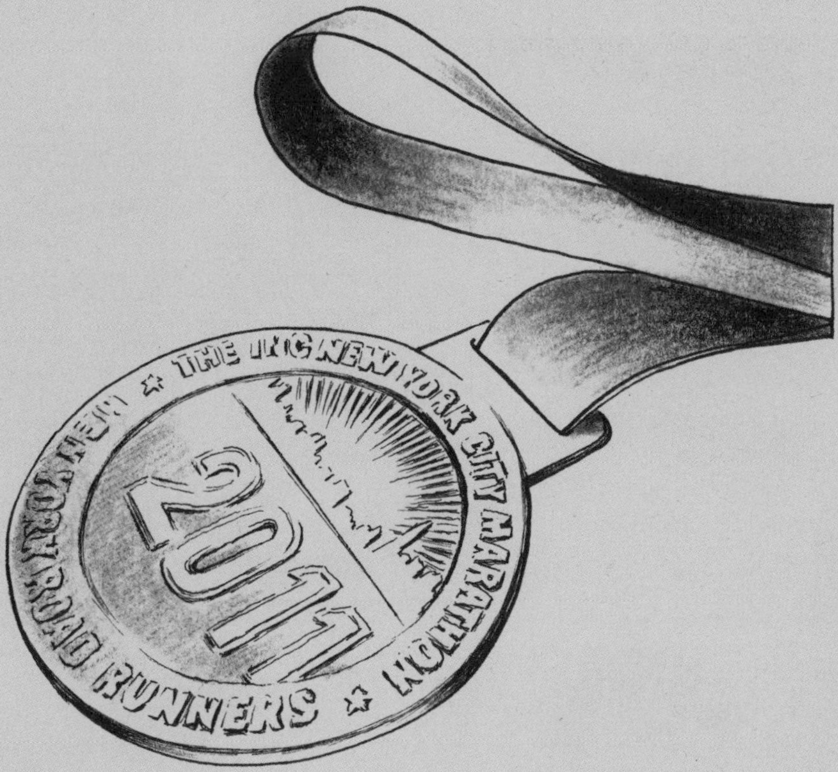
THE ING NEW YORK CITY MARATHON
2011
NEW YORK ROAD RUNNERS

6. AND I FEEL *Fine!*

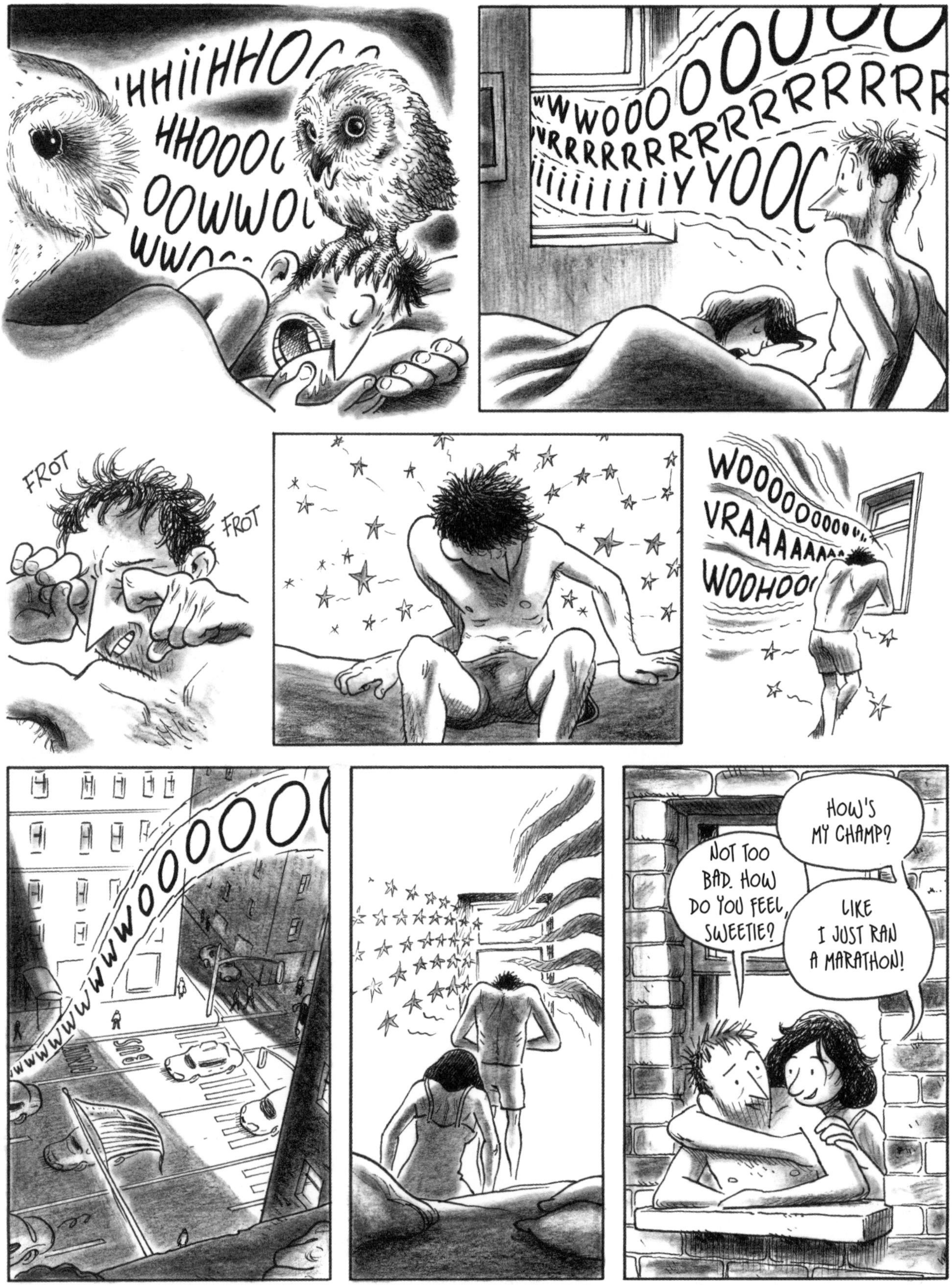

HHHiiHHOO
HHOOOO
OOWWOO
WWO
WWOOOOOOOO
VRRRRRRRRRRRRRRR
iiiiiiiiiiYYOOC
FROT
FROT
WOOOOOOOO
VRAAAAAA
WOOHOO
WWWWWWWWOOOOOOO
HOW'S MY CHAMP?
NOT TOO BAD. HOW DO YOU FEEL, SWEETIE?
LIKE I JUST RAN A MARATHON!

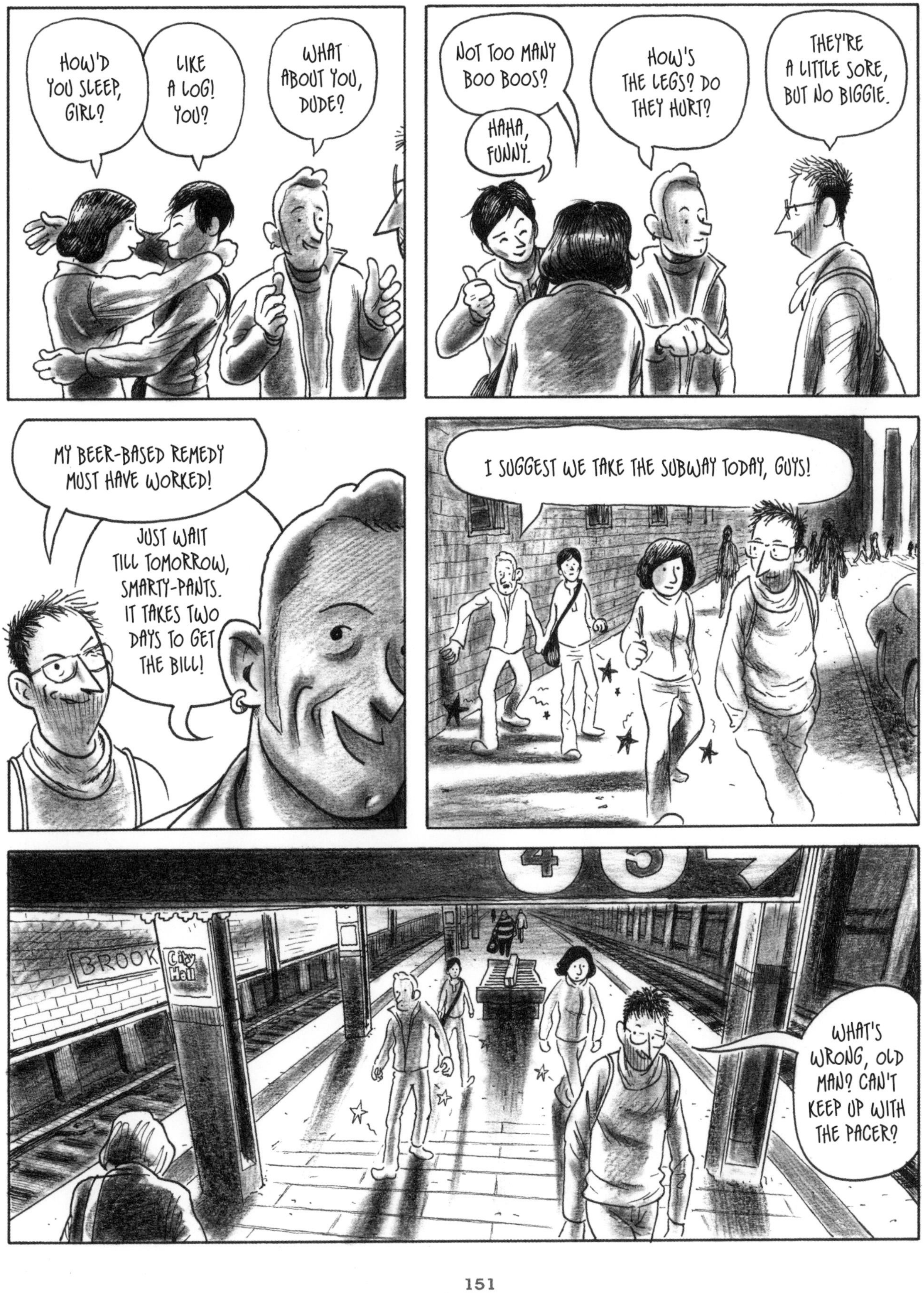
HOW'D YOU SLEEP, GIRL?
LIKE A LOG! YOU?
WHAT ABOUT YOU, DUDE?
NOT TOO MANY BOO BOOS?
HAHA, FUNNY.
HOW'S THE LEGS? DO THEY HURT?
THEY'RE A LITTLE SORE, BUT NO BIGGIE.
MY BEER-BASED REMEDY MUST HAVE WORKED!
JUST WAIT TILL TOMORROW, SMARTY-PANTS. IT TAKES TWO DAYS TO GET THE BILL!
I SUGGEST WE TAKE THE SUBWAY TODAY, GUYS!
BROOK
City Hall
WHAT'S WRONG, OLD MAN? CAN'T KEEP UP WITH THE PACER?

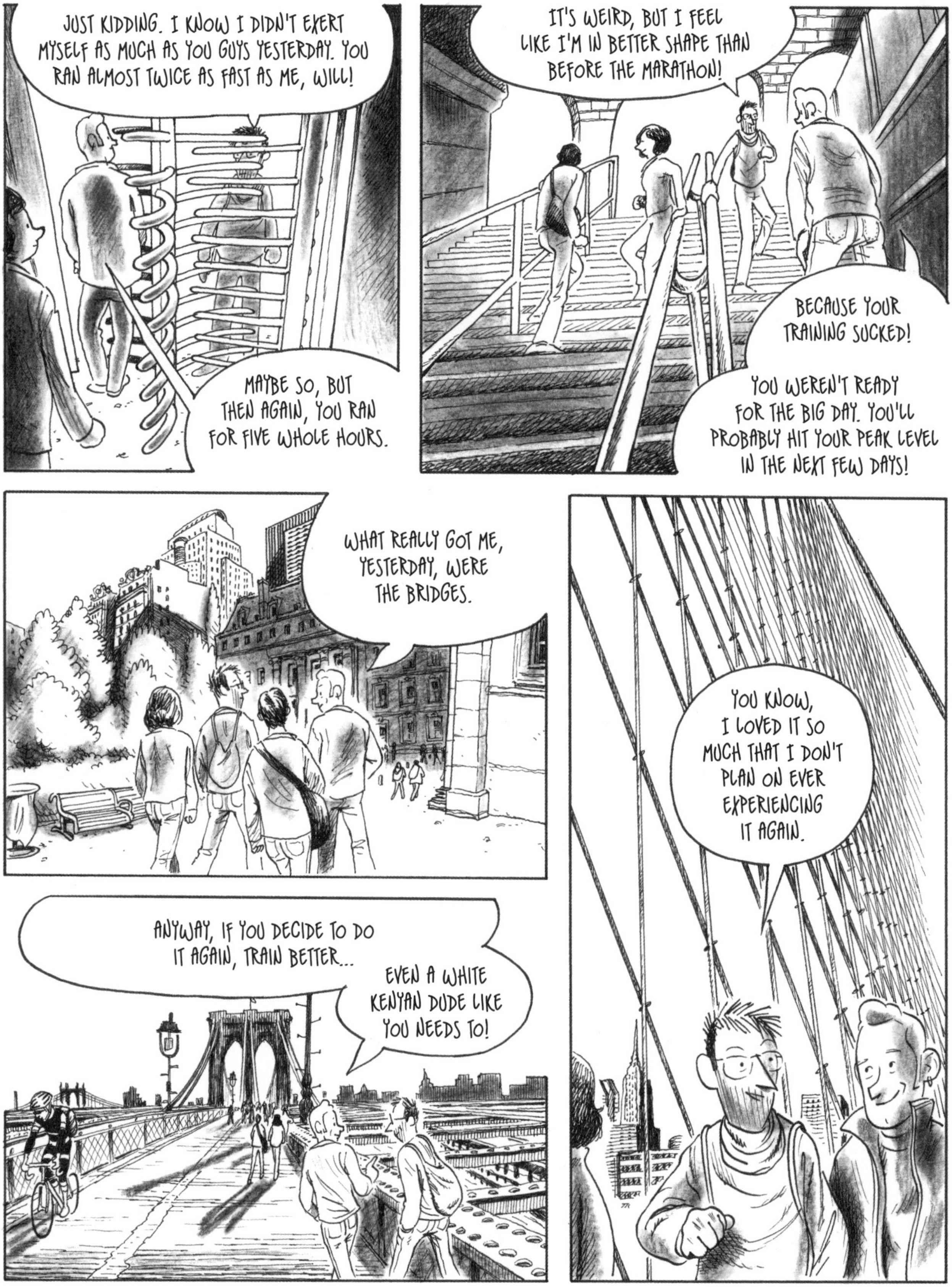
JUST KIDDING. I KNOW I DIDN'T EXERT MYSELF AS MUCH AS YOU GUYS YESTERDAY. YOU RAN ALMOST TWICE AS FAST AS ME, WILL!
MAYBE SO, BUT THEN AGAIN, YOU RAN FOR FIVE WHOLE HOURS.
IT'S WEIRD, BUT I FEEL LIKE I'M IN BETTER SHAPE THAN BEFORE THE MARATHON!
BECAUSE YOUR TRAINING SUCKED!
YOU WEREN'T READY FOR THE BIG DAY. YOU'LL PROBABLY HIT YOUR PEAK LEVEL IN THE NEXT FEW DAYS!
WHAT REALLY GOT ME, YESTERDAY, WERE THE BRIDGES.
YOU KNOW, I LOVED IT SO MUCH THAT I DON'T PLAN ON EVER EXPERIENCING IT AGAIN.
ANYWAY, IF YOU DECIDE TO DO IT AGAIN, TRAIN BETTER...
EVEN A WHITE KENYAN DUDE LIKE YOU NEEDS TO!

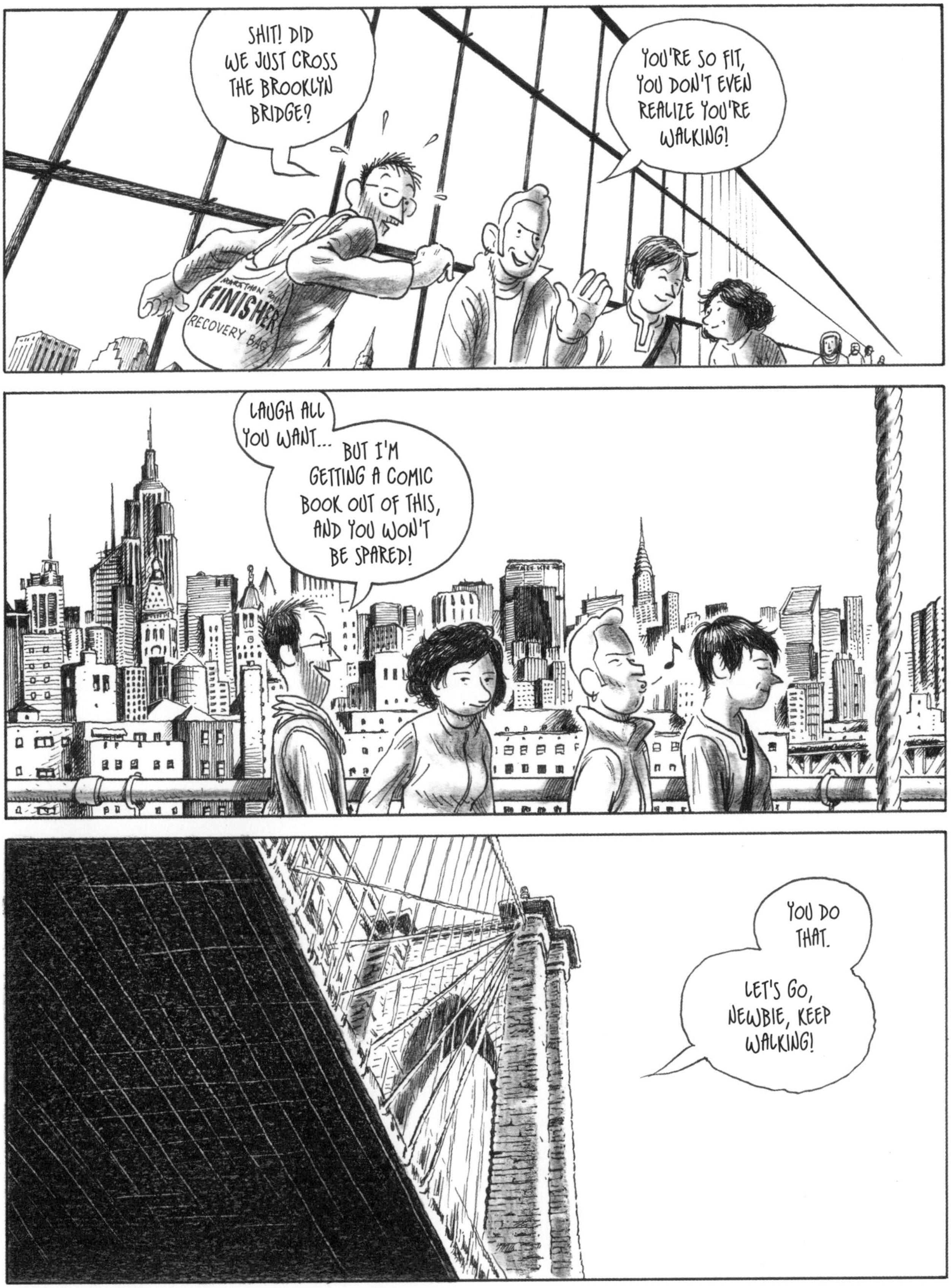
SHIT! DID WE JUST CROSS THE BROOKLYN BRIDGE?
YOU'RE SO FIT, YOU DON'T EVEN REALIZE YOU'RE WALKING!
FINISHER
RECOVERY BAG
LAUGH ALL YOU WANT...
BUT I'M GETTING A COMIC BOOK OUT OF THIS, AND YOU WON'T BE SPARED!
YOU DO THAT.
LET'S GO, NEWBIE, KEEP WALKING!

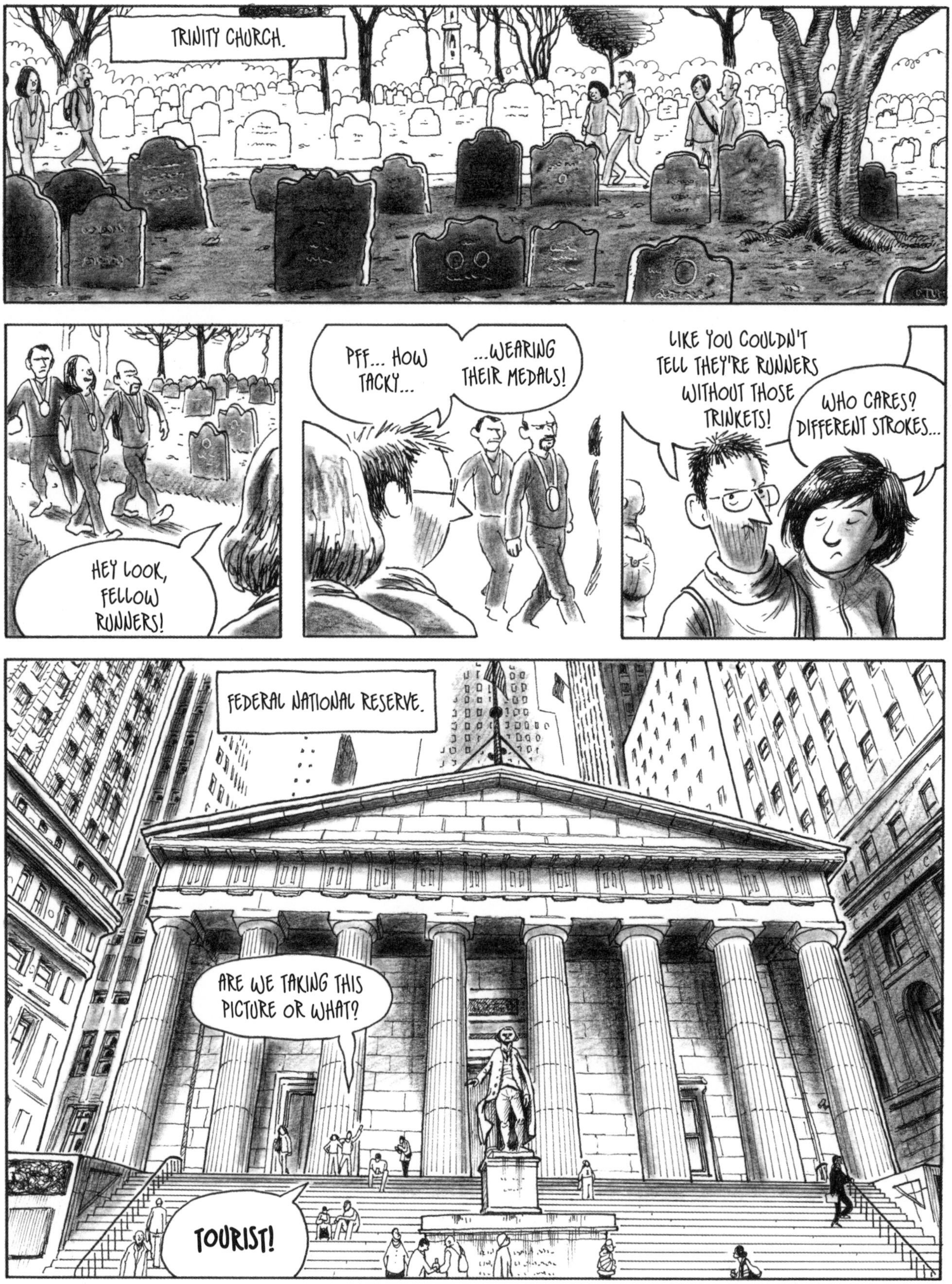
TRINITY CHURCH.
HEY LOOK, FELLOW RUNNERS!
PFF... HOW TACKY...
...WEARING THEIR MEDALS!
LIKE YOU COULDN'T TELL THEY'RE RUNNERS WITHOUT THOSE TRINKETS!
WHO CARES? DIFFERENT STROKES...
FEDERAL NATIONAL RESERVE.
ARE WE TAKING THIS PICTURE OR WHAT?
TOURIST!

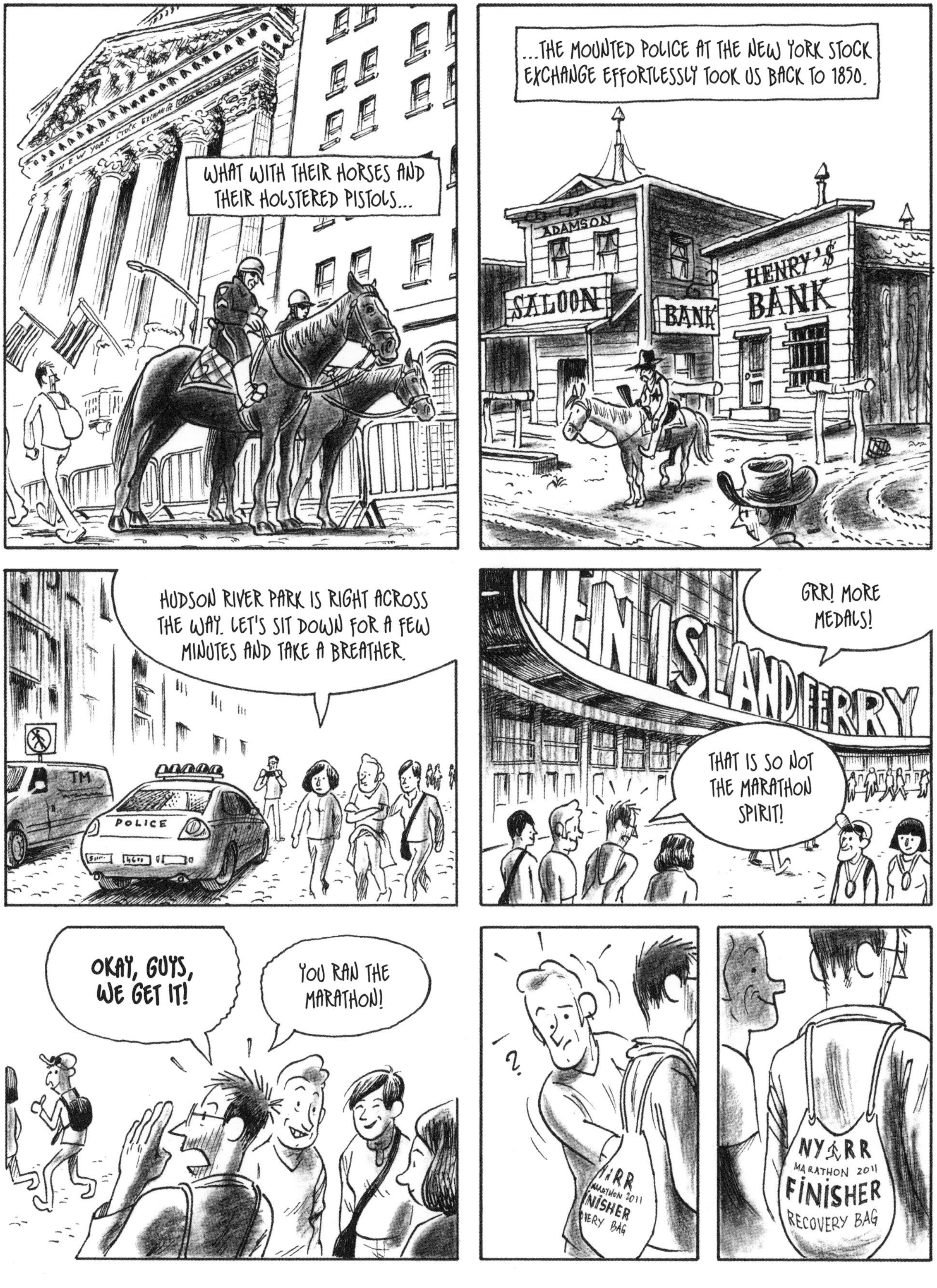
WHAT WITH THEIR HORSES AND THEIR HOLSTERED PISTOLS...
...THE MOUNTED POLICE AT THE NEW YORK STOCK EXCHANGE EFFORTLESSLY TOOK US BACK TO 1850.
ADAMSON
SALOON
BANK
HENRY'S BANK
HUDSON RIVER PARK IS RIGHT ACROSS THE WAY. LET'S SIT DOWN FOR A FEW MINUTES AND TAKE A BREATHER.
POLICE
GRR! MORE MEDALS!
ISLAND FERRY
THAT IS SO NOT THE MARATHON SPIRIT!
OKAY, GUYS, WE GET IT!
YOU RAN THE MARATHON!
?
NYRR MARATHON 2011 FINISHER RECOVERY BAG

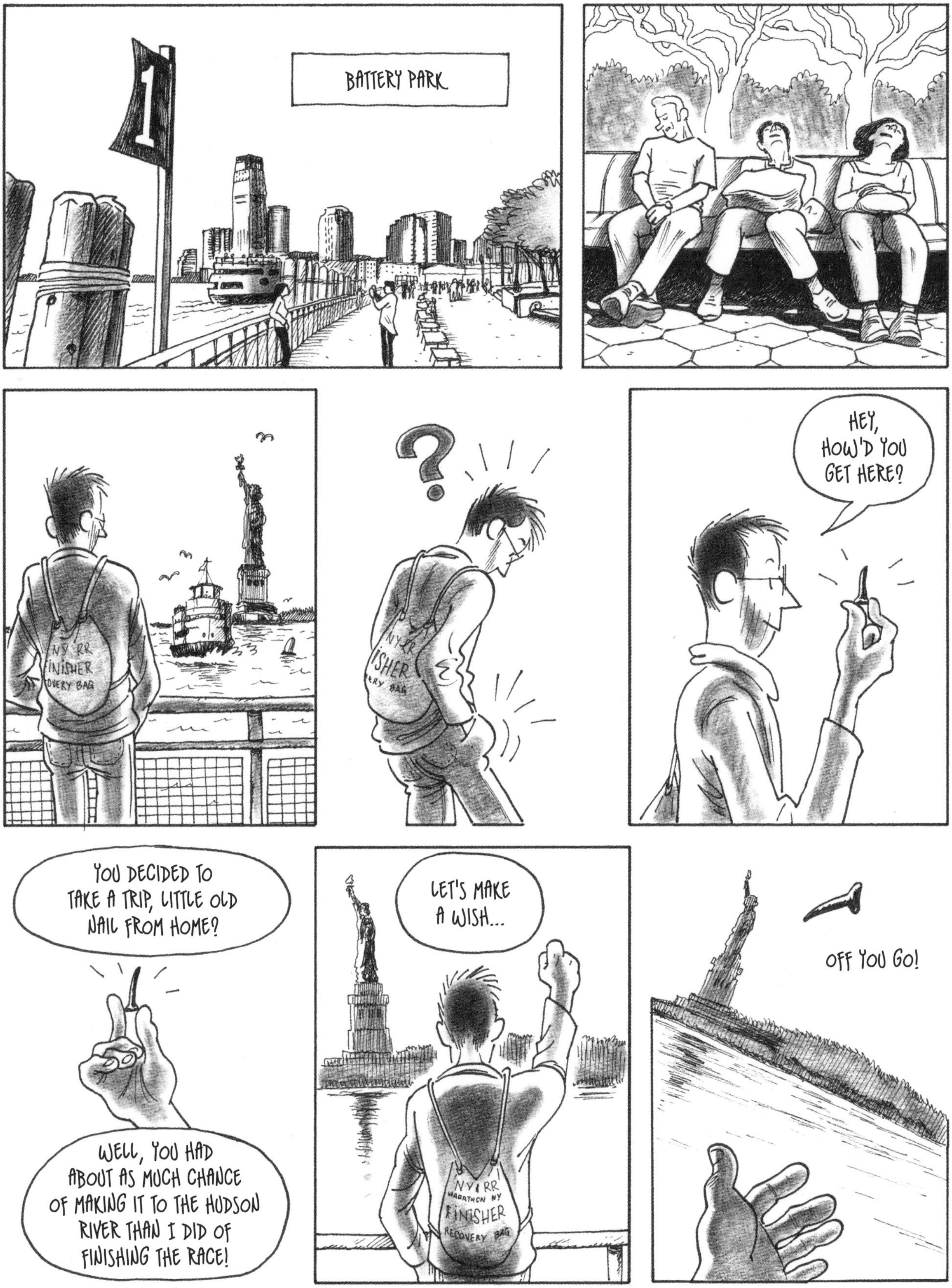
BATTERY PARK
NY RR FINISHER RECOVERY BAG
HEY, HOW'D YOU GET HERE?
YOU DECIDED TO TAKE A TRIP, LITTLE OLD NAIL FROM HOME?
WELL, YOU HAD ABOUT AS MUCH CHANCE OF MAKING IT TO THE HUDSON RIVER THAN I DID OF FINISHING THE RACE!
LET'S MAKE A WISH...
NY RR MARATHON NY FINISHER RECOVERY BAG
OFF YOU GO!

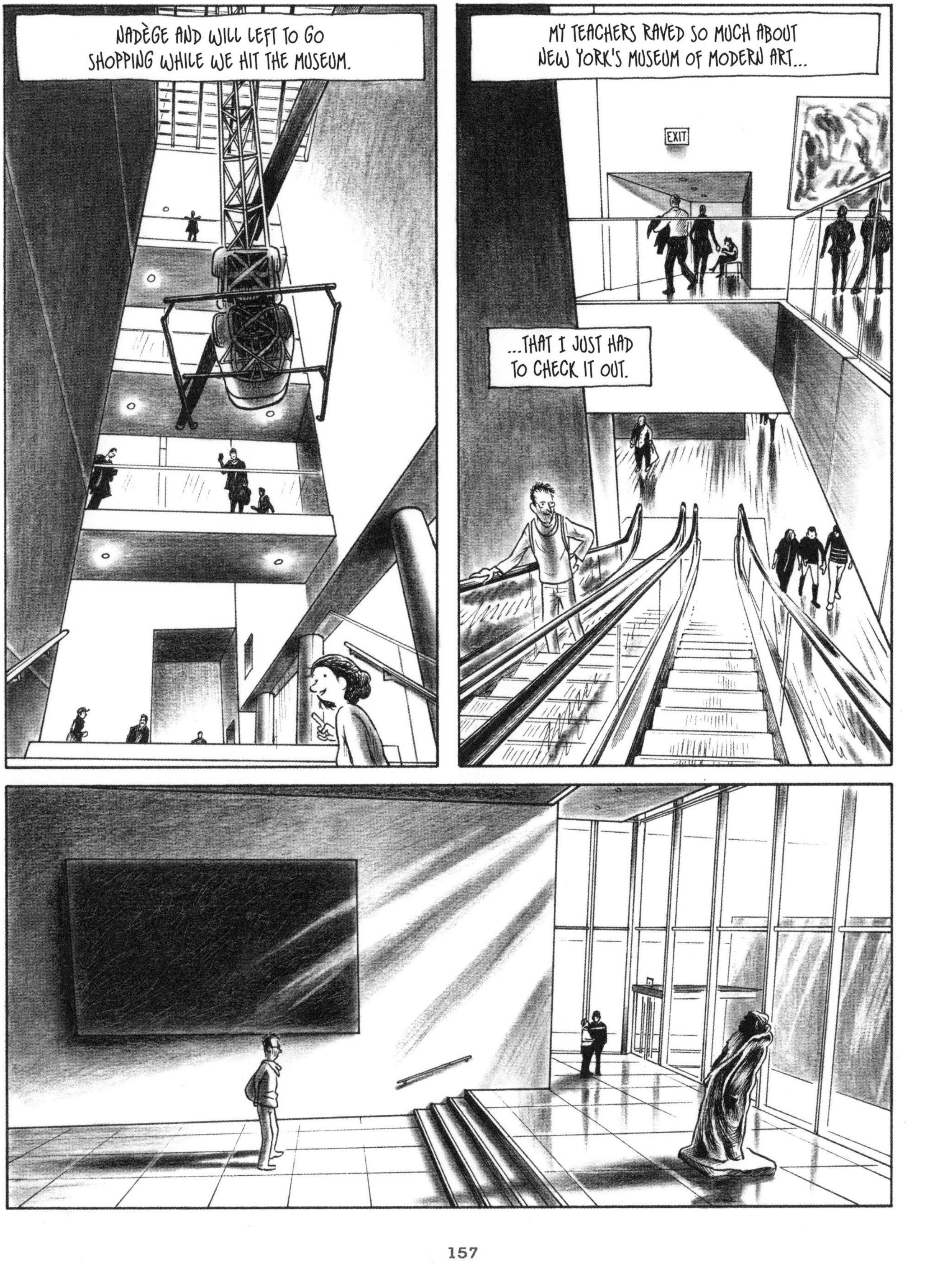
NADÈGE AND WILL LEFT TO GO SHOPPING WHILE WE HIT THE MUSEUM.
MY TEACHERS RAVED SO MUCH ABOUT NEW YORK'S MUSEUM OF MODERN ART...
EXIT
...THAT I JUST HAD TO CHECK IT OUT.

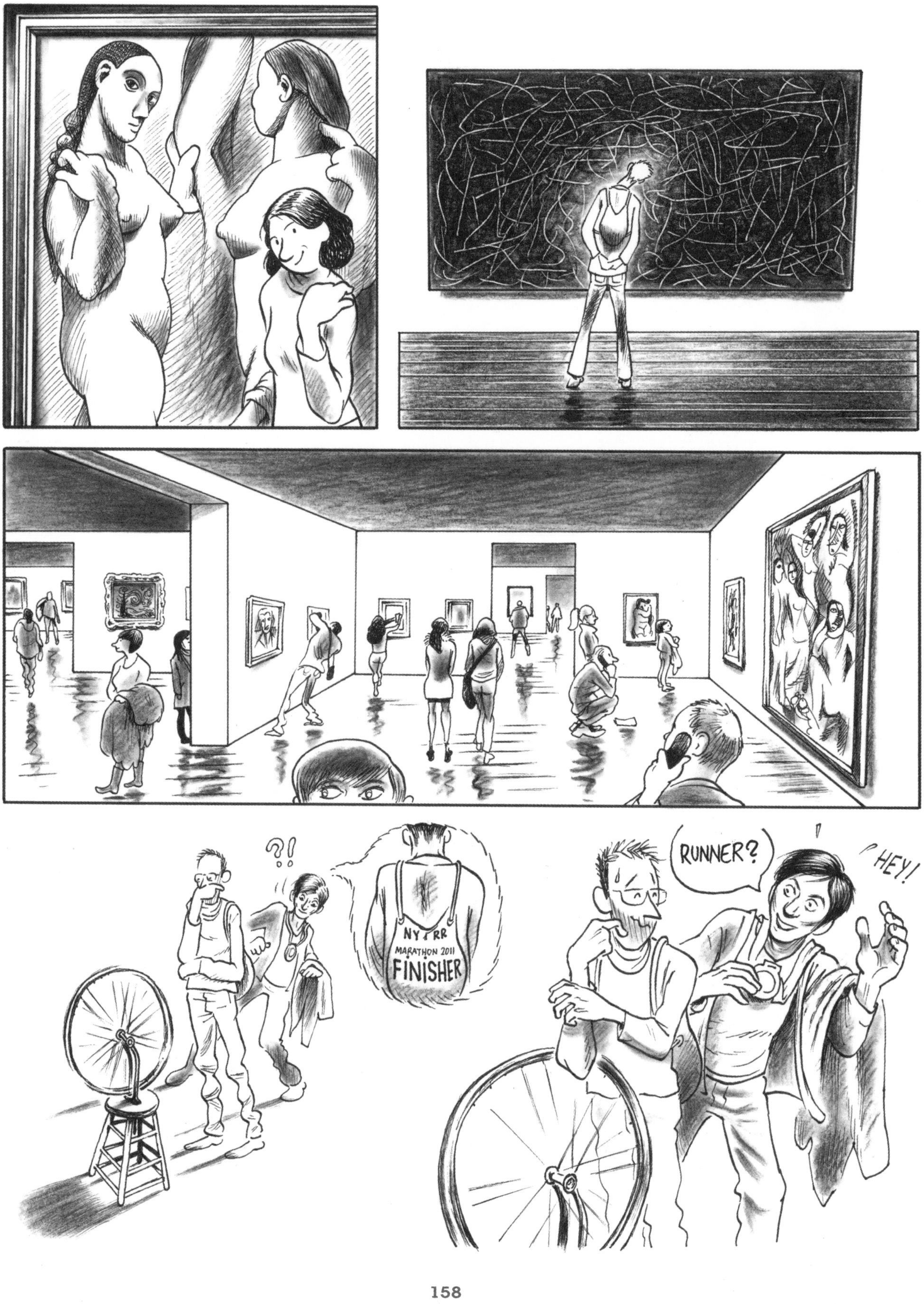
?!
NY RR
MARATHON 2011
FINISHER
RUNNER?
HEY!

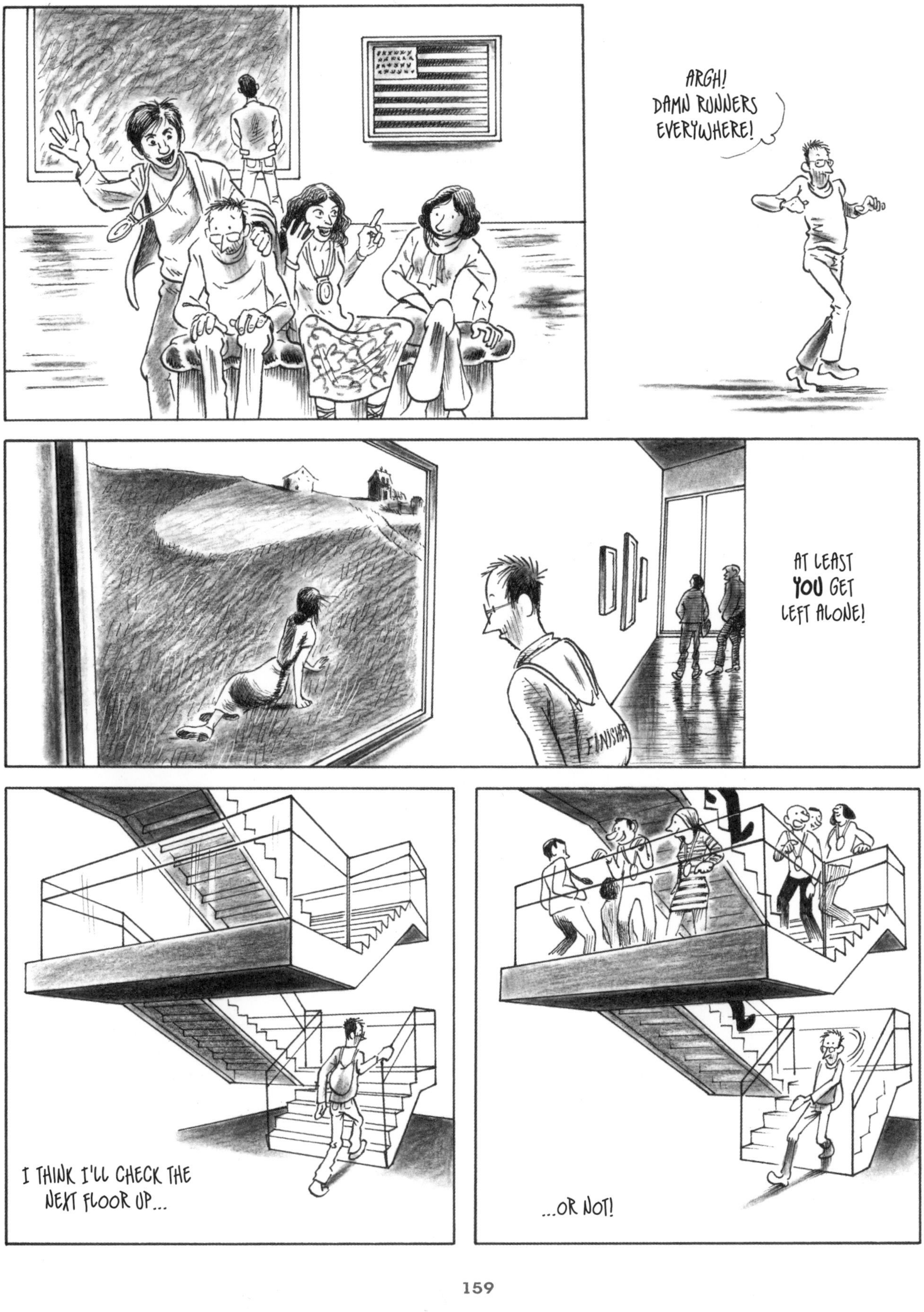
ARGH! DAMN RUNNERS EVERYWHERE!
AT LEAST YOU GET LEFT ALONE!
FINISHER
I THINK I'LL CHECK THE NEXT FLOOR UP...
...OR NOT!

WE HAVE AN HOUR BEFORE WE MEET THE OTHERS.

HOW ABOUT GRABBING A BITE?

WHEW! NO MORE PASTA REGIMEN!

HASTA LA VISTA, PASTA!

AFTER BINGING ON VEGGIES...

BURPS

ARE YOU OK, HONEY?

NO, ACTUALLY.

I THINK I'LL HEAD BACK TO THE HOTEL. YOU GO ON WITHOUT ME.

ARE YOU KIDDING? I'M COMING WITH YOU.

YOU NEED SOME REST.

IT'S THE AFTER-EFFECT OF THE RACE.

LACK OF SLEEP OR MAYBE THE MARATHON BLUES...

WHILE SHE RECUPERATES... ...I'LL DO SOME SKETCHES OF THE NEIGHBORHOOD.

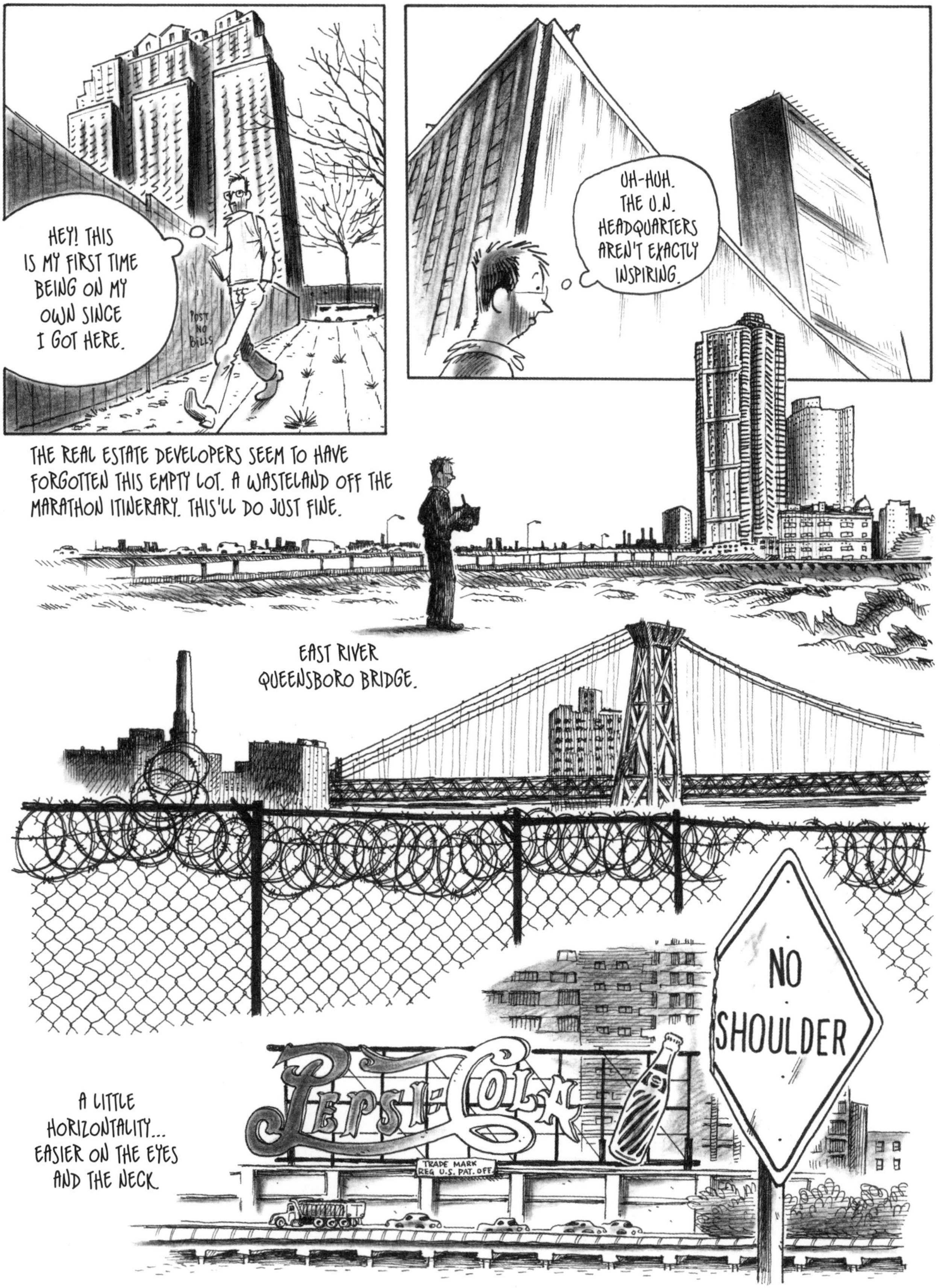
HEY! THIS IS MY FIRST TIME BEING ON MY OWN SINCE I GOT HERE.
POST NO BILLS
UH-HUH. THE U.N. HEADQUARTERS AREN'T EXACTLY INSPIRING.
THE REAL ESTATE DEVELOPERS SEEM TO HAVE FORGOTTEN THIS EMPTY LOT. A WASTELAND OFF THE MARATHON ITINERARY. THIS'LL DO JUST FINE.
EAST RIVER QUEENSBORO BRIDGE.
NO SHOULDER
PEPSI-COLA
TRADE MARK REG U.S. PAT. OFF
A LITTLE HORIZONTALITY... EASIER ON THE EYES AND THE NECK.

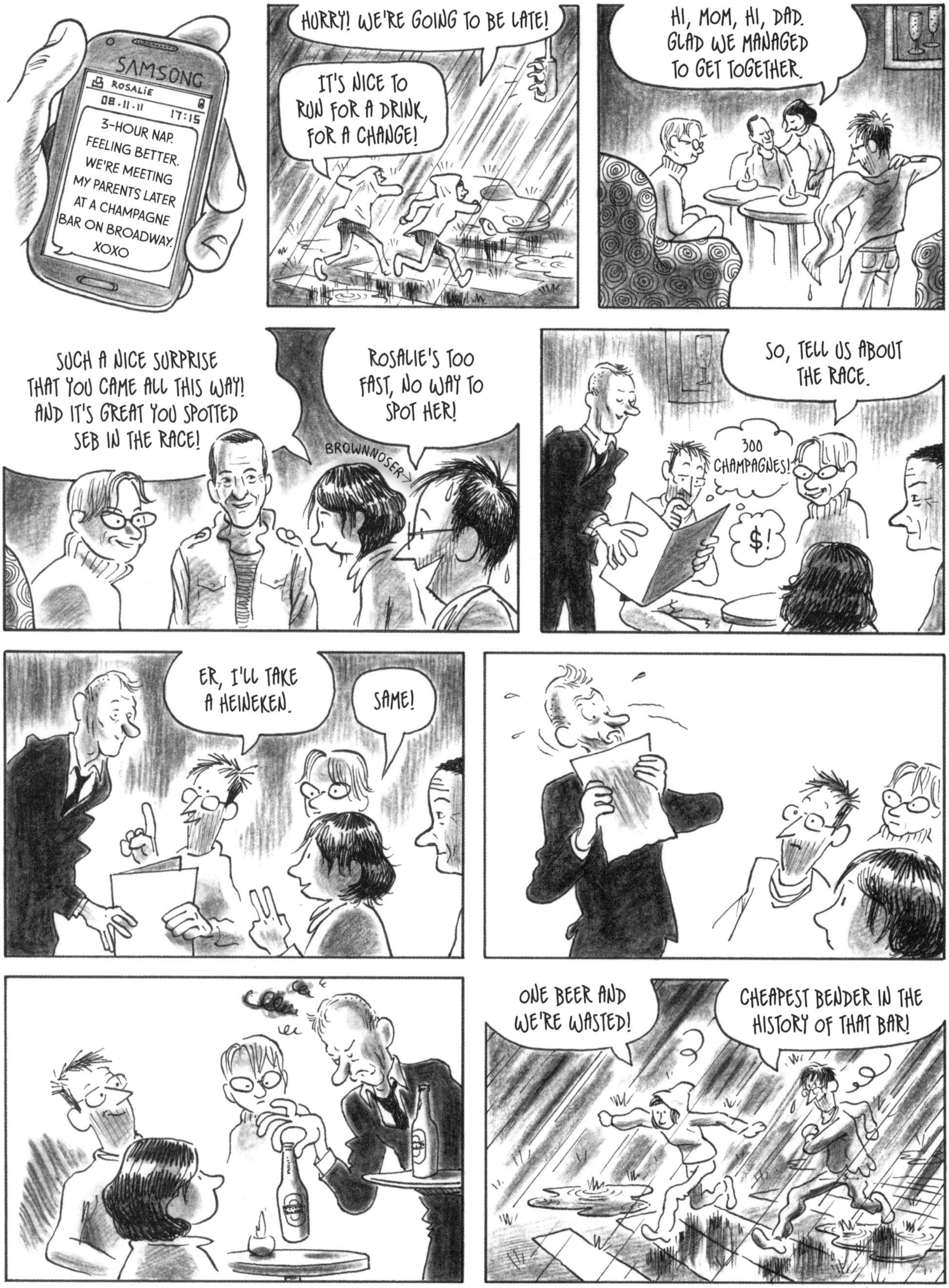
SAMSONG
ROSALIE
08-11-11 17:15
3-HOUR NAP. FEELING BETTER. WE'RE MEETING MY PARENTS LATER AT A CHAMPAGNE BAR ON BROADWAY. XOXO
HURRY! WE'RE GOING TO BE LATE!
IT'S NICE TO RUN FOR A DRINK, FOR A CHANGE!
HI, MOM, HI, DAD. GLAD WE MANAGED TO GET TOGETHER.
SUCH A NICE SURPRISE THAT YOU CAME ALL THIS WAY! AND IT'S GREAT YOU SPOTTED SEB IN THE RACE!
ROSALIE'S TOO FAST, NO WAY TO SPOT HER!
BROWNNOSER
SO, TELL US ABOUT THE RACE.
300 CHAMPAGNES!
$!
ER, I'LL TAKE A HEINEKEN.
SAME!
ONE BEER AND WE'RE WASTED!
CHEAPEST BENDER IN THE HISTORY OF THAT BAR!

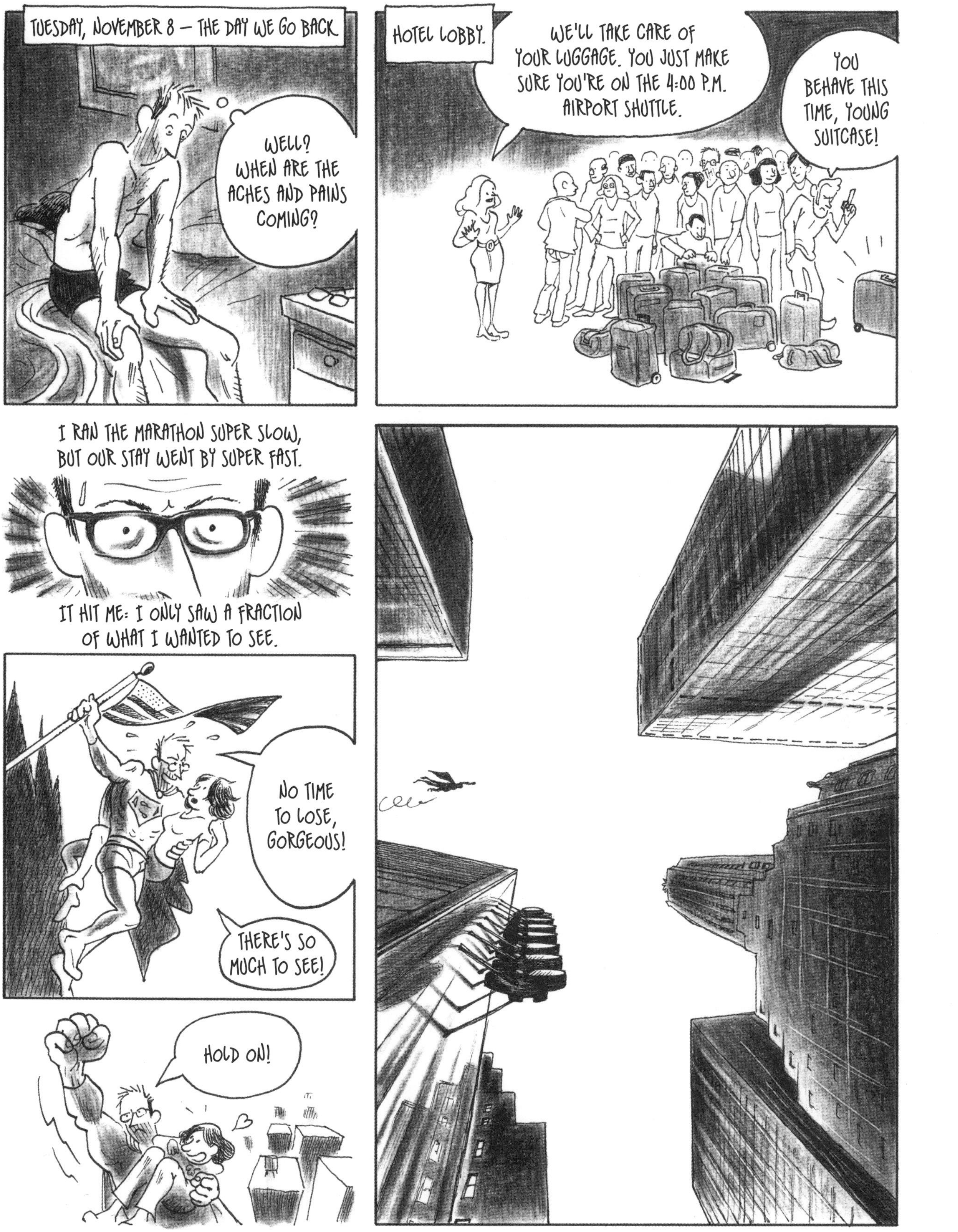
TUESDAY, NOVEMBER 8 — THE DAY WE GO BACK
WELL? WHEN ARE THE ACHES AND PAINS COMING?
HOTEL LOBBY.
WE'LL TAKE CARE OF YOUR LUGGAGE. YOU JUST MAKE SURE YOU'RE ON THE 4:00 P.M. AIRPORT SHUTTLE.
YOU BEHAVE THIS TIME, YOUNG SUITCASE!
I RAN THE MARATHON SUPER SLOW, BUT OUR STAY WENT BY SUPER FAST.
IT HIT ME: I ONLY SAW A FRACTION OF WHAT I WANTED TO SEE.
NO TIME TO LOSE, GORGEOUS!
THERE'S SO MUCH TO SEE!
HOLD ON!

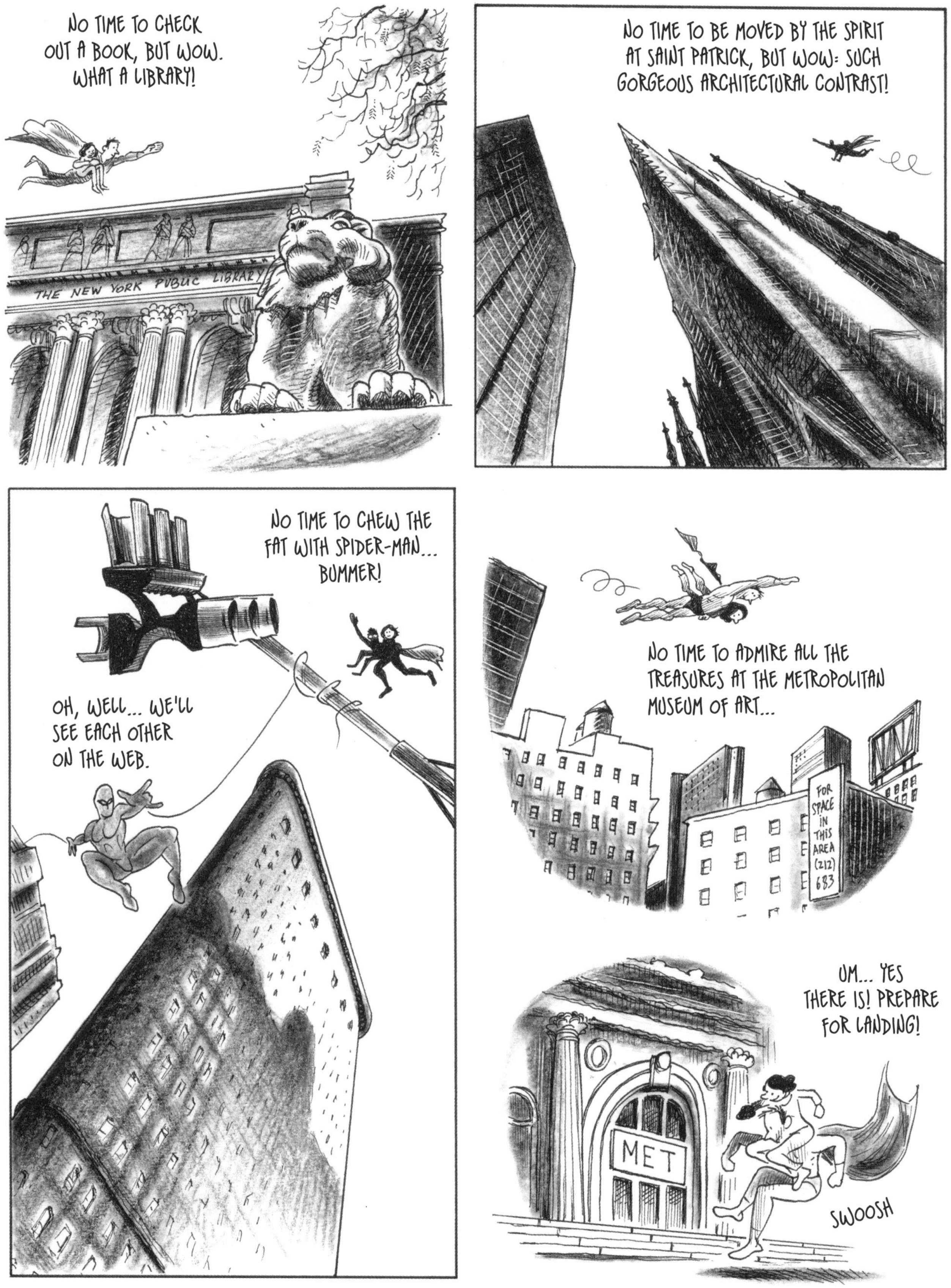
NO TIME TO CHECK OUT A BOOK, BUT WOW. WHAT A LIBRARY!
THE NEW YORK PUBLIC LIBRARY
NO TIME TO BE MOVED BY THE SPIRIT AT SAINT PATRICK, BUT WOW: SUCH GORGEOUS ARCHITECTURAL CONTRAST!
NO TIME TO CHEW THE FAT WITH SPIDER-MAN... BUMMER!
OH, WELL... WE'LL SEE EACH OTHER ON THE WEB.
NO TIME TO ADMIRE ALL THE TREASURES AT THE METROPOLITAN MUSEUM OF ART...
FOR SPACE IN THIS AREA (212) 683
UM... YES THERE IS! PREPARE FOR LANDING!
MET
SWOOSH

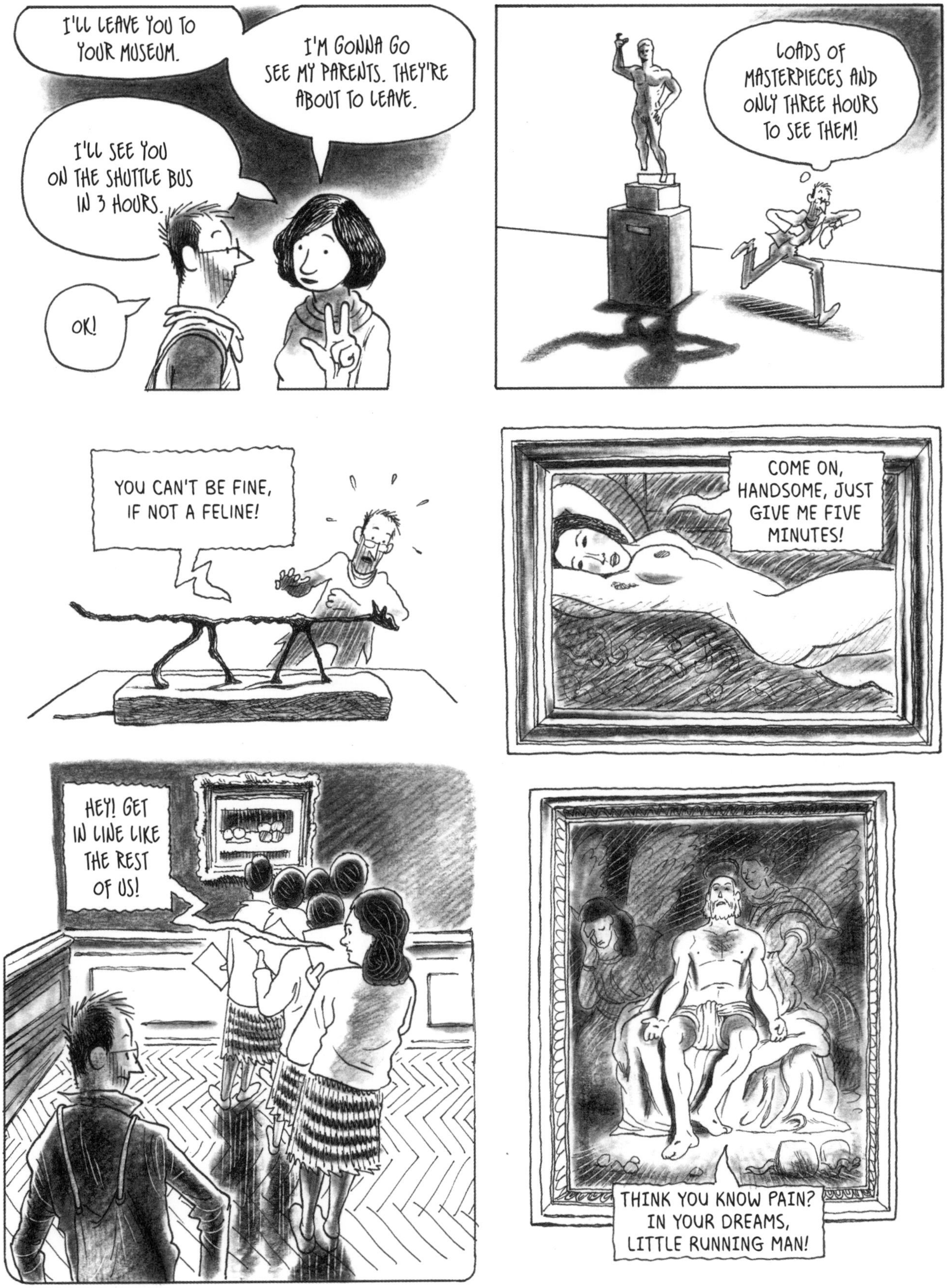
I'LL LEAVE YOU TO YOUR MUSEUM.
I'M GONNA GO SEE MY PARENTS. THEY'RE ABOUT TO LEAVE.
I'LL SEE YOU ON THE SHUTTLE BUS IN 3 HOURS.
OK!
LOADS OF MASTERPIECES AND ONLY THREE HOURS TO SEE THEM!
YOU CAN'T BE FINE, IF NOT A FELINE!
COME ON, HANDSOME, JUST GIVE ME FIVE MINUTES!
HEY! GET IN LINE LIKE THE REST OF US!
THINK YOU KNOW PAIN? IN YOUR DREAMS, LITTLE RUNNING MAN!

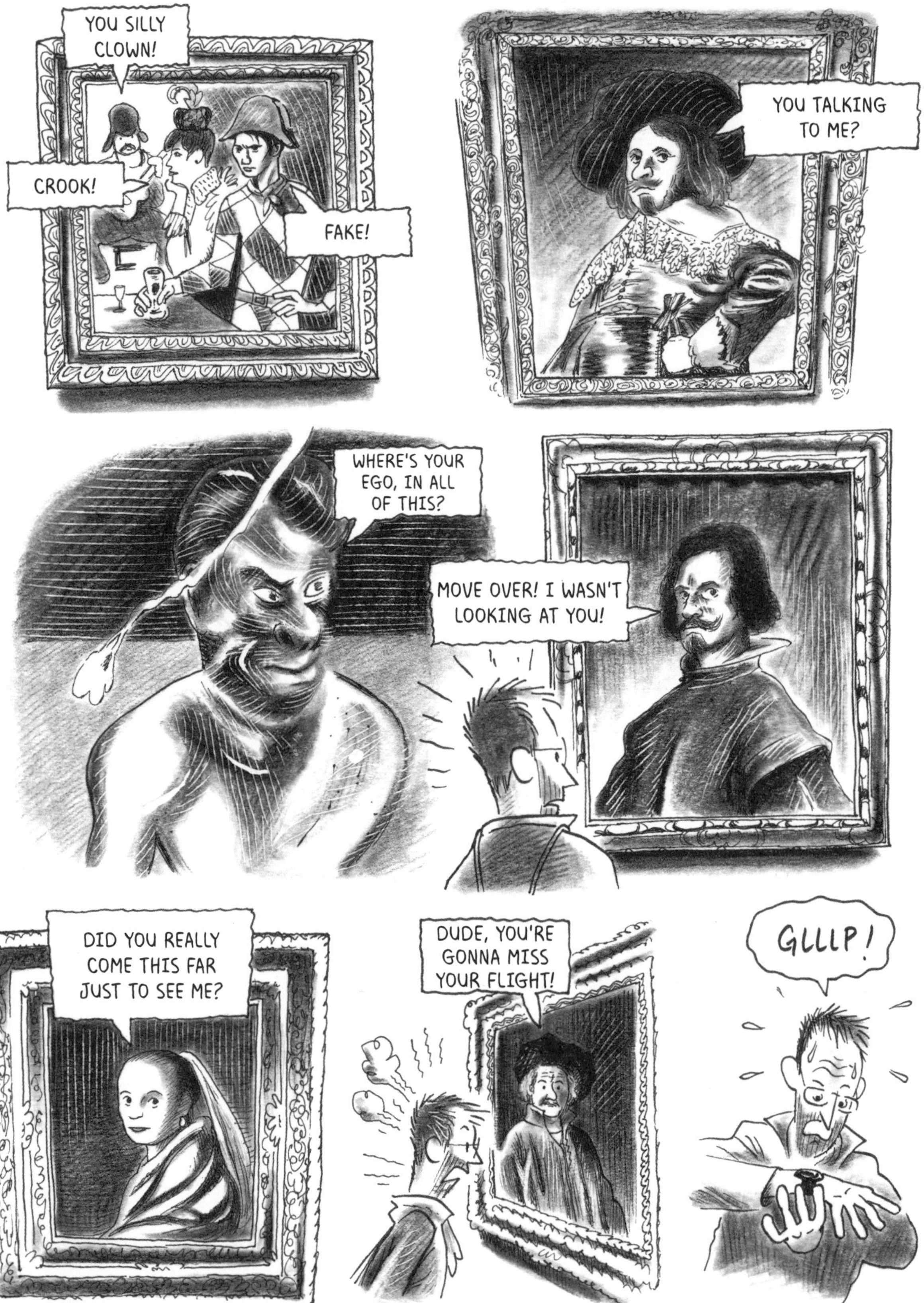
YOU SILLY CLOWN!
CROOK!
FAKE!
YOU TALKING TO ME?
WHERE'S YOUR EGO, IN ALL OF THIS?
MOVE OVER! I WASN'T LOOKING AT YOU!
DID YOU REALLY COME THIS FAR JUST TO SEE ME?
DUDE, YOU'RE GONNA MISS YOUR FLIGHT!
GLLLP!

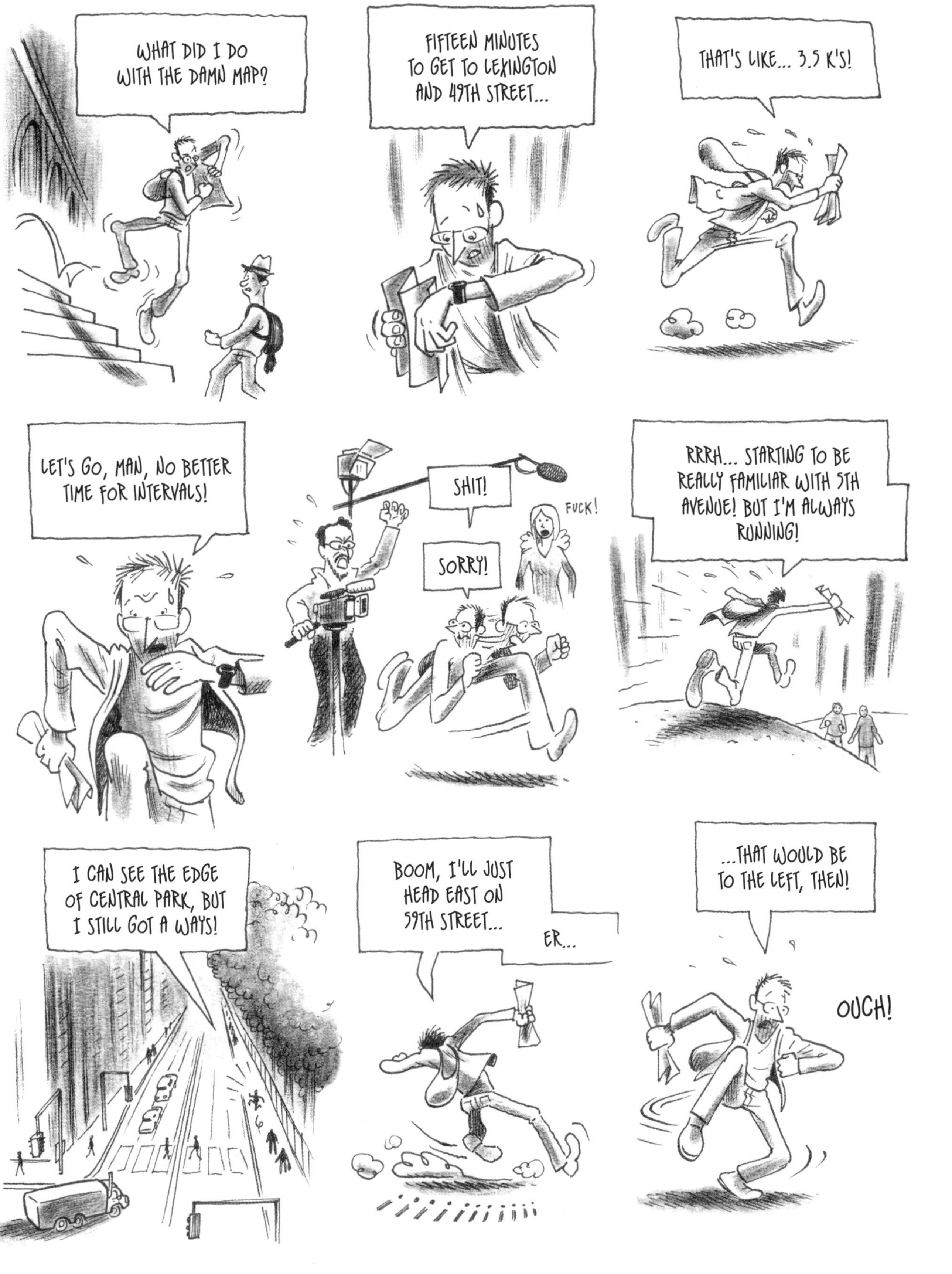
WHAT DID I DO WITH THE DAMN MAP?
FIFTEEN MINUTES TO GET TO LEXINGTON AND 49TH STREET...
THAT'S LIKE... 3.5 K'S!
LET'S GO, MAN, NO BETTER TIME FOR INTERVALS!
SHIT!
FUCK!
SORRY!
RRRH... STARTING TO BE REALLY FAMILIAR WITH 5TH AVENUE! BUT I'M ALWAYS RUNNING!
I CAN SEE THE EDGE OF CENTRAL PARK, BUT I STILL GOT A WAYS!
BOOM, I'LL JUST HEAD EAST ON 59TH STREET...
ER...
...THAT WOULD BE TO THE LEFT, THEN!
OUCH!

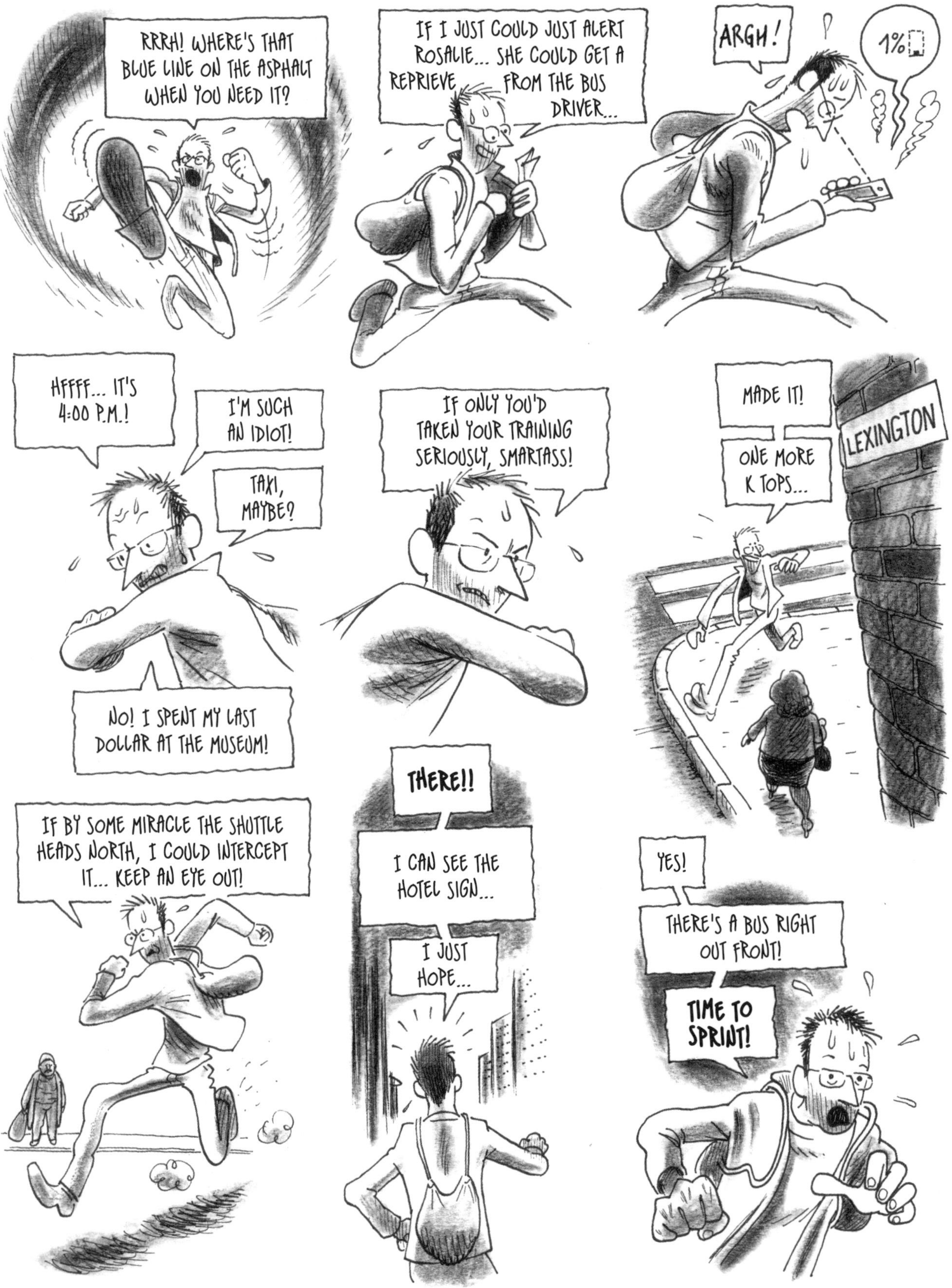
RRRH! WHERE'S THAT BLUE LINE ON THE ASPHALT WHEN YOU NEED IT?
IF I JUST COULD JUST ALERT ROSALIE... SHE COULD GET A REPRIEVE FROM THE BUS DRIVER...
ARGH!
1%
HFFFF... IT'S 4:00 P.M.!
I'M SUCH AN IDIOT!
TAXI, MAYBE?
NO! I SPENT MY LAST DOLLAR AT THE MUSEUM!
IF ONLY YOU'D TAKEN YOUR TRAINING SERIOUSLY, SMARTASS!
MADE IT!
ONE MORE K TOPS...
LEXINGTON
IF BY SOME MIRACLE THE SHUTTLE HEADS NORTH, I COULD INTERCEPT IT... KEEP AN EYE OUT!
THERE!!
I CAN SEE THE HOTEL SIGN...
I JUST HOPE...
YES!
THERE'S A BUS RIGHT OUT FRONT!
TIME TO SPRINT!

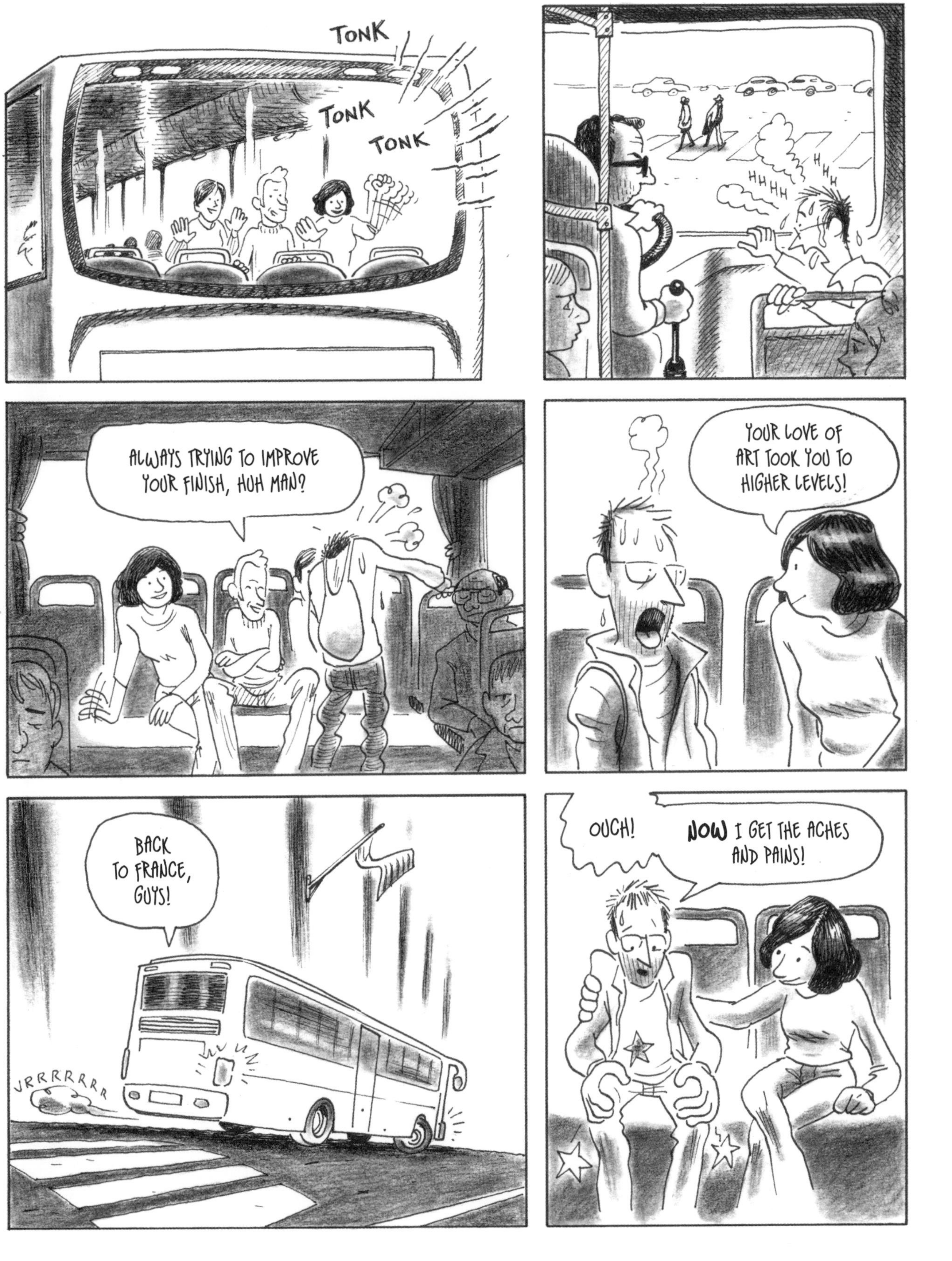
TONK
TONK
TONK
ALWAYS TRYING TO IMPROVE YOUR FINISH, HUH MAN?
YOUR LOVE OF ART TOOK YOU TO HIGHER LEVELS!
BACK TO FRANCE, GUYS!
VRRRRRRR
OUCH!
NOW I GET THE ACHES AND PAINS!

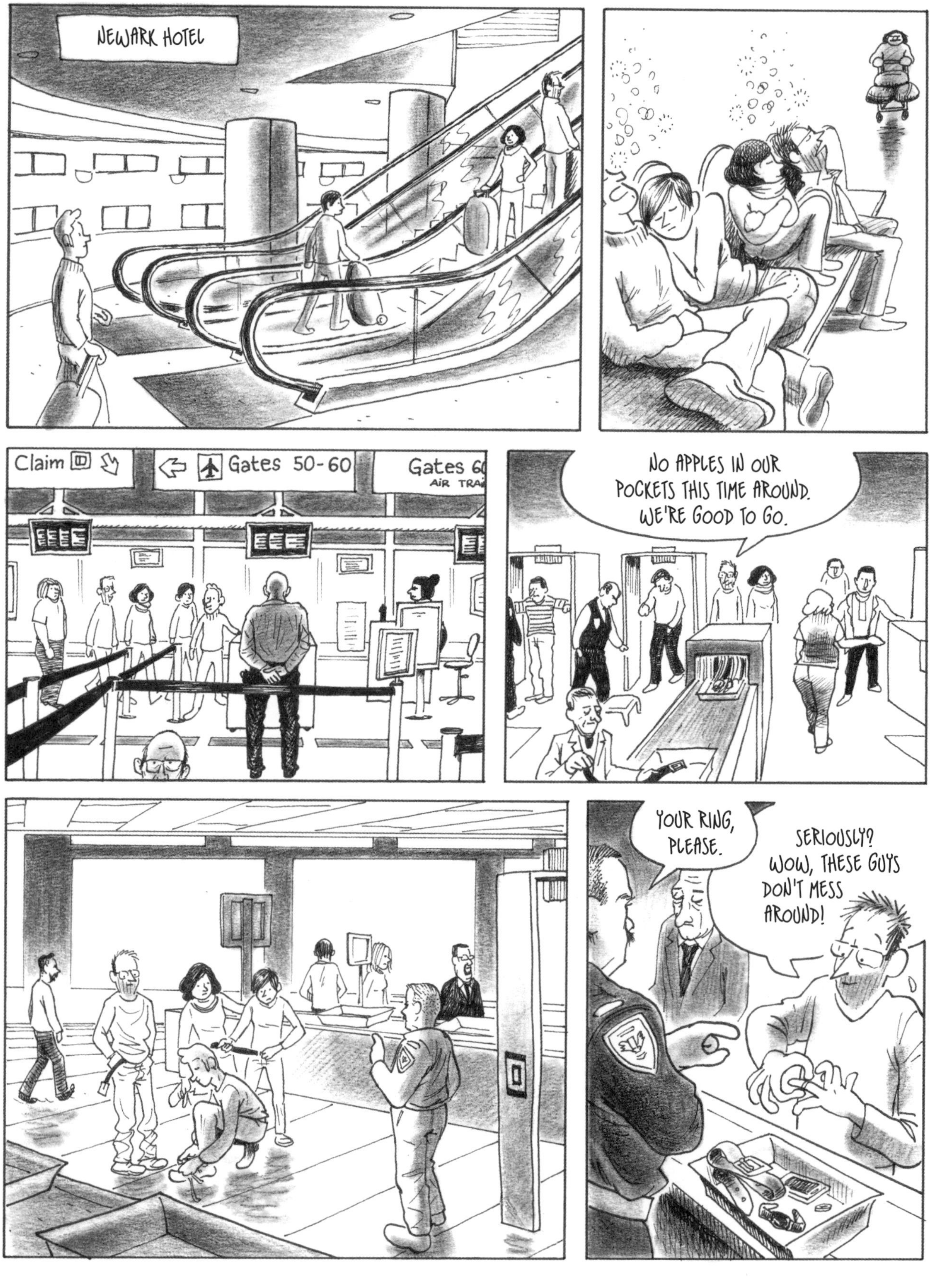
NEWARK HOTEL
Claim D
Gates 50-60
Gates 6
NO APPLES IN OUR POCKETS THIS TIME AROUND. WE'RE GOOD TO GO.
YOUR RING, PLEASE.
SERIOUSLY? WOW, THESE GUYS DON'T MESS AROUND!

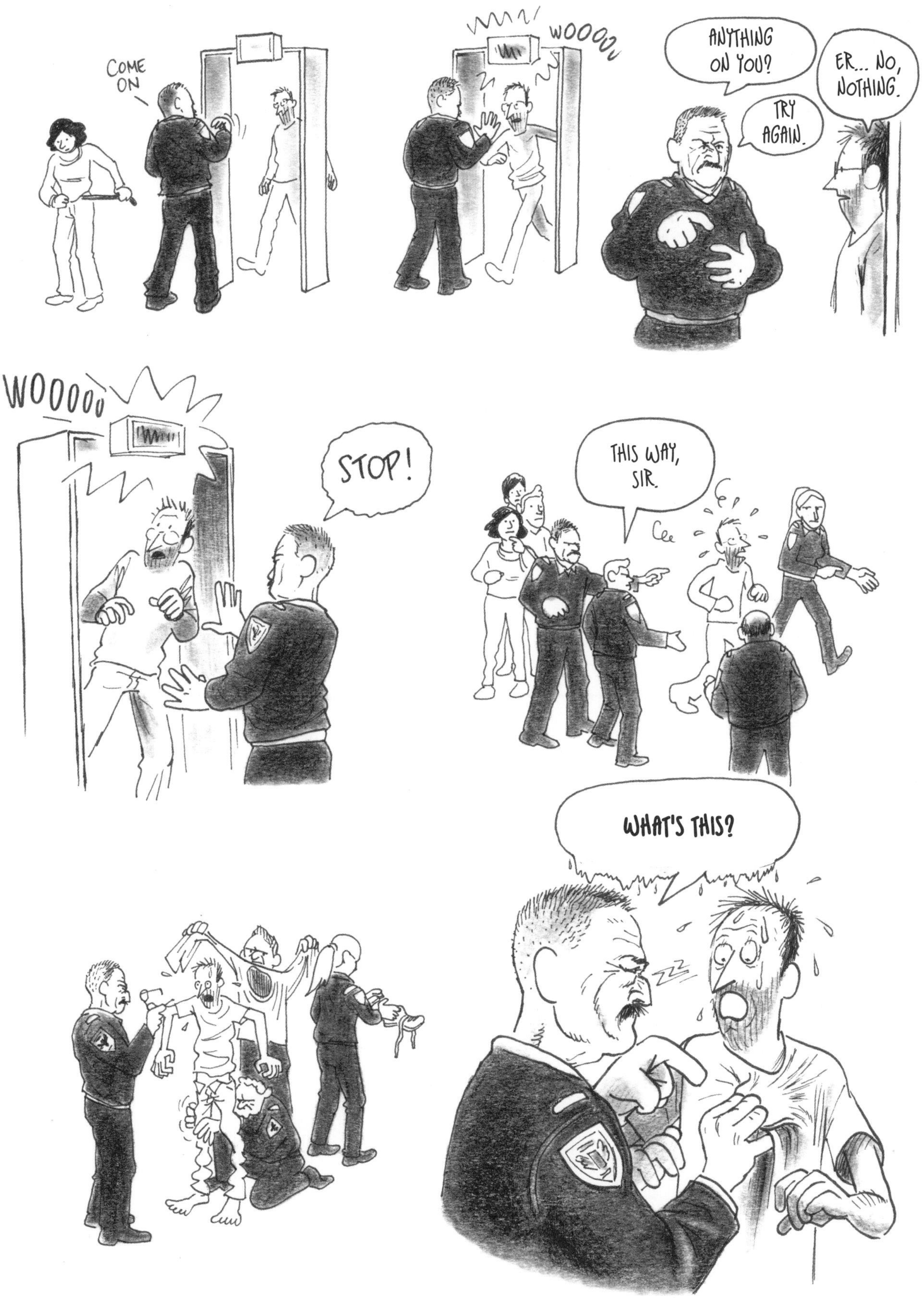
COME ON
WOOOOu
ANYTHING ON YOU?
ER... NO, NOTHING.
TRY AGAIN.
WOOOOOu
STOP!
THIS WAY, SIR.
WHAT'S THIS?

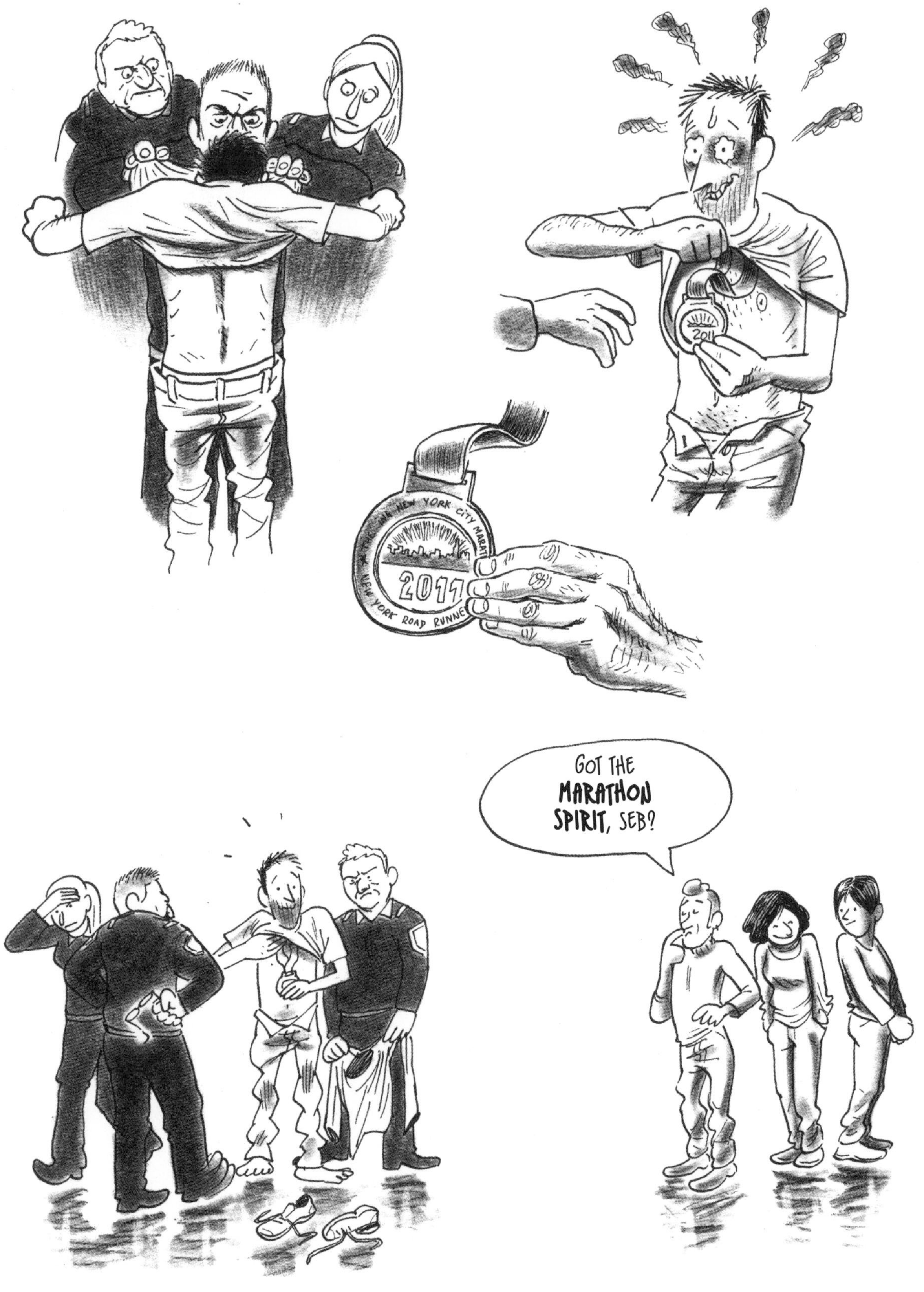
THE ING NEW YORK CITY MARATHON
NEW YORK ROAD RUNNERS
2011
GOT THE MARATHON SPIRIT, SEB?

7.
NOW
What's next?

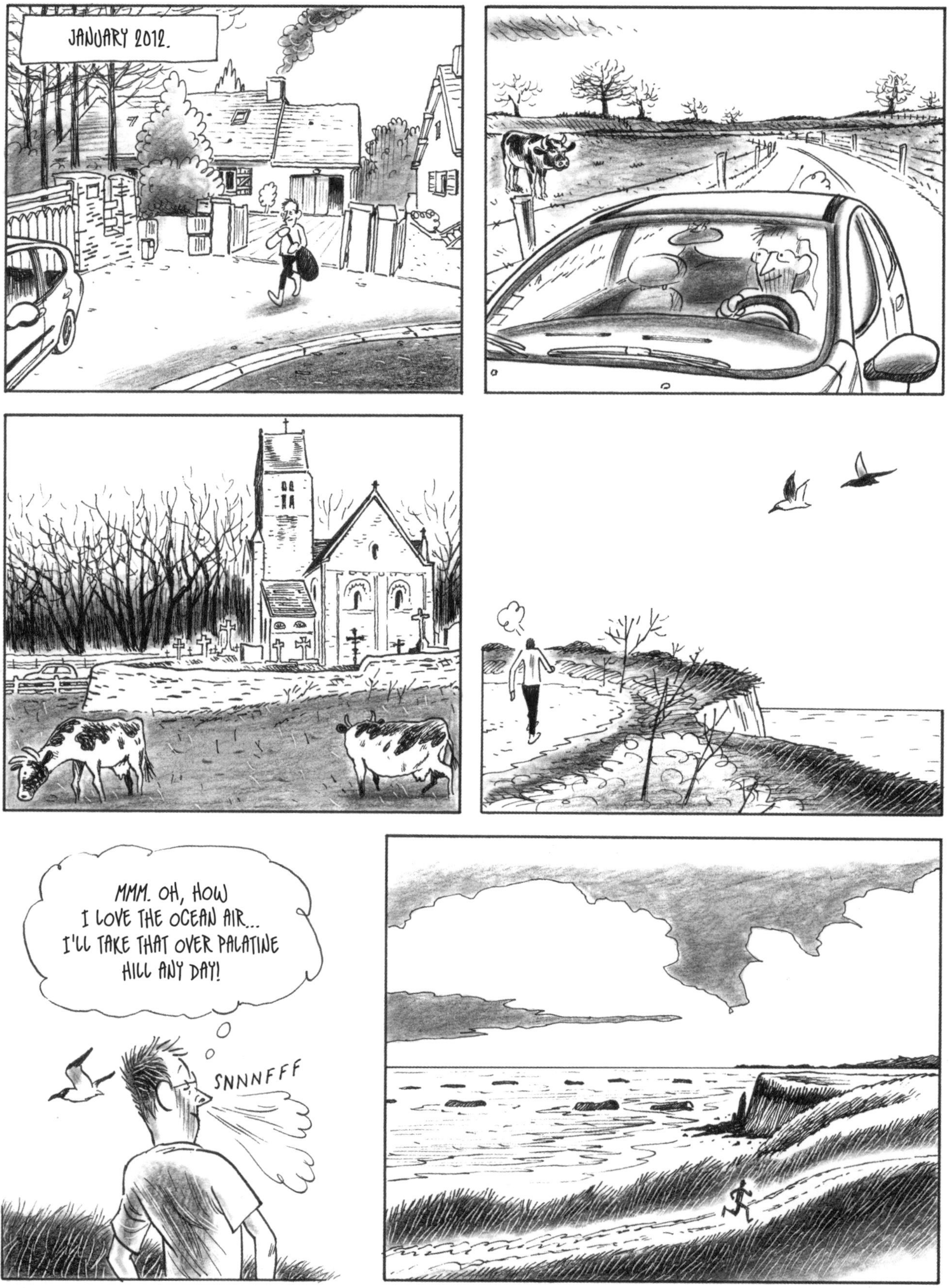
JANUARY 2012.
MMM. OH, HOW I LOVE THE OCEAN AIR... I'LL TAKE THAT OVER PALATINE HILL ANY DAY!
SNNNFFF

I COULDN'T WAIT TO GET
BACK TO RUNNING SOLO.

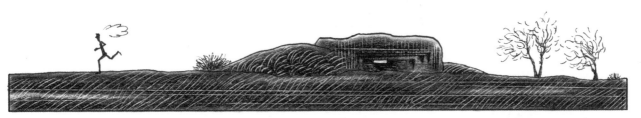

THE TWO MILLION SUPPORTERS? BEEN THERE.
THE 90,000 RUNNING MARATHON LEGS? DONE THAT.

AH... COMING BACK TO THE
MILLIONS OF PARTICLES OF
SILENCE AND SALTY BREEZE.

BUT AM I ANY CLOSER TO
UNDERSTANDING WHAT
I'M RUNNING AFTER?

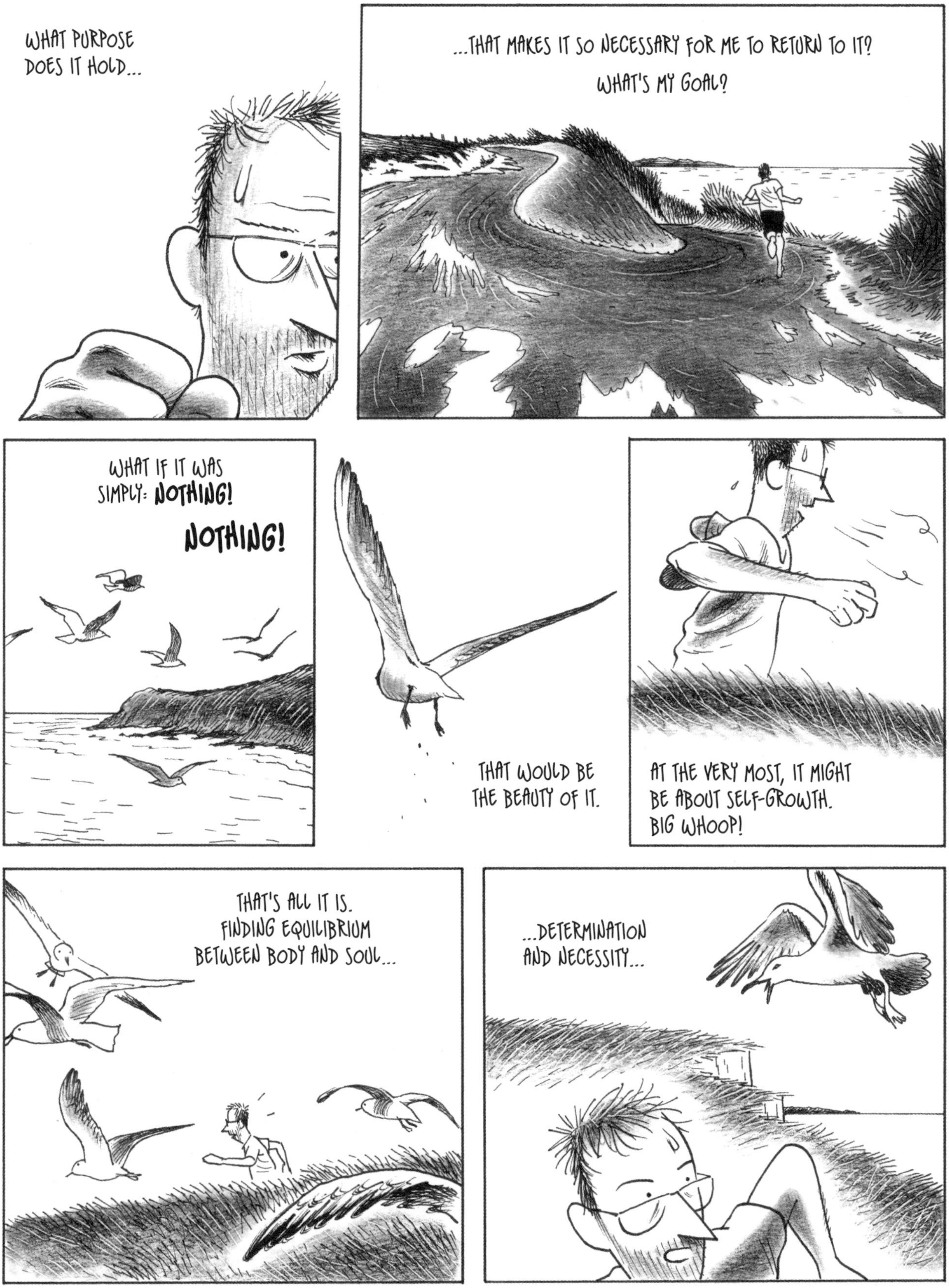
WHAT PURPOSE DOES IT HOLD...
...THAT MAKES IT SO NECESSARY FOR ME TO RETURN TO IT?
WHAT'S MY GOAL?
WHAT IF IT WAS SIMPLY: NOTHING!
NOTHING!
THAT WOULD BE THE BEAUTY OF IT.
AT THE VERY MOST, IT MIGHT BE ABOUT SELF-GROWTH. BIG WHOOP!
THAT'S ALL IT IS. FINDING EQUILIBRIUM BETWEEN BODY AND SOUL...
...DETERMINATION AND NECESSITY...

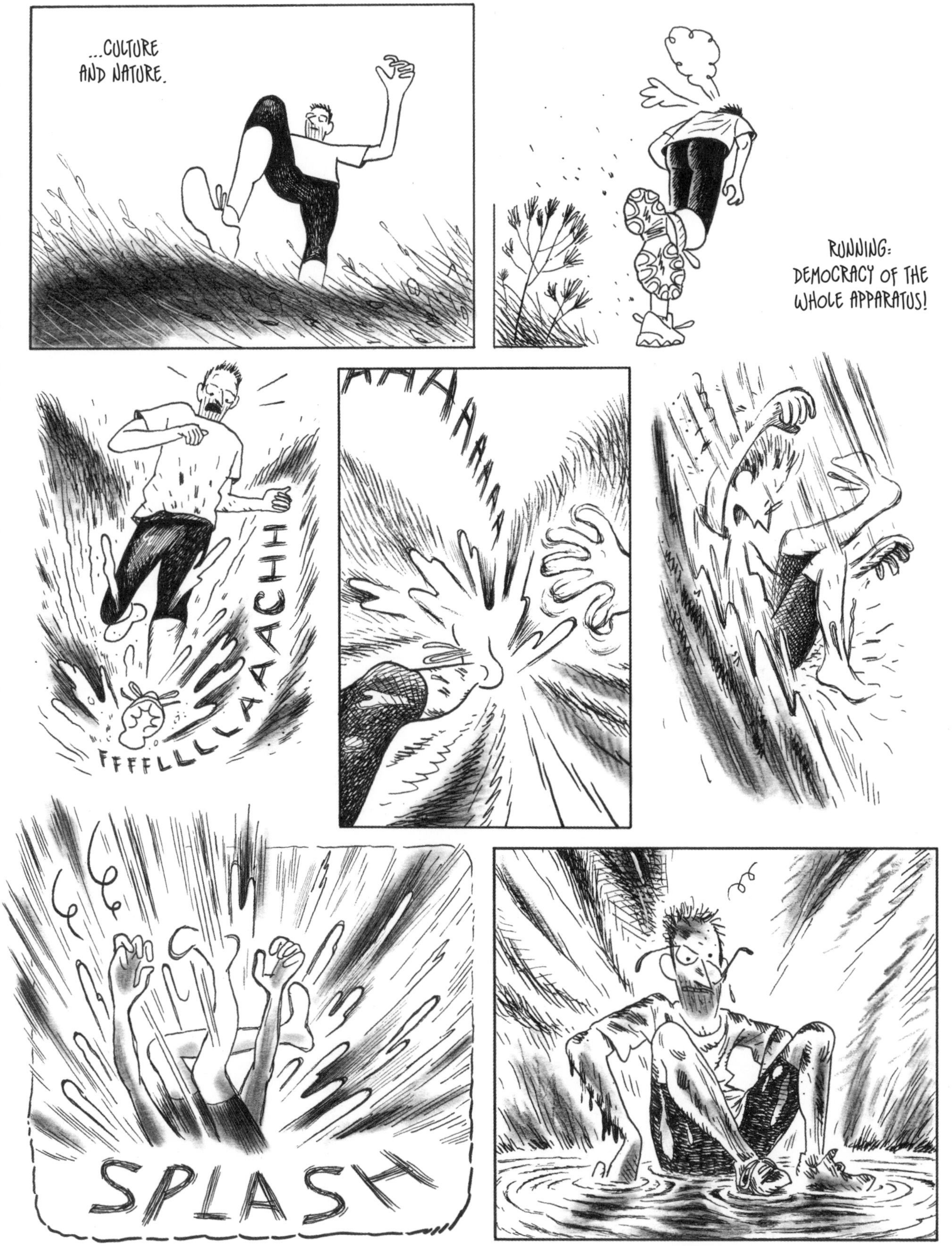
...CULTURE AND NATURE.
RUNNING: DEMOCRACY OF THE WHOLE APPARATUS!
FFFFLLLLLAAACHH
AAAAAAAAAA
SPLASH

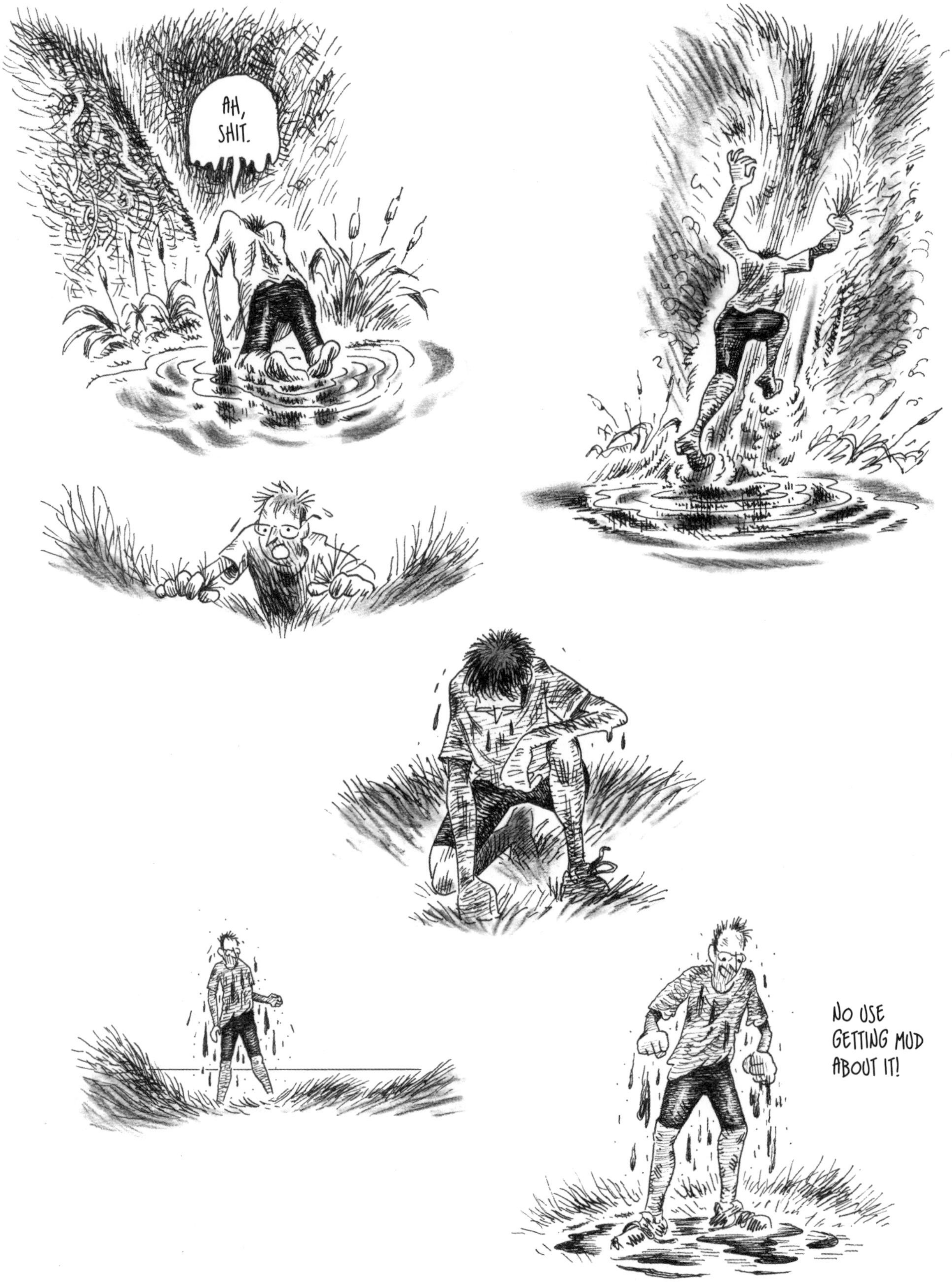
AH, SHIT.
NO USE GETTING MUD ABOUT IT!

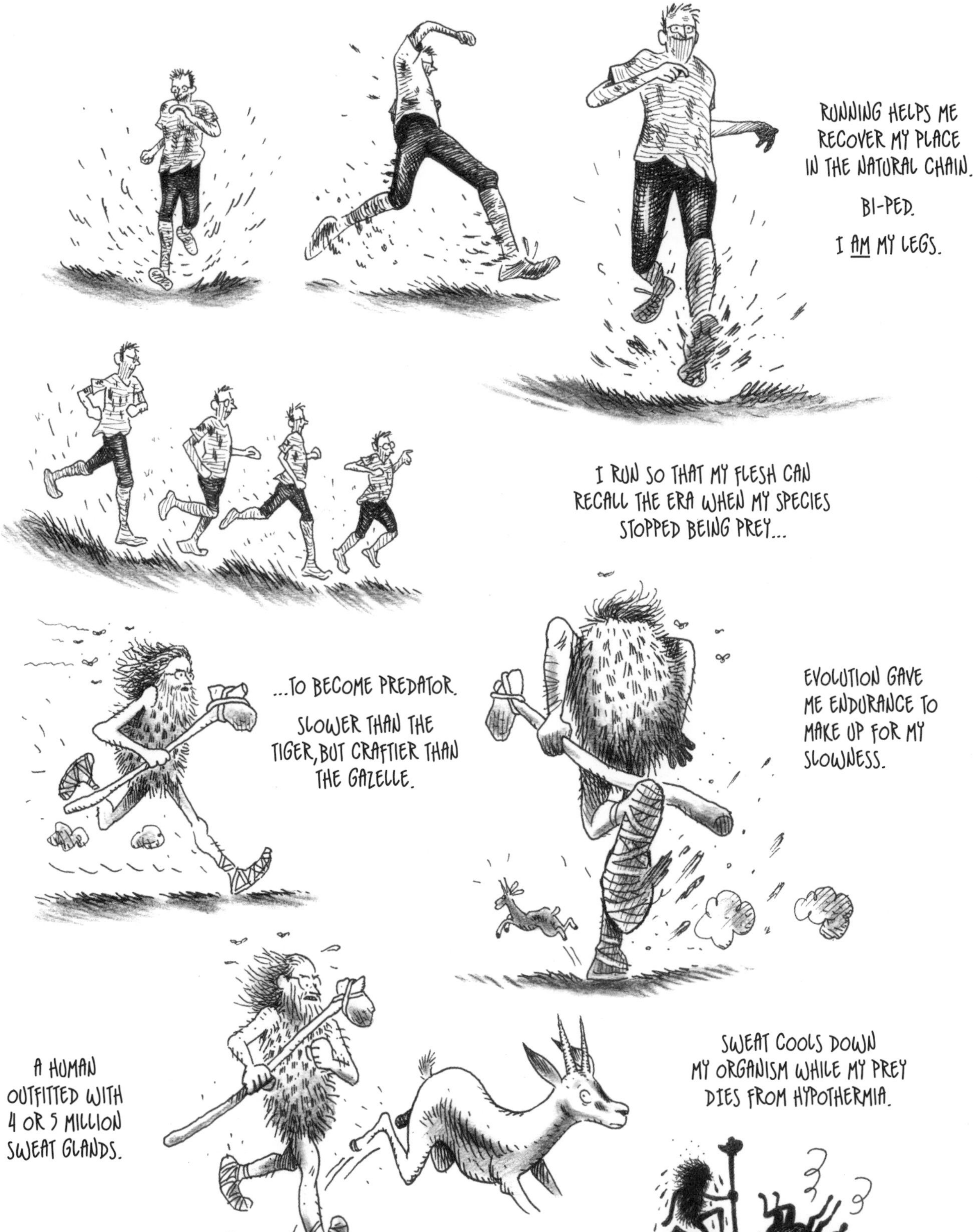
RUNNING HELPS ME RECOVER MY PLACE IN THE NATURAL CHAIN.
BI-PED.
I AM MY LEGS.
I RUN SO THAT MY FLESH CAN RECALL THE ERA WHEN MY SPECIES STOPPED BEING PREY...
...TO BECOME PREDATOR.
SLOWER THAN THE TIGER, BUT CRAFTIER THAN THE GAZELLE.
EVOLUTION GAVE ME ENDURANCE TO MAKE UP FOR MY SLOWNESS.
A HUMAN OUTFITTED WITH 4 OR 5 MILLION SWEAT GLANDS.
SWEAT COOLS DOWN MY ORGANISM WHILE MY PREY DIES FROM HYPOTHERMIA.

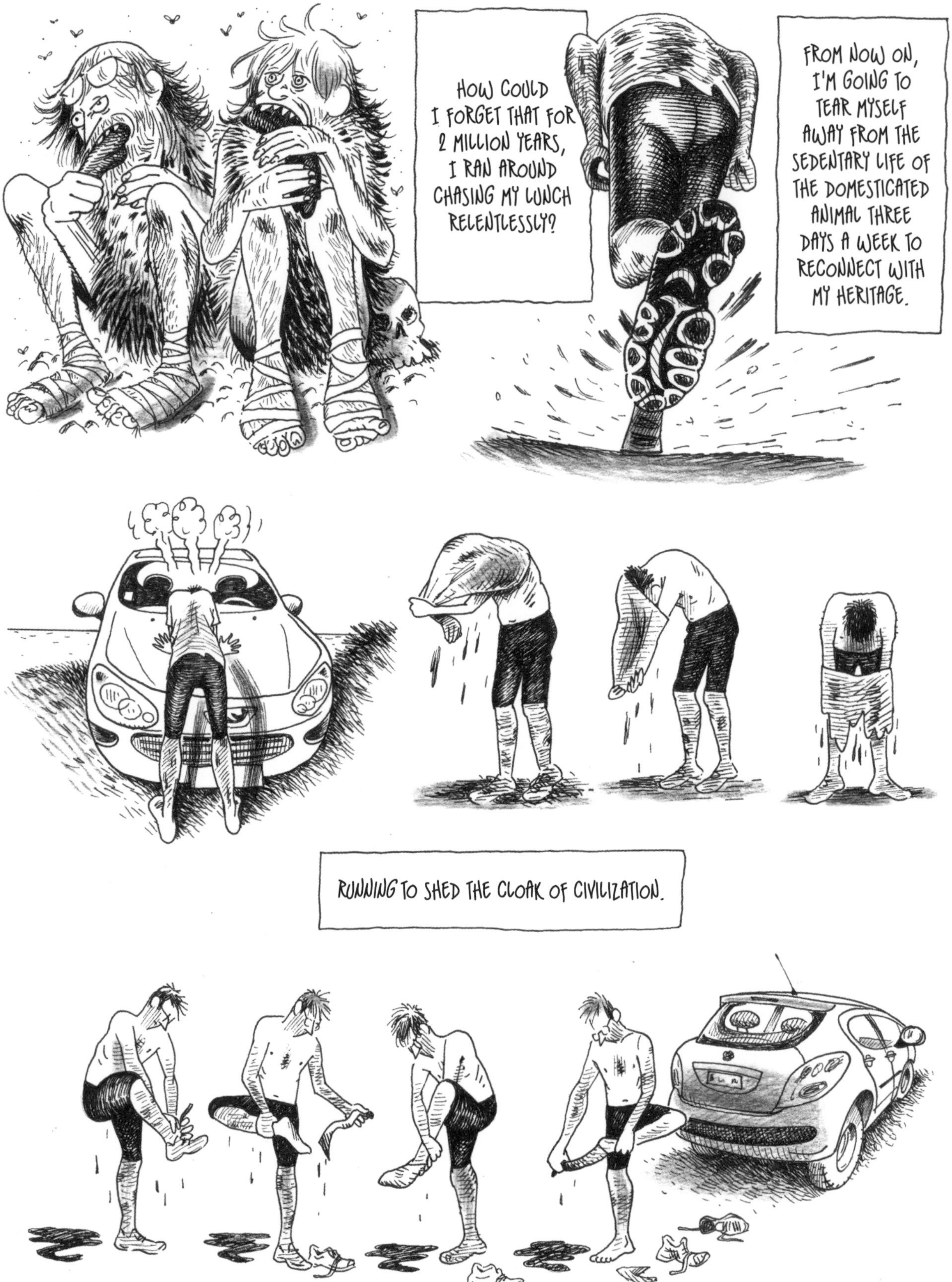
HOW COULD I FORGET THAT FOR 2 MILLION YEARS, I RAN AROUND CHASING MY LUNCH RELENTLESSLY?
FROM NOW ON, I'M GOING TO TEAR MYSELF AWAY FROM THE SEDENTARY LIFE OF THE DOMESTICATED ANIMAL THREE DAYS A WEEK TO RECONNECT WITH MY HERITAGE.
RUNNING TO SHED THE CLOAK OF CIVILIZATION.

RUNNING TO FULLY RELISH IN MY ANIMAL NATURE. OUTSIDE OF LANGUAGE.

FLESH,
WATER,

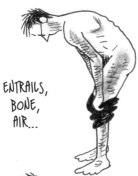

ENTRAILS,
BONE,
AIR...

AS AN ATHEIST,
I DON'T WORSHIP ANY GOD.
RUNNING IS MY RELIGION.

THE FULFILLMENT OF
MY HUMANITY THROUGH
MOVEMENT.

JUST LIKE THE ARTIST, THE RUNNER LOOKS FOR SHORTCUTS. HE EMBRACES SPACE. I RUN UP THE MOUNTAIN OF MY EARTHLY LIMITS TO STIMULATE THE ANIMAL LURKING WITHIN THE CONFINES OF MY PEDESTRIAN SOUL...

...OR, MY DRIVING SOUL.

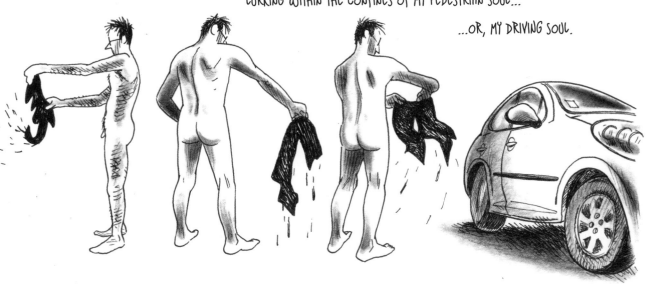

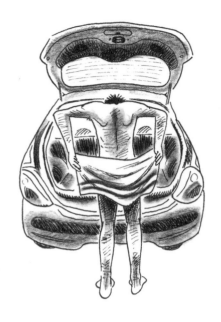

IT'S NOT THE GAZELLE I'M CHASING.

IT'S THAT WHICH IS SUPERFLUOUS.

SEDENTARY LIFESTYLE, ROLLS OF FAT, VANITY... I'M MAKING ROOM FOR WHAT'S PRIMAL.

FOR ESSENCE.

FOR THE COMBUSTIBLE CORE.

RUNNING LIKE I DRAW. EXPERIENCING SPACE ON A PHYSICAL LEVEL.

TO TRAVEL THE IMMENSITY OF THE WORLD.

THE IMMENSITY OF THE WORLD WITHIN.

NO MORE TIME TO WASTE! WHAT'S THE POINT OF SITTING STILL AND NOT FIGHTING BACK AGAINST THE RELENTLESS ADVANCE OF AGE, OF LETTING IT DO ITS THING AND THEN TAKE US BY SURPRISE, ALLOWING IT TO SETTLE IN AND TAKE UP RESIDENCE IN OUR BODIES UNTIL WE'RE RELOCATED TO THAT LITTLE WOODEN BOX.

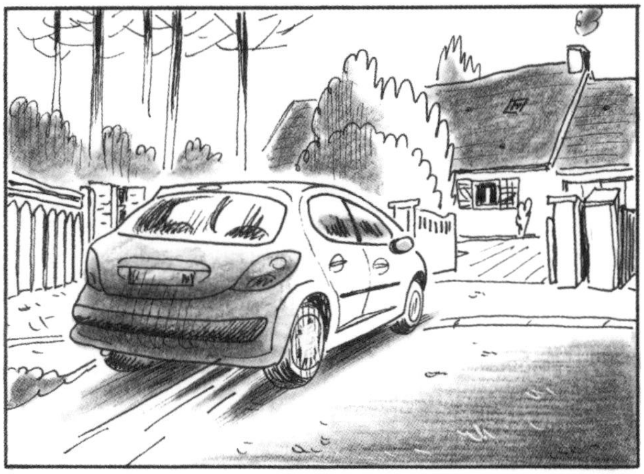

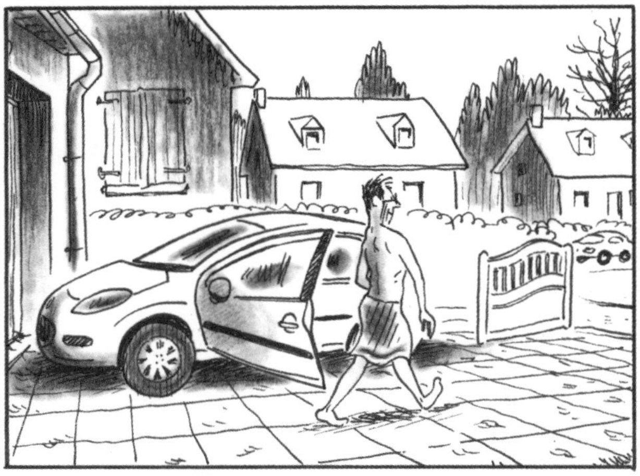

SO REALLY, RUNNING ENABLES US TO STAY ONE STEP AHEAD OF DECAY AND TO FACE IT HEAD (AND RUNNING SHOES) ON!

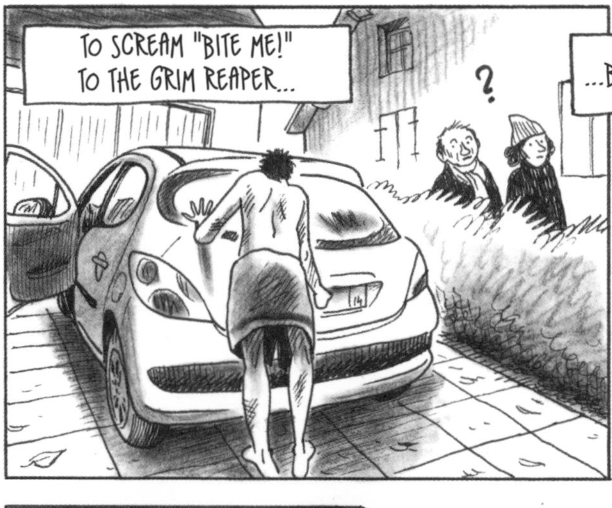
TO SCREAM "BITE ME!" TO THE GRIM REAPER...
?
...BY CELEBRATING LIFE.

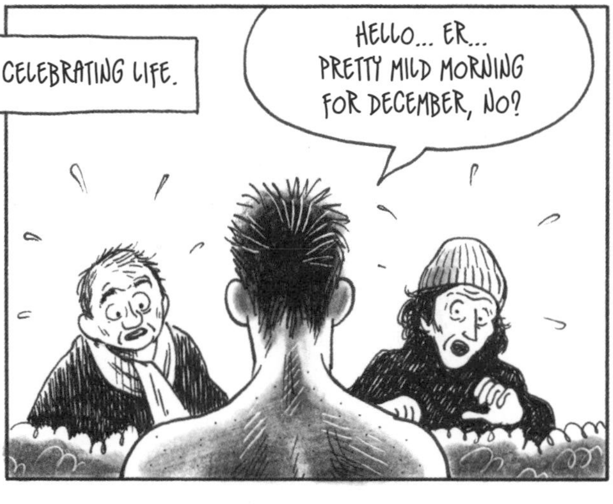
HELLO... ER... PRETTY MILD MORNING FOR DECEMBER, NO?

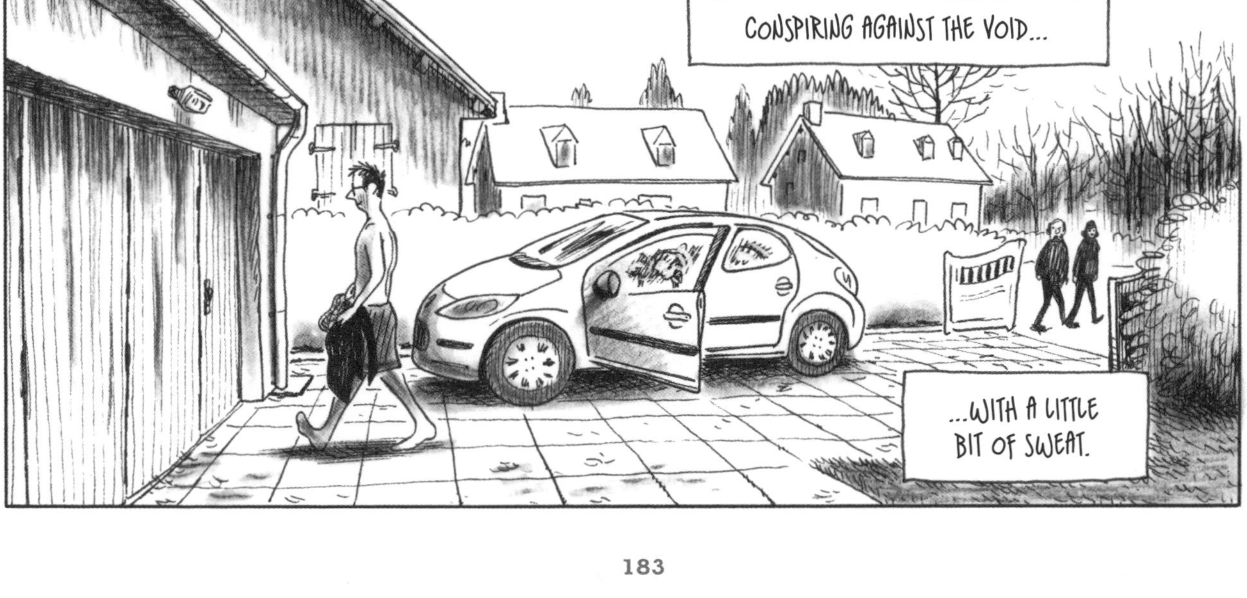
CONSPIRING AGAINST THE VOID...
...WITH A LITTLE BIT OF SWEAT.

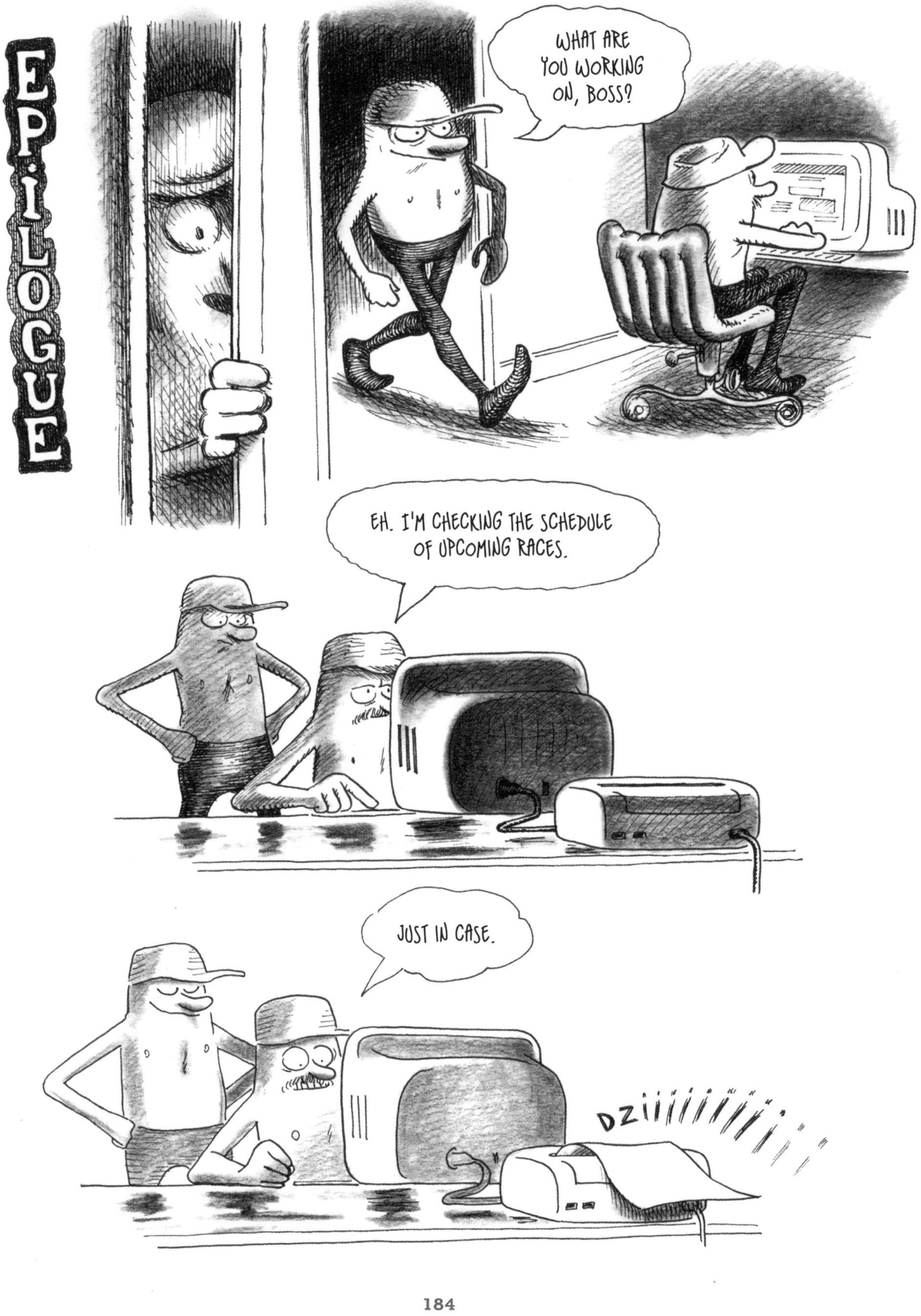
EPILOGUE
WHAT ARE YOU WORKING ON, BOSS?
EH. I'M CHECKING THE SCHEDULE OF UPCOMING RACES.
JUST IN CASE.
DZIIIIIIII

APRIL 2013

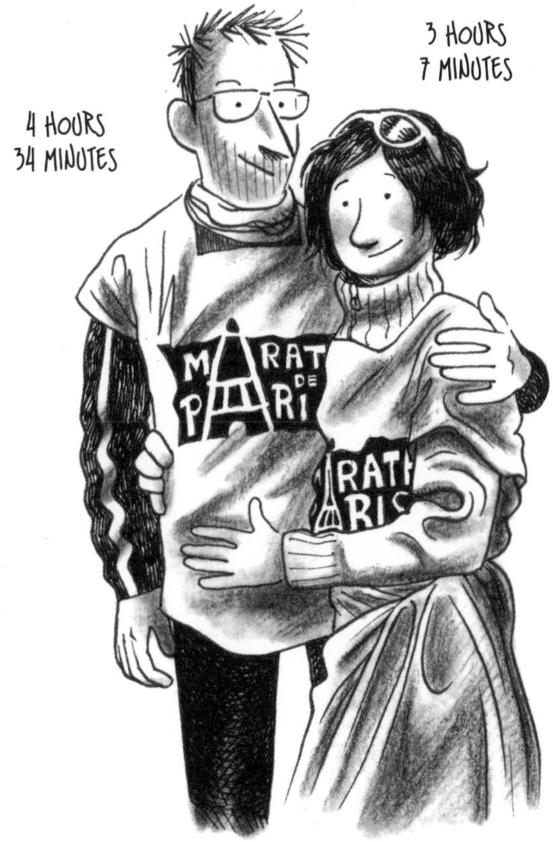
4 HOURS
34 MINUTES
3 HOURS
7 MINUTES

Afterwords

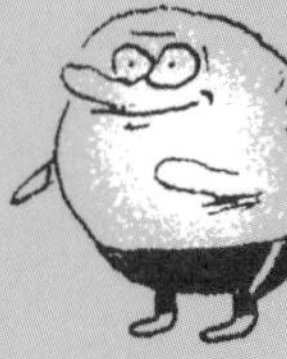

We all know several Sebastiens—friends who aren't sure why they started running, soon enough finish a marathon, and along the way learn how running can change their life. We haven't, however, viewed the story in graphic-novel form. In *My New York Marathon*, Sebastien Samson goes the distance with powerful words and emotions amplified by wonderful cartoon panels. You'll laugh, wince, cheer, and nod your head in agreement.

My favorite moment, from the starting line of the New York Marathon: "Except for being in love, has there ever been a moment in my life when I have felt as intensely alive as right now?"

Probably not. But by reading *My New York Marathon*, you can relive the alluring intensity.

Amby Burfoot
Winner, 1968 Boston Marathon
Runner's World writer and editor

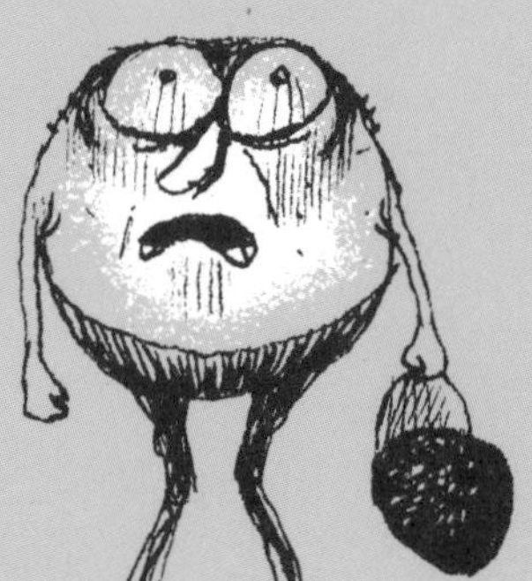

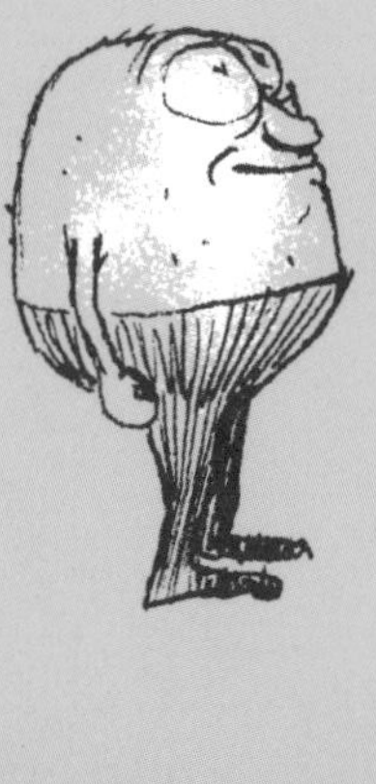

I've looked through hundreds of books and have never experienced anything like this. It entertained me, while telling a life-changing journey to the NYC Marathon.

The drawings were well done and brought out an emotional response to the events in the book. The graphics were arranged to tell the story in a fun and interesting format.

From the inspiration of an average person, to the commitment, the questioning, real issues were presented and dealt with. The challenges were also realistic in the way they were handled.

It is well-documented that endurance running turns on brain circuits for a better attitude, more vitality and personal empowerment—better than any activity that has been studied. There is a series of regular revelations in the story which show that the main character "gets it." I receive such statements from hundreds of runners every week—about how this challenge leads them to the mental benefits for a powerful and positive life-change, at any age. And then...there's the medal!

I guess the sequel could follow the improvements when the characters use the Galloway run walk run® method! I like this book. It has a place in running literature.

Jeff Galloway
US Olympian, 1972, 10,000 meters
Author of North America's best selling running book:
Galloway's Book on Running

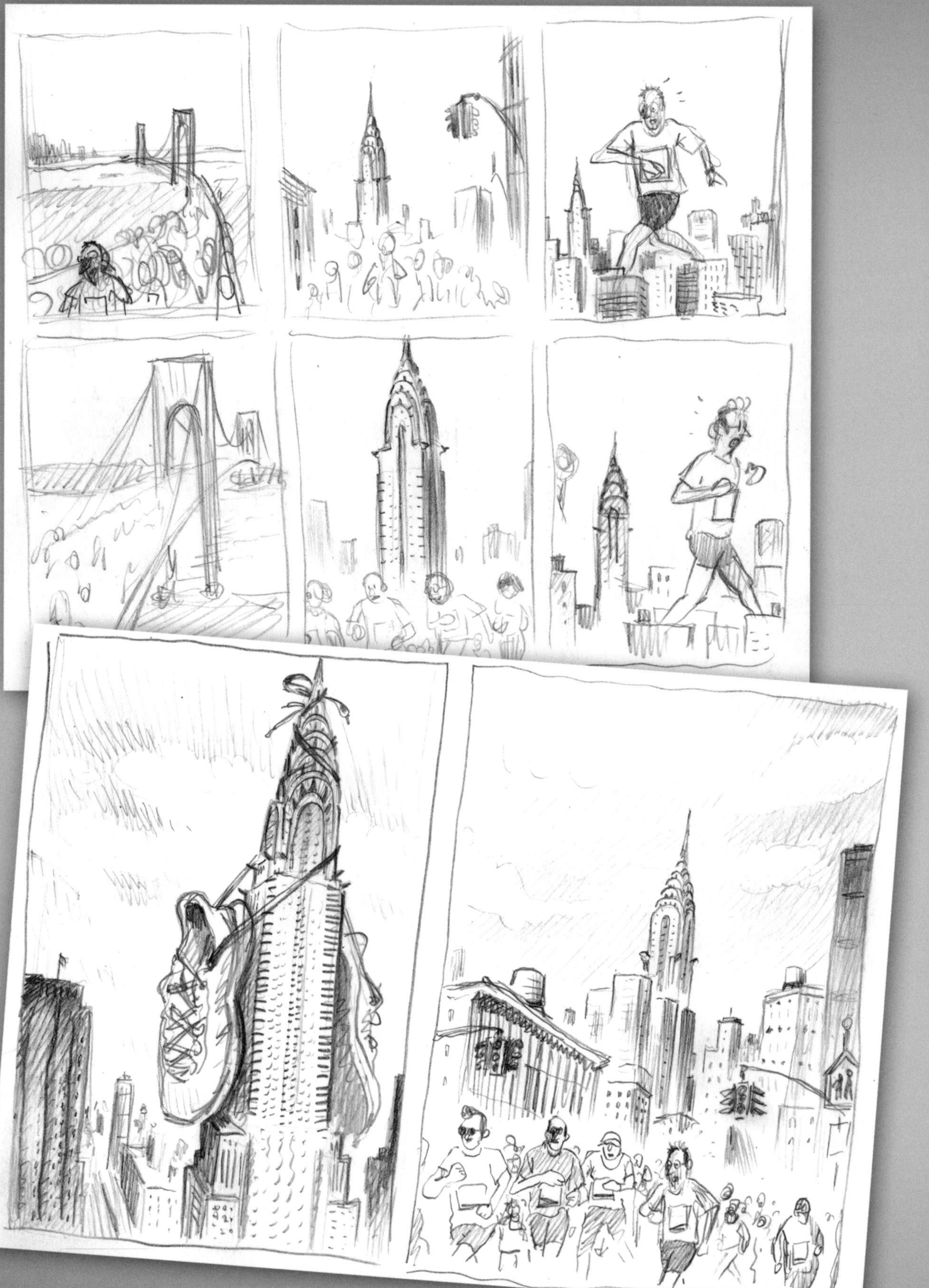

Creating the cover to the US edition of this book was no easy task. But Sebastien had so many ideas...

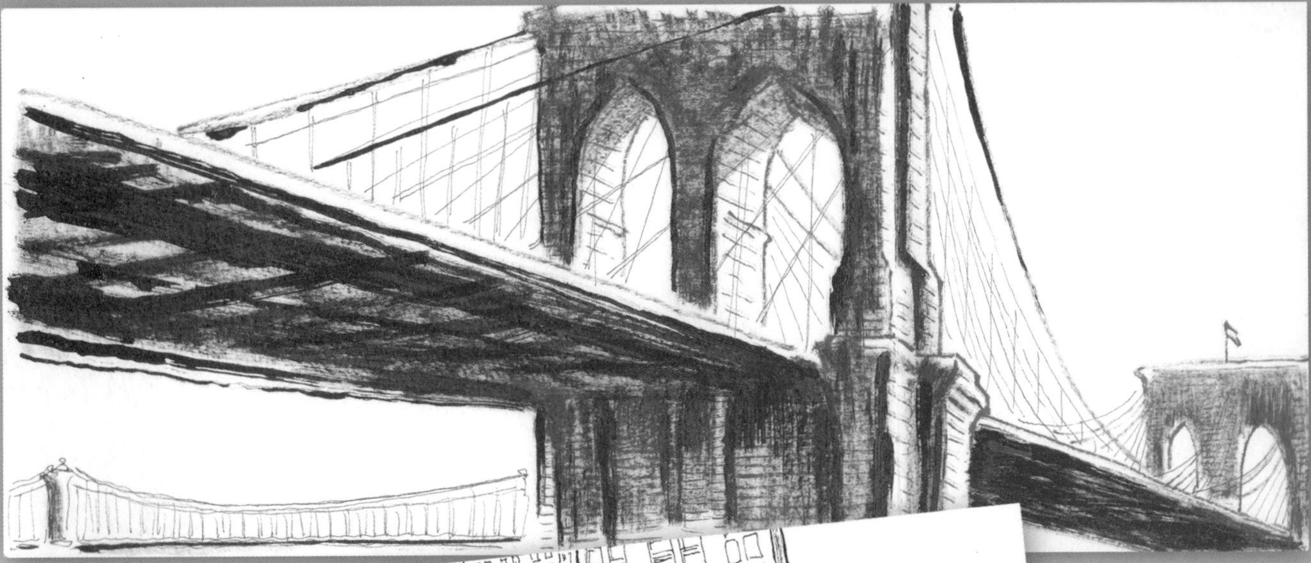

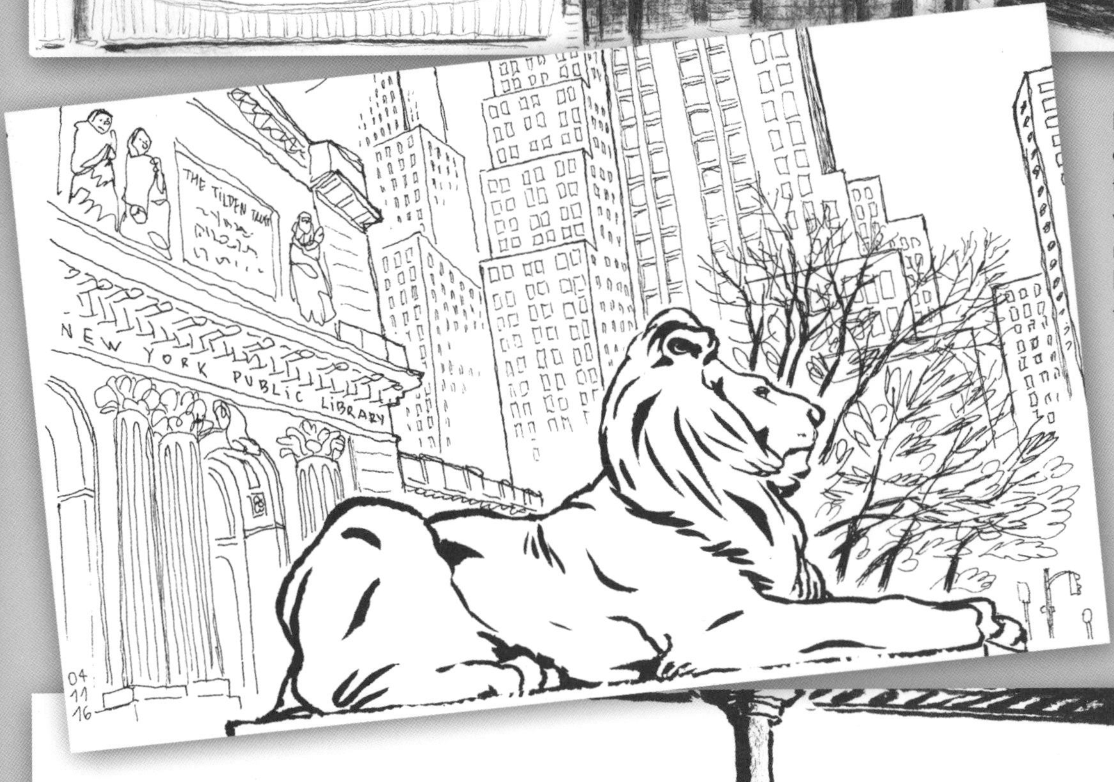
NEW YORK PUBLIC LIBRARY
04
11
16

New York is one of the stars of this book. And you can see how much the creator loved sketching the city.

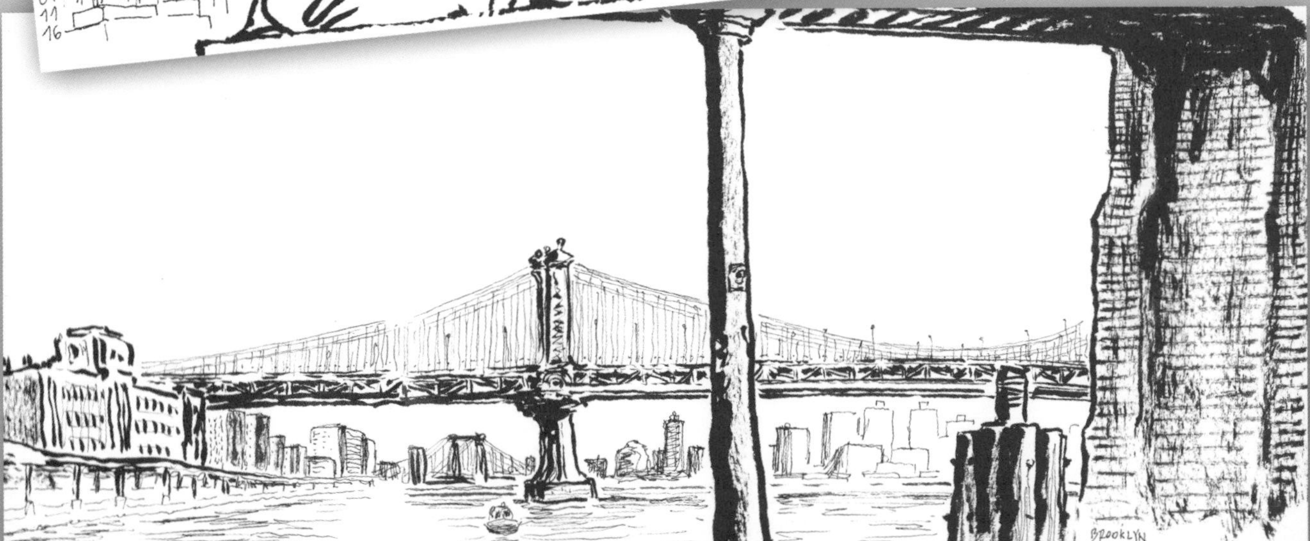
BROOKLYN BRIDGE
05.11.16

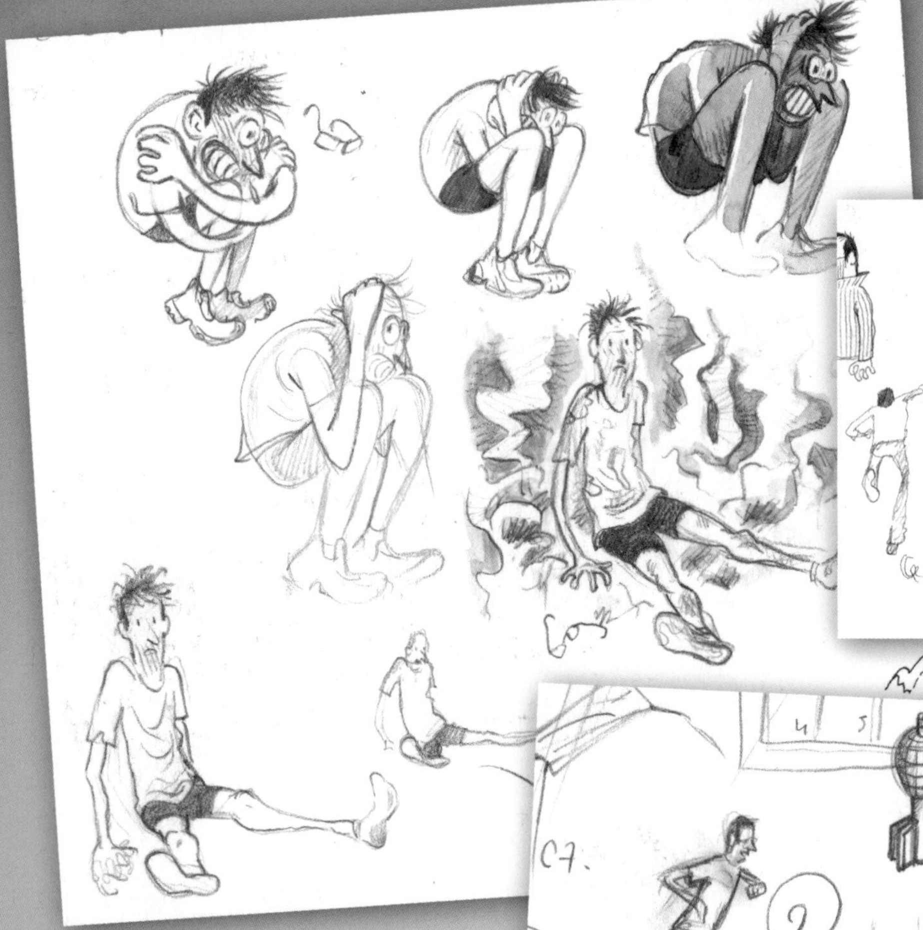

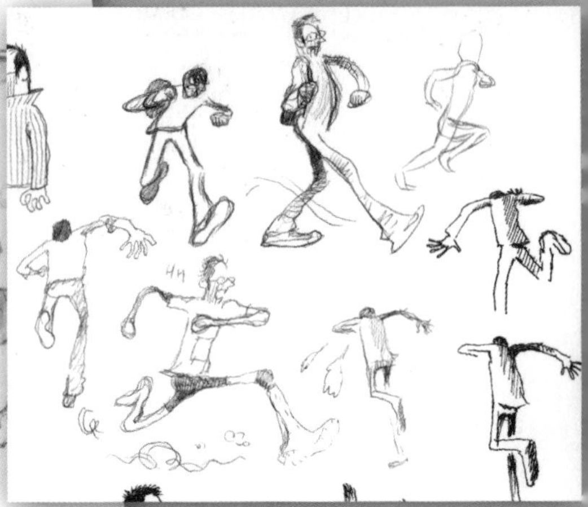
44

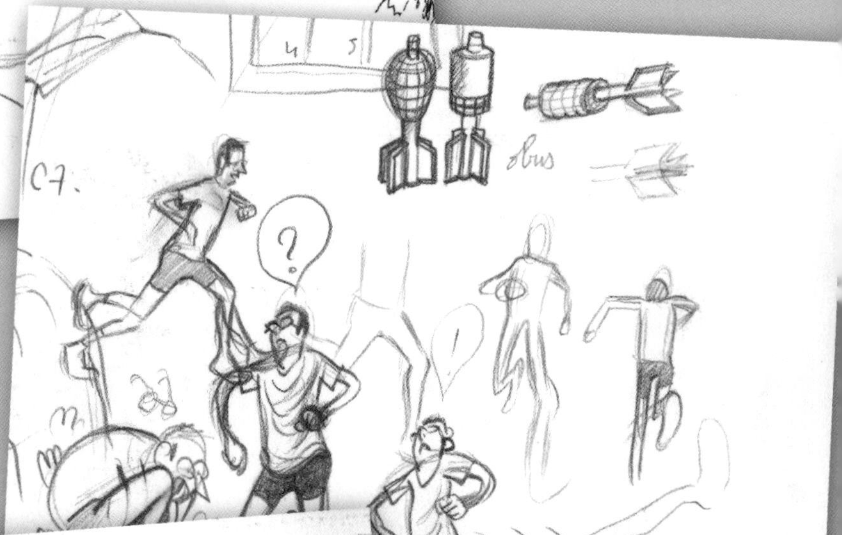
C7.
obus
?

In *My New York Marathon*, Sebastien shows his many different sides... and faces. He spent a lot of time and energy drawing himself in as many positions as possible.

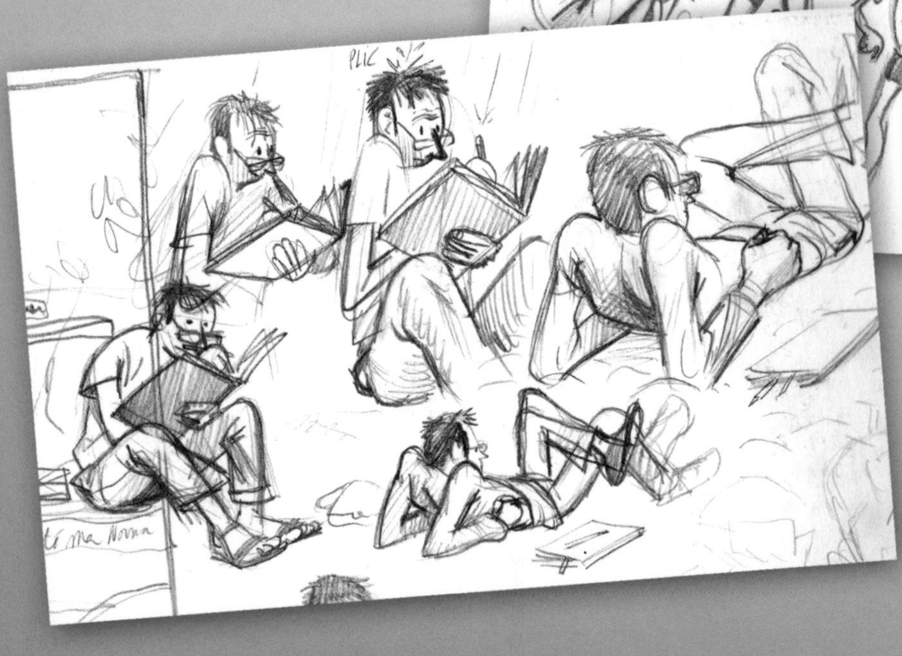
PLIC

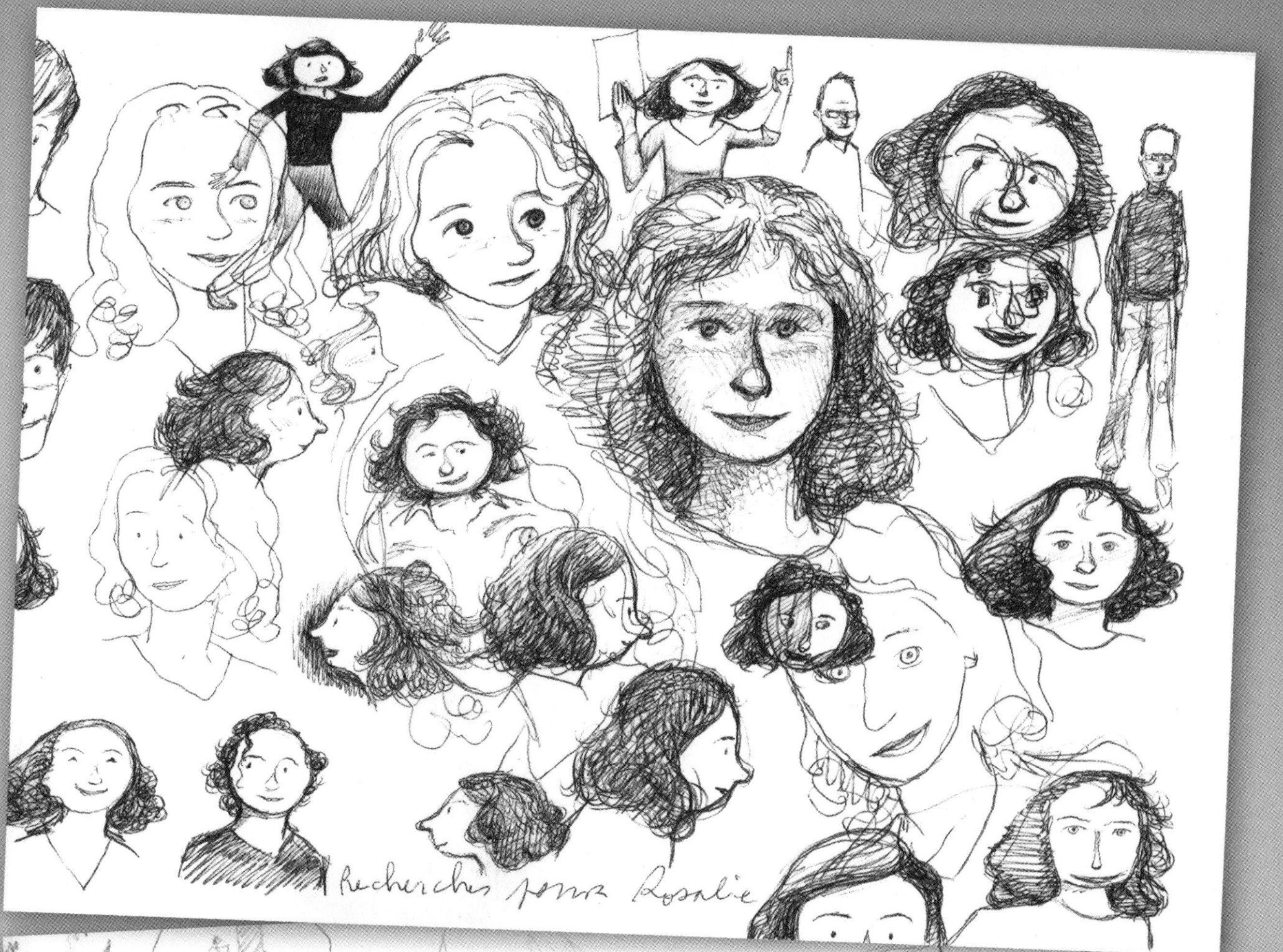
Recherches pour Rosalie

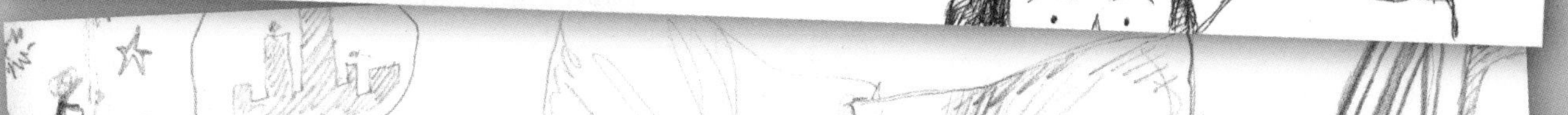

Sebastien spent a lot of time sketching himself and his wife Rosalie, even during their most intimate moments.

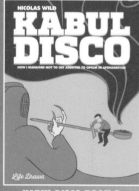
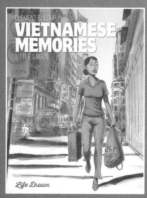